THE NIGHT PARROTS

STEPHEN ORR was born in Adelaide in 1967, studied science and education and taught in a range of country and metropolitan schools. One of his early plays, *Attempts to Draw Jesus*, became his first novel, shortlisted for the *Australian*/Vogel's Literary Award.

Since then he has published eleven novels (most recently, *Shining Like the Sun*) and two volumes of short stories (*Datsunland* and *The Boy in Time*). He has been nominated for awards such as the Commonwealth Writers' Prize, the Miles Franklin Award and the International Dublin Literary Award.

BY THE SAME AUTHOR

Attempts to Draw Jesus
Hill of Grace
Time's Long Ruin
Dissonance
One Boy Missing
The Hands
Datsunland
Incredible Floridas
This Excellent Machine
The Lanternist
Sincerely, Ethel Malley
The Boy in Time
Shining Like the Sun

THE NIGHT PARROTS

STEPHEN ORR

Wakefield Press

Wakefield Press
16 Rose Street
Mile End
South Australia 5031
www.wakefieldpress.com.au

First published 2026

Edited by Maddy Sexton, Wakefield Press
Book design and typesetting by Duncan Blachford

ISBN 978 1 92338 867 3

A catalogue record for this book is available from the National Library of Australia

This project is supported by the Copyright Agency's Cultural Fund as well as a grant from the Government of South Australia.

Wakefield Press thanks Coriole Vineyards for continued support

'The events of the past six weeks had shaken and shattered his faith to its very foundation. And yet he felt strangely reassured as he peered out into the deepening, wet gloom outside.'

T.G.H. Strehlow

'Past or present, there is a human dimension to time, human voices within it and human griefs ordained by it. Our present will become the past of other men and women. We depend on them to remember it with the complexity with which it was suffered. As others, once, depended on us.'

Eavan Boland

Of the night parrot . . .

'Although a desert bird of the interior, it seems to have failed to hold its own, and nothing has now been heard of it for years. I'm afraid we must count it as one of our lost species.'

***Townsville Daily Bulletin*, 1942**

'The night parrot owing, perhaps, to not having contact with the sun, has no gay plumage. It is not unlike the grey cockatoo parrot in size and looks, it has a mottled grey coat and has never been tamed, and we understand will not live in captivity.'

***Centralian Advocate*, 1947**

An approaching storm

On a grey, thundery day in 1971, my brother Anton Gerlach drove his car along a back road west of Leipzig. Past plantation forests, a patchwork of pasture and cattail, soil-warmed rhizomes running down to the shores of a small lake. To his left (as I imagine it), bare-limbed birches and fat sheep, water stretching out blue and boatless to the west; and on his right, smoke from a distant trinity of stacks, an old tractor stirring soil for turnips, smashed-up glasshouses catching early snow. Sitting beside him on that cold December morning was his four-year-old grandson, Max. I imagine him (I've never seen a picture) Gerlach-faced, blue-eyed, fine, pink lips saying something like, 'Mama says we should bring home apples.'

But Anton doesn't reply. He's busy with his own thoughts.

Sometime before 9.38 am, my brother drove up a hill, across train tracks, and either stalled his car, or stopped it. No one will ever know. Less than a minute later, a train came around a corner, tried to stop, but didn't have enough time. The old BMW was pushed a hundred metres south, the train stopped, the driver got out, examined the wreck and noticed a big body (Anton was overweight) and a small body inside an unsolvable puzzle of steel and glass. He knew they were dead. He called along the tracks to the head conductor (who was running towards him), 'There's nothing we can do.'

Anyway, that's how the letter (from Anton's son, Dieter) explained it. I never checked the details. I didn't care. Sitting in my small, hot lounge room in Adelaide – listening to Marcus Welby, sweating (in an old singlet), cataloguing sacred stones with my wife (at the time) Kate – none of this seemed real. After I'd read the letter, I said to Kate, 'What a place to stall a car.' And she (she was always perceptive) said, 'You really think he stalled it, there, then?'

The reason I tell you this so early in my story is that as a creaky eighty-year-old I've worked out the longer you live the less you understand, or at least, can know with any certainty. According to Dieter, Anton had always been moody, suffered from depression, spent time in a sanitorium in Grunewald. He'd had three wives, six or seven kids who wouldn't talk to him. I knew he'd had it rough. But I didn't know *him*. I didn't (couldn't) understand who he was, what he sounded like, the look in his eyes. I hadn't seen him or my other brothers or sister since 1914, since me and Mother and Father climbed onto a cart and drove away from Opa's house in Leipzig. So long ago. The people who'd been closest to me, played with me, flicked food at me, were complete strangers.

As I sit in my fibro house in Hillcrest. Listening to the drills and presses over my back fence. The Monaro across the road that Wayne (Esmay's eldest) tinkers with all afternoon. The bike gang of eleven- and twelve-year-olds that appears after school, riding down the road, throwing lemons into my yard and calling, 'You old poofter!' Tom, my grandson (and motivator, editor, adviser, scribe, cook) went out the other day (in his Scotch College blazer), said he'd fix it. He waited for them, and when they went past (and called *him* a poofter) he accused them of playing around (luckily Jack, my son, wasn't there) with their sisters. They came back, he ran after them, they rode off. He returned, puffed out, and we sat on the dead lawn laughing for ten minutes, until Mrs Wren came past and asked what was so funny and Tom said, 'Just playing around.'

I've been having plenty of fun since Tom came back into my life. In a way, replacing lost siblings. Anton, Alwin, Michael, Julius and Charlotte – five broken satellites orbiting my old, wheezing planet, never getting any closer, never becoming visible.

I remember playing with Julius in the cattle yards at Hermannsburg. Dust, and shit up to my ankles; Ludwig and Oskar telling me not to stand behind the bull. And later, throwing snow at him in Opa's Leipzig yard. According to what I learned from Dieter, Julius never felt right in his skin. He met some girl, got married, moved to Hamburg, but then started wearing dresses, hanging about the Alster Pavilion on a Sunday afternoon. In 1962, a few sailors tried to beat him up somewhere in St Pauli, he defended himself, there was a fight and he was arrested, photographed and charged as 'Justina'. The photo leaked, and he was in the papers (Dieter sent me a clipping). But I never heard what happened to him after that.

Then there was the second-eldest, Alwin. By the time Hitler's war came along he was too old to fight, but he was assigned to an artillery regiment in the east as some sort of clerical officer. At the end of the war the Russians got a hold of him and no one, according to Dieter, heard of him for years. Then, in the early fifties, Michael received a telegram saying Alwin died in a Russian POW camp in 1949. No name. No return address. And despite letters and phone calls and help from the Red Cross, that was the end of Alwin, gone, somewhere into the fog of history.

All of this time, me and my first wife Terese were out in the Western Desert making films and taking photos of sacred ceremonies, or back in Adelaide, painting our Prospect house (this, years before Kate came along). Or back at Hermannsburg, lost in a world of my father's making – the Aranda, their stories and songs, their cut feet dyed purple with Condy's, their fighting and anger at the things that'd been done to them – the whitewashed walls of German Lutheranism made real in the desert. I grew up minus these strangers, these child-ghosts of middle-Europe. Sitting with Father beside a creek, notating the language, collecting ephedra for Mother, watching for the night parrot.

You can never know. What Anton was thinking as that train came at him, braked, tried to stop. Did he hold Max, try to protect him? Did they try to get out? Or did he just sit there, waiting? There was a rumour (there's always a rumour) that Max was his son. A strange, wasn't-meant-to-happen moment with his twenty-eight-year-old daughter-in-law, Eva. Dieter had heard, but never believed it. He and Eva continued until she died in a head-on collision in 1979. Meanwhile, Dieter patented some sort of food wrap, made millions, and never spoke about his son. But the proof of the pudding is in the eating. Max's face was Anton's: his nose, his ears, his eyes. Anton had just been diagnosed with Huntington's chorea. He'd already started shaking, forgetting. But maybe it had nothing to do with that. The fact remains, either that car stalled, or stopped.

Complexity. After all the dramas in the desert, the intervening years, my high school and university, Mother returned to Leipzig. Although, by then, her children had grown up, made their own lives. Out of all of them, Julius was the only one who went to see her. Except me, one time, when I was lecturing in England. I got the boat over, the train to Leipzig, arrived at her front door and said, 'Well?' She just looked at me and said, 'And this is because someone *paid* for you to come?'

Pastor Martin Gerlach was the most complex of all. The most distant. He insisted, but doubted; worked, but wondered why; converted, but came to see that people were better off with their own familiar uncertainties. As I stood beside him on the deck of the boat back to Australia, I said, 'At least I've got this,' and took out a photo of me with my brothers and sister, standing in our prickly-pear yard in Hermannsburg. Father took a moment, bit his lip (as he did when he was thinking) then pulled the photo from my fingers and dropped it into the North Sea. I asked why, but he just shrugged. I never asked again. There was no point. So maybe my final, fumbled thesis (written on Tom's Commodore 64) will make things clearer, to you, if not to me. Why my father gave love in such small, sparing doses. And why, up to and including the end, he conceded nothing to that grey, rumbling sky.

1922
Red Rover

On the first day there was fourteen-year-old Benjamin 'Benno' Gerlach (me), Lucas, Oskar, maybe six, seven of the black kids, and Ludwig. And 'Blind' Silas (not his real name), dressed in his soiled white suit (pants, shoes, socks, shirt) standing in the middle of the dusty compound at Hermannsburg Mission. Imagine. A few stray dogs (covered in sores), Mother sitting in a rocker on the porch of our old house, examining a specimen from her classground, writing in her notebook: 'Ephedra pedunculata woody vine grey bark leaves opposite 0.12 long seed cones 0.3 long with 2 seeds 0.4 long'. Looking up and calling, 'Careful, Benno. It doesn't seem fair.'

And Silas (minus his cane) standing with arms outstretched, like it might help him catch someone.

On the first day there was Father, thirty yards away, cleaning out the church with buckets of water. I can't remember why. Maybe someone had been sick. Maybe he just liked the smell of hospital antiseptic, the stink of God and Jesus and hymn books and acid-eaten, red-rot sermons from his homemade pulpit.

Silas said, 'Red Rover all over.'

Ludwig and us kids ran, straight past Silas, who moved sideways like a crab, hoping he'd catch someone. When we'd all made it over, Mother called, 'It hardly seems fair. Silas, come in out of the sun.'

'It's alright, Mrs Gerlach. It's fun . . . eh, kids?'

Fun. Like my grandson, Tom, running into my room a few weeks ago, showing me his latest computer game (*Desert Fox*), starting it up and saying, 'See, you got to rescue the soldier from the desert.'

'Go on.' Watching him pushing his buttons.

And before long: 'Is this what it was like at, what was it, Hermannburg, Grandpa?'

'*Hermannsburg*. And no, decidedly not.'

'Why?'

'We didn't have any wars going on . . . except for Hitler.'

'Did you fight Hitler?'

'No. That was a long way away, and a long time ago. We didn't have any of this' – indicating a soldier with a machine gun killing a few dozen enemy – 'We just had a lot of boredom.'

'What did you do?'

'Read. Played games. Searched for night parrots.' And what I wanted to say, but didn't, because he wouldn't understand. The outback (as Hoges called it) was a load of nothing. Walking east for a mile, turning around, realising there was nothing there, anywhere, except lemongrass, and perhaps a bronzewing, or skink. No cars, no houses, no people. Just sand and sky and the feeling you were the last, the only person on Earth. 'Growing up like that gave you a sense of . . . resilience,' I said.

He fired a bazooka, and jumped about.

'I was alone.'

'That musta been crap.'

'That's how it was. But we entertained ourselves.'

'How?'

I smiled. 'Silas, remember, I told you, he was blind . . .'

Red Rover. We ran past Silas again, Mother complained again, Father emptied another bucket and called for Adele to fetch more water (although we were low).

'Red Rover!'

This time it was like he could see me, went straight for me, and when I moved left he moved left, right, right, back and forth, till all the other kids (and Ludwig) had got past and Mother called, 'Benno, stop teasing Silas.' I said I wasn't, but she said it was cruel. I stood, waiting, shooshing the other kids and taking a few silent steps. But even then, he heard me. I said, 'It's not fair.'

'Why?'

'You're picking on me.'

He smiled. 'Come on, Benno. There's a time limit.'

Left, but he sensed, or saw? Right, and he smiled and said, 'You know you can't do it.'

'Why?'

'You just can't. Cos you don't understand.'

'What?'

'*And he that sees the world . . .*'

'Bible's not gonna help you now,' I said.

'The Bible always helps, Benno.'

I took off my shoes. I took off my socks. Mother, Ludwig, the kids, everyone waiting. Then I found the softest sand and walked around him. But he turned his head, smiled, sprinted towards me, brought me down, laughing, tumbling, talcum hair and face, and Father saying, 'Nice that some people have the time.'

Silas sat up, brushed off his suit and said, 'You *wanted* to be caught, Benno.'

Oh, and that bit about the desert. Me, standing miles and miles from home, nothing but a blue sky and warm breeze. I can't remember what I was doing there, or how I'd got there, but I remember being alone. And I remember seeing this small speck coming towards me, and waiting, for minutes, maybe half an hour, before I worked out it was a donkey. It got closer, stopped, looked at me. It was old, its fur and skin all ratty, big ribs, red eyes. I reached out, rubbed its head and said, 'Where did you come from?' I turned and headed back to Hermannsburg and it followed me. I told it to go away, but it (she) followed me. When we got back to the mission I put her in the yards, gave her some feed, and water, locked her in and said, 'I think I'll call you Himmel. Is that okay?'

Hermannsburg

Late afternoon gusts lifting iron from the roof, washing from the line – singlets and shirts blown across the compound, against the tannery door. Rain in the night, the leaking roof, Mother calling for Adele to bring buckets. A comedy of brooms and old gal, raised voices, as Father kept moaning from his room. Things settled, and the springs in the matrimonial bed groaned under Mother's weight, Father telling her to keep still, then the wind and rain, again. And me listening for Father, moving between the various remedies of hymn ('If God himself be for me'), charm ('My mouth is growing whole again, is growing whole again') and pleading with God to make him better.

At some point I must have fallen asleep, woken, the rain heavier than ever. I must have walked, on the balls of my feet, on the bits of solid floorboard, into the sitting room. I must have stood listening for Father, trying to understand what was going on (just the word, *oedema*, although I had no idea what it was). I must have sat in Father's chair, and it must have made a noise, because Mother said, 'Benno, is that you?'

'Yes.'

'Go to bed.'

'I've been to bed.'

And Father: 'What's he doing up?'

The sort of morning I remember best: standing in my pyjamas at the kitchen door as Adele, Pauline, and her son, Lucas, made breakfast. Lucas grinning at me, knowing he couldn't come inside and read my books, try Father's cologne, taste his brandy, or sit and talk and work on my clock's broken mechanism (although when my parents weren't around . . .).

Now he just had to knead dough. Now I just stood and watched. My feet on the cold boards, the breeze coming through the front door, into my pyjamas, my underclothes, the faint smell of linseed oil.

Walking back into the sitting room, flowers dropping petals over Mother's lace tablecloth. Usually Mother would make Adele throw them onto the compost pile with the egg shells, tea leaves, soup bones or clippings from overgrown *californica*. Mother and her ephedra, a piney shrub that filled a garden she cultivated around our house – fifty, sixty specimens in rows, carefully labelled, picked, pressed and described in a notebook labelled, simply: EPHEDRA. A difficult, unlovable shrub that, she always stressed, grew everywhere in the world *except* Australia.

I stood in front of the mantlepiece studying photographs of Anton and Alwin, Michael, Julius and Charlotte. Busy at work at St Thomas's School, Leipzig, unaware of their father's feet and legs, his swollen body, his cough. Maybe they were learning Latin, maybe out in the snow, or boiling dumplings with Oma? Maybe they were talking about me: 'What do you think he's up to now?' Alwin saying I was branding cattle, Charlotte, that I was teaching the blacks how to write. I wondered if Mother had written to them about Father.

'Best you get dressed,' Adele said, gliding through the sitting room, puffing up flattened cushions.

Maybe she saw it in my face. 'He's better this morning.'

'Doesn't sound it.'

'Listen, he's been sleeping.'

'I heard him . . .' But what was the point? She only wanted me to feel better; she wanted to comfort me, and did, with a pale hand, small fingers tracing a line of love and consolation across my shoulder.

'Get dressed.' Then she went outside, calling a few of the men.

Bearing in mind I was fourteen and anxious and needed to pee, and everything was in a strange flux; nothing could be explained. Why had my parents left my siblings in Germany? Why was I the only Australian? And Father . . . only fifty years old, but dying (I knew, even then) from an old person's disease.

'Ludwig!'

Ignatz, from the porch. I'll tell you more about him later, but for now, you just need to know he was our schoolmaster (BA in languages, although he had to teach mathematics, science, anything Father thought useful). You need to know he was six feet tall, long arms, spider fingers, timid eyes in wire-framed glasses he kept pushing up the bridge of his nose. You need to know he always wore the same suit, the same frock coat, collarless shirt (even on hot days). And you need to know he had a reedy voice – oh, and a few hairs protruding from his nose (if me or Lucas or Oskar ever laughed it was all over). He stood on the porch calling: 'Ludwig!'

I peered through the gap in the curtain, listened through the few inches open to the last of the storm (as the water kept dripping into a half-full bucket). I heard Ignatz say, 'I have a job for you.' And Ludwig say, 'For the pastor?'

'Yes.'

'Is he getting better?'

'No. That's why I need you. Adele said you can run faster than anyone?'

A short pause then, 'I dunno. I'm old. You want one of them boys. They go quick.'

'I would but . . .' Searching the porch, the compound, the skeletal trees that used to make an orchard. 'I need someone I can rely on, Ludwig. Someone who won't wander off, give up. Go to Alice Springs, get the job done.'

'Alice Springs? Long way.'

I sat, curious. I'd never heard of anyone running all the way to Alice Springs.

'I can trust you?' Ignatz said.

'If it's Pastor Gerlach. He's bad?'

'Yes.'

See, this is how I had to learn about the world, my father's health, death, love, lust, money, all of it – how I had to learn everything when I was fourteen. A childhood of overhearing, digging for hidden notes;

a confusion, a misreading of nearly everything that grew out of keeping me safe – although from what?

'This is what you give them at the telegraph office,' Ignatz said, sitting down on Mother's rocker, flattening a piece of paper on the table. 'It says Pastor Gerlach is very ill, got that?'

'Yes.'

'And they must send a car, they, the Lutheran Mission Board, to collect the pastor. Now, a few days or so . . . that's what we're asking for, that's what you must send. But run fast, fast, like a rabbit.' Showing him with a puppet hand. 'Got that?'

'Yes.'

'The girls have made some food . . . you keep running, right? Drink plenty of water.'

'Plenty. I got plenty of help.'

'How's that?'

He didn't say. Ludwig knew he could tell my father that sort of thing, but not Ignatz Beck. His understanding of the world was limited to newspapers, primers, tables, geometry, even the Bible. No. What he needed to say couldn't be said to Ignatz. 'Can I see the pastor?'

Ignatz thought about it. 'Come on.'

I rushed into my room, waited until Ignatz and Ludwig had passed through the house, then re-emerged at Father's door in time to hear Ludwig say, 'You know how I go? Easy.'

'You needn't,' Father said.

'He does,' Ignatz said, taking command.

'Right . . . I'll be forever grateful,' Father said. 'How long do you think?'

Ludwig didn't reply. It'd take as long as it took. He could fly. He knew he could fly. Plenty of people to help him, but he said, 'Two days, then back, then a car, eh?' Smiling. 'Drive you all the way to Adelaide?'

Adele came up behind me. 'Listening in again?' Pushing me aside, going into the bedroom, hanging a pack over Ludwig's shoulder. But he removed it and said, 'No need.'

'You'll need it,' Ignatz said.

Father saw me and said, 'Benno?'

I stepped into his room. 'Are you feeling better?' I asked.

'I'm fine. What about that rain? Good sign, isn't it? Come here.'

I slowly walked to the side of his bed. He looked me over and said, 'Ludwig's going for help.'

I turned to Ludwig. 'Thanks.'

'Although by the time he gets back I'll be better, won't I, Adele? Won't I, Ignatz?'

Neither replied.

'Righto.' Ignatz, taking Ludwig around the shoulder, hanging his supplies around his neck like a pack horse, leading him to the door. As we listened from the bedroom, and Ignatz said, 'Out of everyone, Ludwig . . .' Again, no reply, just the sound of bare feet in sand, fading.

A year later I was sitting around a fire with Ludwig, Jamy and Silas, and I said to Ludwig, 'That day Ignatz sent you to Alice Springs . . .' He said (something like), 'Long way,' and I asked what had happened. He pulled millet from the sand and said, 'I got the grass and waved it about like this, like it was the sun, and the sun could stay high in the sky so I could get all the way to Alice. I put it in a tree, in a knot-hole, and it stayed there, holding up the sky, and I ran like a rabbit, singing whatever I could think of. "The snake's tail is hissing through the air" or "Jesus Loves Me". I never stopped singing, Benno. I thought I could make it, give them the message and the car would come and ingkata would be fine.' Staring into the embers. '"*Sollt es gleich bisweilen scheinen* . . . this I know, for the Bible tells me so". Running over the dunes, I didn't stop on the way because . . .'

I can't remember what I said then. Maybe something like, 'You tried.'

'Then I got to Alice Springs, and I'm walking along the street saying to people, *Where's the telegraph office?* They're just ignoring me or telling me I should be in my camp, but eventually I explained to some woman and she showed me where to go. I gave the man the telegram, see, here' – and he produced it, because he'd been carrying it for the year or so since – 'and he said, *You got money?* I told him no, but he sent it anyway because he said your dad, Benno, was . . .'

He'd wanted to stop, but I'd insisted.

'So he lets me lie down on his stretcher, and he gets me some water and I tell him I'd just run a hundred and fifty miles, and he says, *Christ, you'd be dead*. But I wasn't, Benno. I wasn't dead. Those people, they ran with me. I slept for a few hours and he made me a brew then some fella brought a stew in from the pub and I gobbled it all down.' Smiling. 'He said his wife was Lutheran, and they knew all about Pastor Gerlach and the work he was doing with the Aborigine people, way out in the never-never (Alice Springs, he said, was bad enough).' He was stirring coals with a stick. 'Anyway, then his machine starts tapping out a message.' He held up the telegram: 'BOARD SAYS NO CAR CURRENTLY AVAILABLE. SEEK HELP AT HORSESHOE BEND'.

Then he folded the telegram and said, 'I told him to send another message, they can't say no, the pastor's sitting at death's door. But the bloke just said if I send the same message I'll get the same reply.'

'But he can't get to Horseshoe Bend. He can barely go to the toilet.'

Back to Hermannsburg, four days later. The rain's cleared, the wind's dropped and the sun's warming the iron roof. Some kids are teasing Himmel, and I tell them to get lost. Adele's cutting up a sheep that's hanging from a tree because none of the men feel up to it. They reckon they're too worried about ingkata, but she tells them people still have to eat. Me, sitting on the porch reading *Robinson Crusoe*. Ludwig runs in, sits down and holds up the telegram. Mother comes out, takes it from him, reads it, and just about collapses. But this soon turns to anger, and she's cursing 'those bastards in their big houses in Adelaide', pacing the old boards, before going in to tell Father. Not so much as a thank you for poor Ludwig. Then Ignatz comes over and asks what's happened, Ludwig manages a few words, the school teacher goes in, then Adele and Pauline, Silas and Jamy. Ludwig says, 'Those rotters. They won't send no one. No one!' A few muttered comments, then, 'Don't even have a car they reckon!'

By which time I could hear Mother crying, Father consoling her, Ignatz trying to make sense of it all: 'We were probably talking to the wrong person. Ludwig needs to go back. We need to tell them it's not a choice. We have no choice, do we, Martin?'

And that time later, around the fire, Ludwig said to me, 'I sorta made a mess of it.'

'How?'

'Shouldn't a come back with a message like that.'

'It wasn't your fault.'

He told me about the journey back – running along the hot Alice Springs roads, stopping to drink at Ellery Creek, to eat at Ntjiakara, another belly full of water at the soak, all the time singing his way through the landscape, full of ghosts, night parrots, *sollt es gleich, in his love we shall grow strong – yes, Jesus loves me!* He told me how he slept at Ndugaduga, but only for a few hours, because he knew everyone at Hermannsburg would be waiting to hear, and how, when he arrived at the far side of the hill and removed the tuft of grass from the tree, given thanks to the old people, he just wanted ingkata to get better – someone to lead us, teach us, preach to us, solve our problems, stop our fights, make us laugh and feel sad and loved, in the arms of God, or anyone. 'This is what I wanted, Benno. But they just said: no car! Like ingkata could just go off and die, because he was too much trouble.'

Eventually everyone drifted back to their shade, their camp, their jobs, discussing what else might be done for the pastor. Later, Father came out on the porch, sat in the sun and told everyone he was fine. He said to Ludwig, 'I'm not sure how to thank you,' but Ludwig just said, 'You get it, don't you? It wasn't me running all them miles.'

Oskar

Pauline's four-year-old niece, Tonia, sat on our kitchen floor playing with a doll. A big, black (Father had painted it) doll with yellow hair and a body that changed from black to white under her dress. Tonia sang: '"Polly put the kettle on . . ."' Adele said to me, 'Why can't you sing like Tonia?' I said, 'I can, I just don't want to.'

'Come on . . . "Abdomens adorned . . ."'

The doll was mine. Mine. I'd been given it one Christmas. I'd said, 'Thanks . . . that's . . . *thanks*.'

Mother had said, 'If we could've got to town . . .'

'Anyway,' Father had said, 'it'll help teach you. It'll help teach him, Alma.'

I didn't dare ask what. To like dolls? Be a girl? But I guess, now, I understand. To realise I was living in some other sort of normal, and what went for other kids didn't go for me. I still have a photo of me on the porch, standing beside the doll in its cane pram. I can see what I was really thinking. But again, that was Father. Complex. The first of many things about him I'd never understand.

But now, Adele said, 'Stay out of that mess, Tonia.'

Because Adele had spilt dripping on the boards, and now there were flies tasting it, and Tonia went between swatting them, combing the doll's hair, sticking her finger in the puddle of muck and tasting it. Adele told her to take the doll outside and play, but Tonia said no, and Adele lifted the wooden spoon, so she stood up and went outside.

'So you don't want to sing?' Adele said to me. 'Too old?'

'*Fourteen?*' Cutting up the cauliflower. Moth-eaten, but full of cowshit-goodness; thrown into the pan, covered with white sauce. As I thought to ask why we were cooking, if Father wasn't eating. Adele could read my thoughts. 'Everyone's hungry.'

'No one likes cauliflower.'

'Everyone, except you.' Touching the end of my nose, flicking it, summoning the honey ants and saying: 'That was ingkata.'

'I know.'

'It'd all be forgotten if he hadn't have listened to the old people, written it all down. And now it's in his books and people will always remember, even if . . .'

'What?'

'If we forget, or drop dead.' Remembering, touching my cheek, picking up a floret and eating it. 'You should be proud of what he's done. It's important you know where you come from.'

'I do.'

'You know *where*, and *when*, but that's different.'

'How many more do you want done?'

'Keep going. That song tells a lotta people who've forgotten . . . some of them twins, like us, eh?'

She must've guessed I was thinking of other things. Father groaning in his room, complaining about the sheet on his foot, just take off the damn leg, someone, please! Laughing with Mother, and Silas, who'd arrived in his best bleached-white, sat with Father to talk about the old days, even before Pastor Kempe, before the Gerlachs arrived in 1894.

'That'll do,' Adele said, covering the last of the cauliflower with sauce.

'What's next?' I asked.

She pointed to a dozen lemons that needed squeezing. I complained, but she wasn't listening, so I started halving them, juicing them, licking my fingers and emptying the liquid into a jar. I worked slowly, interested in what she'd say next. She was the Truth, the encyclopaedia, the better-than-Beck lessons that made sense of my childhood. Father could write the book, he could preach, he could explain (Mother always correcting his small transgressions), Ignatz Beck could make me conjugate verbs, but Adele just said things like, 'I remember.'

'Not again.'

'Just cos you don't like hearing it. I swear – there's your mother on the bed, screaming and shouting, and me and Sally, bless her soul, bringing in the hot water, the towels, and out pops who?'

'Me.'

'Red as coals! No movement, no nothing. *Is he alive?* I say to your mother. *Check him*, she says. And I did, and you were breathing, but just, so I sat patting you, talking to you, until your father comes in and sees and says, *Quick, there's no time*.'

'I think I've done enough.'

'*I'll* decide.'

Father shouting, 'Get that thing off my leg, Alma!'

Adele never missed a beat: '*Follow me*, your father says, running out of the house.'

'You keep telling me this story.'

'You need reminding. People fight to stay alive, don't they, Benjamin?'

'Yes, *Adele*.'

She listened for Father's moans. 'They fight.'

I didn't agree or disagree, but she was right.

'Out the door,' she said, waving a carving knife in the air. 'He's calling to everyone to follow him, and I'm running behind him with you in a blanket. Into the church, fills the font, makes me hold you over the water, pours a little over your head and asks God if it's okay if you become one of His children? And meanwhile . . .'

'Meanwhile the church's full of people, and Mother and Michael and Anton and Alwin, watching Father baptise me before I die . . .'

She didn't growl; she didn't tell me off. 'You can't ever assume, Benno.'

'I don't.'

She just continued with her I-know-better face. 'Your father, I saw it, rode up to Constable Dietrick and Remington when they had six people lined up. Dietrick was aiming his gun, but your father said put it down, and he saved those people's lives. And you think cos he's got some sort of cold or fever or something.' Shaking her head. 'He took that gun off Dietrick and said he'd report him, he'd see him in gaol.'

I'd imagined this story a hundred times. It seemed made up, but it wasn't. 'We've got to find a doctor, or get him to . . . where do you think we could go?'

She took a moment. 'I'm sure your father and Ignatz have a plan.'

'Benno!'

Oskar, bouncing his ball in the dirt outside. Adele messed up my hair and said, 'I'll finish.'

As I went out, she said, 'After your father put that water on your head . . .'

'I know, I started screaming, like Jesus or someone had saved me.'

Calling after me: 'That's how it happened.'

Out of the house, away from the lavender and carbolic acid, talcum powder and body odour it never really disguised. Oskar stood holding what passed as our soccer ball (repaired with twine and glue). 'First to ten goals,' he said.

I licked my fingers, spat in the dust, dunked my head in the horse trough and took my position. Oskar positioned the ball. 'Should we play for something?'

'You haven't got anything.'

'Your knife. Beat me to ten . . .'

Although I didn't care about my knife. He liked carving his name into tables, posts; chopping up insects; walking around showing the other kids, Adele asking me why the hell I'd given it to him. 'The blade's blunt.'

'So what? It's a knife. Oskar, come here, give Benno his knife back!'

'I won it off him.'

Three days before we left Hermannsburg. When Father was bad, but could still get around, when I never (despite what Adele was thinking) thought his life was at risk. The eight-day grass had sprouted. The daubed walls, the wet sand, the yards had dried off and a leftover breeze cooled the huts and houses, the stables, the lean-to they'd once used for making pottery (the wheel in pieces on the ground). Through the graveyard, its wooden crosses and marble reminders ('*Hier Ruht in Gott*') that life was temporary. A board for Trevor Jangala, brought in from where his mother had abandoned him in the desert. Gentle hills and valleys of earth where Father had buried a dozen, fifteen kids who'd died in 1916. I can still remember the starving blacks arriving at the mission at the tail-end of a drought. All bone, sucked-in tummies, drawn faces and bloodied gums. And their kids, sleeping all day, ragdoll-dead, taken from their parents by Mother and Father and blessed and buried in the shade of the church.

Still cool, but it would warm up and we'd be stuck inside, cold flannels on faces, sitting in the bath for hours trying to keep cool with Mother's bamboo fan. So, for now, soccer. Oskar kicked the ball before I noticed, but I was off, after him, blocking his path, taking possession, before he reclaimed it and scored a goal.

We returned to the centre, and I said, 'I'll bet you the slingshot.'

'How's your dad?'

I shrugged.

'What's wrong with him?'

'Adele said there's water, fluid, building up all over and . . .'

Adele was standing on the porch. 'Go on then. You ever got a goal, Benno?'

'Plenty of times.'

So we started again, Oskar got another goal, I tried, but missed, then Adele laughed and went back inside. Oskar said, 'Dad doesn't reckon it's gonna get better . . . I mean, by itself. He says the telegraph bloke kept trying, but every time it came back the same.'

Oskar, son of Ludwig, long-distance runner, singer of sacred songs, maker of charms. Ludwig, totemic brother, soul mate (as the songs say now) of Pastor Gerlach, who'd always (as far as I could tell) had a soft spot for him. Maybe because, after I'd been baptised on that hot day in 1908, wrapped in a blanket, quietened with a black breast and put into my crib until I passed (or rallied), there was Ludwig and his wife, Mary, standing at our door with their own bundle, knocking and saying, 'Is ingkata here?'

Father emerging, seeing the newborn baby, all meat and muscle and black hair, healthy lungs and a horse's kick, saying, 'How old is he?'

'Just now.' Ludwig, smiling.

'What time?'

'Hour ago.'

Oskar and I were born on the sixth of June 1908, Oskar an hour earlier than me. Perhaps that explained his kick, his long legs, his broad shoulders. Perhaps I'd always been playing catch-up.

'That's easy,' Oskar said, lingering over the ball. 'Get to town. The doctors can fix him.'

'If we can . . . I thought maybe there'd be a plane.'

At which point we lost interest in soccer, walked over to the yards and stood watching Himmel searching for grass. Oskar said, 'What's the point of keeping her?'

'She doesn't do any harm.'

'She's just about dead.'

Just watching, as she looked up at us, came over, sniffed my hand.

'Better she gets a bullet,' he said.

'Just cos your dad said it.'

'Look, she's got sores.'

'Come on!' I ran to the house, and Oskar followed. Went in and got a drink, and Oskar was still there. We returned to the porch and sat outside the sitting room. Mother's Leipzig curtains blew in and out of the window (the spot where I'd torn them, where Pauline had sewn them, where the sun and desert air had finished them). They smelled of roses, of liniment; of camomile and a thousand roasts, mint peas, acid-eaten books, everything that added up to my small life. Father, at three am, leaving his piss on the toilet seat; the stains in Mother's underwear.

'Want to see her again?' Oskar asked.

One of his brother's magazines. It showed everything, or at least enough to get you thinking, wondering, exploring. Maybe he thought it would cheer me up, but the promise of more things I couldn't, shouldn't have just made it worse. He took the torn sheet from his pocket and spread it on the table beside Mother's glasses. 'I been thinking about that.'

Just nodding, because it didn't need explaining.

'What do you reckon?'

I shrugged. 'She's a bit old for you.'

'Nah, see, that's where you wanna go.' Studying it, looking up and saying, 'You want to keep this?'

'No.'

'I know what you're thinking, Benno.'

'I doubt it.'

She was nice. But so far removed from anything at Hermannsburg. The Colosseum, overgrown with ferns, the cane lounge, the suspenders she'd pulled down, the hairy bit, and the big bosoms, slinking off to the side, like they were trying to get away. Oskar folded it and handed it to me. 'Go on.'

A little was a lot. Especially when you woke up after it had already happened, fiddling around with the pee-pot, Mother asking what I was doing up in the middle of the night. All in all, another complication of what should've been a simple life.

A few footsteps, and Mother came out, followed by Ignatz. He said, 'It's the only way.'

'Not as he is. And how? In a cart. Iron wheels, and his legs?'

We watched, and listened.

'That's what I think,' Ignatz said. 'There's no other way.'

'We wait.'

'How long? It's going to get worse.'

'I can hear you,' Father called from his room.

So they whispered. Ignatz said, 'Leave it another week, how will we be? How will you feel then?'

'She's right, Ignatz,' Father called. 'It'll sort itself out.'

I put the naked lady in my pocket. Maybe she'd become a charm; maybe she could help me understand. I wanted to add my bit, about how it was a good idea to go to the railhead at Oodnadatta, a train south, hospital, doctors. Why stay and wait for things to get worse?

'We could wait another day,' Ignatz said, 'but it's been two weeks.'

Ludwig held up the ball. 'Best of five then?'

But then the curtain blew out, and Mother saw me and Oskar and said, 'I thought you were helping Adele.'

I went in and said to her, 'Ignatz is right.'

'Wait!' Father called. 'You're some sort of medical expert, are you, Benno?'

Silas emerged with the usual tap of his cane. 'We should pray. The answer's already there.'

'Unlikely,' I mumbled. But, of course, he just knelt and said, 'Should we ask the Lord?'

There was a sort of gathering, but I didn't feel like I was present, like anyone was present: God, honey ants, Adele, standing between the sitting room and kitchen.

Tnokkapaltara

I remember Father standing in St Thomas's church in Leipzig, turning to us kids and saying, 'This is where he stood!' Beaming. Anton saying, 'Who?' Father replying, 'Luther. This is where he stood and preached. See, the plaque.' Indicating, although none of us were interested. But that name, *Luther*, and the rattling words of his hymns ('Commit whatever grieves thee'), his translation of the New Testament, and Father's translation into Aranda. So the blacks might understand what Luther was saying that day in Leipzig, about Jesus and his followers and what they thought about the seven days and nights, the grass trees and wallabies, and how we came to be. All of these things connected, through words, through *the* Word, through what Abraham saw, and the Martins Luther and Gerlach preached.

Here's an example. Oskar and I, four-thirty the next morning, dark, cold, the night full of starlings and snakes, running towards Ntarea ('waterhole'), along the Larapinta ('Finke') in search of Tnokkapaltara ('night parrots'). Two different but identical worlds rubbing against each other, and you could choose whatever explanation you liked. In the end, Father chose both, and tried to make them (not always successfully) coexist. Back then, of course, it was mainly Christian, but things have changed, haven't they? As I write (1988), poor old Henry Ayers's rock changing its name to Uluru. And maybe that's as it should be. Maybe Alice shouldn't be Charles's wife, or Darwin, with his own fascination with parrots; Adelaide, some old German queen with gout – maybe this country's better off being the way it was at the beginning of time.

Back to the desert, just before dawn, October 1922. Back to Hermannsburg, and me, leading Himmel from Mother's ephedra (someone had left her gate open) back to the yards. A pile of branches where Mother had made Ludwig prune her *altissima* (var. *tibestica* – Tibesti Mountains, northern Chad). Further out, past four walls that had once been a hospital, a couple of wild cats, and Venus, burning brightly. I arrived at Oskar's humpy – all iron and sticks and stones and tarps – and shined Father's tungsten lamp through a window. Tapping on the glass. 'Oskar, you awake?'

A shape moving inside, the window opening an inch. 'Turn it off!'

I dimmed it. 'Let's go look for night parrots.'

'Now?'

'*Night.*'

'Where?'

'Ntarea.'

'Why?'

'Before the sun comes up.'

I waited, determined. I was going, either way. Imagine, coming in at seven am, presenting Father with a (living or dead) specimen and saying, 'See, they do exist!' This had been the songline of my childhood – Father telling me about the parrot, its diet, its messy plumage, its temperament – the way it had succumbed to cats and foxes, drought and white men with big guns. Every time we visited a waterhole: 'Look at these prints, Benno, over here!' Although it always turned out to be something else. So that, in the end, I was never quite sure if it was a parrot population of one, living in Father's head.

Now, Oskar said, 'Can't it wait?'

'No. The minute the sun starts to rise . . .'

I waited as he closed the window, watched as he pulled on an old mission shirt, came out and said, 'We better get back before Dad's up.'

We didn't need the lamp. We knew every inch, every pool, every puddle, every spadeflower. We ran barefoot across the compound. Oskar picked up a can and threw it onto the church roof, and laughed, but I told him to be quiet. Over the bloodwood fence, into the hills, following an overgrown path. High grass. Burrs. Oskar gave up on his shirt, ripped it off and stuffed it in a knothole. 'Anyway,' he said, 'that parrot stuff's all made up.'

'There are *specimens*. In museums.'

'What museums?'

'You've never been to one.'

'Have so.'

'When?'

He hadn't. I knew where he'd been every day of his fourteen years.

'When we were in town once. Dad took us.'

'So what else have they got in museums?'

He waited a moment. 'Meteorites.' Sneering at me, shaking his arms, pushing out his chest. '*You* woke me. *You* wanted me to come.'

'But how would you know about night parrots if you've never been to a museum?'

He just walked. 'Probably plenty of them at one time, but your lot shot them all.'

'Not my lot.'

'*Your* lot.' Surly eyes, adjusting to the light.

'I've never seen one, no one has, but I've heard one. Like this.' I made the short, sharp whistle.

Oskar just smiled.

'What? It is!'

He made a long, shrill cattle call. 'That's my parrot. Big bastard.'

We slowed, dragged our feet through the dunes, felt the spinifex between our toes, called out to the night in praise of freedom, in defiance of the small, starchy world we'd left behind. 'If we could find one,' I said, 'it'd cheer Father up, eh?'

'What was he like last night?'

'Alright, I reckon.' Although his groaning had kept me up till two.

'Where we gonna look then?' Oskar asked.

'We just gotta hide, we gotta wait, and watch.'

Sometimes, sitting here in my house in Hillcrest in the year of Our First Fleet 1988, surrounded by fibro homes, a Woolworths, the Ford people dropping spanners on the concrete all day, I remember Hermannsburg. I remember the view to the south on mornings like this, Laikintinerama ('range of doom') and the bluffs of Rutjumba. The way the hills rose out of the desert and hung there, like made-up places, like places from Stevenson and Kipling. I remember the peak of Ltarkalibaka, and I remember wondering why white people never came here. It was more beautiful than Leipzig Station; more fun than sprinting the length of the St Pauli tunnel with Michael and Anton; it was full of ghosts who'd taken over my father's imagination (sitting of a night at his desk, transcribing his notes, the places, the names).

We arrived at Ntarea an hour or so later, and I said to Oskar, 'They go down to the water to drink . . . *shh*.' Finger to my mouth.

We moved through the reeds, our feet sinking into the soggy ground. I listened. As our eyes and ears adjusted to the night. 'There!' I turned up the incandescent bulb, but it was just a Bourke's parrot. A bit longer, and I managed to tell the difference between three or four calls, and tried the lamp again. But this time, a boobook owl.

'No parrots here,' Oskar said.

'*Shh*.'

'Anyway, why's your dad care? He wouldn't want you *catching* one. He wouldn't want it in a cage, or dead, would he?'

Good point. But I said, 'We're here now. We gotta find one.'

An Olympic-sized waterhole hemmed in by east-west walls of rust-red rocks, some smooth, some angular where they'd done a deal with time, some split down the middle. Brackish water lapping at a scaled-down desert with its own hills and valleys, a butcherbird landscape where real and imagined animals came down to drink. Plenty of tracks – wallabies and skinks, what I thought were bustards, although Oskar said unlikely. By now he was in one of his moods, and smiled, and called, 'Jesus, show us your night parrots!' And coming closer to me: 'We should sing, that helps, eh? "I leave all things to God's direction."'

'*Shh*. That's not gonna work. You don't even know your own songs.' And singing my own version of the chant: '"Let the night parrots cover the edge of the pool with their footprints . . ."' Turning to him. 'We better get somewhere to hide.'

We found a spot in the reeds, mud up to our ankles. Flies. Mosquitoes. A bullroarer hum through the grass, although Oskar said it was the old people, shitty we'd woken them. I said shoosh and he shooshed but after a while he lost patience and said, 'He doesn't need a parrot. He needs a doctor.'

'There isn't one.'

'Shoulda gone to town earlier.'

Pissed off, I said, 'He was too busy helping . . .' But returned to the liminal zone. Wondering, guessing there were no parrots. 'Helping all *your* people.'

'*Mine?*No one made yers come.'

'But we did.' Glaring at him. Sometimes I hated him. 'No one else. Just us.'

Sun on the horizon, a grainy, strained-through-muslin light. 'What's that?' I said. The lamp again, but it was just a couple of willie wagtails. 'They probably heard us.'

'Probably.'

'It doesn't matter, I guess.'

'If you wanna show your dad one, we can wait.'

'Nah . . . I'm hungry.'

The walk home was slower. Dragging our feet, leaving a snake trail of disappointment. 'Father was up shouting,' I said.

'At what?'

'The Board. *Thirty years in this place . . . all I ask for's a car, a doctor!*'

'They musta had someone who could come?'

'Course they did.'

Mother was waiting on the porch, arms crossed, as we came down the hill. 'Where have you two been?'

'Exploring.'

'*Exploring?* What?'

'The waterhole.'

'At five in the morning?'

'Before it gets hot.'

She just shook her head and said, 'Clean up and come inside for breakfast. Mary's been looking for you, Oskar.' Before storming inside.

'Sorry,' I said to my best friend.

'*Night parrots?*' Shrugging, running home through the vegetables.

I went over to the trough, climbed in and washed my legs as Himmel watched. Pauline came out for water, saw me, said, 'Your mother's upset.'

'I know.'

'Cosa your dad. You oughta've been here.' She waited as her bucket filled. 'Things are changing, Benno. You're the man now.'

'I'm fourteen.'

'Old enough. Off running around when . . .' Then she shut off the tap and went inside.

I followed, dragging my wet feet on the dry rug, into the cold, polished darkness, the old clock counting every moment, a Bible left open to Revelations. I sat at the table and Adele came in, placed a bowl of porridge in front of me and said, 'Eat that.'

I knew her and Pauline had been talking.

Father sat in the darkness, in the corner, his bare legs outstretched, his pants cut up to the knees to accommodate his swelling legs. 'We woke up and you weren't here.'

'Me and Oskar went out looking for rabbits before it got too hot.'

'Without the rifle?'

'And without asking,' Mother said, coming in, examining my hair and face and muddy clothes and saying, 'You can take a bath.'

Father said, 'I didn't keep you up?'

'No.'

He closed his eyes and grimaced. 'It'll get better soon.' Another thought, and he opened his eyes and tried to sit up. 'Should we have a history lesson?'

'No, we shouldn't,' Mother said. 'What are you thinking, Martin?'

But Father just looked at me, looking at him. 'Battle of Hastings?'

'Ten sixty-six.'

'Between whom?'

'Martin!' Mother, gathering his uneaten breakfast and taking it out to the kitchen.

Father said, 'There are pills for this condition. So once it's taken care of . . .' And a look that said, *I know what you're thinking, Benno*. 'Hard work, that's what matters, isn't it, son?'

'I guess.'

'Remember St Thomas's? Remember Bach? He wrote one cantata a week. He taught the boys to sing, rehearsed them, played on Sundays. He wrote for the keyboard, he had eleven children, he never stopped working. And it kept him going, didn't it?'

'If he had eleven kids to pay for . . .'

'Exactly! And I've got, look over here, boxes of notes to transcribe, books to write . . .'

His way of saying, *I can't afford to die. I won't. So you shouldn't worry. You* should *go exploring with Oskar, you* should *have fun (as much as this place allows).*

'I've decided to go to Horseshoe Bend,' he said. 'There's no alternative. We'll have to do the best we can. Me and Ludwig and Ignatz and you.'

Ignatz was standing in the doorway. 'I'm glad you've seen sense at last.'

'I wouldn't say sense,' Mother said, returning from the kitchen, sitting at the table.

Ignatz surveyed Father from top to toe, asked about his night, and said, 'See, it's *not* getting better.'

'But what *if*,' Mother said, 'what if we go, and you get worse, Martin?'

Sometimes, you just had to ignore my mother. 'Me and Oskar went looking for the night parrot.'

Father's face lit up. 'You did? You and Oskar?'

'Just then.'

'And did you find it?'

'Of course. I saw it, and we ran after it, but it flew away. So that shows you were right, Father. It does exist! We're gonna go back tomorrow and catch it for you.'

'No, you're not,' Mother said.

Father was smiling. 'You actually saw it?'

'Yes.'

'That sounds like a good omen.'

Manual for the Medical Staff Corps (1883)

The church was painted white, mud splashed up the sides, a river red making shade for people to sit and talk before Father's service. There were stories (not that I listened when I was fourteen) about some spirit that lived in the leaves, that drew water from the earth, made life and love, and sugar. I liked standing under it, leaning against it, feeling its skin, its insect trails and hand-carved graffiti ('BM 1891'). Passing into the church, the floorboards worn down to lignin, leaving raw grain; the pews that Pastors Kempe and Schwarz built; the handmade cross under which I and hundreds more had been baptised, confirmed (twelve months earlier), made useful and Christian, given a purpose on Earth.

Walking in, the moon a godly green through the stained glass, colouring the wattle walls. Mother's Hermannsburg Ladies' Choir (before she gave up in frustration, stormed out and said to Father, 'If you want them to sing you can teach them yourself!'). I'd sat and listened as she'd rehearsed them. No melody, no harmony, just a lot of laughing and *we can't remember all that, Mrs Gerlach!* A few snatches, perhaps: 'Nearer, my God, to thee . . .' I could hear them now, and Mother saying, 'If you're provided the opportunity, why wouldn't you take it?'

I sat in my spot on the front pew. In the gap between Mother and Father (when Silas was preaching). The few hard, arse-shaped inches I'd known for fourteen years. I dropped my head and asked God if he could fix Father – today, perhaps, that'd be good. Give him a bullock's heart (still pumping when it was removed), dear Lord. *If God himself be for me, then be for me now.* Today. No more Sunday school stories, no attempts to draw Jesus, no hymns and parables and no Silas, casting off his jacket to show us how Moses stormed down the mountain with his commandments. This was my commandment: 'Don't let my father die.'

'Still, all my songs shall be nearer, my God, to thee . . .' Ignatz pumping the pedals, playing the blocky chords on the harmonium. Mother conducting: 'Watch for your cue, ladies.'

Because it only seemed fair. Me, Oskar and six other kids sitting on our porch, Father saying, 'Benno, a child's duty?'

'Obey your parents, honour your mother and father.'

'Good. Oskar. Young people?'

'Submit yerselves unto the elder . . . be clothed with humility, resist the proud . . .'

'And?'

'Humble yerself under . . . the hand of God?'

'Good.'

Conformation class. Every Thursday afternoon. Our table of duties. Father asked one of the black kids called Tracey: 'And servants?'

'Be obedient to them that are your masters . . . knowing that whatever good thing . . .'

'Any man doeth . . .'

'. . . the same shall he receive from the Lord.'

I went home to see if my prayer had worked. Went inside, waited till my eyes adjusted, and there, Father in his old rocking chair, legs glowing like firesticks, his humpty-dumpty body twisted with cramp. Thanks for nothing, *God*. And what I said at my confirmation – I didn't mean a word of it. Pauline came in, knelt before Father, unrolled pressure stockings over his legs as he grumbled. Mother came running, Adele, Ludwig and Oskar drifted in to see what all the fuss was about.

'I've got to get them on,' Pauline said, working the elastic up the calves, as Father pounded the armrest, called for Mother to do it, but she just said, 'Pauline does it best.'

Father caught his breath and said to everyone in the room, 'It's not a magic lantern show.' Pauline finished, and stood: 'When someone's trying to help you . . .' Glaring at him, before walking out. Father waited for Oskar and Adele to leave.

'It's the only way, Martin,' Mother said.

'I know. I've decided, haven't I?' And to Ludwig, 'Nothing in the mail?'

'Jack'll be here at ten.'

'What are you expecting?' Mother asked.

'A miracle.'

'You don't believe in miracles.'

'I've started.' And noticing me: 'You found a night parrot yet, Benno?'

'No.'

'See, that'd be a miracle. But some things are . . . *withheld*, aren't they, Benno?'

Adele returned with a cup of something, handed it to Father, and he told her he'd rather die than drink it. 'What is it, anyway?'

'Kangaroo apple. The old people take it for their joints.'

He took it, put it aside, and said he'd drink it later.

I sat down and placed my hands in my lap. They'd forgotten me. They always did, like I was a porcelain figurine watching from the mantlepiece. Father said, 'Shall we continue, Mother?' Indicating a letter on the table.

She picked it up, flattened it on the sideboard, sat waiting with her pen. Then, as Father spoke, she wrote: '"Anton, Michael, Alwin, Julius, Charlotte. Here is the matter as it stands . . ."'

'We've explained all that,' Mother said.

'So perhaps: "I anticipate a difficult journey. Eight, nine days. And the weather has me worried. So hot, so early in the season. But not so worried that . . ." What could I put there?'

A sort of back and forth, various versions of assorted thoughts, as I sat in the train compartment, stuffed in beside my brothers and sister, three pairs of pants, a shirt, jacket and two coats, coal smoke coming in the window. Anton leaning forward and saying to me, 'I don't fancy all this.'

'Why?'

'Why would you want to live somewhere so cold?'

He always said stupid things. Cold was cold. Germany was cold, the station at Leipzig (the biggest place I'd seen in my life) was cold. The park on the way to Opa's – cold, icy, a grey sky that had probably never seen sun. Alwin, dragging his case through the station, Father and Mother saying, 'Keep up, it's only a mile or so.'

'"You'll be glad to know this condition is entirely treatable" – is that the word, Mother?'

Without looking up. 'That'll do.'

'"And that once we arrive at Horseshoe Bend, Oodnadatta, the train south, a few weeks of treatment and all will be good. Although this business has precipitated a decision. To give up my calling. To bring Benno and Mother to Germany to see you all."'

It started raining, but Father kept walking, leading us along Kaiser Strasse, saying, 'Only another few houses.' Indicating a block of apartments and saying, 'That place there, second floor, that's where Mendelssohn lived.'

And Julius: 'Who's that?'

'A composer. The *Dream*? You've heard of it?' Humming a few bars of the wedding march. As the rain got heavier and we stumbled over our cases, as Michael fell over, as we marvelled at this strange, new world of five- and six-storey buildings, cobbled roads, and Opa standing at his front door: 'This way, quick, children!'

Father continued his letter to Leipzig, explaining that yes, we were going on a journey, and he was ill, and things might get worse along the way, but God and His son were going with us, and since that was the case, we'd be in good hands. Your brother, Benno, who's been a rod and a staff, is coming with us to make sure we behave, so you should all be proud of him, as indeed we are.

Something, I guessed. Maybe I was more than a Dresden shepherd, pink pants and an overripe apple balanced on the back of my hand. Maybe I'd prove useful along the way? As I lifted my case up Opa's three front steps, looked at this towering old man with his chin whiskers and icy blue eyes and said, 'I'm Benjamin.'

'I know who you are. You're the special one.' Smiling at me.

The special one. But it was never explained.

Father said, '"This is a condition called dropsy."'

Mother stopped writing and said, 'They don't want to know about all that.'

'They should, they need to. Go on.' Indicating. '"Oedema, or a build-up of fluid caused by the heart slowing. Not stopping. Not ending. God has too many plans for me yet."'

'I'm not writing all that. It'll get them worried.'

'They should know the truth. *If* . . . if it came to that, we don't want any surprises.'

'That's just silly.' Although she wrote something – I don't know what.

The truth. There was God's truth, of course, but my father was an enlightened man, and believed books could make our lives better, easier, longer. So he'd sat there (when all this began) with his copy of the British Army's *Manual for the Medical Staff Corps* and searched each page until he found swelling, causes, oedema, treatments. Hidden away between shrapnel wounds and diphtheria, fractured bones and chlorine poisoning. He'd read it to Mother, and she'd told him to stop being so dramatic, and how was a book about war wounds going to help anyway? But he'd insisted. He'd diagnosed dozens, hundreds of blacks with his manual. He'd shown each man, woman and child the precise illustration and said, 'See, this is what's wrong with you, and quinine' – or plasters, double-dipped in arsenic – 'will set things right.'

The word. And the Word. Complementary, in his opinion, although it hadn't done him much good. I'd been through the same bookmarked entries, read the descriptions, studied the drawings, but there was nothing about how to save a fifty-year-old man from his own failing heart.

'"Ignatz will endeavour to keep you all informed,"' Father said, waving his hand, and finishing with, 'That should be enough, for now.'

Pauline came in with a colander, and said, 'Benno?'

I followed her outside to the porch, the boxes of plates and silverware, the books, the towers of Father's notes. We'd spent the last two weeks packing them. Father had decided. If the Board wasn't going to support him . . . so be it! They could find someone else and make him work for no or little pay for the hundreds of people he was meant to save every day. Two chests full of Mother's clothes. All sitting in the morning sun. *Treasure Island* and shattered bones; regrets, pounds and pounds of them. Although, I'd heard him tell Mother he wouldn't leave until someone took his place. Making all of the boxes a form of wishful thinking.

Pauline handed me the colander, and the peas that Ludwig had just picked. 'Come on.'

'Sicka shelling peas.'

'I'm sick of listening to you complain.'

'It's not fair.'

'Don't start all that.'

She was right (as usual). What was fair? Nothing. That's one thing I learned on the mission – God's plans are not your plans. You can fight Him, but He'll win.

Pauline said, 'You okay?'

'I guess.' Peas falling between the wooden boards. There were a few cats. Maybe cats liked peas.

'All ready?'

'Yes.'

She just stared at me. She knew. Her and Adele always knew.

'What?'

'It's risky, isn't it?'

I didn't reply.

'But you've gotta think, it's the best way.'

'I didn't say it wasn't.'

'You haven't said much at all.'

'So?'

She ate a few peas, then said, 'Funny age, fourteen.'

'Why?'

She didn't say. I knew. 'Gotta be fourteen some time.'

Oskar went past and said, 'Coming, Benno?' But Pauline told him

I had work to do, and he should go away. He gave her his look, but she threw peas at him, and he caught some and ate them.

Pauline said, 'Me and Adele are counting on you.'

'For Dad?'

'Come back. The twins, yeah?' She meant the Twins of Ntarea, the totem that was theirs and, by association, mine. She said, 'They all go and leave. None of them come back.'

'I'll come back.'

'We don't want you in town, no? Buncha the old people relying on you.'

'Father's relying on me.'

'You'll be alright. Mr Beck's got it all under control. He's got everything under control.'

And in my best mock Ignatz: '*Today we will prove that the tangent of x is calculated as a function of y.*'

She laughed, then punched me, sort of, and said, 'We'll be waiting.'

And Ignatz, again: '*You can wait all you want, but the Lord Jesus Christ the Redeemer has decided for me, for you, for all of us!*'

But when the moment subsided, she just said, 'You're the one will get him there, fix him up, bring him home. Not Ignatz. All he knows is sums. That don't count for nothing.'

I looked over at Himmel, looking over at me. Like she wanted to tell me something, or knew something I didn't.

'Main thing is,' Pauline said, 'give your dad something to . . . something to hope for.'

'Don't say Samson.'

'Like Samson.'

'Not again!' It felt like she'd dipped my head in a bucket of vinegar.

'Shut up.' She flicked her hand at me. 'That wall . . .'

'I know,' I began, 'that wall there, Benno' (indicating the stone wall running the length of the compound, back, around the dormitories) 'was built by Samson. Samson had just had half of his bowel removed and decided, as . . .?'

'Therapy.'

'. . . to lift hundreds of rocks from the demolished smokehouse and build a wall, and it'd be miles long, and it'd keep his mind occupied, and his hands busy, because that was, and is, what really matters. Keeping busy. But then he died . . .'

'He got sick again.'

'. . . and the wall was never finished, but it was left as a reminder . . .' Smiling. 'There. That saved a few minutes.'

'You are, actually, quite a little shit, Benjamin Gerlach.'

'But at least I get to the point.'

'I'd sit here, every day, watching him move stones . . .' Staring out, like he was still working.

'And I hardly ever repeat myself.'

I saw figures moving in and around the blacks' camp. At first, five or six people, then a dozen, twenty, thirty, gathering and heading towards us. The old people at front, Ludwig and Oskar, Jamy leading Silas, boys running in circles, girls, babies on hips. When they arrived at the house Ludwig said, 'They've written letters.'

Pauline just waited. She knew. She'd written her own.

'For ingkata,' Ludwig said. And the way he said it. It didn't mean ceremonial leader, builder, preacher, none of this. It meant Father. My father. Ludwig looked around and said, 'Me and Mr Beck helped them.'

Each of the old people, holding a sealed envelope. Each of the adults, the teenagers, the kids. Pauline put down her peas, walked down the steps and took Ludwig's letter. Then another, and another. But while she was gathering them, I heard Father saying something to Mother, then his heavy footfalls, then he was at the door, and he said to Pauline, 'What's going on?'

She showed him the letters she'd collected. 'They wrote them, for you, Pastor.'

Father didn't say a word. He managed to move forward, hold the banister, walk down the steps. He took the letters from Pauline and said, 'Thank you.' Then he waited. Ludwig collected the rest, gave them to him and said, 'Just a few lines.' Then everyone turned, and drifted away.

Tuesday 10 October (Day 1)

The previous afternoon, Ludwig, Ted and a bloke called the Greek had gathered a dozen horses from around the waterhole and brought them into the yards. They'd waited until they settled before harnessing them. Watched them graze the winter grass, drink from the trough that me and Oskar kept clean. As the dust settled, and the prospect of the journey was made real. When the horses had quietened they led them up and down the track for an hour. Oskar and I had sat watching. Oskar had said, 'It's gonna be a lot of work, that many horses.'

'I can help.'

'You're no good with horses.'

True. I'd always avoided animals – the muster, the branding, vaccinations, driving them to the railhead. I had a reputation as an indoor kid. Maybe the men had taken pity on me, spared the pastor's son, or maybe they'd just thought I wasn't up to it.

It'd been a big afternoon. Some of the other men had brought in a bullock, cut its throat, strung it up and butchered it. Me and Oskar again, watching from a safe distance, Oskar saying, 'Them dogs eat anything.'

'That one's drinking the blood.' Indicating a three-legged terrier.

Oskar remembering: 'Did you ever find your parrot?'

'No.'

Someone punctured the bowel and a spewy soup drained onto the dry sand, splashing everyone's feet and legs, bile and blood and half-digested grass, hundreds of flies descending.

'I can show you the picture,' I said.

'You did. But that coulda been any bird.'

'This bloke they pay especially to find one of each animal, and he stuffs them and sends them to museums. He found a night parrot and killed it and put it in the mail, and it's in Holland or some place now, which proves it.'

'What?'

'Whether you want to believe or not, it's real. You can go see it.'

I'd shown him one of Father's pictures of a ringneck. But I'd read about this man and his specimens and the special gun that shot a small slug through the heart. He was a good shot. The best. That's why they paid so much for holotypes. No mess, no blood, nothing missing. Unlike the bullock: legs removed with an axe, insides falling to the ground, more blood, the knives coming out. The heart hanging loose, the kidneys collected for pie night, the other organs thrown into a tub for the dogs. A few of the men singing, like they were enjoying it.

They finished the bullock, took the meat to the smokehouse, salted it, wrapped it in cloth for the journey.

Then this morning, the meat was packed into hessian sacks and put into a big ice-box that didn't have ice. Two iron handles, and a little drain for the blood. I said to Oskar, 'If you listen carefully you can still hear it moaning.' And he said, 'Who's going to cook the meat?'

'Me.'

'You can't cook.'

'Pauline's taught me.'

'She hasn't. She's cooked your food while you've sat in there on your bum listening to your dad go on about Jesus.'

I just shook my head. 'Someone's gotta do it.'

Then a few of the women had milked the cows, strained the cheesy-white slop and poured it into a pail. A few days' supply, perhaps. Enough to get us to Henbury, floating in a sea of salted butter, fig jam and condensed milk. But all of this was unknown. Hardly anyone went to Horseshoe Bend, except perhaps Jack, on the mail run.

And that's how it was on this not-hot, not-cold October morning.

How it was as me and Oskar walked around, strangely uncomfortable with each other. Maybe we knew, sensed things were about to change. To ward off this un-charm, Oskar said, 'It's easy. You get to the train, and what's it take? Two days and you're in Adelaide?'

We walked across the compound, Oskar in shorts, me in my best pants (Pauline had laid out my clothes for the journey). Fifty, sixty blacks had already gathered under the ghost gum, beside the lean-to where we stored saddles and harnesses. They were quietly singing, watching Ludwig and Silas, Jamy and Adele and Pauline coming out from the house, loading boxes onto the cart and dray and returning. They were summoning help, I guess – some of the old people who'd travel with us. Ignatz had planned it all the previous evening, sitting around our table, adding up distances and dividing by days, studying a map of the rough country, the places that might have water.

We stopped and watched this growing group. 'You wanna join them?' I asked Oskar, but he just continued into the church, and I followed.

We sat at the back. On Sundays, the place was full. Father had wanted to build a new church, a big, better, cooler place, but of course there was no money, and the Board said, 'It's in the pipeline' (or something similar). The pipeline we'd been waiting for since Father arrived to a collection of huts and stone buildings, good intentions and a box of Bibles. Waiting. Oskar said, 'And what'd happen if . . .?'

'What?'

'I mean *if* . . . you lot wouldn't stay, would you?'

I hadn't thought about it, but couldn't imagine what there'd be to stay for. Mother was no missionary. I couldn't skin a bullock, build a smokehouse, preach, change anyone's life (let alone my own). 'I guess not.'

'They'd send someone else?' Oskar said.

'They might. They mightn't be able to find anyone.'

'Right.' Wringing his hands like he did when he was confused. 'That'd be funny, wouldn't it, because they come here and tell us all about Jesus, then when we're listening . . .'

I walked to the front, splashed the bit of water in the baptismal font. 'Same day. Wonder if it means something?'

Oskar came up behind me. 'Co-in-cidence.'

I dipped my hand, and my fingers made a slow ripple. 'I haven't paid you back yet.'

We were seven or eight, and we'd gone down to Ntarea on a hot day, started jumping into the waterhole. Maybe ten minutes, when I climbed a ledge and (despite Oskar telling me not to) jumped into the middle. Can you imagine Oskar? A few seconds, half a minute, with him calling, 'Benno, you okay?' Then he jumped in, found me lying six feet under, fished me out and dragged me onto the sand. Shouting, demanding I wake up, before he laid me on my side (he later told me) and shook me hard enough to get the water out. I opened my eyes and asked what had happened. And on the way home he said, 'You owe me for that one.'

'Just don't tell my parents, right?'

And he didn't, that day or the next, but a week later he let it slip and Mother was shouting at me, how could I be so stupid, no more unsupervised 'excursions'. Father just sat there smiling, and Mother said, 'Well, aren't you going to tell him off?' Father saying, 'It seems like a good way to learn your lesson, eh, Benno?'

Now, Oskar put his hand in the water, flicked it at me and said, 'And you reckon you're gonna survive eight days to Horseshoe Bend?'

The singing was getting louder. 'I better see if they need help.'

We turned and left, reluctantly. If any place was special, it was here. Special in the hand-hewn floorboards, the wattle and daub walls; in the burn marks the candles left on the walls, and the watercolour stations Isaiah had painted (more about him later). Special in the marble font that confirmed we were alive, and the old table for coffins. Special how everyone had their spot before the big cross, and special how we knew, every time we came in, we were being watched.

And *I* was special, apparently. According to Opa, who must have heard it from Father. Maybe Father had said something to him like, 'You can hold on to the other children, you can send them to school and church, but I think I'll take Benno with me. I think, perhaps, he's special.' Like I said, never explained. But maybe I was the lucky one, sent into the never-never to make new discoveries.

We emerged and saw maybe a hundred people sitting around singing, the women moving rhythmically in the little bit of wind, the kids, even, still and serious and full of purpose. A sight I'll never forget. Sometimes I imagine my own funeral, and the six or seven people who might come. I wonder what I did wrong, less generously, not as wisely as my father. I still remember all of those people, sixty-six years ago, singing us towards salvation and good health, and I realise this is how people are meant to function. None of this better house or school. What's any of that matter? How does it explain why God breathed life into us? But I saw it that day. I saw that my father had become part of something bigger (though not the thing he'd expected).

'Benno!'

Pauline tried to lift a case onto the cart. Oskar and I ran over, climbed up, lifted it, packed it beside the box of books Father had requested. He'd chosen them, as Ignatz had done his sums the previous evening. He'd called out the titles, and Mother, on the porch, had packed them in the Oolong No. 29 box. 'Oh, and *The Odyssey*, put that in too.' He'd been trying to get me to read it for years. Now, with no distractions, he was determined. As he'd been with history, zoology, Greek, Latin – extra studies after class, because although I was a mission boy, soon I'd be sent south to Adelaide, to Immanuel College, for a proper Lutheran education. He didn't want me lagging behind the other kids. He wanted me to be the marvel, the miracle, the scholar he'd never officially become.

Oskar and I returned to the house. We gathered supplies, dragged them back to the cart and dray and managed to load them. Bread that Adele had been baking all night; various meats; small and big water bags; the tents and lean-to, pegs rattling like small change. As the singing got louder, and Ignatz, shittier, asking me where I'd been all morning, just when I was needed (you'll have to do better than that, Benno). I didn't reply. He wasn't in charge. Father was (or probably, Mother). And anyway, I hadn't applied to be a missionary's kid.

I eventually returned to my room and finished packing the clothes Pauline had set out. I checked for a towel, soap, noticed the castor oil Mother put in my hair every Sunday morning (to make it go curly). Like the prime minister was coming to Hermannsburg. I put the oil in my drawer but Mother came in, saw me, reclaimed it and said, 'I can't think what else to take.'

'I've got everything,' I said, sitting on my bed, listening to the songs.

'Just don't get in between him and Ignatz,' she said.

'Is he better this morning?'

'And keep his mind off . . . keep talking to him. That's your job. Read to him. Goethe, that'll do it, I've packed *Faust*.'

Father loved Goethe. He took us to Auerbach's Cellar in Leipzig, bought us a meal and said it was in celebration of our national poet, who came here (here! can you believe it?) to get his ideas.

'Is he better?'

'If he gets bad, tell him. He won't listen to me.' Sitting, taking my knee and squeezing it (she hadn't done this in years).

'But he's better?'

Shaking her head. 'It's a *necessary* trip, isn't it, Benno?'

'Yes.'

'We must do what we can.' Checking out the window for Father before giving up, going into her room and packing the last of his things.

When I emerged into the morning with my carpet bag, Ignatz was helping the men with the harnesses. Four horses on the cart, and four on the dray. Jamy would follow with the spares. Ignatz had worked that out, too. How far we could go before changing; where there was water, feed; which stations would offer food, a bed.

The horses were calm, fat, full of water. Oskar came over and took my bag, threw it onto the dray, indicated the mission blacks and said, 'They want to know how your dad is.'

'He's fine. He's better.'

This is what was expected. This is what my job would be.

'They're worried,' he said.

'They shouldn't be.'

'But don't you . . . *they're worried.* That's why Dad ran so fast . . . because they told him to, he *had* to . . .'

'Who did?'

Even then, I knew Oskar understood more than me. But I wasn't in the mood for sentimentality. I noticed Himmel watching the preparations. 'Come on.' We ran over and I rubbed her muzzle long and hard, like I was scrubbing the kitchen floor. I said, 'It's only a couple of days, Your Majesty.' And to Oskar: 'You promised, right?'

'I'll look after her.'

'Don't forget. And ride her round a bit. She doesn't like sitting in the yards all day.' Running my hand across her head, through her mane, beside her old red eyes. Like she was still trying to talk to me, tell me how it would be.

'I'll make sure no one eats her.'

I gave him my Ignatz glare.

'*What?*'

Mother came out of the house, shouted at me to get ready, stood in front of her ephedra, plucked a few samples and placed them in her botanical notebook. Changed her mind, said, '*Holoptera*,' picked a few more and added them to her collection. Then, from inside, Father called, 'Alma!' and she cursed him, and went in.

We waited. Magic lantern time, the skeleton-and-keys telling us we were in for a hell of a ride. Father emerged in his best shirt, frock coat, pants cut open to reveal his stockings, the leftovers tied with string so he wouldn't look like some leper, cast out into the desert. Mother walked with him, steadied him, supported him as he came down the steps. The blacks stood, fell silent, watching. Slowly, as Ludwig finished securing the load, as Silas felt his way to his seat, as Oskar said to me, 'Just don't go jumping into any waterholes.'

Across the compound to the ladder that'd been placed against the dray. Father waited, then managed to lift his leg to the first rung.

The blacks came closer. A few men said, 'Jakai, ingkata nunka!' An out-of-phase chant spread, before Beck called for a hymn. '*Karerai, wolambarinjai!*' Slowly stirring, one by one, in a failed harmony that sounded like one of Mother's choir practices. The German words Father had crossed out and written in Aranda in the hymn books so everyone would understand. '*Wake, awake! Proclaim with power the watchman's voices from the tower. Jerusalem awake!*'

The second rung, third, as Ignatz helped Father up, Mother half-pushing him from behind. Through this awkward arrangement, and Father's perseverance and shaky hands and legs, he eventually climbed onto the dray. Then, with Ignatz holding him, he took three or four steps and sat down in his ingkata's chair, with its upholstered red seat, its hand-carved armrests, spindles and top slat. Jamy had lashed it to the dray with a series of uncompromising knots.

'*Midnight's solemn hour has sounded; the criers call with joy unbounded . . .*'

Mother climbed aboard the dray, sat on the driving seat beside Ludwig, already holding the reins. By now, the blacks were close, and stopped singing. Father said, 'It's only a small trip, and I'll be back soon. In the meantime, the best thing is to keep things running as normal. Jobs. Do your jobs.' But then he was out of breath.

I climbed aboard the cart and sat beside Ignatz. He said, 'Wouldn't you rather be with your father?'

'We've got plenty of time,' I replied.

Finally, Blind Silas – fresh white pants and shoes, old cane, sitting on a tea chest – said something in Father's ear. Then we were off, followed by a dozen women trailing Jamy and the fresh horses. They, and the old people, would accompany us until they were sure we were safe.

Tjamangkura

It's country you have to see (although very few people do). Red, orange and Kenyan coffee where the grass runs down to the water (if there is any). Reeds thickening at the edges as you wade in, wait in the lukewarm pool. Like the Bible stories Ignatz would tell us, the Jews sacrificing their goats and children and short, hot lives to God. Water tannin-brown from overhanging trees as, in the near distance, hills rise imperfect and purple against a clear sky. We travelled the first few miles and Ignatz, full of thoughts, leaned forward on his knees, barely touching the reins. He pointed to a rabbit and said, 'There weren't so many when I arrived. Some fool let them in. That's why the numbers of native animals have dropped.'

'Why?'

'That's how nature works if you upset the balance. If you bring in something that doesn't have a rightful place.'

This is how the journey would be. Me stuck next to schoolmaster Beck, complaining about everything. I bet he wasn't happy about Father, and his heart, and all this drama. He just wanted to get on with knowing more.

'And how are you?' he managed, glancing at me.

'How am I?'

'With all this . . . with your father?' He moved the reins like some sort of business scribbled in his script. 'Worried, I bet?'

I didn't reply. Of course I was worried. For a smart man he could ask some dumb questions. I knew what he was like. At the front of the class with his cane, Oskar stumbling over some basic English, a verb, or a sum he couldn't understand, Ignatz saying, 'It's really quite simple,' and Oskar replying, 'For you perhaps.'

Ignatz staring at him. 'A bit of respect?'

'You've been to university, but I haven't. Never left this place, so how am I meant to know when to carry the remainder?'

'Because I taught you!'

'I don't understand what you say.'

'Well, listen!'

'I do!'

At which point Oskar (or one of the other kids) would be summoned to the front, told to raise a hand, and Ignatz would say something like, 'This is going to hurt me more than it hurts you.' Oskar might reply, 'Why do it then?' And Ignatz would say, 'You'll thank me for this one day.'

'No, I won't.'

But it'd proceed. It always proceeded. Finger-thick bamboo lifted to the light, back, back, further, brought down on knuckle and bone; the wincing, the bitten lip, the protesting, none of it making any difference. Again, a full arc, harder (it seemed) this time, the victim saying something like *it hurts* or *isn't that enough?* But that's the strange thing. It never seemed enough for Ignatz, continuing, despite the sign on the wall promising God was Love.

'He'll get better,' I managed.

Ignatz didn't say anything. Maybe he didn't want to raise false hopes, or any hopes. Better to be careful, to praise the rules and recite the lessons of the worst-case scenario. That way everyone knew where they stood, even Oskar, at the front of the room, reclaiming his hand and saying, 'No.'

'Pardon?'

'You're hurting me cos of a sum.'

'Put out your hand.'

At this point I'd always watch the artery pumping blood across Ignatz's forehead, the few drops of sweat on his brow, his hand shaking with anger. I'd know that whatever God had said, whatever Jesus had practised, had been lost in translation (or at least implementation).

I watched Father moving from side to side on his throne, trying to steady himself on the armrests, a low moan, but no complaints. Sometimes one leg would lift, and Silas would try and hold him still. The rattle through the road would make it a long, painful trip. Silas sang part of some hymn, but Father lifted a finger to stop him. Mother turned back to check him, Father reassured her, the dray plodded on, nice and slow, amplifying every rock, every corrugation, every pothole and soft edge.

'How's it going?' Ignatz called to them. Silas looked back and said, 'As long as we go slow,' and Father said something, too, although we couldn't hear him.

Ludwig shook the reins every few minutes, but the horses knew what was expected. They just plodded, one leg after another, shoes coming down hard and flinty on the road.

'You should keep it in perspective,' Ignatz said to me.

'What?'

'Millions have this condition and live quite comfortably.'

But they don't live at Hermannsburg, I wanted to say, but didn't, because he'd take it as disrespect. The same words, the same look in Oskar's eyes as he wiped his hand on his canvas pants, said he, Mr Beck, wasn't to do that no more, and ran out to tell his parents. Then it was on – Ludwig and Mary versus Father and Ignatz, shouting, Ludwig demanding to know how a bamboo cane made anything better. Father agreeing but supporting Ignatz, Ludwig asking him who he really cared about, Father becoming indignant and saying how dare he question what he'd done for *your people*.

'You can't make someone's heart better, can you?' I said.

'It can be *managed*, Benno.'

'Didn't Pastor Kempe die of a heart attack?'

'Everyone dies of something.'

'But he was only fifty-four.'

Ignatz just flicked the reins and said, 'You've brought some books?'

'Yes.'

'We're in for some long nights. Maybe we can read something together? Your father said he doesn't want you behind when you go to school.'

The landscape didn't change – the rise and fall of ridges, each feature, each rock, grain of sand, shard of granite (off the old people's tools); each stunted bloodwood offering sacrificial limbs; the mess of mulga; dragonfly wings disturbing water. Horses flicking tails full of flies. I said, 'I'd hate to be a horse.'

Ignatz shook his head. He didn't understand. He didn't have any sense of the abstract, or imagination. 'Why would you hate to be a horse?'

'Not much to look forward to.'

'They're brains aren't like ours. They don't *expect* anything.'

'Does God save horses as well?'

'What?' Wiping dust from his eyes.

'Do horses go to Heaven?'

'They just accept that we harness them, they pull. And in return we feed them, water them, protect them. Not such a bad arrangement.'

'Even if they don't go to Heaven?'

Silas stood, looked around and said, 'That's a mile already.' And to Father: 'We'll be there in no time.' The dray dropped into a rut, and he nearly fell, but Father grabbed his arm. Silas raised his cane and said, 'I can see the hills, Lord! Nothing's hidden, eh, Pastor?'

Father told him to sit down before he fell off.

Ignatz mumbled, 'Fool.'

'Why did he have to come?' I asked.

'Your father asked for him.'

For once I agreed with Ignatz. Silas was half-batty, his brain cooked in God juice. Someone else we'd have to care for. But if Father wanted him.

'I've never understood,' Ignatz said. 'I think your father feels bad.'

'Why?'

'That year, 1906, there were visitors. People didn't know at the time, but their daughter had measles, but it wasn't until after they'd left . . .'

I'd never heard the story.

'A week later some of the children came down with it.' Encouraging the horses up an incline with a few quiet words. 'And when we knew . . . but by then five, six people had it, and an old bloke died, and some of the kids . . . Most of them got better, except Silas. It was on his face, in his eyes, everywhere. And like now, there wasn't any medical help.'

I watched Silas, surveying a landscape he could only smell, hear and taste.

'Your father's always looked out for him. Like you and Oskar, and Ludwig.'

The old people were everywhere, watching us, apparently. The women following behind were still singing, some talking to no one in particular. At fourteen my understanding was that people died, were reincarnated, and this kept happening for thousands of years, crab-bodies popping in and out of new shells. A nice idea. The songs were nice, the way you accepted others as all others, who've ever lived, who've ever walked the Earth.

'He shouldn't have come,' I said.

'In for a penny in for a pound,' Ignatz said.

The women called to us, told us we were safe, turned and headed back to Hermannsburg. Father managed a wave, and Silas blessed them, but they didn't see or hear any of this. Their job was done.

'Anyway, you understand all about, what was it – *I can do all things through he who strengthens me?*' Ignatz said.

My confirmation talk, my little message to God, that I was still happy about all the baptism business, and wanted to join His club, become a decent Christian, draw on my reserves of inner strength.

'I thought you did a good job,' Ignatz said.

'I had to do it.'

'Not necessarily. If you didn't want to. But I think your father was happy. Talking about your brothers and sister and how you missed them but had to stay strong, for your parents, for the blacks, for the mission. Impressive.'

Me and Oskar and the other kids kneeling at the front of the church, Father moving along, confirming us, asking what we'd like to say to God. Ironed pants and starchy tie, oiled hair and scrubbed face (Pauline thinking she could still come into my bathroom). Cut nails, cufflinks, even, and enough talcum powder to hide the devil. Father looking down at me.

'And what would you like to say, Benno?' Mother and Adele and Pauline watching from the front pew.

'I'd like to talk about . . .' Staring up at this big, black, fat figure. 'About . . . when you don't feel you're up to the challenge.'

'What challenge?'

Shrugging. 'Like with Michael and Anton and . . .'

'Go on, tell us about it.'

'Like when I miss them and want to see them but know I can't, and I have to remind myself why I'm here.'

'And why's that?'

'Cos God wants me here, with you.'

Father smiling. Although the whole thing felt fake, staged, all the rubbish about *eat your bread with joy*, when I just wanted to play with my brothers.

We managed three miles before stopping at Tjamangkura waterhole just before two. I filled the kettle, gathered wood, lit a fire and put the water on to boil. We ate Pauline's damper, beef sandwiches and sweet biscuits. Father stayed in his chair, held an umbrella over his head, watched us from the dray. A small orbit of lost souls looking like they'd been travelling for days, not hours. Jamy called up to Father, 'Them horses are fine so far, eh, Pastor?'

'Musta been whoever broke them in.'

'That was me and Ludwig!' Glowing, because Jamy was still the same twelve-year-old who'd fallen from a horse during a muster, kicked in the head, destined to remain a permanent boy (maybe that's why Father favoured him, too).

I spooned tea into the water and waited for it to boil. I told Father I had his coffee if he liked, but he said no, I'll take tea like everyone else. Then Mother asked how he was feeling and he said fine, don't keep asking. As a distraction, perhaps, he started opening the letters the blacks had given him. He read one, he said: '"Pastor go a long way, but not so far . . ." Who was that?' Checking the name. 'The children have written.'

'All of them,' Ludwig said. 'We made sure.'

'And here's Oskar: "I've told Benno what needs to be done so keep an eye on him, Pastor."' Looking down at me. 'Hear that, Benno? *What needs to be done.*'

I knew, and I'd made a start. I'd be the tea and coffee boy, the damper boy, the snack boy. I'd be the fryer of food, the keeper of bush biscuits. And by doing all this, I'd play my part in making my father better.

'It's touching, what they've done,' Father said, adjusting the umbrella. 'Makes me think . . .'

No one asked what. We knew. Mother told me to hurry up with the tea. 'We can't sit here all day, Benno.'

That's how it was, for the rest of the trip. The lot of us sitting around waiting for the water to boil, counting the miles, realising we were going too slow. Ignatz said, 'I was hoping we'd pass this waterhole earlier.'

'The horses can only go so fast,' Ludwig told him.

'It's this track,' Mother said to Ignatz. 'And Martin's . . .'

'But we've counted on eight days.'

'And eight it will be,' Father said, still reading, laughing.

Ignatz fell silent, choosing to wait. His was the way, the truth. Once, in 1919, he stormed into our house and said, 'I gave you until last Wednesday, Martin.'

'Gave me? You're *threatening* me?'

Ignatz's mother, sick in Germany. He wanted to go home to see her.

'I've sent the Board three telegrams,' Father said.

'I've asked Ludwig to harness a few horses. We'll ride together.'

'And who'll teach the children?'

'You. For a few weeks.'

Standing a few feet apart, staring into each other's eyes.

'I'll be back as soon as I can.'

Mother daring to say, 'Perhaps he needs to, Martin?'

'No.' Glaring at her (I could tell), then him. 'She's not *dying*, is she?'

After he'd gone, Father had said to Mother, 'Last time I talked to him he said he never wanted to see her again.' Explaining how, after Ignatz's father was killed in a forestry accident, she'd sent him to St John's

German Orphan Asylum – years and years of scrubbed floors and chopped wood, cold porridge and canes, every day, correcting his behaviour.

'But it's different, at a time like this,' Mother had said.

And over the years, the rest of the story – how all of these stray boys were shepherded into the seminary, taught how to serve the Lord in some of the world's most inhospitable places. The long nights, the safety lights, the discipline that was everywhere, the love of God taught as pluperfect verbs.

Mother removed the beef from her sandwich and said, 'Who killed this?'

Ludwig looked up, sheepishly.

'You took too long.' She sipped my tea, flicked ants from her dress. 'Martin, keep that umbrella up.'

I ripped the damper into chunks, covered them with butter and jam, handed them around. Silas with his hand extended, waiting; Jamy tearing at a length of jerky; Ignatz, busy with a notebook, adding up the hours. 'It's a good job, Benno.'

It? I assumed he meant me. One of those well-placed shots he used when the classroom descended into silence, the blacks lost in cloud through filthy windows, me, the token white kid in the mission school. But black or white, what was the point of knowing the difference between longitude and latitude if you didn't have bearings, if you lived on a false pole, as far from anywhere as possible; if there was no high school, no university to look forward to; if you'd just be sent to work on a station whose owner bled money back to the mission. The stuff I worked out in the years after – the theory, and the practice; the good intentions, and the scene I saw just outside Alice in 1975, when I visited Isaiah's kids. The flagons and cans and dogs and snotty children who'd started out like Oskar and Jamy and hundreds of others.

The food was packed away, the boxes and carts and baskets secured. Ignatz checked his watch and said, 'We need to get to Rubula by six, half past at the latest.'

Towards Rubula

This time I made sure. I sat on the dray beside Ludwig. Mother stood in the millet with her hands on her hips. 'You sitting there, are you?'

'I didn't think it mattered.' I turned to Father and said, 'I could read to you?'

'You haven't got a book.'

But it didn't matter, because Mother was already climbing onto the cart.

So we began. Where there was water, the Finke offered life – pink everlasting and poached egg daisies, a couple of bettongs hiding in the spinifex. And the things, the spirits I couldn't see, I guess. A giant barking spider crawling across the sky, battling a stick-nest rat for a cloud to lie down on, and sleep. As wind from the west summoned curlews, and I said to Ludwig, 'How many miles?'

He showed me with his hand, describing the sun from where it was to where it would be if we made good time. I turned to Father and said, 'I found some old postcards.'

'Let's have them.' Wincing, trying to move in his chair.

I found them in my pocket, checked the names, showed him St Thomas's, covered in fog. 'This one was from Julius.'

He took it, admired the view for a full minute before saying, 'I can still hear the boys singing.' Turning it over and reading: '"Dear Benno, just a quick note about Leipzig . . ."' Going on to describe a St Thomas's master who picked his nose, flicked it across the room as he was teaching them Greek.

'We may be back soon,' Father said, returning it. 'Remember Grimmaische Strasse?'

'Yes.'

'Those few days before Christmas, the markets in the Old Town Square. Remember the town hall and . . .?' Descending into memories, as the horses slowed, Ludwig applied the whip, the last of the track gave way to paperbark. Silas said, 'What's it all about, Pastor?'

'Leipzig's main street, Silas. The view of the church where Bach worked, where *St Matthew* was first performed. The half-timbered houses in the background.'

'I'd like to go there.'

'You can smell the place, Silas. Taste it. Maybe one day I'll take you.'

This seemed unfair. I couldn't imagine a time, a reason he'd take Silas anywhere. Or that Silas would need to go, *want* to. This place was all he knew. God sprinkling daisy seeds across the desert. Still, it was funny to imagine Silas tapping his cane along Grimmaische Strasse.

'Julius has excellent handwriting, don't you think, Benno?'

'At least you can understand it now.'

'How long since you got this one?'

I checked. 'Two months.'

'Good to see they're improving, don't you think?'

This seemed some consolation – his children were being civilised, taught properly, made to learn and act, to think and behave the accepted German way. I showed him another postcard: 'Eckmeier Toy Factory'. A dozen dolls lined up in a frosted window, and on the back Charlotte had written: 'Opa bought me the one third from left. I've called her Trudl!' Father took the postcard, studied the image, felt it, even, with his thumb.

'What is it?' I asked.

Returning the postcard. 'What else?'

A copse of birch leaning over a lake. My older brother, my (one time) protector and best friend Alwin writing they'd spent the day boating, hiking through the riverside forest. Father seemed pleased with this, too, describing the country on the banks of the White Elster to Silas, who said, 'Bet they'd prefer to be here.'

Father said, 'This is a bit of a scrawl.' Trying to read the message Alwin had written. I reclaimed the postcard and read: '"An excellent day outdoors. We were lucky, this far into winter, but Opa said it was because he'd asked God, and God enjoyed the Elster as much as anyone."'

All of my siblings had written a postcard, and all of them had the same stamp, and postmark. I guessed this meant Opa or Oma had sat them down, put a postcard in front of them and said, 'Write to your brother.' I could imagine them lined up, scribbling, asking each other what to write, completing the job with a minimum of words, and fuss, before offering their efforts to Oma. If something was designed to make me feel apart from them, this was it. Still, I'd taught myself to unthink this thought; it never led anywhere. I gave Father all five postcards, and he described the scenes to Silas, then told me: 'You must write back, Benno.'

'I guess.' Because somehow this would be good for me.

'If they've taken the time. Don't you agree, Ludwig?'

'Yes, Pastor.' Turning around to check on Ignatz, Mother (who waved), Jamy, sitting high in his saddle.

Silas said, 'This one's just as good, eh, Pastor?' Reaching into his shirt pocket, unfolding an old watercolour. 'Is this Isaiah's painting, Benno?'

'It's the waterhole.'

'Look at it! He's no cleverer than me. And yet they reckon these paintings he does . . .'

Maybe Silas could see with his fingers, pick up some trace of light or colour through his full-moon eyes. More likely people had told him, and he'd believed them. He even described the scene. 'See, you've got the old white gum here, and it looks like the real thing, doesn't it, Pastor?'

Father agreed.

'And the reeds around the pool.' His wiry fingers found the right spot. 'And here, this is best. How the grass gets darker up high, then it's hills – just blurs, doesn't it, Pastor?'

'It does, Silas.'

'He's a real talent is Isaiah. They offered him twenty quid for this one but he said no, it's for you, Silas, cos it shows your country, where the euros go.'

'You should put it in a frame, Silas.'

'I will, when I get one.'

But he never did – just left the fragments in his pocket, soaking up years of sweat, till the painting was a blur of colour and line. He was still showing it to people years later when I went back to Hermannsburg with Terese. Still getting it out of his pocket and explaining how Isaiah had painted it for him, because it was *his* country. It was still there (so the story goes) when they laid out his body, years later.

The day was getting warmer. Sweat running down my side. I sniffed for the stink, because it always came (despite Mother's talc). I pocketed the postcards and Father said, 'Don't worry, you'll be seeing them soon.'

I surveyed the sand and tried to forget, tried to think of progress, Ignatz's numbers, a bottle of medicine that would make my father better. I tried to focus on this. Even when (like now), Father stretched back in his chair, let the umbrella fall (Silas fixing it), closed his eyes and muttered something about Rebecca.

'Who?' I asked.

'That business was never settled satisfactorily,' he said. 'We owed her more than . . . that little girl, Benno.' Just looking at me.

'Rebecca?'

'Terrible, the injuries. Terrible, Benno. Although . . .' Through some sort of haze. '. . . whether that justifies killing a man.'

'Who?'

'Norman? You remember, Norman? No, of course not. Why would you?'

Silas said, 'Are you okay, Pastor?'

Father sat up. 'This rocking makes you tired, doesn't it?' He attempted to turn back to the cart and called, 'It makes you tired, doesn't it, Alma?'

'What?'

But he didn't have enough energy to explain.

Meanwhile, Ludwig said, 'The horses are finding it tough going.'

'Get onto the hard ground,' Father said.

Ludwig pulled the horses left, but the dray kept dropping into the sand. The team struggled, and he tried more whip. 'Don't want them getting tired, eh, Pastor?'

Ignatz overheard and said, 'We've only just left Hermannsburg.'

'Paul!' Silas called. 'Just when he was full of doubt, that he wouldn't make it, you know what happened, Pastor?'

'Yes, Silas.'

'On the road to Damascus. You know, eh, Benno?'

Generally, about this point, Silas would produce a coloured illustration to show what he meant. He'd hold it up and ask if he had the right one, and when he did he'd start preaching, telling us about (for example) Paul and his faith, sorely tested, and it was only at his lowest moment, his greatest time of despair, that God appeared to him blah blah. But this time Father said, 'It's a good story, isn't it, Silas?'

'Paul saw this light, brighter than the sun, the moon, than anything . . .'

'But maybe,' Father said, 'we should hear the story tonight, when people can *concentrate* on the message, Silas?'

Only Father could stop Silas. Only he could silence him without hurting his feelings. Maybe because he was the official one, the on-behalf-of-God messenger the Lutherans had sent. Either way, Silas stopped, pulled his hat over his eyes and returned to the watercolour landscape.

'Damn!' Ludwig.

The front right wheel sunk into the sand up to its spokes. Ludwig encouraged the horses. They pulled together, and we lurched forward, back, into a deep rut. Again, two, three more times before Ignatz (who'd pulled up) said, 'Careful of the horses, Ludwig.'

Ludwig kept going, applying the whip, and Father's head went back and Mother saw this and called, 'It's not doing any good.'

And Ludwig, 'We gotta get out.'

Again and again, and the horses started groaning. Ignatz put on his brake, jumped down, came over to Ludwig and said, 'You're just making it worse.'

We all got down and checked the wheel, six inches into the sand. Ludwig said, 'We hardly gone nowhere already, Pastor.'

Father didn't react, but I knew what he was thinking. How this wasn't a good start, a good omen, a good anything. How the numbers, in no sense, could add up to much. But he just said, 'We can't expect these poor animals . . .' He managed to stand, and to say to Silas, 'Come on, help me down.' Silas climbed up, helped Father to the steps, and he turned and searched for a foothold. 'Benno, go get something to put under the wheel.'

'Stay still, Martin,' Mother said.

As I wandered through a small forest of desert oaks, I watched Father trying to get down – the slow steps, the unsure hands. Silas helped, Mother helped, all of them, even Jamy, who said, 'We could try with the fresh horses.'

'No,' Father said. 'We'll need them.' Reaching the bottom, examining the wheel and saying, 'It can be done.' Looking out. 'Benno?'

A few sticks, termite-eaten bloodwood. 'It's all little stuff,' I called. Thinking, *of course!* I ran back, pulled a few boards off the dray, dragged them through the sand and laid them, lengthways, under the wheel. 'That should be enough.'

Ignatz didn't look impressed. Like I hadn't thought it through, and there was a simpler way. Mother said it was worth a try, but Father suggested there was too much weight on the dray. So I stood on top and handed down boxes, baskets, the books and pots and pans. Eventually Father said, 'That should be enough.' He, Jamy, Ignatz and Ludwig went around behind the cart, and I was made driver. Father put his shoulder to the back of the dray but Mother told him not to be stupid, and led him, under protest, to shade.

Then it began – me applying the whip (too lightly, Ludwig said), the others pushing with shoulders, strong backs and legs anchored in the sand, shouting directions at each other as the dray rocked forward, back, nearly out, then Mother shouted, 'Martin!'

Fear. Hiding inside the broom closet, a mop wet on my bare feet, a bucket smelling of bleach. I peered through a gap in the door. *Dear Jesus* . . . Frightened to the point of pissing, because I'd run in to escape Adele's furious hand. 'Benno!' But then some bloke came in, pushed her back over the bench, his hand up her dress, and they were so close together, and she was saying, 'I gotta find him.' I ran out, stood punching him, thumping him hard, telling him to get off my mum, my mum, leave her. Before I ran out – across the compound, past the tannery (men busy boiling skins) – into the desert, voices calling for me to come back. But maybe you misremember this sort of stuff. Re-stage it in your head, over and over. The train's whistle, the unreliable pulse of Kate's ECG, the way Father laid sideways, his arm trussed up under his body.

Mother got to him first, lifted him, laid him in her lap and called for someone to bring water. I found a canteen, jumped down, ran over and offered it to him. 'Father?' But he just looked at me and said, 'Warm, isn't it?' He tried to lift his body, wipe his forehead, before drinking. 'That's nice and cold.'

The others had gathered around. Ignatz said, 'You must have fainted,' but Father just said, 'The warm . . . it makes you want to sleep, doesn't it?'

Silence, as he sat up. 'I felt light-headed.'

After a few more tries, we freed the dray. Then we reloaded, Mother and Silas helped Father back to his throne, and we continued in silence, mostly. For the next hour. The ground got harder, and we found the remains of an old track. But we were all hot, tired, and Ignatz called from the cart, 'We need to make another two miles. Rubula. We have to get to Rubula.'

As we rolled on, following the Finke, as it spread its waters, reclaimed them, shrunk into a creek, waterholes, nothing, for long stretches. No one said anything. Silas, asleep sitting up. Me, trying to pick the splinters from the boards from my fingers.

Eucalyptus sessilis

I only saw my father cry twice, both times because of Mozart. Firstly, when we were in Leipzig, and he insisted we listen to some proper music. Rows C8–16 at the second Gewandhaus, lights dimming, everyone falling silent, a harp and flute sharing a melody. I watched him – I watched my father sit forward, caught up in the music. The slow movement, the way the harp played with the flute, long arpeggios drifting into the rafters, me and Julius and the others thinking, *How long does this go for?* Father, again, sitting forward, but now I could see his lips moving, his head low, eyes squinting, like he did when he was lost in thought. I saw him wiping a tear from his eye. I remember Michael, the others looking, all of us shocked that Martin Gerlach would do such a thing.

A few days later, Father bought the recording, took it back to a neighbour's apartment and sat listening, over and over, as we kids drifted back to Opa's. He returned a few hours later with the disc in its sleeve, protected by an extra layer of paper.

Though it didn't end well. Getting off the boat in Port Adelaide six weeks later, a bus to our Grenfell Street hotel, Father unpacking his duffle bag and there, in three equally-sized pieces, his Mozart. I remember him cursing it, dropping it and crushing the bits of shellac, blaming the purser for throwing our stuff about. And the next day, going from store to store in search of a replacement, finding only a music box (no bigger than a snuff box) with a small brass handle. Father turning it, hearing the slow movement from his concerto. Handing over his money, placing it in his pocket and, that night, playing it again and again, Mother calling for him to stop.

The reason I tell you this (apart from showing you my father did have a soft side) is because that night at our camp at Rubula, Father found the music box in his pocket and started cranking the handle. Silas knew the piece and said, 'We always meant to get more Mozart.'

'We did,' Father replied. 'And we will. Won't we, Mother?'

Busy stirring the stew I'd made. 'I've been telling you. Always too busy with your honey ants.'

'When we get to town . . . when I retire and when we return to Leipzig, there'll be plenty more Mozart. What do you think, Benno?'

'Plenty more.' Smiling, because Mozart was a good sign. I emptied my sliced carrots into the stew and said, 'Another half hour, I reckon.'

The last miles hadn't been so bad. A track that followed the Finke – hard ground, the horses sure-footed, picking up the pace as the afternoon cooled. Grey clouds following us, overtaking us, raining for ten or fifteen minutes as Mother said, 'Shall we stop, Martin?'

'No, a little bit of water never hurt anyone.'

After the storm, the afternoon steamed up, sweat-soaks, wiping our faces with mud-coloured handkerchiefs. Silas's suit was already soiled, but he had another. It was important, he said, to always be well-dressed ('I don't fancy standing at the pearly gates in boots and a cabbage hat'). Stone country, steam rising off the pavement; wet granite picking up the sun, spilling red and violet as Ignatz explained how a nearby mesa was made.

Father stopped turning the handle and said, 'That smells excellent, Benno.'

'Thanks.' It'd been a lot of work. Another fire, good coals for even heat, the cast iron pot, the meat, the various vegetables thrown in, and Mother's gravy. I'd said I could do it, and I could. I had it all planned – breakfasts, lunches, dinners.

'Can you hear them?' Jamy said, sitting playing solitaire, looking out across the woolly oats and beard grass. 'Funny how you hear the songs better out here.'

'Which ones?' Father asked, sitting on a cushion on his chair on a high ledge.

Jamy listened, and after a moment: 'Hear it?'

'We wrote it down, didn't we?' Father asked.

'Yeah . . . but they're singing it.' Chanting the song.

Now, everything was in the stew. I sat stirring, listening to Jamy; to Michael, telling me Father would never let us see him cry; to Mother, stirring the goat plum on the coals; Silas, sitting in hip-high grass, staring out at a biblical landscape; Ludwig slicing the bread; Ignatz doing the sums, again. 'If we keep this pace up we should make it in time.'

Jamy said they were getting louder, and Father smiled and said, 'I wish I could hear them.'

Mother asked if I'd added turnips, and I told her I'd forgotten, but it didn't matter because no one liked turnips. She asked, and everyone agreed with me, although Ignatz said, 'You can't taste them in a stew.'

Silas said, 'I know why they're singing.'

'Why's that?' Father asked.

But he wouldn't explain.

Ignatz closed his journal and wandered over to the bit of bush near our camp. He picked a small branch from a gum and said to Father, 'What's this one?'

'Finke River Mallee.'

'Or is it?' Examining it.

Jamy said, 'They're loud . . .'

'It's still happening,' Silas said, dropping his head.

Ignatz returned with the branch, sat down, examining it.

Mother handed me the bowls and I began serving. We sat eating, listening for the old people, for Mozart, for some explanation, some summing up that made sense. Ignatz said, 'This is something different to *Eucalyptus sessilis*, Martin.'

'Of course it is,' Father said. 'It's Finke River . . .' His expression asking why it mattered now. But Ignatz brought the branch over and said, 'Maybe it's something we haven't described yet?'

'Not now,' Mother said to him. 'Martin, try and eat something.'

'I could press it?' Ignatz said. 'At least if I . . .?'

'Ignatz!'

So he returned to his spot, and his stew.

'It's not a scientific expedition,' Mother said. 'It's . . .'

'Plentya stew make you strong,' Silas said to Father. 'There's only one of us.' Tracing a circle in the air. 'One of us, see.' And to Ignatz. 'You can hear when they sing. *One of us*. That's all.'

Then Jamy said, 'They've stopped.'

Later, I took the plates down to the creek and washed them with sand, rinsed them, left them on a rock to dry. I noticed a wall, part of a roof. Up a small hill and there, an abandoned homestead. I walked around it, past a semi-submerged water tank – concrete walls intact, the domed top collapsed into a mix of old fence wire, a rusted bike, rotted vegetation. Father had organised the men to build something similar at Hermannsburg – two earth-insulated water tanks in which hung, from twine, bottles of Ignatz's home-brewed beer. Sometimes the lines would break, and the bottles would fall in, and some kid, Oskar, once, would dive in and retrieve them. And beside this tank, an old well, six-foot diameter, a rotten pop-head on top. Like ours, too. The story went (although I kept asking, and never got a clear answer) that some kid had fallen in, miles to the bottom, broken a heap of bones, and by the time they got to him . . . Because there were lots of ways to die on the mission. Lots. Before the pipeline was put in I always thought I could taste something strange in the water.

A three-roomed cottage, collapsed in on itself. What was once a kitchen – fireplace, iron tripod, most of a chimney. Floor cavities a mix of boards, rubble, rabbit shit and, in one room, a leg – porcelain, pulled from a hip, a small shoe still attached. I picked it up, felt it, spat on it and rubbed it clean. Then I noticed Ignatz watching me from the kitchen. He said, 'You Father doesn't seem any worse.'

'Or better.'

He came towards me, and for some reason I offered him the leg, but he said, 'That was a nice stew.'

'Thanks.'

He took the leg, but then threw it away. 'Just don't listen to any of that nonsense.'

'What?'

'Hearing people singing.'

'Maybe there's something to it.'

'And what's that?'

I wasn't sure. I wasn't sure for many years, until I took up where my father left off. When I wandered with him through the bush on long, hot summer evenings collecting samples, hearing (second-hand) creation stories the men had told him. Once, I remember, we walked two miles from the mission and stood outside a cave called Manangananga. Father said, 'Only initiated men can go in.'

'What's in there?'

'Paintings. Tjurunga. Things we're not meant to know about.'

'No one would know if we went in. And you're studying that sort of thing.'

'Well . . . we could take a peek, I guess.'

So we went inside, into the dark, and Father said, 'We shouldn't go any further.' But by that point he'd seen the paintings on the wall. 'Look, see, that one, a euro passing along the river.'

I said, 'I can't see why it's so special.'

'Maybe because you don't understand what they believe.'

Back in the ruin, Ignatz said, 'You don't want to get caught up in all of that business.'

'What?'

'The old people singing. If you believe that you can't believe in God.' Looking me all over. 'I'm relying on you, Benno. For your dad's sake. You and me, right? Ludwig, Silas, Jamy.' Shaking his head. 'Just you and me.'

Later, I packed the plates, helped Jamy lay out the swags, pitch a tent for Mother and Father. I helped him hobble the horses in the green grass, beside the little bit of flowing water. Father laid in his tent, clothes packed under his legs, his body, his bum. He settled in to try and sleep, and called to me, '*David Copperfield*. Chapter Six.' So I fetched it from the cart and started reading. After a while I heard Mozart, and Mother say, 'For God's sake, put that thing away.'

And here I sit, Hillcrest, 1988, turning the same handle, poor old Mozart competing with the clunk of tyre machines from the Ford garage over my back fence. The same melody, the same missing notes from the same broken sprockets, since my father gave me his music box. My second wife, Kate (she died in 1982, but I'm getting to her), used to sit here playing it, asking about Martin, and if I missed him. I'd tell her about those days beside the Finke, and how I remembered every puff of wind, what we ate each night, when so and so got shit on the liver and stormed off. All of it. She wouldn't believe that I remembered, but I did.

'"I had led this life about a month, when the man with the wooden leg began to stump about . . ."' I read to Father.

'Slow down,' he called from his tent. 'Enjoy the words. Enjoy saying them, Benno.'

'". . . stump about with a mop and a bucket of water . . ."'

The rest on their swags, half-asleep, then Father saying, 'I think you might be right, Ignatz. An entirely different venation.'

Wednesday 11 October (Day 2)

By nine the next morning we'd slowed, and I'd lost interest, so I jumped down from the dray (Mother: 'Benno, what are you doing?'), dropped back past Ignatz, found a few carrots and started feeding the spare horses. Yesterday's – two from the cart, two from the dray, all of them tired, heads low, legs heavy. Jamy said to me, 'Whatever happened to Anton?'

'You know,' I said.

'He stayed in Germany?'

I'd told him a hundred times, but he never remembered, never made a complete picture from the parts. It was strange, because he *could* remember certain things, like why the police took his uncle away, and why they put a rope around his neck and hanged him. But now he just said, 'Bet it was cold over there?'

'It was. But that was years ago.'

'They like carrots.'

'I know.'

'That one, Teddy, he'd eat them all day if you let him. Your one though . . .'

'Himmel?'

'She's no good with hard stuff. Her teeth are bad.'

'That's why we gotta look after her. You will, eh, if I go?'

He shrugged. 'Gets like it's not fair to keep them . . .' But he changed his mind and said, 'I won't need to cos you can.'

'But if I can't?'

'But you can.'

I think Jamy preferred animals to people. He knew the horses; he knew the cattle; he knew all of them, and talked to them, understood their problems, knew they'd rather not be here, pulling us towards Horseshoe Bend.

'How long ago?' he said.

'Coupla years.'

'Are you going to see them when we get to Horseshoe Bend? You're going on the train, aren't you?'

'Yes.'

'Well, you'll get to see Anton, won't you?'

'Perhaps.'

He tilted his head. 'Don't let Teddy hog it all. Give some to Charlie.'

We walked in silence for a minute, Mother calling for me to stop bothering Jamy, Father cursing something. Jamy said, 'I wouldn't like not to be with my brothers and sister.'

'They left years ago, Jamy.'

I couldn't tell what he was thinking. Maybe back then was now; maybe people didn't come and go; maybe they were the voices he heard.

'So you go to Germany and see them, and will you stay there or come back?'

'I don't know. We need to get Father to the railhead, to get help. Then when he gets better and retires . . .'

'He'll go away?'

'Yes.'

'*Ah*.' This seemed to concern him, but he knew, he'd known for months, the packing, the boxes on the porch. 'But who'll be the pastor?'

'The people in Adelaide will find someone.'

'But what if they can't?'

'They will. That's their job. Although at some point, I guess, you'll want to look out for yourselves, won't you?'

'Why?'

'You can't have white people, missionaries, there forever.'

He chewed this thought over, told me to share the carrots around.

'I remember that day,' he said, 'when you and Anton and Lucas were being naughty, remember, and Pauline comes out and she's chasing you with her wooden spoon, telling you she'll tan yer hide. I remember that day.'

I was out of carrot, but I said, 'Do you remember the names of my brothers?'

'You'd always be playing, and me and Teddy would ask but . . .'

'And my sister?'

He studied the sky, squinted, then said, 'Charlotte?'

'They went to Germany to get away from you mob. They didn't fancy blacks, Jamy.'

I know what you're thinking, but I've never claimed to be perfect. The days were long and boring and Jamy made good entertainment. But if it's any consolation, I always felt bad after, or Mother would find out and hit my arse, shouting at me because I wasn't the son she'd brought into the world.

'They didn't like me?'

'They thought the blacks, even the kids, had a funny smell.'

'Benno!' Mother called. Perhaps she knew what I was doing.

'That's why they went away, Jamy.'

I watched him, then the usual thing happened, and I thought I was the world's worst person, and said, 'That was just a joke, Jamy. They liked you.'

'Really?'

'Of course. Out of all the kids, you were their favourite. The main thing is, don't tell my parents any of this.'

'Benno, get here now! Jamy, is he annoying you?'

Calling: 'No, Mrs Gerlach.'

'Promise?' I said to him. 'Or else I'll get my arse tanned.'

It'd already been a long day – six am, helping Ludwig and Jamy bring in the horses, harness them, load the pots and pans, the tents and swags that Mother and Ignatz had packed. Father up the ladder, slower than yesterday, stopping on each rung to wait for the pain, the few steps to his chair. Settling in and smiling at us and saying, 'Another beautiful day.' Invoking verses from Matthew (alternating lines with Silas), before interlocking his hands across his belly. A few words to the horses, and they moved off, a foot, a few feet at a time, the whole thing repeating.

I left Jamy and ran back towards the dray. I'd only gone a few yards when I stopped and looked into the bush. An old Afghan, seventy, older, with baggy clothes, head wrapped in rags. Standing like a ghost, holding the reins of a camel. An old, sagging thing, loaded down with packs, bedding, a few tools. I lifted a hand, said, 'Hi,' but he didn't reply. I said, 'We're going to Horseshoe Bend.'

He smiled and said, 'You were the boy?' He held a hand at knee-height.

'Sorry?'

'This high, you remember?' He patted his chest and said, 'Aalem.'

'Did we . . .?'

And Mother calling: 'Benno!'

'Horseshoe Bend,' he said. 'Remember? They made me leave.'

'Who?'

'Boss, and his offsider.'

'Father?'

'You were just little, and you'd pray.'

The others were too far away. I said, 'I've gotta go,' and ran off, looking back, saying, 'Aalem?'

'We prayed.'

I ran over the hill, past Jamy and Teddy and Charlie, Ignatz, jumping up next to Ludwig.

'I told you not to bother Jamy,' Mother said.

'Who's Aalem?'

'The old Ghan,' Father said.

'Did I know him?'

'You wouldn't remember.'

I tried. I knew I'd seen him. I knew the face. 'He said hello.'

'Who?' Mother asked, handing me a sheet of paper, a pen, a book to rest on.

'Aalem. Back there.' Indicating.

Mother shook her head and said, 'You're dreaming,' but Father said, 'He was there?' Attempting to look back.

'I saw him.'

'Well . . . he was bad news.'

'Why?'

'Start with Anton,' Mother said, tapping the letter.

'You should remember him. You spent long enough with him,' Father said.

'When?'

'Few months before we went overseas. So you must have been six. You and the other kids.'

'What happened?'

'He was one of the cameleers, used to take people from Oodnadatta to Alice. But he got old and slow, they told him to . . . he had some argument and left the camp at Marree. He ended up at Hermannsburg, stayed with us for months, didn't he, Alma? Set up his camp near the schoolroom, cooked his food every night. And five times a day, out comes the prayer mat, and off he goes, *Allahu Akbar* . . . You and Anton prayed with him, and me and your mother laughed, at first . . .'

'Until it became obvious he wasn't leaving,' Mother said.

'I said to him, listen, Aalem, as much as I want to help, this is a Lutheran mission . . . but he stayed and stayed and in the end me and Ignatz . . . But he liked you, Benno. He'd sit there and talk to you for hours, read you some of his books. You don't remember?'

'No.'

'In the end,' Father said, 'it was muscular . . . Ignatz and some of the men, carrying him off.'

'You threw him out?'

Mother had heard enough. 'Let's write to them, Benno.'

Now I remembered. The book with the strange script, the brown hands with liver marks, the camel sitting, waiting, watching. I said, 'He wasn't hurting anyone, was he?'

'You were young,' Father said. 'All of you. And we didn't want him around when we left for Europe.'

'If *they* took the time to write to you,' Mother said.

'He looked like a nice old man,' I said to Father.

'He was a horror,' Mother said.' Now, come on.'

You're the one left them in Leipzig, I wanted to say to Mother. I wanted to remind her of the day, the morning, we dragged our cases down the steps of number eight Kaiser Strasse, waited for the cart, stood in light snow, Michael and Anton at the window watching us. I wanted to remind her of all of this, and of the night before our departure when Charlotte cried, for an hour perhaps, because her favourite brother would be going back to Australia and she'd be left with Oma. But all I could do was write: 'Dear Michael. This is in response to your postcard. I bet they made you write it, didn't they? I bet they told you what to put in so I wouldn't feel so bad. I bet they said, nothing about the hikes, the markets, the chestnuts. But I don't care. It's not your fault.'

Father examined Ignatz's specimen. He'd already sketched a branch, noted the alternate leaves, described the fruits, the shape and size and the colour of the anthers and filaments. He waved the specimen in the air and said, 'This one could be named after you, Benno. *Eucalyptus benjaminii*?'

Some consolation perhaps. Julius, who didn't understand these things, had said, 'Why don't we all stay together?'

I'd said, 'Mother and Father will need someone to help.'

'Well, that should be me,' Anton said.

He'd already had this discussion with Father – surely I'd be the logical choice? I can do things, I can ride a horse, and Benno can't. He'd tried to make an argument for me staying, but Father was having none of it.

'I need you to look after the others,' he'd said.

'But Benno—'

'You!' Thundering, like it'd already been decided, argued over (Mother), set in stone, and *had to be this way*.

I thought I should remind my parents. How the kids' faces were lined up, and their breath fogged the window, and after a while Opa and Oma came along and took them in and closed the curtain.

'So we're on this trip to Horseshoe Bend, remember, Michael?'

Mother noticed what I was writing and said, 'Maybe don't mention . . . I mean, *why*?'

'I shouldn't tell them?'

'They don't need to know,' Father said. 'They'll just worry, and Oma and Opa, then there'll be letters and Opa on a boat, and all sorts of dramas.'

'But they *should* know,' I said.

'No.' Father.

So I screwed up the letter and threw it into the scrub.

'Without the dramas,' Mother said.

Me? Dramas? But I tried again: 'Hi Anton. I've been instructed to tell you that life in Central Australia is the most idyllic –'

'Benno!' Mother, but this time, the same serve from Father.

So I turned away from her, and wrote, and told Anton things were as usual, the same dreary rubbish from Ignatz (you remember, eh?), the same Sunday mornings hearing about the battle with Lucifer, the same three cuts of meat, stews, hot days. I finished and Mother asked to hear it, but I said no, if you want me to do it this is how it'll be done. More criticism of my attitude, my sniping, worse, somehow, because it had turned my beautiful voice low and gravelly and angry.

'Angry?'

'Yes.'

'Benjamin,' Father said. 'Just write one letter, okay?'

So I continued: 'Dear Anton, Alwin, Michael, Julius and Charlotte. You can't expect me to write five letters, can you? And to be fair, your postcards were only a few lines long. So maybe if I told you about Ignatz and the lesson he gave us on human anatomy. It's important to understand that people have a choice about having babies.'

'Tell them we're keeping well,' Mother said.

'I have.' Continuing: 'And sometimes the hardest thing is to stay strong.'

I could imagine my brothers and sister, Anton reading my letter, all of them laughing, Julius repeating something like, 'Willy willy willy!' That's how it'd be. And all I could think was I wished I could be there with them.

'A unique specimen,' Father said, placing the branch between tissue paper, attempting to press it inside *David Copperfield*. '*Benjaminii*,' he said to me, smiling.

I thought, *maybe there's another way to look at it.* Me and Dad, at eleven at night; him at his desk, writing, and me sitting beside him; his piles of ethnographic notes, songs and stories, his Aranda translation of the Bible (doing what Luther had done), his dictionary of native words, terms, all of it, piled high. Years and years of it, gathering dust (as it still does, in my Hillcrest lounge room). No brothers, no sister, just me, *special*, listening to him say, 'The hard part's going to be finding a sympathetic publisher.'

'Why?'

'I'm not sure anyone'd think there's a market for . . . ethnography.'

'But that doesn't matter.'

'No, it doesn't.' Messing my hair. 'See, you understand what I'm doing, Benno. Why I came, why *we* came, despite . . .'

'What?'

'That doesn't matter. All these stories, see, and one day you can finish the job.'

'You do it.'

'It's too much, Benno.'

I finished my letter, but refused to let Mother see. I sealed it in an envelope and addressed it to 8 Kaiser Strasse, Leipzig, Germany. And on the back I wrote: 'No Adults. NUR FÜR KINDER'.

Alitera

Within an hour things had changed. The sky clearing, the sun moving in and out of phase, Mother studying *distachya*, its ripe, red cones full of seed. Sketching a branchlet and writing *subsp. distachya, s. europe, sw-central asia*. Telling Father it contained ephedrine, and it might do him some good. But he said, 'It's just a plant.'

'It's good for rheumatism.'

'Well, this isn't rheumatism!'

Father was a rag doll, bits and pieces plucked from the rubble, left arm falling to his side (Silas placing it back in his lap), head rolling on his shoulders, as he fought for breath. Mother asked if we should stop, but Father said, 'No, keep going, Alitera, at least.' Ignatz said this was the right decision, and Mother: 'What does it matter if he's dead?' I sat on the back of the dray reading bits of the Bible. Jesus on his cross.

Father said, 'Remember, Silas, when you played Christ?'

'I remember.' Proudly, head high, blue-sky eyes.

'What year was that?'

'Don't know, Pastor. Maybe when they were having that war?'

'I reckon you're right. In 1915, perhaps? That year, you were sick, remember, but *you* kept going, didn't you?'

'Yes, Pastor.'

'A hot December but you just . . .' He tried to sit up, to get his breath, and Mother said, 'Ludwig, you'll have to stop.'

'No. Alitera,' Father said. 'You were my best Christ, Silas.'

'Your only Christ. After that no one else wanted to do it.'

'The third station: "Jesus, the cross you are carrying has become very heavy. You are becoming weak and ready to faint . . ." You remember, Alma?'

The Hermannsburg Passion. An outback reimagining of Christ's suffering, fourteen stations of tragedy that lasted three years before Father gave up. Mother's (and the girls') costumes, a shaky old script, weeks of rehearsals and the final, candlelit performance. Comical, in retrospect, but Father had been convinced it'd do the job – bring the whole drama alive, show (without having to trawl through the Scriptures) the central message.

'That couldn't have been 1915,' Father said. 'Benno, do you remember? You were the infant child.'

'Was I?'

'What year was it, Mother?'

'That wasn't the Passion. That was the *nativity*. It was 1909. He was a fatty.'

'I was never fat.'

'I mean you *were* a baby!'

There was even a photo: my legs sticking out of a sheet, a donkey that wouldn't stand still, three wise Aborigines emerging from the girls' dormitory.

Repeating. It always repeats. So there's me sitting in my Prospect lounge room in 1952 – light classics on the radio, Terese sewing a hole in Jack's pants – looking through an old box of Father's sacred stones, spearheads, grinding stones. Telling Jack all about them, offering them, saying, 'Feel it,' but he and Sharon busy with god knows what. 'They call these tjurunga. Say that, *tjurunga*.'

And Jack, humouring me: '*Tjurunga*'

'Sharon?'

'What?'

'Tjurunga?'

'What's a tjurunga?'

'*Ah*.' Picking up the handwritten draft of Father's English-German-Aranda dictionary, finding the entry and reading: '*Tju*, hidden, or secret . . .

runga, something personal. See, a secret stone. Something personal like a pocket knife or . . . a bangle.'

Sharon laughed. 'So that rock's the same as a bangle?'

'Yes.'

Terese told me to put away my rocks because no one was interested. 'Didn't you say they belonged to someone else?'

'Perhaps, although how can I return them?'

'Put them in the post.'

'See, they're carved,' I said to my kids, showing them, but something more interesting was on the radio. So I reached in to see what Father had packed away, forty years earlier, and produced a halo – wire with the barbs flattened (Ludwig's work), formed into a small circle, woven with straw, Mother's lace, a few strands of tinsel. Terese looked at me and said, 'What's that?'

'My halo. From when I was Jesus. When we had the nativity play.'

'You were Jesus?' Laughing at me. 'Hear that Sharon? Your father was Jesus.'

'When?'

'When I was a baby.' I put the halo on my head, and it fit. I offered it to the kids and they tried it on. Jack said, 'It's falling apart.'

'It's old.'

Eventually I hung it on the lounge room wall and Terese kept taking it down, saying it was a piece of old rubbish and the rats had got to it. And it was still there, that day in 1955, when I left. Thirty-three years till I saw it again. But that story can wait.

'You must remember, Alma?' Father said. 'Pauline was the best Virgin we ever heard.'

'You're living in the past,' Mother said to him.

'And Silas, I forgot what you played?'

'Martin!' Mother said. 'Write your memoirs when you're sixty, seventy . . . not now.'

'There it is!' Ignatz called.

Alitera. Scattered grevillea, honey myrtle limbs sweeping the ground.

A grassy bank spreading around and growing into the waterhole. Granite boulders making a bay, of sorts, where a wallaby drank, looked up at us, continued. And on the other side, carpet daisy halfway up a steep bank, a pair of bean trees. Mother placed her ephedra in her notebook, surveyed the place and said, 'Could be worse.'

We stopped and unpacked. Silas and Ludwig helped Father down, settled him on a log in the shade. Ignatz started filling canteens. 'Martin, wasn't this the only place the police would water their horses?'

Father didn't reply. Long, deep breaths. Starting from nothing, filling his lungs, releasing. Mother tried to help him drink. I stood waiting, unsure what to do. Mother said, 'I told you we shouldn't have come, Martin.'

'Don't start that.'

'I said stay and wait. At least that way we could've looked after you.'

Silas stood at the water's edge, studying the gums.

'You can't have it both ways,' Ignatz said to Mother. 'If we'd stayed you'd be saying we should've gone for help.'

'Nonsense. It's obvious. Look at him.'

'*Alma*,' Father said.

Ignatz threw the canteens onto the dray and said, 'Dietrick and Remington . . . remember, Martin?'

'I remember.'

'This was their favourite watering hole. They'd wait, over in the reeds' – indicating – 'for a group of blacks to come along.'

'I remember,' Father said. 'He got what he deserved.'

Father remembering the day he rode up to Constable Dietrick and demanded his rifle. 'Being an officer of the law doesn't give you the right to go around killing.' Dietrick said the men he'd shot were outlaws, but Father said, 'That's not for you to decide.'

'That must have taken some doing?' Ignatz said.

'No, he was a coward. And his offsider. He never would've . . . I didn't think that for a moment.'

'But he wouldn't give you his gun?'

'No, but as he rode off' – struggling – 'I said these men saw what you did and you'll answer for it.'

'Do we need to go over this *now*?' Mother said.

'I'm feeling better,' Father said. 'It was the sun.'

'I think we should go back. A day or so, and we can look after you properly, Martin. Another seven days. Who knows what'll happen?'

'It's not a good idea,' Ignatz said.

Mother wasn't finished. 'I've said, all the way along . . . out in the middle of nowhere, if things get bad, worse than this, then what?'

She sat on Father's log and mumbled. Father invoked the fourth station, but she said how does that help, Martin? Then he said it was a pity, wasn't it, we stopped the Passion, but she reminded him that no one wanted to do it anymore. She said something about an eternal optimist, and where did that get you (the Board couldn't give a shit about the Passion, or you, me, our children). Father said, 'We've had the opportunity to change lives. We've told these people about Jesus. Now they're ready for Heaven. What a thought, Alma! Imagine, Benno! They were lost, but now they'll be with us and millions of souls who've . . .' Looking around at the vacant faces. 'See, I'm better.'

And Mother: 'We've only just begun.'

I wandered down to the soggy sand. Squatted, drinking, then splashing my face. I could already smell myself, so I undid a few buttons, flicked water under my arms. Maybe it'd help, maybe not. Mother would soon tell me. I looked up – two camels, standing watching me. One stepped forward, drank. Then the other. Old, with patches of missing hair, scabby around the mouth, feet all worn and knobbly. Look, camels, I wanted to call, but didn't dare scare them off.

Camels weren't easy to get along with.

Somewhere in the Western Desert, 1932. The National Research Council had given me money to return to the desert (stopping at Hermannsburg to see the old folks), find wandering bands of Pintupi people, use my (and Father's) knowledge to transcribe their stories, their songs. I'd been travelling for two weeks, and found no one. As if they were trying to avoid me. Long days, dry biscuits and warm water, as I wondered, again, what I was doing out here. Then, one day, packing my swag, my notes, my few boxes of things, this camel decided she'd had enough (or had sniffed a bull). She shook me off, threw off her saddle then bolted. I held tightly to the reins, and she dragged me – along the sand, standing, on my arse. I knew if she got away it'd all be over. The middle of nowhere. Maybe I could last a few days, but no water, no supplies. Holding on for dear life, until she realised I wasn't about to give up, slowed, stopped and waited. Then I led her back to camp, loaded her, cursed her, but in the end, relied upon her for the next few weeks.

Now, I stood, took a few steps closer, reached out and rubbed her flank. She didn't care. She just drank. I knew if I called to the others these two would bolt. So I spent a few minutes stroking them, before returning to camp.

We sat and watched the small fire, the water on to boil. Silas said, 'It's all been decided, hasn't it, Pastor?'

'It has, Silas.'

Silas's white clothes had turned coffee-cream, but this didn't bother him. Dirt, I guess, made it real, and worthwhile. Jesus was dirty. Martin was dirty. Everything that was, and was with God, was dirty. Silas said, 'Don't know it's much like them pictures say, Pastor.'

'What pictures?'

'The Spain pictures.'

Silas turned to me, said, 'Benno?'

I went over to the cart, searched his duffle bag, returned with one of his pictures. He'd ordered a set of Bible scenes from a Spanish publishing company – portraits of the main players, parted oceans, whales, Jesus and his disciples resting on paper daisies. He showed this picture around, stood holding it like a banner. '"Looking for that blessed hope, and the glorious appearing of the great God and our saviour Jesus Christ."'

'Maybe later,' Father said to him.

But he knew it was the right time. He always sensed these things and began preaching in the middle of a meal, morning tea, halfway through the branding or vaccinating. He'd just stand, hand around his Spanish visions, and the words would come.

'"Jesus will come again, he will *come quickly*."' He told us it was from Revelations. 'Just shake me flowers, don't I, Pastor?' Looking and smiling at Father, who said, 'That's right, Silas.'

'Shake it, one with the other, boy and girl, eh, Pastor? Boy tree. Girl tree?' He stood, found a branch, and started shaking it. '". . . the great God and our saviour . . ."'

'Enough!' Mother said to him.

'Boy and girl, and what happens, Pastor?'

'I think we all know,' Father said, smiling.

Mother stood and shouted, 'Stop this at once, Silas!'

But he didn't. He just danced around, handed me the branch and said, 'You can climb this time, Benno. You can make one touch the other. You can get them all sexy, eh, Benno?'

I dared not speak. Mother was fuming. But I knew what it was. I knew date palms were dioecious. I knew one palm was male, the other female, and I knew (I'd seen) if you could get the man bit, break it off, rub it on the girl bit, the dates would come thicker and faster. Common enough, for Ignatz to ask some of the boys to climb ('little monkeys!') some of the taller palms and inoculate them with Silas's love dreams.

'You sit down now!' Mother shouted at him.

But Silas was on a roll. 'Climb up like a monkey . . .' And he demonstrated.

Of course, this was all Father's fault. Because one Sunday he'd given a sermon in which he portrayed the male palm as native, dark, Aboriginal, and the female as white, European, Christian. He'd said if they got together the result would be far superior. In fact, he'd explained, one couldn't exist without the other. And isn't that, he'd said, just like us? Nature as metaphor. He liked this sort of preaching. And it was the only way most of the blacks would understand.

'Maybe that's enough?' Father said to Silas.

Mother joined in. 'If you're going to behave like this, Silas, you can get your things and walk back to the mission . . . now! Do you want that?'

'It's like the monkey,' Silas said. And to me: 'You were the monkey once, weren't you, Benno?'

I nodded. I'd climbed a date palm once. But only got halfway before falling. Oskar had got up, and done the job properly.

'Well?' Mother said, indicating the way back to Hermannsburg.

'Alma,' Father managed. 'He doesn't mean to . . . leave him be.'

So Mother sat. But she was furious. She said to Silas, 'We've come on this trip for one and one reason only.'

Silas looked at her and said, 'But it's not the reason you think, Mrs Gerlach.'

Along the Finke

1954. Me at my desk, my research assistant, Kate Monteath, leaning over me, putting her face close to mine, whispering, 'What are you doing?'

'I'm trying to work this out.'

I'd been studying some of Father's old photos – small, sepia snaps from our 1922 trip to Horseshoe Bend. And this shot, showing nothing but sky, a few clouds, the tops of trees. 'I have no idea why he took this one.'

She kissed the top of my head. 'Maybe he liked the sky?'

'*Oh*, I remember. He was trying to pee. Then we heard this noise, an engine . . .'

That was it! Father standing in front of a ruined house, waiting for his stream, Mother in the dray calling, 'Do you want a hand?'

'No, I can still pee, can't I?'

Jamy was waiting in the cart, and Ludwig was in charge of the (not-so) fresh horses.

'Then this packs up, too,' Father said.

'No rush,' Silas called, from his usual spot beside Father's chair. 'I have the same problem.'

'There's no problem,' Father said.

It'd been my job to help him down, walk him across the yard, wait while he managed to undo his buttons and (almost) begin. Then I went into an old bedroom, dragged my feet through the rubble, stopped and knelt to examine shards of green glass mixed with bits of pottery. Pieces no bigger than pennies, as I heard Father starting and stopping, cursing his waterworks.

'Benno, what are you doing?' Mother called.

'Waiting.' Placing my foot on the shards, pressing down, hearing them break, seeing a skink run out, chasing it and blocking it with a stick. I wondered whether I should just step on him, or her. Maybe being dead was easier than anything?

Then the engine, growling, tappets working at full throttle as the biplane approached us and Father said, 'What's he doing all the way out here?'

A small plane held together with wires, and a pilot with goggles looking down at us.

'Get my camera!' Father said.

I ran from the house, and Ignatz had the Box Brownie ready, handed it to me, and I returned to Father. He said, 'Quick, it'll be gone,' as he stumbled, steadied himself against the wall, and I uncapped the camera and tried to get the plane in shot. 'I can't see it.'

'Just press the damn button!'

So I did. Then looked up, and the pilot was waving.

Mother said, 'Who flies a plane out here?'

And Ignatz: 'Maybe it's the mail?'

Father: 'Maybe he thinks we're lost?'

'We are,' Silas said, looking up to see the plane. But then it got quieter, and smaller, and Father said to me, 'Did you get it?'

'I reckon.'

A small dot in the sky, and it was gone.

Back in my office, I told Kate about the plane, and she said, 'What was it doing out there? Sure you didn't dream it?'

'What, I'm that stupid?'

'I didn't say you were stupid, but you are prone to *fantasy*, Benjamin Gerlach.'

'There was a plane, and I tried to . . . see, that's proof.'

She examined the photo again. 'There's no plane.'

'Look.' A small dot that might've been a plane, or a bird. 'An Avro.'

'Avro?' Smiling. 'Do you even know what an Avro is?'

'Yes, as a matter of fact,' grabbing her, pulling her onto my lap, pushing Father's photos aside. Then she said, 'You're fascinated by that trip, aren't you?'

'It was . . . epic.'

'Why don't you write it all down? It'd make a good movie.' A finger under my chin, lifting my head, kissing me.

After the failed photo, I helped Father back to the dray. Mother asked if he'd actually gone, and he said he'd got something out. She said, 'Well, go finish, or else we'll have to stop in another ten minutes.'

We continued chasing the midday sun, the dray and cart lifting and dropping over rocks, Ignatz finding a smooth path, Father clutching the arms of his chair. Mother, busy with her bamboo fan, and me, on the back again, reading a comic about English schoolboys playing rugby, hiding in the library when they should've been in bed, telling stories about Africa and lions and tigers and missionaries in pots. 'Stupid story.'

'What?' Father asked.

I showed him a picture of a priest in a cauldron, bubbling away, tasting the carrots and turnips. Father laughed and said, 'It doesn't end well, this job, does it, Benno?'

'"Having civilised the Benoto people, Reverend Smyth was seasoned and prepared for dinner."'

'At least you avoided that,' Mother said.

'"The reverend said, The eyes of the Lord are upon you, but the chief replied, The Lord has provided!" Look, he's grinning. I think it's meant to be funny.'

Ignatz said, 'If *you're* retiring, Pastor . . .' Gazing into the mid-distance, occasionally shaking the reins, a strange sort of tch-tch. 'I think I might try somewhere in the city.'

'You wouldn't stay at Hermannsburg?' Father asked.

'Not saying straight away. Maybe a year, maybe . . .'

'And why's that?' Mother asked. 'Martin's been going thirty years . . . thirty, isn't it, Martin?'

'That doesn't matter,' Father said. 'If you've decided, Ignatz.'

'And here,' I said, showing them. 'Look, the chief drawing who gets what bit.'

But they ignored me. Father said, 'You can only do it for so long.'

Ignatz just drove.

'My only concern's succession. If I were to go, then you . . .'

We passed two big palms. Out in the open, full sun, flourishing. Fronds moving in the breeze, dates dropping to the ground. A wide, brown, welcoming path leading to an unreliable Bethlehem, a crowd of ghosts cheering the chosen ones.

'And what's caused this decision?' Father asked.

'Nothing's caused it,' Ignatz replied. 'Except the passage of time. And the necessity of living alone.'

'You're not alone.'

'I am, Martin. I've asked the Lord why, and if I should continue, and he's said, Keep going, a bit longer won't hurt you. But I'm still there, every evening, by myself.'

'Maybe if you went to town, met someone?'

'The job's too much for one person,' Ignatz said. 'I know, Pastor, what *you've* achieved but . . . lessons, every day, and the kids are hardly receptive.'

'Martin did it for ten years,' Mother said.

'I've asked myself, if they don't want to learn, and they're just destined to work with cattle, station kitchens, or worse, so many of them pregnant.'

Father managed to sit up. 'But we're not here to judge, Ignatz. We're here to provide an example. And if we do this, and the blacks see the benefit of the way we live . . .'

I'd guessed Ignatz had been thinking this way. You could tell. How he sat at his desk staring out of the window, or lost patience with us for the smallest thing, shouted at us, slammed books on desks, called the blacks names he shouldn't have.

'We could ask the Board for someone to help you,' Father said.

'The Board?' Ignatz laughed. 'Rubbing ointment on skin at three in the morning, vaccinations, organising the muster, trying to keep them at it, get the animals to the railhead. See, none of that's my job. I was sent to teach.'

'And what about Martin's job?' Mother said. 'He was sent to minister.'

'Alma,' Father said, taking a moment before saying, 'When we arrived in 1894—'

'I've heard all of that,' Ignatz said.

'—there was nothing but a few stick huts, a few lay workers – Kempe had been there for years and done nothing except drink himself silly. That church, that school house, that kitchen, the wagon shed, storehouse – how did it all get there?'

Ignatz took a deep breath and said, 'I just thought I'd tell you.'

It was funny how they'd drawn the priest – half a body, but his head still saying, 'I hope you don't think this is funny?' As the natives ate his freshly-roasted legs. The women and children giggling, and someone saying, 'Have you finished with your arms yet, Reverend?'

'All I'm saying,' Father continued, 'is that we've been given a task, Ignatz.'

'And I've carried it out.'

'Remember, Martin?' Mother said. 'Having to slaughter cattle? Never been near a steer, and there's me cutting its arteries. And we had to teach them, didn't we, Martin, how to grow their own food? For years and years.'

We continued towards low, green welcoming country, whole swathes of cassia moving in the wind. Ignatz said, 'I don't think I'm being unreasonable.'

'We've all been let down.' And after a while. 'It's just the blacks. Can you imagine, if we all left? What would it have all been for?'

An hour later, Jack Fountain came along on his camel. Old Jack. Our once-a-week Jack, heading for Hermannsburg on His Majesty's Postal Service. Hooves, blinkers and long lashes; the way his body moved as an extension of Irene's. The two of them, no rush; the various mail bags and pots and pans hanging off the old girl's hump. Back at the mission he'd sit, drink a few glasses of barley water, hand out the letters ('Ah, you haven't heard from Alwin for a while'), wait until everything had been opened, read, discussed. Looking at me and saying, 'What's Julius been up to, Benno?'

'Just school.'

'And your Oma . . . is she better?'

'Opa says so.'

But now he just rode down the track, stopped and said, 'I didn't reckon you woulda got this far yet.'

'We've been making good time,' Ignatz said.

'How are you?' Father asked, but Jack just looked at his legs, his big, puffy body, and said, 'Get you to a doctor, you'll be better in no time.'

So we stopped (despite Ignatz's concerns), made the usual camp, boiled the usual kettle (or at least I did). Jack said, 'It's right along the way, Pastor. Everyone's ready for you. So it shouldn't be such a drama getting there.'

Father turned to Mother and said, 'See, I told you.'

Silas asked about a doctor, but Jack said he didn't know. 'The hard part's getting to the train. They got some good doctors in town. My old girl, remember Juicy, how she left me? She got a liver infection, and they got that out, and she was fine.'

Father said, 'Alma wanted to wait at Hermannsburg but I said . . .'

'No, no, no, Alma. This sort of thing' – indicating – 'you wanna get that looked at quick smart, eh, Pastor?'

'As I said.' Smiling at Mother, but she said, 'How's Gus?'

'Gus is all right . . . but *Harry*.'

'Causing problems?'

'He, I think' – looking around, whispering, although I wasn't sure why – 'will be the death of them both.'

A few moments' silence, as everyone took it in, digested it, formed an opinion based on what they knew about the Elliots' fourteen-year-old son, Harry. Father said, 'It wasn't anything him or Lou did . . . sometimes they're just born bad.'

'The other day, without a word of a lie,' Jack said to Father, 'the stock inspector was there, and while he was inside talking to Gus, Harry comes out, gets in his car, starts it up . . .'

'True?'

'Oath. Drives it straight into the yards. Crushed a coupla steers, too. You oughta heard what came next.'

'You were there?'

'Not for long. Me and Irene made tracks, quick smart, get me?'

Father shrugged and said, 'Maybe he'll grow out of it?'

'You oughta be grateful for a good lad,' Jack said, pointing me out, like they might've forgotten I was their son.

'We are, we're grateful,' Father said, but of course, Mother said, 'Most of the time.'

Jack distributed his letters and Mother went through them – for Ignatz, from Immanuel College. She handed it to him and said, 'Maybe it's good news.' A few supportive parishioners, Alwin, Julius, the Board. Father snatched this one and ripped it open. 'Maybe, Alma?' Reading, but then shaking his head, Mother saying typical, Jack saying bad news is it, and Silas saying it doesn't matter, Pastor, we're well on the way. And Ignatz: 'In their oak-lined board room making decisions about people's lives.'

Father said, 'They reckon they're trying to find someone with a car. "'Ideally, come and fetch you from Oodnadatta, Martin, but if not, somewhere close. Ideally, soon, but these things take time."'

Jack said, 'See, that's a good sign, Martin.'

'How?' he asked.

'That Jesus of yours, he's got it all planned, hasn't he?'

We drank, and eventually Father asked if I could help him to the nearest tree.

Irene

Back then (as the photos show, a fourteen-year-old with a big smile, summer freckles, strange little teardrop eyes falling off the side of his face) I was happy. Back then (the silver nitrate faded, leaving this ghost of the boy Gerlach and his stodgy, cotton-trimmed parents) life just washed over me, and I thought nothing of it – jumping from bed, out the door (Pauline: 'Benno, get back here and eat breakfast!'), down to Oskar's place, though the rooms, ('Hi, Ludwig, Hi, Mary!'), outside with my best friend, down to the yards, up to the top of the cattle shed, gathering my arms and saying, 'It's easy, you'll never hurt yourself if you roll.' Standing on the edge (twelve feet up), refusing to allow the thought of *what might happen*, jumping, rolling, standing up and saying, 'See, as long as you don't land on your feet.' And done once, you have to prove it to yourself – up, jump, over and over, both of us, till even the risk of broken bones seemed boring. Back then. Compared with now. Because I haven't really told you about my eighty-year-old self, have I? The same eyes, but generally swollen, tired, red from reading. A cabbage patch of liver spots on my cheeks. A bigger, fatter nose with porcupine hairs, and my teeth, they've never been right. Down to a saggy neck, and chest, with trainer bra boobs (Sarah Fielke, but more on that later). The Gerlach girth. I've had to be careful with that, too, because it is, was, what caused all of the problems in the first place. Fluid retention, heart failure, the journey to Horseshoe Bend. But it's managed now. With pills. But my legs are as thick and firm and determined as that day me and Oskar jumped off the shed. Back then. Back then I wasn't scared of anything. A broken leg, at a time and place where it couldn't be fixed. But who cared? A broken neck? No problem.

Back then (as a fourteen-year-old, the biting gale blowing in my face) I was a different person. We all are, aren't we? Before life removes the rough edges, or the keenness we're born with. Back then I was a porcelain bird flying across a whitewashed wall. Taking it all in (the various opinions, facts, lies), wanting to share my own thoughts but realising no one was interested. That's how I remember it. My whole childhood, really. For example, Father sitting at his desk talking to two men from the Aboriginal Protection Board (me, in the hallway listening) and one man saying, 'It's not a matter of what *we* think, Pastor,' and Father saying, 'I won't give them up,' and the man replying, 'The half-castes are never accepted in the proper black community.'

'How would you know?'

'Well, that doesn't matter. The government has said we should take them so we will. Next Friday, perhaps?'

'I'm not agreeing to that.'

'I have the paperwork.'

That's what I remember hearing, and later, these two men in rough, cotton suits leaving the house, mumbling to each other, 'I don't care if the old bastard wants to make trouble.'

I didn't want them taking my friends – the kids I learned with, played with, got in trouble with (Lucas, always Lucas). Apparently they were half-castes, quarters, eighths. Like the way the men separated the steers, the cows, the potties during muster. And anyway, everyone knew about St Mark's, the clothes, the haircuts, woodworking for boys, sewing for girls, the early mornings and late finishes and, on a Saturday, the dances where you could meet someone nice, someone white, and start the process of bleaching, of giving up your black bits. I went in to Father and said, 'Cos they're not black enough?'

'Whatever you or I think doesn't matter, Benno.'

'We should refuse.'

Father waved the letter in the air. 'We can't. We'll have to talk to Pauline and Adele – the parents will listen to them.'

As I stood at the edge of our improvised camp, Jack Fountain said to Father, 'Yours won't be the first.'

'You've heard?'

'They're getting out of the soul-saving game, Martin. People don't see it that way anymore.'

'My thoughts exactly,' Ignatz replied.

'And you heard all this from where?' Father asked.

'Someone who knows someone on the Board.'

'Who?'

'Sounds right,' Ignatz said.

'What would you care?' Mother said to Father. 'You don't want to go back, Martin.'

Remember, me on the edge of all this. No one conceding I was fourteen, I had a man's body, and brain. I could form my own opinions, and each was the product of deep thought, the study of facts, the reading of history, the understanding (we special children have) of people. Instead, Jack called to me, 'How's school, Benno?'

'Fine.'

Ignatz mumbled something and there were whispered comments. I wanted to say, Sorry, I didn't hear that, *Herr Beck*.

Jack said, 'How do you spell diarrhoea, Benno?'

I couldn't see the point of the question, but I told him, and Father said, 'No, that's not right, is it?' And for once, Ignatz defended me. Then Jack said, 'I always admire someone who can spell diarrhoea. Not many can. It's a good sign, isn't it, Benno?'

'Of what?'

'What sort of brain you've got. Your dad reckons you got a good head on your shoulders.'

I shrugged. I couldn't imagine him saying it.

Then Jack asked me a few more words, and I spelt them, and he said, 'There's no stopping this boy, is there?'

Enough. I waited until they started whispering between themselves again, fetched a dozen squares of newspaper I'd torn (always my job), snuck into the bush, found a big tree and pulled down my pants. Worked my arse free, and sat waiting.

'Benno, you watching for snakes?' Mother called.

I refused to answer. I could never get away from her. I looked up and noticed a parrot. A night parrot? Yes, of course! I wanted to run and tell Father, but realised this wasn't the moment. He or she walked towards me (without noticing me), picked through leaf litter and found something. As I cast my mind back, Father sitting at his desk saying, 'Not to be confused with a ground parrot.'

'How?'

'A night parrot is green, but yellowish-green, all mottled, dark brown. And smaller than a ground parrot.'

It was the right colouring, and it seemed small enough.

'A sort of croak, right? Some with a drawn out whistle.'

I wanted to throw a few twigs, see if it made any sounds, or flew (I knew night parrots didn't like to fly). But I couldn't find anything, and anyway, I wasn't finished. I just had to watch, and wait.

Father had said, 'Purely nocturnal.'

'So what do they do all day?'

'Sleep.'

'Where?'

'In a hole.'

'They sleep in a hole?'

'Yes, no, I don't know, but you'll never see them during the day. You'd be very lucky to see one at night.'

A ground parrot, surely. I finished the job, cleaned my hands in the dirt, stood and fixed my pants. I took a step towards the bird, but it still didn't notice me.

'Benno! Come on, we're waiting.'

Another step, but this time it looked up. I knelt, put out a hand and said, 'Hungry?' But it turned, and half-flew, half-ran into the bushes.

As I emerged from the spinifex, Jack said, 'Come on, let's have yer, Benno.'

He was waiting beside Irene, and told me he wanted to travel on the dray. 'Smoothest ride available, young man.'

'The camel?'

'How do you spell available?'

'*Irene*?'

I didn't have any choice. Father in his chair, Silas at his feet, and Mother and Ignatz ready on the dray; Jamy back with his horses, and Ludwig on the cart.

'*A-v-a-l-a-b-e-l*?' he said.

'It's got an i.'

He was standing with his hands cupped, ready to help me up. Father said, 'Go on, Benno. You've been on a camel before.'

'That was years ago.'

Nothing for it. So I clambered up, settled in the saddle, adjusted the few bits of rug and said, 'She stinks.'

'Not what you say to a lady.' Climbing up beside Mother and saying, 'Let's go.'

Camels are shit. They jag from side to side, up and down, bruise your arse bone. They have one speed, and attitude, and they smell like piss. I felt like I was falling off, though I never did. I watched the others, comfortable on the dray, and said, 'Does anyone want a go?'

'You'll get used to it,' Jack said. 'Just do what she does.'

'How do you mean?'

'The rhythm, Benno. Feel the rhythm and give into it, eh, Alma?' Who slapped him and smiled and said, 'He's only fourteen.'

'That's old enough. When I was his age . . .'

'Alright, Jack.' Father.

'Give her a pat, say her name. She likes it. Goodnight, Irene.'

'Is she going to sleep?'

Jack broke up again, shook my mother's arm and said, 'You don't need to be able to spell everything, eh, Alma?'

I said, 'Father, I saw a night parrot.'

'In the middle of the day?'

'He mighta been a blind one.'

'Why?'

'I was standing right next to him, but he didn't see me. Or didn't mind me being there.'

'So why didn't you grab him?'

'I was busy at the time.'

Jack roared, and Ignatz said, 'A time and place for everything, I would've thought.'

We travelled like this for half an hour. Jack was right, you just had to give in, jiggle like you're doing eurhythmics, or whatever it's called these days. *Aerobics.* In their leotards and leg warmers. Eventually I heard Jack say to Ignatz, 'No, that's not the case at all.'

'Well, it's what I've decided.'

'I travel up and down the length of this track, and I hear what people say, Ignatz.'

He didn't reply. I stroked Irene's neck – before she shat, reached down and ripped grass from the ground. Continuing.

'They're very grateful, Ignatz,' Jack said. 'Most people think if left to their own devices these blacks would be back in the stone age, roaming . . . and worse, you know what it's like when they get to town.'

'It's too much for one person,' Ignatz said. 'If I'm going to do something . . .'

'They're not going to send anyone else. The blacks have learned to rely on you. You ought to hear what people say, Ignatz.'

'I don't care what people say.'

'The way he's schooled them, plenty of them getting to town, to high school, a few to university, haven't you?'

'One. One. In how many years?'

'That's a start.'

Father adjusted himself, lifted himself from his chair. 'This is my concern, Ignatz.'

'I've decided.'

'What they say,' Jack said, 'is if a few get educated, they can return and lead their own people. And they see that's down to you and Martin.'

'Listen to that,' Mother told Ignatz. 'You could be running the place.'

For a few minutes, nothing was said. I wondered whether Ignatz mightn't change his mind.

We'd been travelling close to the river, and now it widened, took on a pattern of ripples and dents as it flowed south. Shallows, and a sort of beach, variable daisy stopping short of an escarpment that rose a hundred feet, more, in a matter of moments. Father asked Jack if the water was deep, and he said four of five feet. He asked Jamy if the horses were up to it, and he seemed to think so. 'Straight here . . . over there, not so deep.'

So we lined up – the dray, the cart, the fresh horses, and me and Irene. Just waiting, like the waters might part.

'You sure?' Father asked Jack.

'You gotta get across, Martin.'

Ignatz said, 'Someone should try first,' and Jamy tied the horses to the cart, and began, his old mare up to its saddle, struggling, but then emerging on the other side. He called back to Ignatz, 'Just keep moving. Don't stop.'

'What about Irene?' I said.

'She'll be fine,' Jack replied.

There's a photo of this – 1937 perhaps, Terese and me (a few years before Sharon and Jack) standing with Father's old Brownie, the Finke in flood, water halfway up the cliffs. A slightly wonky shot, as I said, 'I reckon this is where we tried to cross.'

'All of you?'

'Me on Jack's camel. Shitting myself. Father in his chair, Silas holding on for dear life, and Mother and Ignatz at the front . . . you oughta seen it.'

We'd only been married a couple of years, and here we were, a thousand miles from anywhere, me telling her this story about a bunch of idiots on a cart and dray trying to follow the Finke. I think she said something like, 'I woulda turned back.'

'We couldn't. There was nowhere else to cross, and Father had to get to hospital.'

'Well, where are *we* going to cross?'

'We're not.'

'How are we going to get home?'

Me telling her this was her home now. The Western Desert. Patrol Officer Benjamin Gerlach.

But now, Jamy called, 'She's solid on the bottom.'

Ignatz thought about it, flicked the reins, and the four horses moved forward, in, up to their knees, big, sweaty legs, a pop-eyed terror of water. The dray dropped into the river, the tray flooded, the boxes and baskets soaked, and Ludwig said, 'No point muckin' about.' Then he shot forward, went around the dray, his horses working against the current. Jack looked back and called, 'Come on, Benno, she's up for it!'

I kicked Irene in the ribs and she sauntered into the water, but then stood, waiting. I kept shouting at her, but she wouldn't move, and Jack called back, 'Come on, old girl!'

By now the dray was heading up the opposite bank, the cart, the spare horses, but Irene didn't care.

'It was just me,' I said to Terese, fifteen years later, and she laughed. 'I coulda died.'

'How deep?'

'Eight foot, easy.'

'You just said four.'

'Eight, at least. And that bitch of a camel just stood there.'

As it was – the others all safe, calling for me to keep up. 'Get up, Irene,' as I slapped her rump and she let out a moan that rolled along the river. Eventually she decided, took a few steps, changed her mind, jumped about, and I was in the water. Clinging to the reins as the current tried to take me, as Ludwig jumped in and swam across.

Now I was telling Terese about Oskar – about this black kid playing in the Finke, and idiot me knocking myself out, Oskar saving me. 'Otherwise,' I said, 'I wouldn'ta been here talking to you.'

'You've had an exciting life.'

'Although Father only ever saw it as settling a debt.'

'How's that?'

'Years before, just after they'd arrived, this policeman, Dietrick (I've told you about him), rocks up to the mission saying he's looking for Ludwig, cos he's been involved in stealing cattle, something. Father says yep, I got him, but you're not having him. Dietrick goes, but then returns later, finds Ludwig, drags him off, and Father follows and says, I told you he hasn't done anything. Thing being, when Dietrick got a hold of you . . .'

There were various versions of this story. Oskar had one with Father walking up to Dietrick, taking his gun, and him and Ludwig returning to the mission. Either way, it was like the favour had been returned.

Ludwig grabbed me around the scruff, dragged me up onto the sand. Mother came running down and Father said, 'What sort of animal is that, Jack?'

Me, drying out, as Irene slowly crossed the river, came up on the bank and started eating more grass.

Running Waters

As we moved through patchy grass – a couple of cycads, pumice from some long-gone volcano – it'd already begun. Silas up front, head low, mumbling about flowering crests of countless stalks. Jamy singing under his breath, his chant becoming an animal groan, a charm against hurt he sang in time with his body.

'What's going on?' Father said to Silas, but he didn't look up, didn't say a thing. Father asked Jamy, and all he managed was, 'So many of them, Pastor.'

Father knew, Mother, Ignatz, Ludwig, all of us. Irbmangkara was a place to be avoided; Running Waters, a fattening of the Finke, a chance to water your animals, rest, tell the old stories. But not for years now. Now the blacks found other ways around. Silas said, 'Should we keep going, Pastor?'

'We're going to stop.'

'Lunch,' Ignatz agreed.

'But further up,' Silas insisted.

'This'll do,' Mother said. 'That was a long time ago, Silas. There's nothing you can do for those people now.'

Jack had gone. He'd reclaimed Irene, pecked cheeks, shaken hands, wished us the best, but said he had mail to deliver. He'd asked if we'd be okay, and Ignatz had said, 'As long as we stick to the schedule.' Then he'd ridden away, calling, 'Make sure they look after you, Martin.'

Now we continued through scrub, the cart and dray lifting over anthills, rotten trunks and branches. I saw an eagle watching us. She tried to fly, but couldn't, one wing completely useless; tried again, lifted a few feet, veered left and crashed into the ground. It seemed a shame. Jamy described her to Silas, and he said, 'That's cos she's hung about here too long, Pastor.'

'Where?' Father asked.

'*Here*. Irbmangkara. Bad place. Hear it?'

We found a clearing beside a pool. A dozen paperbarks hanging across the water, shedding skin, dropping leaves. Father said, 'This'll do.'

But the double-chant continued, and Mother said, 'For goodness sake, Silas, Jamy.'

Canopies joining, welcoming us, lifting limbs as He made his way into Jerusalem. And behind this, a mess of turpentine, witchetty, wattle and God knows what. Father had described it all in his guide to desert flora. Pressed each specimen, mounted them, drawn up labels with binomial Latin, habitat, soil. He knew all of this country. Maybe not like Silas, Jamy, the other blacks, but like Darwin, Sturt, the mad explorers. This was a place to be studied, understood, documented – so that, in time, it wouldn't seem so threatening.

Ignatz and Ludwig started unharnessing the horses. Silas and Jamy waited on the cart and dray, so Ignatz said, 'Are you going to sit there all day?'

Silas helped Father down, settled him on a tea chest, turned and looked across the waters and said, 'No good.' Then he walked up a hill, until he found a log to sit on. Jamy followed him. They rested together, just out of sight, and Mother said, 'This sort of nonsense . . .'

'You helping?' Ignatz called through the bush. 'Silas?'

But I guess (now I understand) they were hearing other voices, forming some sort of chorus, demanding some sort of action.

'Unreliable,' Mother said, settling beside Father, taking the rest of the mail Jack had brought, and sorting through it.

Meanwhile, I helped Ignatz and Ludwig hobble the horses beside the pool. Ludwig said they were tired, and Ignatz agreed. 'There's no rush. As long as we can get to the ranges by night.' Then it was down to me (again) to produce the damper, break it up and butter it, make mutton sandwiches and hand them around. Calling: 'Silas, Jamy, you eating?'

No reply.

Father said, 'Leave them be.'

Mother opened a letter, produced a packet of photos and said, 'At last.'

Two dozen shots Father had taken around the mission when he was still mobile. Me, Mother, Pauline and Adele standing on the porch, smiling; Lucas in the background, grinning. Mother handed the photo to Father and he said, 'I thought I'd have problems with that camera.'

'You've got boxes of these photos, Martin.'

'I must assemble them. I was thinking of some sort of book.'

'To go with your other books?'

'And find a publisher. I'm sure someone would be interested. Look at what that Bates woman did.'

'She was an idiot,' Ignatz said.

'No, she had a mission, too.'

'Mad. Living in the desert for thirty-five years. She said the blacks were cannibals, and they'd become extinct.'

Mother said, 'But she looked after them, Ignatz.'

He wasn't convinced. 'She did that to draw attention to herself.'

A photo of all the kids – Ignatz beside the schoolhouse, me, Oskar, Lucas and the girls, a few boys grinning at Father as he lined us up, said *no silly stuff*. I said, 'You've cut half of me out.' Ignatz said, 'Well, you were only ever half there.'

'At least I came.' Filling mugs with barley water, handing them around, navigating a fog of flies that lived beside the water.

'I would've thought Benno's your best student,' Mother said to Ignatz.

'Perhaps.' Turning to me. 'We've had our days, eh, Benno?'

I knew what he meant. When I'd been the only student. At the front, centre, thirty empty desks, Ignatz saying, 'Should we try some maths?'

'Is there any point?'

'Your parents still want you educated.'

'We could try again tomorrow.'

'Will anyone be here tomorrow?'

Which is why he'd had enough, I guess.

Ignatz shook his head and said, 'I don't think you'll desert them, Martin. If you were gonna go, you'd have done it years ago. You'll be back.'

'I wouldn't be so sure,' Mother said.

'You were the one telling me,' he said, 'how you'd go around serving them, feed their kids – remember – when you made ice cream that time? All the children running about, and they didn't know what to do with the stuff. You're not going anywhere, Martin.'

Father just rubbed his legs. 'It doesn't matter what I want, Ignatz.'

A photo of Silas in a clean suit holding a picture of the Last Supper, telling a group what'd happened in the end. Some attempt at Christmas decorations (Pauline's job, every year), a tree, and Silas in the middle of a rant. Father said, 'Maybe he can take over?'

Ignatz almost laughed.

Mother said, 'Silas? The inmates running the asylum?'

'His heart's in the right place.'

We could hear the chants from the mid-distance.

'They'd all starve to death.'

'Well, then . . . maybe you, Ludwig?'

But he just drank, shook his head and said, 'That water looks cool.'

The rest of the photos were handed around. Father wiped his face and neck with his handkerchief. 'Benno, take them something to eat.'

I walked the hundred yards, flattening sickle-leafed scrub with a stick, an afternoon smelling of kero and night-lights, the acid of a billion dead ants. Silas, on an old log, and Jamy at his feet. I approached them, handed them damper, but Silas said, 'I'm not hungry, Benno.' The same with Jamy.

'Don't you want to be here?' I said. Stupid question. I knew they didn't; knew why they sat, hunched over, heads as heavy and tired as the horses. I put the damper on the log and said, 'Maybe later, eh?' Then I sat beside Silas and said, 'You should write about what happened here.'

'Why? It happened. You can't stop it happening. It's always happening.'

'But if you write something down, and people read about it, then it might not happen again.'

I guess he thought this was stupid; I was stupid for saying it. I didn't even know what the tribes had argued about in 1875. It wasn't much, apparently. But Silas (I knew) had seen it all. As a three-year-old, holding his mother's hand. He'd been here, this spot, perhaps, eating seed cakes, when eighty men came out of the bush with spears. 'And you remember?' I said to him.

'I remember. Just down there.' He indicated.

'And you were, what?'

'Three, a little fella, but I remember, Benno.'

Something about territory, something someone had said or did. Eighty of these blokes running down the hill, waving spears, shouting, the women and children too scared to move. An hour, probably less, dozens of bodies lying about where we sat now.

'So we shouldn't have stopped here?' I said.

'No,' Jamy said. 'Your father oughta known better.'

'You can hear them,' Silas said. 'Listen. They're running in all directions, but it doesn't help, Benno. Can you hear them?'

'Maybe.'

'My mum, she put me behind this old log, and I sat there and watched and . . .'

I waited. 'What?'

'My two best friends, no older than me, no younger than me, got hit on the head, and they went down, and they just slept, like that' – and he showed me – 'and they never got up, Benno.'

If you stopped and looked you could see everything, and you could understand why it had been, and why it would persist. Nothing we could say would change this; nothing we could write down; nothing we could study. It just was. You either got it, or you didn't. The birds escaping the bush; skinks scattering in the leaf litter; lizards dragging fly-full bellies towards termite mounds.

'You can't hear?' Silas said.

'No.'

'Then all the Matuntara men left and there were people everywhere. I came out and saw them, and some were still alive, but not for long. Here, there!' Indicating. 'Blood everywhere.'

As far as he was concerned, they were still there. No one had attended to them. No one had collected their bodies. No one had sung songs of healing (like Father's) for them.

'Hoo-bloody-ray!' Mother said, from a distance.

I left the damper and said, 'You better eat it, you'll be hungry tonight,' and half-ran, fell, scratched my arms on thorns, sprinted and arrived back beside the dray. Mother was waving a letter, and told me to sit down. Father was grinning, his fingers interlocked on his belly.

'It's from Gotthold Wurst,' Mother said.

'Who's he?'

'A wheat farmer. Don't you remember, he visited us at Hermannsburg about a year ago? His daughters went into your room and you complained they'd gone through your things?'

'I remember.'

'Well, he's written again.'

'What's it say?'

I noticed Ludwig in the pool. His shirt, his pants hanging from a branch, his boots and socks on the ground. Jumping up and down, splashing, diving under the water. And Ignatz, too, preparing to go in. He'd half-hidden himself in bushes, taken off his shirt, laid it on a rock. I watched as he emerged from his hiding spot, tried the water with his foot, put in his leg and, slowly, his whole body.

'"We were sad to hear what has happened to Martin,"' Mother read. '"I've had some experience with the condition. My grandfather. It came and went. Painfully, as I remember."'

Ludwig floated. He let his head go under, raised it, spat water, looked at me and said, 'You should come in, Benno.'

'"The Board's actions are completely unacceptable,"' Mother read. '"Thirty years of service and you've been forgotten, Martin. I think it's a disgrace, and I've written to express my concerns."'

The water looked cool. Ludwig was sitting on a rock, listening.

'"But there's no point waiting, Martin. I've decided. If I put my car on the train, get off at Oodnadatta, I could make it to Horseshoe Bend in two days. Not that I can wait for you to agree, or disagree, so by the time you get this letter I should be at the railhead. Straight to town. The Austin could make it in good time, and she has good suspension."' Mother held up the letter. 'Isn't that wonderful, Benno?'

'That's great,' I said. 'So if we made it in a few days?'

'We could,' Ignatz said, attempting a backstroke, stopping, standing up to his hips.

Father said, 'It's a wonderful thing he's done. He's a good man, isn't he, Mother? A proper Christian. Not like those people on the Board. They've lost the spirit, eh, Ignatz?'

'More businessmen than Christians, Martin.'

'Exactly.' Then to Mother: 'Although it wouldn't have done us much good if we were still back at Hermannsburg.'

'Don't talk about that.'

'It's true,' Ludwig called.

'And you just keep swimming,' Mother said. 'See Martin. One man, driving all this way, in his car, *his* car – not the Board's, not any of that. *His* car.' Re-reading the letter and saying, 'He's given us money too, hasn't he, Martin?'

'Not us. But the mission. And yes, he has. A hundred pounds, maybe more, over the years. One of our true believers, Alma. One of the few.'

'"I'm sure this could be of help, Martin, and I look forward to seeing you soon. Trude has packed some medicines that might be of assistance. But all we can do is try and believe that the Lord is with us, if not the Board."'

'Coming in?' Ignatz called to me.

I looked at Mother. 'Go on,' she said. 'But make it quick.'

I walked around, found a spot, took off my shirt and revealed my white skin. Pauline knew every rib, every freckle, my bony legs, the spinifex under my arms. A beginner's body, she called it, coming into the washhouse while I was in the bath, as I covered myself with my flannel, and she laughed and said, 'Nothing I haven't see a thousand times before.'

Father was still looking at his photos. Maybe he thought things were looking up.

Ignatz said, 'What are you scared of, Benno?'

I unbuttoned my pants, pulled them down, folded them over my shirt. Mother said, 'You look like a polar bear.'

I went in, one step at a time, with Ignatz watching, his head half below the water. Then I sat on a half-submerged rock and said, 'It's cold.' I folded my arms.

Ignatz said, 'Come in, I'll give you a race.'

'Go on,' Father called, watching.

So I slipped in, raced him from side to side, and won. He took my arm, my forearm, my wrist, held my hand in the air and said, 'See, he's a little champ!'

That was enough. I got out. Stood, drying myself with my shirt, as Ignatz watched me. 'What's the rush?' he asked.

'Didn't you say we had to get to the ranges?'

Parke's Pass

Today, people call the Finke River *spectacular*, although I don't think any of us saw it that way in October 1922. Now people look at it and say, 'What about those ranges, stretching out forever?' Or 'Can you believe how the river just stops and there's a waterfall?' They go on about cormorants and spoonbills, and they see something we didn't. Back then the bush was a prison, keeping us from the world, from hospitals and civilisation, other people, siblings, orchestras. It was a cholera ward, an asylum. No *ooh* and *ah* over how the waterholes lay still and quiet and cold; no adoration of ancient caves and paintings of long-extinct animals. Just me, Mother, Father and Ignatz on our dray, Silas lying down on the back, trying to get some sleep; Ludwig on the cart, and Jamy back with the horses. This time I had the reins. Ignatz shook his wet head and said, 'He paid for it in the end.'

'He did,' Father agreed.

Contrast this with where I'm sitting now. Street after street of fibro homes, a patch of lawn, viburnum and pittosporum. This is the world people were making while we were trying to get to Horseshoe Bend. A few vegetables out back, a swing for the kids. Endless acres of suburb that grew in the Australian imagination while we were lost in the never-never.

Father said, 'I don't reckon they'll ever know the actual number.'

And Ignatz. 'It'd have to be in thousands.'

'The problem was, and is,' Father said, searching the stony pavement, 'they let those people do what they want. Dietrick *was* the law. Whatever he thought, whatever he said. There was no accountability.'

'Still isn't,' Ignatz said.

'They were frontier days.'

'Still are.'

'I think we've got rid of that type.'

But Ignatz said, 'How do we know what people will think, one day, about what we've done?'

'Helping the blacks?' Father said.

'*Helping* them?' Shrugging. 'Time will tell.'

'What's that mean?'

Dietrick's life was an anti-legend. The station (the ruins still there) had been built by the government to protect pastoralists or, more correctly, allow Dietrick to shoot the blacks who strayed onto leases, who took animals. Drought years, the Aranda had got hungry, wandered, wondered where their animals had gone, taken a few from such-and-such Downs, or so-and-so Station, stupidly thinking life was all about sharing.

'All of this country,' Father said. 'Between Running Waters and Tempe Downs. Every day, along these tracks probably, rifle at the ready . . .'

Later, they put in a road and more people came and saw the ruins and asked what we'd been doing here. They said, 'I can't believe they did that!' They shook their heads and put it down to a 'colonial mindset'. But to me, at fourteen, it was just bush, standing between me, my father's life, and the real world.

So why do I bring this up? Why do I skip sixty-six years (becoming an adult, marriage, children, jobs), take you a thousand miles south, along these miserable little streets, this small asbestos house, and me, looking up from my dad's journals, wondering *who's knocking on my door*? I never have visitors. Except Mrs Wright, asking if I've seen her cats. The knock, again, and I called, 'Who is it?'

No reply.

'If you're selling something I don't want it.'

And again – the slow, tapping on the glass.

'Fuck!'

Imagine me (this is only a few months ago) in my trackpants, an old business shirt, a dressing gown. Unshaved, halitosis, yellow teeth, reading the notes Father had left: 'Firstly, the Kangaroo Song (9 verses) everlasting daisies &c.'

I had no intention of getting up.

'Night parrots speaking, tree tops &c.' Thinking, when I get all this down, when people read it, it'll sell thousands, hundreds of thousands of copies. Translated. Thirty languages. A documentary. The world will finally understand what Father did (apart from saving souls). I'll call it *The Night Parrots*. Something enigmatic, hard to pin down, elusive, real but not real, imagined but physical, factual but spiritual; something full of regret, but possibility; something that lived in the gaps between words.

Knock, knock, knock. *Fuck off!*

Back in the scrub, trundling along, Father said to me, 'Leaving this place won't be any loss, will it, Benno?' Looking out, although I knew he'd learned to love it in those twenty-eight years.

'But when you get better, you'll want to come back?' I said.

'I think I've done what I set out to achieve.'

'What's that?'

He gazed at me strangely, like he couldn't understand how I couldn't understand. 'Left things better, don't you think?'

I shrugged. I was fourteen, and stupid, and saw the world for what it was – trees and buildings and people and clouds. I didn't see *beneath* things. 'I guess.'

'You guess?' Smiling, reaching out to touch me, but realising I was too far away.

So we just travelled, people nodding in and out of their dreamtimes, following their songlines, minus the bitumen and give way, stop, go, think about it carefully. Father said, 'When I started, Benno, when me and your mother arrived in 1894, these people, the blacks, none of them lived longer than thirty-five, forty, and look now.'

'That's right,' Mother managed.

'They had basic conditions, they died. Most of their children died. That's what it was like back then. None of them could read or write.

They were ignorant. But now, most of them have basic skills, don't they, Ignatz?'

'Basic.'

'And their understanding of an afterlife. Well, they didn't know the Truth. I think they understand now, don't they, Silas?'

No reply.

'Silas? They understand who Jesus is now, don't they?'

'Who?'

But he left it at that. 'They grow their own food, they understand nutrition, and their kids have got a better chance than they had.'

This seemed important to him – so I agreed. 'Things are much better.'

'Of course.' Smiling, reaching out to touch me again. 'Maybe it'd make a good film?'

'I reckon.'

'Who do you reckon could play me, chasing all those wandering blacks killing all our stock? Remember that, Alma?'

'Yes.'

'Or maybe a scene with me serving them food, or ministering to them, washing their feet – that'd be particularly symbolic, eh, Benno?'

'I guess.'

'You could be in it, too, Alma. And you Ignatz, Silas . . .'

If they were excited, they didn't say.

'I'm not saying it because I want praise. Just so people might know that despite what Dietrick and his mob got up to, there were others who tried to *help* the blacks.' He closed his eyes, and remembered. 'That fella killing all our stock. And he told me, he told me, Benno, he said, This is our land! Get off. But I said to him, We've come to teach you to share.'

'We had a pretty decent idea,' Silas said.

'I mean this tribal mentality. That's another thing I'm proud of, Benno. Teaching them that we're all one people under God.'

'We were.' Silas.

'Not always. The way he raised his spear, remember, Alma? And pulled back like he was going to throw it at me, and I just stood there – and he backed off. That was an important moment.'

'Why?' I said.

'Because the other blacks saw that violence solved nothing. No more Running Waters after that, eh, Silas?'

'No. You fixed all that, ingkata.'

'Yours was a violent society, Silas. It couldn't continue.'

Silas sat up and said, 'So there are no regrets, Pastor?'

'No one gets it all right. I think, perhaps, when I gave those children up . . .'

When the same two men in their rough cotton suits returned a few days later with a motor bus. When they handed Father a removal order and said, 'This is the list of kiddies, Pastor.'

'I didn't decide,' Father said. 'I didn't make that list.'

'Who did?' I asked.

'He said these are the children, he had the parents marked, which were black and which were white, and he said, Are you going to help us, Pastor?'

'That's enough,' Mother said. 'We know the story.'

Father reached out to me again. 'I refused to help, but I can still remember sitting in my chair and hearing the arguments from the camp and the parents shouting and screaming and I can still remember (Lord forgive me!) putting on my Mozart, and when the screaming got louder, turning it up and . . . I can still remember, and that, I think, is my biggest regret, Benno.'

'But some of those kids got to go to good homes?' I said.

Father hadn't convinced himself. 'Ten minutes later their parents were at our door, Benno. They were saying where are they taking our kids, when can we see them? I had to say, I couldn't do anything about it, and they argued and shouted before going back to the camp . . . And they returned, every day for weeks, saying, You can fix it, ingkata. You can get them back. I said I'll try. I wrote letters, and I tried but . . .'

Mother said, 'What's this achieving, Martin?'

'Your son asked.'

'It's done, finished. Benno, leave your father alone.'

Can you hear it? Can you hear the knocking? It's the sound of something you got wrong a long time ago, and can't make right. So there's me, eighty years old, smelling like wallaby piss, throwing down my pen and saying, 'Damn you!' There's me, storming to the door, opening it, stepping out and saying, 'What the hell are you selling?' A half-familiar face.

'Dad?'

'Jack?'

'How are you, Dad?'

'You . . .' Looking down the crumbling drive, the footpath, across the road to that stinking Nielsen bastard, for some explanation as to why the son I hadn't seen for thirty years was standing at my front door.

'I saw you the other day at the shops. I followed you.'

'You followed me?'

'All the way – watching you with your trolley. You're not meant to take them out of the shops.'

I admit, there were seven or eight left at the end of the street, just so they couldn't work out who'd taken them.

'Why didn't you . . . Jesus, Jack, you're all grown up.'

'Surprised? I couldn't come in, but then I spent last night thinking about it, and I didn't sleep a wink.'

I welcomed him into my house, and he said, 'You got a lot of books and stuff.'

'Some of it's mine. Some of it's your opa's.' Clearing a spot on the couch, sitting him down and saying, 'You shoulda said something yesterday.'

'I saw you and I thought, *Jesus, it's not, is it*? But I knew. I went home and thought, *I'm not saying anything to that old bastard*, sorry . . . but I thought . . .'

'What?'

I might leave it there, for now. There's a lot to tell you about Jack (born in 1944, Sharon in 1942), but it's after midnight and I'm tired, and like Father, sitting on the dray, sometimes you just have to give in to sleep.

The Krichauff Ranges

I was telling you about Jack, about shame, the one thing we all regret. For Father it was giving up those kids, and for me . . . I've been skirting around it, haven't I? It was 1955, I was married to Terese and we had a nice place in Prospect. I had a university job lecturing about the thing I knew best, loved best (as I hope these pages show) and I had a research assistant called Kate Monteath. We spent a lot of time together, she liked my sense of humour, and I found her quirky, dark, cynical in a very non-Terese sort of way. We worked together, got lunch together, and it just grew until . . . Even with Jack sitting home waiting for me, Sharon, my wife, a nice place with red Berber, good neighbours. All of this. So my 1915 was 1955.

A few days after the first knock on the door, Jack returned. I brought him in, switched off the telly, sat him on the couch and asked if he wanted a drink.

'Coffee . . . white with two.' Staring at me, like he couldn't understand who or what I was, why I lived in a hovel smelling of old books, photos, fifty thousand feet of unprinted Ektachrome 35mm reversal; a room full of artefacts (I showed him these later); plates and mouldy coffee cups in the gaps between shoe boxes full of hundred year old handwritten notes about birds, trees, totems. He noticed all of this, but he just said, 'I had no idea.'

'What?' Going out to the kitchen, filling the kettle and putting it on.

'Hillcrest.'

'I know. Kate . . .' Looking into the lounge room. 'You remember, Kate?'

He didn't say.

'She bought this place in 1952, and when we . . . white? Two?'

'Ta.'

I returned to the kettle, waited, wondered what to say. Was he here to make amends, or get even? Or was he like his father, his grandfather – curious about why people did things? 'What were you doing in Hillcrest?'

'Woolies. Then I looked across and . . . I knew.'

'I've shopped there for thirty years.'

'First time. We, that's me and Steph and Tom, live at Highgate.'

'Steph? Tom?' Emerging from the kitchen.

'Steph's my wife. Tom's my son.'

'Your son?' Smiling. 'There's another one of us?'

'I guess.'

'I'd like to . . .' No, too soon. 'How old?'

'Twelve.'

'Twelve! *My* god. I'm a grandfather. And you decided, when you saw me?'

'I wasn't sure.'

Eventually the kettle boiled. I made coffee; fucked around, half-shocked, excited, terrified, full of hope and maybe a bit of lost love, until he called, 'This is Martin's stuff?'

'Some of it. Some's mine. I was thirty years in the desert, too.' Emerging with the coffees. 'You remember?'

'I remember you taking us to Hermannsburg that time.'

'That's right.' Sitting down between piles of books.

'And introducing us to a few black people.'

'Who?'

'Can't remember.'

'Oskar, perhaps? Pauline, Adele? Any of them ring a bell?'

'No.'

'Still, you remember. That's fantastic. And Sharon, she'd remember, too?'

He shrugged. 'She hasn't mentioned you for years. In the late fifties, when she was at uni, you were like . . . Satan.'

'And your mum?'

He stared at me for a moment. 'Thirty, forty years to explain. How long have you got?'

'Look around.' I indicated the Bach and Mendelssohn piled beside the record player. 'I've got plenty of time, Jack.'

He took a book from a pile, studied the front and said, 'It was mainly all Aranda, eh?'

'It was.'

'And they're still . . . do you ever go back?'

'Not anymore.'

He replaced the book, tried to drink the crap coffee, said, 'So, this was your thing?'

'My thing? I guess.'

'And now . . .?'

I upset a cushion and a pile of notes nearly collapsed. 'I took over from Father.'

'*Father*?'

'My dad. Martin. I inherited all his stuff, and he asked if I'd try and make sense of it and . . . perhaps you're thinking I've wasted my time.'

He shrugged. 'It was what you wanted to do.'

Muddy. I decided against taking it further. It was too late to say sorry. Jack said, 'I just saw you, and followed you, and here I am.'

'Right. Well. Twelve, eh? And where's he go to school?'

'Scotch College.'

'*Posh*. Does he like music, sport?'

'He likes history.'

'See!' Waving a finger. 'You're stuck with another Gerlach. And what do *you* do?'

'Teach. High school. Like old Ignatz. Remember him?'

'You remember Ignatz?'

'I remember you telling us about him and his . . . predilections.' Smiling.

'God. Teach! And, sorry, what was her name?'

'Steph. She's an accountant.'

'Well, that comes in useful, I guess. So I suppose you have lots of money?'

'Some.' Looking around the room, the Leipzig postcards pinned to the wall, portraits of Father and Mother, a few of Isaiah's watercolours in broken frames. A whole life, scraped together, served up as a memorial to what we'd tried to achieve, but failed to grasp. Jack noticed and said, 'That's one of Isaiah's paintings?'

'Running Waters. Remember? I took you and Sharon and your mum once, but that was late forties, you wouldn't remember.'

'I remember the old church where Martin preached. And the house you grew up in. And the waterhole where you hit your head and nearly drowned, but some kid saved you.'

'Oskar. That was Oskar. He saved me.'

He wouldn't have come, he wouldn't have drunk my coffee, he wouldn't have sat and listened if all he'd wanted to do was punish me.

'And that time,' Jack said, 'when you had to get Martin to hospital. On some old cart, and he was screaming in pain. You always told us about that, and how shit-scared you were that he was gonna die along the way.'

I couldn't remember telling him this, but I must've. I must've gathered them around the telly, and started my stories. 'Yes, they were a rotten couple of days.'

'You still remember them?'

'I do.'

In fact, I could hear Jamy calling from somewhere deep in the bush. He was saying, 'He's over here, Ludwig.'

'It was his heart, wasn't it?' Jack said.

'Yes. But we still had hope. Some farmer was going to drive up from Kapunda but . . .'

'You don't remember? You took us and Mum along the same route, and showed us the places, and what happened where.'

Jamy was still calling, 'I got him over here, Ludwig. You want me to kill him?'

'Go on.'

'He's just a little one.'

'So what? I'm hungry.'

I said to Jack, 'If you decided to come in, you must have thought . . .?'

But he just put down the coffee and said, 'Lotta maybes, eh?' He stood, saw one of Silas's old Bible pictures and said, 'What was that mad bastard's name?'

'Silas.'

'And he was all in white, wasn't he?'

'He was.'

'Because?'

'Father saved him when his parents were killed.'

'That's right. You used to always talk about him, and how we needed a preacher like him at school so we didn't fall asleep in chapel.' He looked around again, satisfied. 'It was good to see you.'

'You don't want to . . . I mean I could . . .'

But he smiled and said, 'Now I know where you live, Benno. Father. That's what you always called Martin?'

'Those days, your father was your god. You didn't dare . . . no Brady Bunch back then, Jack.' We waited beside the bubble-glass door. 'There's a lot I could explain,' I managed. 'I'm not saying it as an excuse but . . . I could *explain*.'

I'll leave all the Jack business there for now. All the stuff about regrets, and how it's never too late to fix things. I won't tell you about how I watched him walk down the drive, get into a new BMW, look back, then drive off. I won't tell you I was thinking, *Shit, was that it*?

Back in the bush, Jamy raised his rifle, and Ludwig said, 'Go on, kill it.' The wallaby stood watching us with its Himmel-brown eyes, the surely-you-wouldn't expression that masked (I guess) fear. Jamy pulled the trigger and it moved like it was drunk, before falling. It seemed a shame, but I hadn't been brought up in a finishing school. 'I could cook it?'

'Nah, on the coals.'

'Kanga curry?'

On the way back, I took the wallaby from Jamy and said, 'I've got it.' He said, 'I'll cut her up,' but I told him I would. He laughed and pushed me and said, 'You can't do nothing like that.'

I was determined. I returned, showed Mother and Father, said how the wallaby nearly got away. 'But I'm gonna cook it.'

Me, trying to be king-of-the-bush, lying it in the grass, cutting it (slowly, awkwardly) from top to bottom, removing the guts, the organs, throwing them away, as Jamy, Ludwig and Ignatz watched, and Silas shouted from the distance, 'And when he returned, he was man. He was a member of the tribe!'

I skinned it – legs, arms, body. Then cut the meat into chunks as Jamy laughed and said, 'You're making a mess of it.'

'If you want to do something useful, get the cast iron pot.'

Father said, 'After, we can try a cake, Benno.' A schoolboy grin. That's what I imagined he was like as a kid: affable, few words, many thoughts, dropping jokes like farts in a hot tub. Light. Until, perhaps, the Lutherans got to him. He said, 'I can help you.'

Mother looked confused.

'The banana cake,' I reminded her, and she shook her head and said to the others, 'Do you remember that?'

Mother's Day. Father and I and six overripe bananas, Pauline standing back with her arms crossed as I said, 'We'll take over, you can lie down.' But she wanted to watch. I chose a bowl and she said, 'Too small.' Butter, and she said, 'Salted.' Like this, until Father glared at her, and she went out. Then we began our cake. The only time I got to give orders. 'Take that . . . mix the flour and butter . . . not so fast . . . then, when you've got a minute, you need to mash the bananas.' Father got it. He said, 'If it pleases thou, Sir Benjamin.'

That's how I remember it. Me and my dad, cooking. A few words, a grunt, banging into each other. And then it was ready, and we went out to the porch, put it in the brick oven, and Pauline said, 'Not so close to the heat.'

'I'm in charge!' I told her. 'Aren't I, Father?'

'He is.'

So Pauline backed off, and Father and I went in to make tea, then, half an hour later, we brought the cake to Mother, in bed, sitting up, arms crossed. 'It's burnt on the edges.' And Pauline: 'I told them – a cool oven.' Then Mother cut a slice and tried it, stopped, grimaced. 'It's not cooked in the middle.' Pauline, smiling. Father, pointing to me and saying, 'He was in charge!'

'I wasn't!'

'You were giving the orders.'

I went over to him (something never generally allowed), stood an inch in front of him, waved my finger at him and, perhaps, poked his chest. That's how I remember it, anyway. Mother's Day. Or Father's. And now, he said, 'Maybe we should've brought Pauline along.'

'It's a stew. You can't get it wrong.'

'No?' Smiling.

And Mother: 'If anyone can . . .'

Over the next ten minutes: the meat in the pot, the pot on the coals, the water, the curry powder, the bay leaves, the chopped carrots and onions, all of it bubbling away. I gave it a stir and said, 'An hour perhaps.' I washed my hands in a waterhole, dried them on my pants and said, 'Anyway, if I'm doing all the cooking . . .'

Father just smiled.

'What?' Grinning.

'I didn't say a word.'

Thursday 12 October (Day 3)

The night refused to cool. Seven people tossing and turning, Mother and Father complaining to each other. I lay bare-chested, waiting for a breeze; watching an ant cross my ribs; humming the Honey Ant song (Father saying he was glad I remembered). Swiss movement stars, distance, futility. At one point, three wild donkeys came down to drink and Ludwig sprang up, chased them away, squatted and laughed.

The next morning we harnessed the fresh horses, boiled the billy and cracked the tent. No one had slept. We were all tired. Father, especially, telling Mother (so we wouldn't hear) he'd had a bad night. He said he could barely feel his legs, move them, for the pain. Northerlies picking up by seven, burnt necks and arms, raw shoulders, Mother saying, 'You'd think He could keep it cool.' Father telling her He had someone for that job. Porridge slopped in plates, sugared. Strong tea that tasted like piss smelt.

Father said he didn't want to sit today so we spread rugs on the dray and he laid down and said, 'Maybe that'll be better?'

We started off just before eight. Ignatz said it was too late, we'd have to make it up. The horses accepted their lot, pulled slowly, the wind lifted dirt from the ranges and blew it in our hair, ears, up noses and in mouths. Settling in sweat, a vanishing cream of everything (for what it was worth) civilised. Mother said, 'After today we're nearly a third of the way, aren't we, Ignatz?'

'Nearly.'

'A third, Martin! A few more days.'

The dray lifting and dropping into corrugations, the old boards rattling, Father saying, 'I can't do it.'

So we stopped, Ludwig and Jamy re-lashed the chair to the dray and Father mounted his throne again, apologising, saying, 'If there was another way,' Silas telling him none of us minded, we were here to help. As we set off, Father prayed, something from Psalms, Silas joined in and the rhythm repeated for another day.

An hour later, Father asked for his notes and a pen, and sat correcting his work. 'The more I look at it the worse it seems,' he said to me.

'You'll have plenty of time to fix it,' I said.

'Maybe you need a second set of eyes?' Ignatz called from the cart.

'Exactly,' Father said. 'No matter how well you *think* you write, Benno. I never quite got the Australian argot, the way words . . . German grammar is . . . Schulz, I told you about Schulz, didn't I, Benno?'

'Yes.'

'He could strip a sentence and put it back together like a motor car. But somehow, in Australia, it doesn't matter.'

He descended, reading a page of handwritten notes that had already been crossed out and rewritten until the page was mostly scribble. 'And if you got it wrong – if you confused a passive verb for an active verb, out came the cane. But you remembered, next time.'

Ignatz was silent. He had his own cane. I have plenty of stories about what he did to some of the boys. Sometimes he'd walk up and down the aisle, slam his cane on a desk, some boy would piss himself, there'd be shouting and the parents at our door that night. But Ignatz would never admit he'd done anything wrong.

'"The assemblage of words,"' Father read, '"mostly fails to capture the essence of what I want to say."'

Mother told him not to bother with all that, but he said, 'To keep our minds from this place.' Indicating. '"The challenges of form have proved too difficult to—"'

'Martin!'

'It doesn't read . . . it's not smooth, is it, Benno? But what I'm saying is someone, you, could rewrite it so it flows, so it appeals to a wider audience?'

'It's fine.'

'Ignatz?'

'Fine.'

'No' – studying it over – 'something's not right. The syntax. I'm still sitting in that classroom in Leipzig, conjugating verbs, trying to avoid the cane. You can't learn with a cane behind your ear.'

We passed gibbers, salty margins and a few grey bushes. A hot wind full of grass seeds and fine dirt. We shrunk into our seats, waited for it to pass, wiped our eyes. Ignatz spat dirt from his mouth and said, 'Sometimes the most hostile environments produce the most, what would you call it, *ecstatic* effects.'

'How?' Father asked.

'The Old Testament?' Ignatz said.

Although there was nothing ecstatic about our sweaty clothes, wet armpits, numb arses. Nothing romantic about the crust around our mouths. But Father was used to it. He said, 'It's important, isn't it, to remember?' He wiped his forehead with his handkerchief. 'The way the ranges were made.' Trying to turn his head to admire them, again. 'The rainbow serpent thrashing about – that's how it was, wasn't it, Ludwig?'

'Yes, Pastor.'

'And the three caterpillars? Who were they, Ludwig?'

He took a moment to think: 'Yeperenye, Utnerrengatye and . . .'

'What a story,' Father said, sitting forward. 'Arriving somewhere around here, and encountering the stink bug – imagine that! A stink bug – and their battle. I tell you, the gospels have got nothing on that!'

'A stink bug?' Ignatz called.

'Ripping off its head, going underground, perhaps over there' – throwing his hands about – 'before making these ranges.'

Ignatz said, 'It wasn't really like that.'

Father ignored him. He was seeping into the fissures, through the caves, into the aquifers with the caterpillars. He was determined to make the

McDonell Ranges. But Ignatz said, 'The Finke is the oldest river on the planet.'

'We know all that,' Father said.

'A hundred and fifty million years. These ranges, Benno, were made by tectonic plates pushing against each other. And they're still pushing, and getting an inch taller every year.'

I wanted to tell him to shut up. I'd heard this, and a thousand other scraps and footnotes, too many times. They had no juice, no spunk, no love. They might have been right, but what did that matter?

'The rock formations, the trees, all of it,' Father said, lighting up, as if he knew it was true, as if this explanation made no claim on God, or his seven-day narrative. 'Imagine these three caterpillars, down there still, pushing life up through the sand, the rocks, the water.'

'Like Genesis?' Silas said.

'Exactly! The same thing. An explanation . . . I've written it all down, all of these myths (thanks for your help, Ludwig) and they're in a box, another box, labelled, what was it, Alma?'

'Kangkaita.'

'*Kangkaita*. All of those stories. Just like God opening his hand, the earth dropping into its pot, cooking away, and you have life.'

'The only way the Finke could cut through all that granite,' Ignatz called, 'was hundreds of millions of years, a few grains every year, so slow we can't imagine it.'

'That doesn't *explain* the thing, Ignatz. People need to *understand*.'

'I don't know what you mean.'

Ignatz was off – how Stuart mapped the Finke, made peace with the blacks, opened up the country for grazing, for civilisation, for geologists who'd classify rocks and make sense of how Australia was made. The telegraph. Todd and his wife Alice, all of it. A rock by rock, tree by tree description of a country he never understood (especially its people).

Here's an example. I remember when I was eleven or twelve, sitting beside Oskar at the front of the class, Ignatz giving a speech about how Australia was an ancient continent, once covered in forests, but then the climate changed and bang, we were a desert. I remember the black kids listening, accepting his version of Creation, going home and telling their parents. Later that day, a crowd gathered outside our house, and Father said to them, 'What's all this about?' Someone said, 'What he's telling them – it's no good.'

A few questions from Father, then he said, 'We can hear about both, can't we? People can make up their own minds, can't they?'

But then Ignatz appeared and said, 'I thought this was a mission.'

'Sorry?' Father.

'A mission. God. Genesis. And on the seventh day he rested.'

Someone at the front said they wanted their kids to know about the rainbow serpent, and the three caterpillars. They wanted them to understand this was the Aranda way, and to them, the correct explanation. They had no problem with their kids learning about geography, geology, physics, the chemicals in water. In fact, this was good. Necessary. But to say the world was *only* granite and sand . . .

So, the next day. There's (just) me, up the front, with Ignatz saying (something like), 'It's important we get a clear understanding, Benno.'

'Pardon?'

'They don't want to learn, do they? They want to keep believing what they've believed for years. That's what I'm battling against. That group, turning on me.'

'I don't think they—'

'I came thousands of miles to teach their kids and look what they do. So it's important I teach you, at least.'

That's how I remember it. Just me and Ignatz, again. Having to read about Cromwell, or how Alexander the Great was defeated. Writing responses – full sentences, subject, object, predicate. Reading my answers, Ignatz filling the blanks with more facts, as I glanced at the clock, and he said, 'Am I boring you?' My first ten years of education. As I wrote, Ignatz peered out the window at the black kids, playing, and said, 'You have to be sure what you do with your life, Benno.'

'How's that?'

'You think one thing, but years later . . . does your Father still enjoy his work, do you think?'

'I guess.'

Taking a moment. 'Have you finished yet?'

Back outside our house, the leader of the group (I have no memory) said, 'They don't wanna learn what he's got to teach.'

Ignatz: 'Education's not about having a good time. What would you have me teach them? If you want your kids to have *opportunity*.'

'They got jobs on the stations.'

'So they'll have what you've had? And that's enough, is it?'

Ignatz believed in a system that had, even then, let him down. But he stuck with it. After all the talk about land rights, they took the children, and abuse, and all this tent embassy business in Canberra. He died believing, I guess. Which is one thing for Father – he saw the light, too soon, too late.

It was nine-thirty, the part of the day that'd lost whatever relief the night had brought. The sun in our faces, Father with his umbrella, drifting off, Silas forever straightening him. I watched him breathing; the thirty seconds (it seemed) he tried to inhale, the time he took to expel it. His notes, still in his hand. Silas removed them, and returned them to their folder.

I looked back. Ignatz alone on the cart. No one wanted to sit with him. Jamy, with the tired horses, a little wave, and 'They're feeling the heat, I reckon.'

Mother was going through the rest of the mail. Opening each letter, reading a few lines to see what it was about, folding it and putting it in her pocket. One by one. I said, 'Who are they from?'

'No one.'

'Have to be from someone.'

She didn't reply. I said, 'Ignatz shouldn't be so mean.'

She screwed up a letter and threw it into the bush.

'Do you know, once, when it was just me and him, he took me to Mananganaga.'

'He shouldn't have done that.'

'He said, Enough of this, Benno, let's go. We walked in the rain and when we got there I said, We can't go in, but he said, Why not?'

She was still reading, or at least pretending to.

'So he grabbed my hand and we went in, and I said, It's only for initiated men. He said, It's just a cave, for God's sake.' I looked back at him. Nothing. Though he probably knew we were talking about him.

'Mother?'

'What?'

'I was telling you . . .'

'That doesn't surprise me.'

'Then these paintings, all the sorts of food, like a message from hunter to hunter, and I said, They've been there for thousands of years, and do you know what he did?'

'No.'

'He got his water, and he splashed it on them, and he said, Thousands of years my arse. Then he used his hand to rub them off.'

I'm sure Mother didn't see that as any great loss, but when I told Father that night, he said, 'That's not right, Benno.'

'So, what are you gonna do?'

Thinking and thinking and then, 'Nothing.'

'Why?'

'Unfortunately, I need him more than he needs us.'

The next day, I did say to Ignatz, 'Mr Beck, you oughtn't have done that to the paintings. They're sacred.'

'There are plenty more.'

I never understood why he did it. Was he trying to prove something about himself, them, what they believed? I said, 'Maybe we should tell them they got damaged?'

'They can have another go.'

Our worlds were at war with each other. One thing, or another. The look on Ignatz's face as he entered the cave; one of the 'wild Abos' (Ignatz's term) walking around Hermannsburg wearing nothing but a corset he'd taken from the line. Mother coming out and shouting at him to take it off, as he laughed at her. As she grabbed it, told him to cover up (she always turned away when they were naked). A schoolroom crammed with a hundred kids with no shoes, no pants, no books. Just Ignatz, ranting. A portrait of the King. And Ludwig's hand-painted sign: 'Thou God Loveth Me'. The weekly line for potato rations (boxes stacked to the church rafters, the dust from the gunny sacks, the body odour and flies, everywhere). Morning calisthenics. The same kids spaced out, squatting, standing, over and over, arms out, deep breaths. Once, in 1919, the Governor of South Australia came to visit. In a big tourer, with his wife and aides. I remember showing him around – the church, the tannery, the pottery, the dormitories full of pressed sheets and Bibles. Back to the house, and scones and tea, the governor looking at me and saying, 'Quite a unique life you live here, Benjamin.'

'Just like anywhere else,' I said.

'Really? As far from anywhere as I can imagine. Which makes your Father's work so valuable.'

His wife reached over and squeezed my earlobe.

We heard the car horn and went out and the tourer was full of thirty, more, kids. One of the aides tried to shoo them, and they laughed and pretended to drive, but wouldn't get out. And the wife (old bitch) said (something like), 'They're just in from the desert, are they?'

'No,' Father replied. 'Just the novelty . . .'

The novelty. The Hermannsburg novelty. Until it wore off, years later, and we weren't so much saints, as sinners, then criminals, then dogs. But I'm getting to that. But to credit the governor, he said to the kids, 'If you all get out you can have a ride . . . up and back to the gate.' Which took most of the afternoon, and a tank of petrol.

The box gums

Not *in* the Krichauff Range as much as skirting it, Ludwig finding tracks between folds of mountains, sandy plains and spring-fed pools persisting through the hot, wet afternoon. He was talking to the horses, explaining the geography, and how they might continue: 'Come on, up, over there, over!' Flicking the reins, telling us we should stop to let them rest. Ignatz insisted it was out of the question.

A sheer cliff, layers of salt and schist, a conglomerate of burnt banana cake, Father explaining the mystery of Creation. In fact, he said, 'Six thousand years seems unlikely, doesn't it?'

'Not at all,' Silas replied.

'Looks that way.' Ignatz.

I asked about the copper-green rock, the white-stained strata, rust bleeding into a billion years of history. Ignatz blamed dissolved minerals, but Father said unlikely. The fault lines in the faces, the piles of rock at the bottom, and in between, a mix of box gums and cycads. We'd already passed some of Henbury's cattle yards, full of shit and withered balls, a crushed calf left to dry in the sun. Enough room to bring in a hundred cattle, sort them, select the culls for market. Some sign of civilisation, at least.

Father held his armrests as the dray moved through sand, sunk, found hard ground. Silas smelt the air and said, 'Something rotten.'

'What's that?' Father said.

'Something dead. Can't you smell it?'

On and on, Ignatz alone, again, me between Ludwig and Mother, Silas staring at the loose boards, Father cranking his music box and saying, 'The two least popular instruments.'

'What?' Mother.

'The flute, the harp. But Mozart put them together and made them work.'

The heat persisted. The sun on my arms, Mother warning me I should've worn long sleeves.

I was back on Opa's cart. Rattling along Kaiser Strasse as Julius sat holding his arm, the tea-cloth Oma had used as a bandage, around and around, tight, to stop the bleeding. The horse they called Bismarck, and some man, I forget his name, who ran the stables. Julius calling: 'It stings!'

Father and Opa up with the driver, me beside my brother saying, 'It's stopped bleeding.'

Julius stared at the blood. 'There's so much of it.'

And Father: 'Stop being so dramatic, Julius.'

An ice-blue night, coal and sulphur sleet, a southerly that cut through clothes, skin, bones. Around nine, because us kids had just got ready for bed, and Julius was running around in the front room, tripped on a rug, fell through a window, cut his arm, Father shouting how could he be so stupid, neighbours coming in and Julius saying, 'I didn't mean to.'

I can still remember the corrugated road; the limping horse; the back of the three men's heads; and Julius's small eyes, his fat cheeks, his high-parted hair. I can smell Leipzig – larks and sweet doughnuts, boiled cabbage and menthol. Like it was yesterday. The driver flicking the reins, asking which hospital and Opa saying, 'St Elisabeth.' Julius lifting the tea-cloth, seeing the gash and saying, 'Do you think I might die, Benno?'

'No, you can't die from a cut.'

And Opa: 'Stop being so dramatic, Julius.'

It was a long way to St Elisabeth's, and after fifteen minutes Father turned and said to Julius, 'What were you doing, anyway?'

'Nothing.'

'No running inside. You were told.'

Julius started crying, and I had to tell him to stop. Father got shittier, Opa said, 'I thought you'd toughened them up a bit, Martin?'

'If you let them fix you up,' I said to Julius, 'I'll give you that cross. You want it?'

'Yes.'

'Do you remember the story?'

And he called out, 'Hey, Opa, tell us— '

'No, don't bother him. The story, remember, when he was fighting the French and he outflanked a whole column, came up behind a command post, found Napoleon and all his generals . . .'

'Wasn't Napoleon earlier?'

'No. And he captured the lot of them, remember? So they gave him an iron cross.'

'And I could . . .?'

'When you get better. They'll have to sew up your arm.'

'That doesn't matter. It's stopped bleeding, see?'

Eventually we arrived at the hospital, I helped Julius down, the nurse came out and said it was a decent gash and would take *at least* a dozen stitches. Then a doctor (who thought he was funny) said, 'Get me the big needle, nurse.'

'The one we use for horses?'

'No, for elephants. On second thoughts, I think it'd be easier to remove the limb. Don't you agree, nurse?'

'Yes, Doctor.'

'Do we still have that tree saw?'

'Yes, should I get it?'

And to Julius, 'It will save all that sewing. Agreed?'

But he was on to them, and said, 'How big's the needle?

That night I sorted through my pockets, found the cross Opa had given me (me, not the others, because it'd already been decided – *I* was the special one, *I* was the one returning to Australia). I handed it to Julius and said, 'Iron Cross second class. For bravery and *con-spick-u-us* attention to duty, I, Benjamin Gerlach, award you, Julius Gerlach, this cross.'

We emerged from the last of the sandhills and settled on the plains. Silas said there'd been flooding. Father asked how he knew, but he just replied, 'I bet there are branches, aren't there, Pastor? And I bet you can see where the sand's been washed up?'

I heard what sounded like a radio, off its station, amplified across a grassy clearing in front of us. A violin, an alto, the static of hundreds of budgerigars crowding every inch of a couple of ironwoods, extending out to branch tips, where they moved in the breeze. Getting closer, a white noise of green and yellow bird atomising the day, the valley, the peace of a place where no one ever came. Father covered his ears, and Mother stood and clapped and shouted, 'Get away!' And each of the hundreds of birds lifted from their branch and flew away. We pulled up on the riverbank beside what looked like a shallow spot and Mother said, 'Is it safe?'

'Of course,' Ludwig said.

'I can't see the bottom.'

'It's there.' He cracked his whip and the horses shot forward, into the water, splashing, resisting, more whip. They kept going, up to their flanks, their bellies. I held onto the dray, but the wheels sank, and Father said, 'It's no good.'

Ludwig continued. The throne rocked and Father reached for Silas. Mother shouted, 'Ludwig!'

It wasn't all bad – we were soaked, and I felt cool, and laughed, and Father said, 'What's so funny?' I said, 'Nothing.'

Ludwig kept thrashing the whip. 'Come on, you dumb animals.'

Father's music box played a few notes.

Mother said, 'Benno, watch your father!'

The wheels fell into a hole, the dray dropped and Father tumbled into the water. I jumped in after him and tried to swim. But of course, I'd never been able to. My head popped up and I heard mother saying, 'He can't swim,' and I remember thinking, *Who? Me or Father?* But I was in, and so was Father, and I had to save him. I raised my head, saw him a few feet away, splashed my hands in an attempt to breaststroke. This was how it was done. This would propel me through the water (though I'd never done it before). This would get me to Father, and I could save him.

'Father!'

I could see him, further along, bobbing in the current, and I saw Ignatz running along the bank taking off his shirt, his pants, his shoes, and jumping in. Swimming (he seemed to know how) towards Father. Then, arms around my chest, someone pulling me from the water. Mouthfuls of it. When Ludwig deposited me on the sand (as Oskar had done) I coughed, tried to vomit an empty stomach. Mother came running towards me and I noticed the dray, high on the opposite bank.

Ludwig (wearing underpants) knelt beside me and said, 'You okay?'

'Fine.'

'You coulda drowned.'

Mother asked what I was thinking, reminded me, no, told me I couldn't swim, I never had, never would, that's why she'd given up on lessons. I said, 'Father fell in.' I coughed up more phlegm, and noticed Ignatz helping Father from the water. He managed to stand, and looked at me and said, 'Benno!'

Ignatz helped him hobble along the bank, then Father stood a few feet away and said, 'Stupid thing to do. Just what I need – a body to –'

'I thought I could get you. It didn't look that deep.'

'Well, it was, wasn't it? Jesus, Benno.'

And with that, he extended an arm, and Ludwig and Ignatz helped him back to the dray. Mother said to me, 'You're here to help, not make things worse. We've got enough to worry about, Benno.'

'Next time just wait till you're told what to do,' Father called back to me.

Sixty-six years later, I get it. I was the one asset he couldn't, wouldn't risk losing. Having brought me back from Germany, invested so much time, so many insights and explanations ('Listen, there, when the harp comes in'). The one thing, the one object, the one person he wouldn't risk leaving in Leipzig. To go and drown . . . but he just turned again and said, 'There's no point sitting there in wet clothes, is there?'

Mother shook her head and returned to him.

I took off my shirt and laid it on a rock; my pants, on the sand.

'What are you doing?' Mother called to me, helping Father dry off.

I didn't reply. I wasn't sure what any other son would've, should've done. I wanted to stand, to march over to my father and say, 'You were the one who brought me here!' And maybe he'd say, 'Because I thought you'd have more common sense.'

But it didn't happen like that. Instead, over the next twenty minutes, Mother and Ignatz helped Father change into dry clothes. They sat him down, gave him barley water, examined his legs and arms and fussed over him. A while later, Father managed to walk over to where I sat, half-naked, in the sun. 'You've got nothing to prove, Benno.'

I just looked up.

'I know you're up to the job but . . . that could've ended badly.'

The *job*? What was the job?

'For your mother's sake – stick to the damper.'

Thinking back, it seems strange he didn't understand. How I was worried about him; how I was scared, how I was terrified that the man I admired most, needed most, might not survive the journey. That's all I was thinking. Not in actual thoughts, perhaps, but in the way moments came and went so quickly; the way I was always ill-prepared, too late, not tall enough, unable to understand, make myself understood.

It was all explained a few days later. When I sat in my room, clean shirt and tie, as the others sat in their pyjamas. Julius saying, 'Mother says a few months, and if you can't come and see us we'll come and see you.'

Charlotte, Michael, all of them said something similar. Until, eventually, Father and Opa came up for my case, but I told them I'd carry it. Down the stairs, hands shaken, Oma kissing me on the lips, Opa saying he was jealous he couldn't go. I felt like saying, 'Well, if you hadn't put all those stupid ideas about Jesus into his head . . .' Then the maid opened the door, kissed me and said I was in for a big adventure.

Out on the footpath, looking back, five faces softened with muslin, gas light, the glow of the fire. Father said, 'It's important you keep going, Benno. No point dwelling on things.'

I didn't look back. I just climbed aboard the carriage, waited for my parents, and we drove off.

Pantjimdana

We moved a hundred yards upstream from our failed crossing, found dappled shade beside Pantjimdana waterhole and unloaded. I waited short, tasting native tomatoes, spitting them out, throwing them at budgies. Eventually I joined the others, drying out beside a shot of spadeflower.

Pantjimdana is the sort of place where Christopher Skase might've tried to build a resort, a big pool, the locals serving cocktails and making beds for minimum wage. There'd be flights in, helicopters, photo shoots with U2, Paul Hogan going on about some version of Australia more LA than Hermannsburg. Pantjimdana ('the feather crests are lying about') might have been (if not for its isolation) a victim of its own beauty. Not that we saw it that way at the time. As we sat on what might've been a beach (if they framed the shot properly), admiring the cliffs, the caves the blacks had lived in, the fresh springs bubbling up into pools. Cycad postcards, a soundtrack of rustling grass and cabbage palms that stood above, but with their feet in, the water. Father said, 'It was a long way to come.'

'How far?' I asked, sitting in the shade of a *Macrozamia macdonnellii*, named after the explorer who'd walked this stretch of river in search of cattle country, minerals, glory.

'Katherine, Mt Isa,' Father said.

'Not that far,' Ignatz said.

'At one time all of this was a tropical forest.'

Mother and Ludwig had sat Father on a lump of granite to recover from his *Boys' Own* moment. Maybe he felt bad for having shouted at me (how I remember it, although he'd just raised his voice). Maybe. Because he looked at me, sitting in my underpants and singlet, and said something like, 'We tried to teach you,' and I said, 'Why's a kid in the bush need to know how to swim?' He pointed to the waterhole and said, 'You don't need an ocean to drown in.'

I've found that to be the case – a puddle, a bath will do. A small life, a bucket full of regrets, a dozen things you should've done. More than enough. But anyway, he said to me, 'We've got to watch out for each other, don't we, Benno?'

'I guess.'

'If we do that we'll be fine.' Descending into reverie. 'What do you say, Silas?'

'We've only got each other.'

'Exactly! That's how it is, Benno. Each other. You and your mother and me and Ignatz, Jamy . . . Where is he?'

Silas called for him, but his words just settled in the bush.

Me and my parents, the mad preacher, the angry teacher, Ludwig looking after the horses. He'd unharnessed them, allowed them a sand bath. Twelve of them (in various states of rib and bone and boredom) rolling in the white sand beside the water. That's something I should've made clear about Ludwig and Jamy – they loved horses. They loved (I guess) the way they didn't argue, or laugh at them; the way they just did as you asked, day after day, year after year, until they laid down and died.

'We should eat now,' Mother said to me.

So I stood, made for the cart, Ignatz watching my progress.

'Jamy?' Mother called.

'He's probably gone to the toilet,' Father said.

'He didn't take any paper.'

I found the basket full of rock-hard damper and said, 'Will this do?'

'It'll have to,' Mother said. 'And salted pork.'

'Again?'

'Again.'

I found the pork, unwrapped it, looked at Ignatz and said, 'Are you having some?'

Ludwig started brushing the horses that'd walked down to the water to drink. One by one, checking their legs, running a hand over twitching muscles.

'Katherine?' Ignatz said.

'Exactly.'

'And yet each of these palms has survived here for a million years?'

'Much longer. Although if you don't like that explanation there's the story of the ancestor who gathered the seeds in Queensland and came here, scattered them, and they started growing.'

I sliced the damper, added the pork, Pauline's chutney (to make it edible). A small collection of little lunches, laid out for the sake of the flies as much as anything.

'All along the Finke,' Father said.

'God was busy on the second day, wasn't he, Martin?'

'He was.'

'He had a lot of trees to make?'

'He did. Including these.' Stopping, realising he was being drawn in, again.

'Ignatz, how does any of this matter?' Mother said.

'It doesn't.'

'Well, why do we need to talk about it?'

Mother's voice shook the fronds on the cabbage palms, the grass, the gum leaves, the water in the hole, the sand between our toes. That's what my mother could do. Equal to any serpent or caterpillar – when she spoke the world listened, shuddered, shut down (for a moment, anyway).

'We're out of chutney,' I said, showing them the jar.

'We'll get by,' Father said.

And Mother shouting again: 'Jamy!'

'All I was saying,' Ignatz suggested, 'is that there can't be some figure spreading seeds when we believe, *we believe*, don't we, Martin, that God laid his eyes upon this land and decided what it should look like, and then set to work.'

'These things go together,' Father said.

I handed the sandwiches around. Ludwig sat down to eat. Mother called for Jamy again. Father said, 'I believe, Ignatz, that life is a multiplicity of events, of people, of beliefs, and these are all one thing. Maybe you can't see that?'

'You arrived as a missionary.'

'I am! I always have been, and will be! I was taught that God is love, weren't you? And if that's the case, why would I waste my time?' Settling, attempting to eat the damper.

Mother said, 'If you want to do something useful, Ignatz, go and find Jamy.'

'Fine.' Eating his own damper, pulling pork from the middle and throwing it into the bush. Then he stood, and Mother pointed and said, 'I saw him going that way.' And he walked off.

The horses were happy enough. Drinking, touching muzzles, rubbing up against each other, returning to the sand and soothing sore flesh. Mother said to Father, 'We never should have brought him.'

'You shouldn't encourage him,' Silas said. 'Just ignore him, unless he has something useful to say, which isn't very often.'

I watched Ignatz disappearing into the bush, calling for Jamy, clearing a path with his arm.

'At least my suit's clean again. Is it clean, Alma?' Silas said.

'Yes.'

White, glowing, hanging on a branch to dry.

'The Lord wanted me pure again, Martin. That's why he deposited you in the water.'

Mother said to Father, 'Ignatz has been at it again. When I hung out his clothes . . .' Placing her damper on the ground and taking a letter from her pocket. 'It's smudged, but you can read it.' She flattened it on her knee, showed Father (who refused to look) and read: '"Dear Ignatz, thank you for your latest letter . . ." See, *latest*,' Mother said. 'I know of at least five others.'

Ignatz was calling for Jamy.

'"Firstly, your concerns. Pastor Gerlach has been working with the mission blacks for thirty years. In that time he has built Hermannsburg into the biggest, the most important Lutheran mission in Australia. You, no doubt, are aware of his achievements."'

'Alma!' Father said.

'"So when you wrote to us with your concerns, and what amounts to allegations . . ."'

'That's no good,' Ludwig said. 'We don't need to hear any of it, do we, Pastor?'

'We don't, Ludwig. Alma, enough.'

'You need to hear it. You need to know what he's been saying behind your back.'

None of this was a revelation. Mother, Father, all of us knew Ignatz had been writing to the Board for years. He'd been outlining every concern, saying you needn't act if you don't want to but *if* . . . But it hadn't worked. The Board had written to Father and he'd told them Ignatz was an idiot, and he'd deal with him. And anyway, Jack Fountain had caught on, and every time Ignatz handed him a letter he'd check (steam from a billy). He'd read, and report to Father. Once he copied a letter so Father could read it. Ignatz had caught on and hidden his letters in others, but Jack was good, and could tell, and when he arrived at Hermannsburg he pulled Father aside and said, 'He's written another one, Martin.'

But now, Mother read: '"We don't have any concerns about the management of the mission. If Pastor Gerlach chooses to let families live together, that is his choice. If he allows traditional ceremonies and initiations and even circumcision that is also his choice. None of these things runs counter to His teachings, and indeed, might form some bridge between cultures."'

'See!' Father said to Mother. 'They don't care. So why should I?' Leaning forward and rubbing his calves, his thighs.

'Because he's going behind your back,' Mother said. 'It's time we confronted him.'

'They haven't got anyone else to send, Alma. Who? And *he does his job*, doesn't he?'

She just sat, reading the letter again.

'That is his one fault. But we all have faults.'

'It's unforgivable,' Mother said. 'It's better we do the work ourselves.'

'How?' Shaking his head, leaning back and resting on straightened arms. 'Can I just get better? Can I not hear this? Alma?'

She folded the letter and placed it in her pocket so she wouldn't forget. 'I'm willing to speak to him.'

'You won't. Just be quiet.'

But she wasn't happy. She said to me, 'Get dressed, we need to keep going.'

I stood, threw the rest of my damper away, pulled on my pants, my shirt, my shoes and socks. Ludwig gathered the horses, led them to the dray, the cart, and harnessed them. All the time, Mother complaining about Ignatz. When she'd run out of steam she said, 'Benno, go see where he's got to, will you?' Standing, helping Father up, walking him towards the dray.

I followed Ignatz's path, calling, 'Herr Beck? Jamy?'

As I went, all I could hear was Silas, invoking Jesus, mixing half a sermon with half a hymn, and in the gaps, a few lines of Aranda, the sort of mixing Father suggested might work. 'Herr Beck?'

After a few minutes, I emerged into a clearing and there, on the other side, in a stand of what might've been paperback – Ignatz and Jamy. Close, half-leaning on a low branch. I stood trying to work out what was happening; I took a few steps back, a few more, and watched from the bush. I saw Ignatz saying something, then continuing.

'Jesus.'

Mother? Father? Ludwig, perhaps, he'd know best? But then Ignatz was fixing himself, talking to Jamy.

Back, checking every step to make sure I wouldn't give myself away. Then I ran, a hundred yards perhaps, and without thinking, called, 'Herr Beck? Jamy? We're leaving.'

Ignatz called, 'I found him.'

This is when I worked out things were getting stranger, when, like Father, I'd have to decide how to manage a difficult situation. Someone had to look out for Jamy. We'd all been taught this, for years, ever since he'd fallen off his horse: *You must take care of Jamy. You must make sure nothing happens to him, kids.*

When I arrived back at our camp, Father was already on his throne. Mother beside him, Ludwig holding the reins, waiting. I tried to climb aboard the dray, but Mother said, 'Why don't you go on the cart, Benno?'

I walked back, climbed up, waited, and soon Ignatz was sitting beside me, taking the reins, saying, 'I can't wait for some proper food, eh, Benno?'

'We need to cook damper.'

'Tonight, perhaps?'

I watched Jamy get onto his horse, and start leading the spares. I wondered how a man of learning, of God, of facts, of history and geology and mathematics, could just sit there, telling the horses to get up, as if nothing had happened.

David Copperfield

The best thing for it was Dickens. Oolong No. 29, returning to my spot beside Ignatz, trying to avoid his face, his eyes, his hands. He said, 'We're making good progress.'

I read from the start, again: *Whether I turn out to be the hero of my own life* . . . Maybe this should've been the title of my book. But I didn't feel like a hero. A hero would've said something to Father, shouted and defended Jamy, dragged him away from the monster beside me. But what did I do? Stop, think, consider. Bullshit. Looking back at Jamy, low in his saddle, his arms loose, his head hanging towards a strange infinity.

To begin my life with the beginning of my life . . .

I wasn't really reading. Just forcing my eyes to follow the words, in lieu of other things. Anti-reading, perhaps? I wondered if I could *become* David Copperfield. 'I am born.' *I was born in a wattle and daub house and appeared so sickly that the nurse rushed me to the church to be baptised* . . . Continuing in my head, so I didn't have to look at his fingers, his nails, the way he held the reins; so I didn't have to listen when he said, 'What are you reading?'

'*David Copperfield*.'

He rested his arm on his leg and said, 'Dickens is overrated. Read for an hour and nothing's happened. And worst of all, the melodrama. I'm not sure Dickens has dated well.'

'He's still popular.' Shit. It slipped. It was hard not to argue with Ignatz, but I returned to the book. *I was born with a caul, which was advertised for sale* . . .

I was born in a big, brass bed, with Pauline and Adele helping Mother, and me refusing to emerge, and when I did (I was told later) everyone looked at my small, pink body and thought my god, is that it? A disappointment, perhaps, although Father always said it was another run on the board. He was good at making people. But as for what Mother thought . . .

It was working. Ten minutes into the journey and I'd avoided his raspy, teacher voice, his facts, his lectures about nothing that meant anything to anyone. Sometimes I'd stop reading and glance at him. Sometimes, until I corrected myself.

'Your Father was concerned about you,' he said.

No reply.

'Benno?'

'I know.'

'He was scared you might drown.'

Nothing.

'If someone's talking to you, Benno.'

But I was stuck on a cart next to him, and could be for hours. 'I know he was worried.'

'So you should do everything you can to make it easier for him.'

Make it easier? Jesus. But I just said, 'I do.'

Chapter one was more interesting than Genesis. So I returned. *There was something strange, even now, in the reflection that he never saw* . . . Until, of course, Pauline raced into the church, presented me, and asked Father to save me. Which he did.

'When you think about it, it's strange,' Ignatz said. 'That we create life, and that child grows up to write novels, like Dickens (bad ones, admittedly), travel the world and see icecaps, deserts, fall in love and . . . it's a miracle, isn't it?'

'Yes.'

'What are the chances, Benno? That you'd be sitting here, beside me, reading that book? Billions to one.'

Maybe, if I tried enough, I could *become* David Copperfield. I am born. I observe. I have a change. With the Gerlach details inserted. A million words, published serially in the *Australasian Post*. Imagine? But Copperfield was funnier, smarter, better-spoken than me. And his life (I'd read the book three times) was more interesting.

'All I'm saying,' Ignatz continued, 'is that we come from nothing, and we get to see the world, like some giant Cook's tour. You must admit, that's something to be grateful for. Are you grateful, Benno?'

'Yes.'

'Then you should show it.'

Idiot. I continued reading.

'And if he dies—'

'He's not going to die!' Enough. Shut up.

'*If. If* he does. How glad you'd be that you'd thanked him for all of this.' Showing me with an open hand.

'He's just a bit sick,' I said.

'Show him, Benno.'

'It's none of your business.'

There might be a chapter saying: 'I observe the wayward schoolmaster', in which I tell the reader how, as I sat in the front of the cart, things became clearer. How I recalled his eyes surveying my legs, my body; how he popped into the bathroom to tell Pauline (busy scrubbing nine-year-old Benno) the vegetables would be brought in, presently. I said, 'Did you find Jamy?'

He took a moment. 'Yes.'

'Was he lost?'

'He's always lost.'

'You found him in the bush?'

'Yes.'

I looked him right in the eyes. 'You helped him?'

'Yes, I did.'

Maybe I cocked my head, because I wanted him to feel the terror. 'I saw, and I didn't understand *how* you were helping him.'

He clutched the reins and said, 'Maybe you should read your book?'

'I'm sick of it.' So I threw it back in the tea chest.

Then he handed me the reins and said, 'You can drive.'

So I drove. I'd said what I'd needed, for now. Maybe he'd stop. Or maybe I'd tell Father. How would that work? A confrontation, Ignatz storming off, no one left to carry on at the mission, the kids coming forward, police? He reached back, found a map, pointed to a hill and said, 'This map isn't so good. No heights, but you can tell we're here.'

I turned back, I called, 'You okay, Jamy?' He sat up in his saddle and said, 'All good.'

'James Range,' Ignatz said, 'although it's not clear . . . if you were relying on this map. No longitude, latitude.'

Now, he descended into grid lines, roads and tracks. 'Army ordnance is the best type, Benno, but this is all we have.' He tried to show me where he'd measured the track, made calculations, written a date beside it. 'We need to be here before we make camp, so another two hours perhaps.'

For once, I felt like *I* was standing at the front of the room with the cane, up and down the aisles, slapping people on the back of the head. I said, 'I wasn't sure what . . .?' Looking at him again.

'What?'

But I'd done enough, for now. I handed him the reins, jumped down from the cart, chased the dray for a few moments, then jumped on. Father looked back and said, 'What's wrong?'

'I'm bored.'

And Mother: 'If you didn't *say* you were bored then you wouldn't be bored.'

I looked back. He'd thrown the map into the tea chest. He was sitting forward, watching me, before turning his gaze to the bush.

'You should keep Ignatz company,' Father said.

I said to Silas, 'Chapter nine: I am taken to Sunday school. In which the Lord descends and saves my soul, and I become a good Christian.'

'Don't be stupid,' Father said.

'Part one: I am placed in the front row of the church and hear the prophet Silas preaching to the masses. A thousand souls, covering each of the hills of Jerusalem, and Silas says . . .?'

'And that time, remember, Martin,' Mother said, 'he wrote to the Board to tell them two hundred pounds had gone missing and you, *you*, Martin, were the only other person with access to the safe?'

'It didn't happen like that,' Father said. 'It was about the security of keeping large amounts of money . . .'

'It was not. And if it were, why couldn't he come and see you first? No. I still have the reply. The Board asked you to explain.'

'That was a long time ago, Alma.'

Silas stood, lifted his head to the sky and said, '*If you forgive men their trespasses your Heavenly father will also forgive you.* Matthew 6:14. Are they listening to me, Benno?'

'Of course, Silas. They're on their feet, they're cheering you.' I turned to Ignatz, and smiled. 'It's about choices,' I said. 'And whether we should forgive.'

Mother said, 'I've had enough of the man.'

'Enough, Alma!'

'Listen to me . . . are you all listening to me?' Silas said.

'Benno, don't encourage him.' Mother.

But I said, 'We're listening, Silas!'

'*I* had a choice,' he said, trying to steady himself, as Ludwig turned and said, 'You oughta sit down, Silas.'

'Go through the rest of my life *hating* the people who'd killed my family. My friends. I. Had. That. Choice.'

'You did,' I called.

'I grew up at war with the world! I didn't make friends. I didn't trust people. I didn't love! I was the kid sitting under a tree, and if people came close I'd run away. That's how it was, for years, until Pastor Gerlach approached me and said, Listen Silas, there's someone I want you to meet. Then he took my hand and led me to the church and opened this big book . . .' Of course, Silas had his Bible handy, and he held it up and said, 'He showed me someone was watching out for me.'

'Who?' I said.

'Jesus Christ, my Saviour! And from that day . . . I'd return to the church in the morning, at lunch, at night, for hours, by candlelight, reading this book.'

Father didn't care. Maybe he'd heard the story more than me. Mother just said, 'Forgiveness is one thing.' Taking the letter from her pocket, opening it again, reading it again.

'God asked one thing of me,' Silas said.

'What was that?' I said.

'He told me I should forgive. He appeared to me . . . do you want to hear that story?'

'Perhaps later.' Father.

Mother had no intention of forgiving. She told Ludwig to pull up, got down, walked back to the cart and handed Ignatz the letter. 'This came for you, from the Board.'

He took it, read a few lines.

'In reply to your latest complaint,' she said.

'I wasn't complaining.'

'No?' Hands on hips.

'I was just explaining . . .'

'What?'

'Alma!' Father called. 'Enough of this!'

But she just said to Ignatz, 'None of this was necessary. If you'd just come and spoken to us.' She stormed back, climbed aboard, and we continued. Father said, 'Why do you need to create such conflict?'

There was something magical (not in a happy sense), magnetic, electric between my mother and father. Between all couples, perhaps. Whatever held them together was a function of whatever pulled them apart. Whatever they gained as a couple, they lost as people. Like that night in our Grenfell Street hotel, Mother in the bath and Father standing at the door, saying, 'Well, what should I do, then?'

'Nothing.'

Because it'd been a mistake, she'd said, to leave the children in Germany. A mistake, for her to agree to return to this godforsaken country and the desert and the mission and . . . all the rest. 'You go back. I'll get the next boat to Europe.'

'Don't be stupid . . .' Staring at me, almost apologetically.

'It was a mistake, Martin. I can't take it again.'

'We're committed.'

'You're committed!'

'What do you want from me?'

Silence for a few minutes. Then father found his coat and left the room, and I sat waiting, wondering how it would end. But it always ended the same way. This reversal of poles, alternation of current. On the train back to Hermannsburg. And maybe, I think, that was me and Terese (some sort of fuse burning out too soon). Or Kate. Maybe me and Kate might've been as perfect as Martin and Alma. This part-warring, part-adoring couple that couldn't help but attract. Either way, back on the dray, Father said, 'Sometimes I think, Alma, you're so full of anger.'

'Someone has to be.'

And that was it. Just the steel rims, sparks on stone, the storm and stress of each of the spokes, as we continued.

Tunga

Another hour and a half, two hours, I can't remember, it was sixty years ago. And then you say, *Well, how can you remember the rest of it?* Don't worry, I can. We'd settled into our new camp, the tea-in-water boiling, Mother brushing crumbs from her apron, Jamy sitting close to the fire (as he always did), shuffling a pack of cards. Father praying: 'Dear Lord, I trust you've been enjoying the journey so far. We've been trying to keep it comfortable for you, provide some entertainment, eh, Silas?'

'It's not entertainment.'

'I hope you're feeling well-fed, courtesy of Benno, and his miraculous damper.'

Like this – far easier to remember a thousand details than any Biblical narrative; how Mother sat with a twig cleaning her ears, instead of drawing morals; how Silas walked around in his white-again suit, instead of claiming kinship with Jesus; how I sat, quietly, wondering what Oskar was up to, instead of going off into the bush to blubber, or shout at God for fucking around with my Father.

Two hours, let's say. All the time, following the Finke, and whatever it felt like doing. Big sandy beaches and, at one time, an acre or two (as I remember) of wild paddy melons, Silas saying he could smell them, taste them. 'It's all the Afghans' fault.'

Me: 'How?' (although I'd heard this story a thousand times).

'They didn't think there'd be enough for their camels to eat, so they planted a few, and look now.' Indicating the green melons growing beside the Finke. Telling Ludwig to be careful because there was nothing worse for a ruminant's gut than paddy melons.

On and on, Ignatz alone on the cart again, Father stretched out, muffling moans, Mother asking if he was okay, Father saying, 'There's no point asking me all the time.'

'We can stop.'

'We can't.' Ignatz.

Mother whispering, 'As if anyone's listening to you, Herr Beck.'

'Herr *Ignatz* Beck,' I said. 'Master of long division.'

'I'd like to teach him long division.'

'What does that mean?' And smiling, because Mother was funny when she got angry.

Father said, 'You sound like a couple of schoolkids, don't they, Silas?'

But he was busy surveying the melons, the flowers moving in the breeze, the vines that spread seeds into waterholes, up cliffs, everywhere. He said, 'Those melons might take over the whole country.'

Although they already had. Along with the goats and donkeys, the willows along the water lines, the feral pigs and dogs, the rabbits. The thousands of animals (including us, perhaps) who'd changed the land forever. And in the end, forced out the small, shy, nocturnal animals – the marsupial moles and bandicoots, the night parrots and lizards, black emus and giant goannas.

Towards sunset we stopped beside the river. Silas helped Father down, and he rested under a tree, taking time to settle his breathing, shake the pain from his limbs. Ludwig and Jamy unharnessed the horses and hobbled them beside the water. Sweaty bodies and twitching muscles, but they brushed them down again, waited until they stopped snorting bulldust. We were still a few hundred yards short of the Henbury waterhole (Tunga), but that would have to do for the day. We were tired. So we spread our groundsheets and started unloading. I noticed smoke rising in the distance and said, 'Henbury?' Ignatz said yes, the station, why would we make camp so close? Pots, pans, water on to boil; Mother wiping Father's face and neck with a flannel, him telling her to go away. And Silas, pants rolled up, into the water up to his ankles, saying, 'We've got company.'

'Who?' Father asked.

Two of the Henbury blacks appeared in the distance. The horses got closer, louder, stopped short of our camp, and one of the blacks (I can't remember his name) climbed down and said, 'Ingkata!' He came forward, shook Father's hand and said, 'They're waiting.'

'They'll have to wait until tomorrow,' Father said.

The second man shook Father's hand, sat opposite him with his legs crossed. 'We heard you were coming.'

The blacks knew we'd arrived. Smelled us, miles off, heard our wheels, Silas babbling, Ignatz calling directions; whispered voices telling them they had visitors. The men sat and talked with Father for ten minutes as we unpacked. Father told them about the previous days, the decision that had been made at Hermannsburg. 'That first day out was rough, wasn't it, Silas?'

'Bad for your legs, Pastor.'

'But we got there, didn't we, Benno? And if we did that, we can make it the whole way, can't we, Mother?'

'We can.'

One of the blacks got up, went over to his horse, opened a saddle-bag and produced a freshly-plucked chicken. He brought it over, and Mother told him I was the cook, so he gave it to me and said, 'Killed this afternoon.'

Great. Wet, warm and clammy in my hands. Damper and salted meat seemed so much easier, but Ludwig said he'd help me, tied off the horses and came over. The same man produced potatoes, carrots, a small bag of apples, and said, 'Bob's coming over later.'

'He is, is he?' Father said, smiling.

'And Alf maybe.'

'He alright?'

'Yeah, alright.' Just laughing. At who knows what.

I found the pot – dropped in the chicken, a pint of water, stock – and started chopping the potatoes and carrots. Ignatz said, 'If we got to Henbury we could eat there.'

But everyone ignored him.

The second man went over to his horse, unhitched some sort of box wrapped in a rug, brought it back and said, 'Alf reckons you'd like this.' He produced a small phonograph, laid it on the sand and said, 'Bach!'

Father's face lit up. '*Bach*? He reckoned I'd like a bit of Bach?'

'*Bach.*' Taking a disc out of an oven mitt, placing it on the phonograph and saying, 'Strange sort of music?'

'It is. The strangest anywhere. But in Leipzig . . .' He stopped, because he knew they'd have no idea about Leipzig, St Thomas's, or Bach.

This small, bony black man cranked the handle (as, no doubt, Alf had shown him) and a *Well-Tempered* fugue started playing – clunkety keys, the hiss of sandpapered shellac, but Bach, nonetheless. Rising through the box gums, spreading along the plains as everyone stopped to listen. Father closed his eyes and said, 'Perfect.' Two songlines that could exist alone, but together made something more perfect. In and out, up and down, never repeating the same idea twice. 'How did he do it?' Father asked. There was a scratch, the same phrase repeated, so Father knocked the box and it continued. Fugue, prelude, fugue, as we kept chopping, adding vegetables to the pot, as Father hummed along, and the blacks sat grinning, cranking the handle to keep Bach singing beside the Finke.

Well, that's how I remember it. This little Gewandhaus moment in the outback. Although it was a long time ago. I remember finishing the stew, hanging it on the tripod above the flames. Then I wandered into the bush, fifty, a hundred yards, music of perpetual motion stripped back to basics, broadcast through the reeds. I sat and thought, perhaps, *things would get better now*. Maybe we were through the worst of it and maybe, one day, we'd be thanking Ignatz for the discipline. Father would be fixed, and we'd be back at Hermannsburg. That's how I saw it – for a while, anyway. The idea of hope. Me, sitting in my back yard wondering if Jack would ever return.

A quarter acre block, 1988 (as I might've already told you), mostly grass I'd given up mowing years before. There was a concrete slab and, on this, a table and chair I'd bought when I moved in with Kate. I was reading, sipping Earl Grey, something playing on the stereo, wafting out of the window. Maybe it was Bach; maybe the same piece. The Finke as Hillcrest, and Hillcrest as Finke. My old jocks and singlets hanging on the line, the dog barking next door, planes flying overhead (I'm under the flight path) and a voice, 'You there?'

I looked up. 'Shit. Jack!'

This must've been a few weeks after our first meeting, and I guess I'd decided I'd never see my son again. But there he was, looking over the gate between the drive and back yard. 'You busy?'

'No, of course not.'

I went over, opened the gate, shook his hand. 'Good to see you . . . I was thinking maybe . . . it's good to see you.'

He smiled. 'What, you thought you'd never see me again?'

'No . . . perhaps. Come on.'

I took him over to my little oasis, apologised on behalf of the Ford factory, the angle grinder guy, the planes and cat shit all over the place from Mrs Wright's cats. Jack placed a shopping bag on the table and said, 'These are from Steph.'

'Steph?'

'She said we had millions, and had to get rid of them.'

I opened the bag. Peaches. Soft, red and scented. 'Thanks. They're expensive.'

'I know. No point throwing them away. Steph said take them to your dad.'

'You told her about me?'

'Of course. And I told Tom.'

'And what did he say?'

'He wants to meet you. He's very curious. Would you like to meet him?'

Can you imagine the moment? After so many years. After so long imagining what they thought about me, how much they resented me, there was my son with a bag full of peaches from his wife, talking about my grandson and how he was interested in meeting this miserable old man who'd shat all over his father in 1955. Imagine! That was one of those turning points, like that day I was sitting in the bush listening to Bach, and I heard Father walking towards me.

But now I smelled the peach, bit into it, tasted the syrup and felt happy as the juice rolled down my chin. I wiped it and said, 'They're good.'

'They should be. Watered every day. Fed. Pruned. There's no mucking about at our place. And we've got plenty of others. Pears. You like apricots? I can bring you those, too.'

See, like this, like he'd been looking for some reason to come back and see me. Hope! That things could and would get better. Soon. After so long sitting in the dark and assuming the worst and hearing my son telling me he hated me and wished I'd died years ago.

'You can bring him over anytime,' I said.

'When are you free?'

I almost laughed. When was I free? 'I'm free anytime, Jack.'

'He plays soccer. Would you like to see one of his games?'

'Yes. Please.'

'He has a semi-final on Saturday.'

'Fine. Would I . . . would I meet you there?'

'No. I'll come and get you. What, about ten? They kick off at eleven.'

I can remember fifty years ago, but I can't remember that day, a few weeks ago. I was knocked over, and probably a bit teary (although a Lutheran upbringing knocks that out of you). My son telling me my mistakes could be made good with a soccer game, a bag of peaches. 'It's not much of a yard,' I said.

'You kidding? A block this size? Anyway, just needs a bit of work.'

'A bit! I haven't done any gardening for years. The old girl next door complained to the council. Said I had snakes and one had bitten her cat and it'd died. But I haven't got snakes. If I did, with my luck, one woulda bitten me.'

'Your luck?'

'No snakes!' I called, loudly.

'I can see you've had your own fruit trees?' Indicating the skeletons of a few apricot trees me and Kate used to water, but gave up on. 'This was Kate's place?'

'When I moved in . . . but she died six years ago. So it serves me right, doesn't it, Jack?'

'Why?'

I didn't reply. It seemed too obvious. 'I think about it, but I don't know why I did it. Still . . . soccer, eh? Is he any good?'

Jack sat up, thought about it for a moment and said, 'I think he *thinks* he's okay but . . . his ball control needs work.'

'That can be fixed.'

'Exactly! Like this place.'

'I don't know.'

'You gotta have faith, Dad.'

Just staring at this boy, who seemed to have more knowledge, more wisdom than his father. As my father sat down beside me and said, 'You can hear Bach from here?'

'Just.'

'Why are you sitting by yourself?'

I didn't reply.

'You know,' he said, 'there's no reason to worry. There are lots of good people, and they'll help me, help us, and things will come good.'

I don't know what I said then.

'So you shouldn't . . .' He took my knee, squeezed it.

I asked him if his feet, his legs hurt.

'Of course. But God's here with me and he'll . . .' He thought for a moment then decided. 'There's a lot you don't know at fourteen.' Dropping his head, thinking about it, saying, 'Hungry?'

He stood, and waited, and I helped him back to camp.

The Mollys

The dusk a chattering of starlings lifting, dropping and twisting above the water, a couple of cormorants, a lost pelican. The cries and songs competing with Bach, still. A breeze picking up resin and gum, algae and black mud before drifting up to our camp. Me serving everyone chicken stew, saying, 'There's plenty more.'

Alf sitting on a camp chair, a bottle of ale, wiping his mouth and saying to Father, 'But that wasn't the worst of it, was it, Martin?'

'That's why it only lasted two years,' Father said.

'Was it that long?' Laughing again, shaking his head and saying to his daughter, Elsie, 'I told you about it, eh?'

She just smiled at him. She never said much. The story (as Father told me) was that Alf had met Molly E. at Henbury (she was working in the kitchen), there'd been some sort of romance, she'd fallen pregnant and moved to the mission. Elsie was educated by Father and Ignatz (sewing and cooking courtesy of Mother) before returning to Henbury with Molly to work in the kitchen. Like that. On and off. She just said, 'I didn't know if you'd made it up.'

'Me?' Alf said. 'Have I ever made anything up? Eh, Martin? Alma?'

'Never,' Father replied.

I finished serving the stew – the mushy, pond-bottom vegetables, chicken torn from the bone, split peas and stale damper to thicken it.

'I won't hear it said!' Father called, as loud as his lungs allowed, as the cormorants screeched, dragged their feet across the water and flew away.

'No one's said a thing,' Bob Buck replied.

Alf and Bob were a pigeon pair. Whereas Alf had married (Father's favour, after hours) Molly E., Bob had married Molly T. (at the same ceremony). Whereas Alf had produced Elsie, Bob had produced Ettie, a year earlier. Elsie now fourteen (sitting, smiling at me) and Ettie fifteen. Of course, I knew them well. These two girls, half-in, half-out, black and white, cattlemen fathers and domestic mothers, sitting behind me in class for years as Ignatz went on about Homer and long division; hanging around outside my window (giggling) as I tried to get to sleep, saying, 'Bet she's got you tucked in nice, eh, Benno?' A continuo, a female accompaniment to my singular, stupid childhood. Ettie looked over the fire at me and said, 'I never knew you could cook, Benno.'

'It's easy.'

'Needs salt.' Elsie.

Father said, 'No, when I look back, Alf.'

'And you should remember, Pastor. It should all be written down.'

'Exactly what I told him,' Silas said, flicking chicken from his suit.

Father grimaced, sat back, took a few breaths and said, 'Just a succession of . . .'

Silence. Spoons in bowls, slurping, Ludwig saying it was the best thing I'd made yet.

'Though it was pretty tough how I got that part,' Alf said.

'You asked!' Father said.

'Did I?'

'You did, you said someone's gotta do it.'

I wasn't there, of course. Neither Elsie nor Ettie, but we'd heard the story plenty of times. Alf approaching Father (at the head of a crowd of blacks carrying clubs), touching his shoulder, kissing him, and greeting him as Rabbi, before the others rushed forward to grab him, and Father called, 'This is not how we rehearsed it.'

'I never knew why you wanted to do it,' Bob said, turning to Ettie and saying, 'I told you, eh? The Passion that time.'

She said, 'I heard,' but glanced at me, then back into the fire.

'It's when I thought I could do some good,' Father said. 'Before ... there are lots of things left undone, Bob.'

'Plenty done.'

'When I look back ...'

Mother said, 'Nonsense. The church, the vegetable gardens ... that was you and me, Martin, bending over day and night, planting and weeding and watering, picking off the grubs, so they'd know how it was done.'

Father didn't reply.

'And the first year, remember, when the donkeys got in and ate the lot?'

Bob reminded Father of his St Peter, the two denials: 'I do not know the man!'

'But you got that wrong,' Alf said, followed by a short argument, then Bob said, 'What was it? Before the cock crows?'

'You will deny me three times,' Father said.

'That's it.'

'Two years. Then the spirit deserted us, didn't it, Alf? Bob?'

'You shouldn't say that,' Mother continued. 'We were living off a few pounds from six, seven parishioners.'

'That's right,' Silas said.

'I remember you, Martin, walking up to your first bullock, that old rifle of your father's, remember? You placed the muzzle to its head and said, What now, Alma?' This time she started laughing.

'First thing I killed,' Father said.

'But you did it, you pulled the trigger.'

Elsie was prettier. She had Alf's straight nose, his flat face, and Molly E.'s mouth and forehead. She used to (every day, as we waited for Ignatz) put her hair up in a bun, and she looked smart and sexy. Around twelve, perhaps, I started thinking about her more. What was under her corset, the dress Mother had taught her and the other girls to make, her slip, her bra – I just sat listening to my Father, studying the way her shoulders lifted and dropped, her long neck with its single freckle, the little wisps of hair that had escaped the bun. And then, at lunch, I'd come over and say, 'There's no one in the church this time.'

'What are you saying?'

'If you want to go somewhere and talk?'

Ettie was fatter in the face, and always complained. I think she'd worked out that I preferred Elsie. That I only ever tolerated her as a means to an end, or a beginning. So when Elsie and I got to the church I said, 'Sorry about my dad.'

'What?'

'Going on like that. And his jokes. He thinks he's funny – I got to listen to that all day.'

Sitting across from each other, eventually holding hands, although that's as far as it went. In the end, Ettie stopped being friends with Elsie, and two gangs formed – the Elsies and the Etties. They were always bitching about each other, pushing and shoving, until one day Ettie punched some girl in the face and she lost her front teeth and her parents took her to live in Alice. But Ettie and Elsie were close again now. Working in the kitchen at Henbury, making thirty meals a day, taking a cart out to the muster camps.

The next ten minutes was a summary of the journey so far. As I returned with my pot for a second round, spooned out the dregs, Father said, 'We're making good progress.'

Ignatz agreed.

'And this arrangement with the chair' – indicating – 'seems to be working, eh, Benno?'

Cranking the Bach, topping up drinks, then Bob said, 'That was the easy bit.'

Alf agreed. The Finke was predictable, navigable between Hermannsburg and Henbury, but things were about to change. He surveyed the horses and said, 'They're tired.'

'They'll make it,' Ludwig said.

'I don't reckon. Not through the Britannia sandhills.'

Bob said, 'You might make it some of the way, but those last miles along the Finke from Hell's Gate to Idracowra . . .'

The birds had settled. Just a few twigs falling into the waterhole, making concentric circles. *Let the night parrots cover the edge of the pool with their footprints!* Although I couldn't see any. Maybe they were still hiding, waiting, unwilling to reveal themselves. The previous day, Father had said to me, 'Are there really any night parrots, Benno? Or are they just made up?'

'You said . . .'

'*I believe*. Either way, they serve a purpose. If we think such a thing exists. People need to feel secure, Benno.'

'How?'

'The parrot. I'm not saying anyone's time's been wasted. I mean, we came here in good faith. We've worked hard, haven't we? *We've done good*. And that's something.'

I didn't understand.

'So when it comes to be written about, and if someone says we did more harm than good . . .'

'Who's saying that?'

'*If*. Then . . . we can feel we've achieved something, eh?' The serving of meals, the washing of feet (and sheets and clothes and socks and underwear), the slaughtering of cattle and the growing of onions; the teaching of Latin, and the love of David Copperfield; a shed full of Singers and a dozen black girls sewing neat seams; the pottery workshop; how Father showed Isaiah how to paint in watercolour, and how Micah followed, years later. All of it. Worthwhile. In the name of God (minus the various betrayals).

Bob Buck said, 'I wouldn't want to risk it, Pastor. Stuck out there, and they're trying to pull you through the sand.'

'They're pretty tired,' Jamy said.

'See,' Alf said. 'Needn't be any big deal, Martin.'

'This is what we do,' Bob said. 'We've got a yard full of fresh donks. You can take some of those.'

'Donkeys?' Father asked.

'Dozens of them, eating our food, drinking our water. Get them to work, I reckon, eh, Alf?'

'Good idea.'

'Donks are better in sand,' Bob explained. 'And we can give you four for the cart, four the dray, and spares. You alright with that, Jamy?'

Busy beside the fire playing solitaire. 'I reckon.'

'I can't ask you to do that,' Father said.

'Why? They're donks. Pests. You can leave your horses here and get them on the way back.'

Mother said, 'That sounds like a good idea.'

And Father: 'I dunno, Bob.'

'I'm telling you,' Bob said, 'You won't get through those sandhills with them horses. It's a long drag.'

I collected the plates and started scraping them off. Father said, 'Should've thought that through, I suppose.'

'It's decided,' Bob said. 'Best way. What you've done for us over the years, Martin. Ettie, she can talk all that German cosa you. Go on, Ettie, show us.'

'*Ich wünsche dir eine gute Reise, Pastor*.'

Bob smiled. 'And she can do her maths, speak proper English, the first Buck to write her name. When me and Alf got too much for the Mollys, for the girls, you took them in. You've done that for hundreds of people. Seems to me, none of us can repay what you've done. So I reckon that's decided. We'll be down in the morning. You wanna get started early?'

'Six, if possible,' Ignatz said.

I walked down to the water with the plates. Then I squatted and cleaned them with sand, rinsed them, laid them on a cloth to dry. When I looked up Elsie was standing behind me, arms crossed. 'Wanna hand?'

'I'm done.'

Just waiting, with Ettie perhaps ten or fifteen yards further off, watching us. Elsie said, 'Bad not seeing you round anymore.'

'Why'd you leave?' Although I knew. And it had already been a year, or longer.

'Dad said I'd learned enough. Had to get working.'

'You like cooking?'

'That woman, Ted's wife, she says wash them clothes, them sheets, dry them, fold them, and I say to Ettie, don't I, Ettie, what we gotta do all this for?'

I wasn't sure what she wanted me to say or do. 'Maybe you could go to Alice and get a job? Or Adelaide. You want to study?'

She didn't reply.

'You should get out of here.'

She sat beside me, lifted her dress a few inches above her knees and said, 'Better at the mission.'

'Yeah.' I sat beside her. Ettie kept watching.

'Liked it when we got to . . . you miss me?'

I wasn't sure. What was left of what had begun? 'Maybe you can ask to come back, and help Adele and Pauline?'

'Six in the morning shelling peas, and if any of the women say, We gotta teach yer proper, Elsie, the old cow says none of that anymore. But your dad didn't mind, did he?'

She was pretty in the moonlight. She still had a child's face, and I wanted to run my finger across her cheeks, her lips. I wanted to feel how smooth she was, how warm, and I wanted (tried) to smell how nice she was. She had bigger things up front now, and I thought, if the adults weren't around, and Ettie, forever watching . . . the bit of me that had its own brain started deciding, and then she reached out and covered my hand, and it moved some more, and she saw and said, 'You thinking about me?'

'No.'

I was thinking about Oskar's brother's pictures. The world stripped bare – shoulders and chest and breasts. 'I could come back.'

'You could.'

Then she giggled and pointed and said, 'It's gone all funny,' and I gathered my knees and told myself to stop thinking about it, stop it, stop it, but her shoulders, and her calves, her sepia belly and the hair at the bottom – pulling my legs closer, Elsie laughing, Ettie jumping around because she knew what was happening. So to stop it I said, 'I'm fourteen now.'

'Me too.'

'So things are different.'

'How?'

I stopped and thought, not because of that, but because whatever used to be okay wasn't anymore. The way we were kids, but had entered a world with different rules. Where the blacks were sent off to play while I was taught calculus; where they were taken to learn about the Dreamtime, and I was given Dickens; where they got to wander with their old people, but I had to stay with Ignatz and Mother.

'Seems a pity,' I said. 'If you just stayed at Henbury. You were a good drawer, weren't you?'

She shrugged. But she was. 'She makes us sew all day, and I just wanna go outside for a walk, think about you, Benno.'

Ettie had settled, but still watched, arms crossed. Father and Bob and Alf were laughing again. Mother called for me to hurry up and I called back, 'Nearly done.' I gathered the plates and said, 'Maybe when we get back to Hermannsburg you can come and . . .'

Although what was the point? She'd never go to university. She'd never marry Benjamin Gerlach. She'd never leave Henbury, the Finke, the desert.

I walked back, Elsie ten steps behind me, Ettie ten steps behind her. Alf said, 'What you two been up to?' And howled with laughter. Mother slapped his arm and said, 'There are other things in life, Alf.'

'Such as?'

The Eighth Station

Around seven, Bob sent one of the blacks to Henbury for his hessian sack. Tied up, left in a laundry trough, waiting. Twenty minutes later the boy returned with Bob's stash, laid it on the ground and said, 'Plenty of grog?'

'Plenty,' Bob said, producing a dozen bottles of home brew. Him, Alf, Father, and even Mother. He offered me one, but Mother decided on my behalf. 'He's only fourteen.'

'That's old enough. I'd been drinking for years at his age.'

Father was consulted (he could still overrule Mother) but said no, 'Bad habits start early' (or words to that effect).

So they sat sculling (Bob and Alf), sipping (Mother and Father), as a group of blacks gathered further up the hill, a few coming down to greet ingkata, shake his hand, thank him for what he'd done for their kids, for the pox problem (Silas's sermons, but more on that later), for the canvases, the expeditions to the creek to gather clay for the pottery classes. Father thanked them and said he'd be back past Henbury soon. I noticed Molly T. and Molly E. in the group, calling for Ettie and Elsie to come home. But they wouldn't. Bob and Alf were getting drunk.

After a while, talk turned to confirmations, and Bob said, 'Remember that day, Martin?'

Only a few months before, Bob, Alf, the Mollys and Elsie and Ettie arriving in a cart, Mother dressing the girls in skirts they'd sewn, me in a pair of pants and a jacket she'd made, the other boys in white shirts with the top button done up. All of us, presented to God for His approval.

'Like this, wasn't it?' Bob said, and he stood me up, the girls, called for some of the boys to come down, arranged us tallest to shortest. 'Lord, look at this sorry lot!' Walking up and down the line and making the sign of the cross on everyone's forehead.

'Bob!' Mother said.

Molly T. repeated this, telling him to stop drinking. But he didn't care, up and down the line saying, 'I, Pastor Gerlach, confirm you in the Lutheran Church . . . is that right, Martin?'

'No.'

'I present your souls to God and hope he approves of what we've done to make you good Christians.' Dropping to his knees. 'What was next, Martin?'

'The prayer.'

'How did it go?'

'We didn't stand like this,' I said. 'We were at the front, and we knelt.'

Bob managed to stand, finish his drink, throw his bottle into the scrub and call for another. 'Martin, you finished?'

'He shouldn't be drinking,' Mother said.

Ettie fetched two more, Bob opened his and drank, Alf called for another, and it went on like this. Ignatz tried one, but said it was awful; Jamy, Ludwig, and even I snuck in a few mouthfuls when Mother wasn't watching. But Bob wasn't finished with the confirmation: 'I place the threefold sign of the cross upon thee, the holy paraclete—'

Alf said, 'Parakeet,' and walked up and down the line blessing us. 'I reckon you lot are well and truly confirmed, so you can piss off now.'

We did as we were told. I sat near the fire, Elsie sat beside me, and beside her, Ettie. Alf said, 'They got a pill for everything these days, Martin. They'll put you in hospital and a coupla days later . . .'

'Yes,' Father said, looking at me. 'A pill for everything.'

'Then we can get you back,' Bob said, 'and you know what I reckon? We need to start things over again. Me, you, all of us, get the Passion up and running again.'

Mother laughed. She said the beer was awful and poured it into the sand, but Bob lurched forward, saved it and returned to his spot near the fire. 'I'm serious, Martin. We need to get it going again. Silas, remember when you were Jesus that time?' He stood, grabbed Silas under his arms, lifted him and said, 'You were going down the road with your cross' – and he led him across the camp – 'and you came across this group of women and stopped to talk to them, remember?'

Bob led Silas towards the women. Silas didn't resist, but I could tell he wasn't happy.

'And you said to them?'

'I said – don't cry for me. I'm going to meet my father.'

'That's it!' Bob said. 'You were a good Jesus, Silas. See, Martin, why the hell did we stop? It was fun, them few days putting it on. We should try again, when you get back, when you're better . . . soon, eh, Martin?'

I guess Bob only wanted Father to return to the people he'd taught, protected from the bureaucrats, fed and housed and shown another safer, warmer, more secure (when we saw it like that) way to live.

'Quick!' Jamy said, running over to the cart, finding the rifle, returning to the camp, grabbing my arm and saying, 'Come on, Benno.'

'What is it?' Bob asked.

'Rabbit.' Running away, coming back, pulling me along.

As we headed over a few dunes, as the singing and laughing faded, Jamy said to me, 'Enough of that, eh, Benno?' Smiling, and I smiled back and said, 'What, you've had enough?'

'I reckon.'

'Did you see a rabbit?'

He grinned. 'Gotta be one around here somewhere.'

We walked, searching, and he said, 'What do you reckon about that mob?'

'They're okay.'

Screwing up his nose. 'You reckon?'

It wasn't that Jamy was quiet, inward, strange. He just needed time to get to know someone, work them out, how to talk to them, understand, be understood. He didn't like noise. He didn't like movement. He just liked sitting around the fire with his cards, listening. That's what I remember most about Jamy. Me and him, a hand of twenty-one, him saying, 'What d'yer reckon about them girls, Benno?'

'They're okay.'

'Bit loud, eh?'

Like this. Like I was the only one who might understand him.

'They rabbit on a bit, don't they, Benno?'

'They do, Jamy.'

'And they don't make any sense, do they?'

'No, they don't.'

'You should keep away from them, I reckon.'

'I reckon.'

You just agreed with him. Tried to remember, or maybe forget, the person he used to be. Running around with me and Oskar and Lucas, poking the bulls to get them angry, running off to find the next thing to get us in trouble. But that wasn't him anymore. Now, he said, 'Bob and Alf are idiots, aren't they, Benno?'

'How can they be idiots? They're just having a drink.'

He didn't like it when I didn't agree. 'You oughtn't be scared though, Benno.'

'About what?'

'You know . . . look!'

A small euro stood watching us. Jamy said, 'That'll do,' and lifted the rifle.

'Why are you doing that?' I said.

'It's good eating.'

'We can get fresh meat from Henbury.'

He stared at me, like there was something he couldn't understand, no matter how hard he tried to think it through. Eventually he lowered the rifle and said, 'We should go back, I reckon.'

The drinking continued. An hour later, Elsie went down to the water, went in, ankle deep. I checked no one was watching and followed, took off my shoes, joined her and said, 'You should see if you can come with us.'

'To town?'

'Perhaps.' Going in deeper, letting my feet sink into the sand, pulling them out and laughing at the suck, repeating, until we were up to our ankles. She said, 'Where will you go?'

'Immanuel College. Then university, and study what Father does ... languages.'

'I should do that!' Glowing, pointing to herself.

'You should.'

'But they'd never let me into university. And anyway, that school'd charge money, wouldn't it?'

'I reckon.'

Now she was in deeper, and had to push harder with her feet, her legs. 'Plenty of girls in town, I reckon.'

'Just cos there's girls doesn't mean ... I'll get married when I'm thirty. But I got a lot of other stuff I want to do first. You should come to town. The Lutherans have scholarships at their schools and if Father says you're good they'll definitely let you in. They want black kids to teach other kids, Aranda, you could do that. Better than living here cooking for the ...'

She was up past her knees, and I moved in and stood opposite her.

'You gotta try and imagine, Elsie. Something different. It's good to learn. To know stuff.'

'Dad wouldn't want me going.'

'We could talk him around.'

She lifted her head, caught my eyes and said, 'Anyway, there's Danny.'

'Sorry?'

'Danny. He's only little, but he reckons ... his dad's Pete, the guy who comes to do the yards.'

I didn't know what she was talking about. Danny? Pete? I'd never heard of them. 'What, they've just come?'

'Danny reckons that me and him ...'

'What?'

'He took me out and we slept in the gorge, up that way, with all the birds. And we were there all night and ...' Smiling. 'And then he ...'

'Danny?'

'He reckons if I went with him we could get together and . . . he did what we did, Benno.'

I knew what she meant. One night, a few months before she left, out in the middle of nowhere. A few minutes I'd gone over in my head a thousand times. What she could make me do, and what I could do to her. 'So there's someone called Danny, and he likes you, and you and him . . .?'

She wasn't so sure now. 'Daniel, I reckon he's called.'

'*Really*?'

I could see what was happening. 'And you like him?'

'He didn't muck around like you did.'

'You shouldn't just stay and . . . with *Danny*.' I had an idea, reached into my pocket, produced Opa's cross and said, 'You can take this.'

'Why?'

'Hold onto it for me. And when you come to town, give it back to me.'

She didn't get it. 'I'm gonna marry Danny, I reckon.'

I put the cross back in my pocket and said, 'If that's what you want.'

I couldn't sleep that night. Too much on my mind. Then, sometime around two, I heard hooves and saw horses, fifty, a hundred, who knows, coming down to the water to drink. Lingering, as I laid on my tummy, content, admiring them. I watched Father straightening his legs, shifting his arse, trying his side but unable to get over. And Mother, dead to the world, snoring.

Then I heard Jamy say, 'Thirsty bastards, eh, Benno?'

Friday 13 October (Day 4)

I was woken by the sun on my face, or maybe Bob, sitting beside the fire cooking bacon and eggs, muttering something to Father (propped up on a tea chest). I spat dirt from my mouth, moved my head into the shade, smelt the earth, as Alf (on the other side of the fire) said, 'With something this common.'

'I knew when it started,' Father said.

'How long ago?'

'What was it, Alma, six weeks?'

Mother said, 'Something like that.'

I could just lay here, I could pretend, forever. I could refuse to admit there was a problem or that it had anything to do with me.

'Just gotta stay positive,' Alf said.

'We're nearly there,' Jamy said, and Ludwig agreed.

'Day four of what . . . eight?' Father said.

I heard Ludwig getting up, going over to the horses and calling to Alf: 'You reckon, if I take them up . . .?'

'Ted's up there. He'll help you.'

So Ludwig led them up the hill, calling as he went, 'I'll meet you up there, ten, fifteen minutes?'

Bob finished cooking and said, 'Who's hungry?'

I was starving. I felt I should've sat up, got my bit of bacon and egg and eaten it. But something made me lie there, eyes closed, listening.

Father took his plate, tasted the bacon (I could hear): 'I'm a bit worried.'

'Martin, not now,' Mother said.

'They won't send anyone else.'

'Why would they, if you're gonna get better?' Alf said.

'The place'll be chaos. Probably is now. I can just imagine.'

'No point worrying about what you can't control,' Bob said, serving more bacon, more eggs. God I was hungry! But I wanted to hear what came next.

'If it is, it is,' Mother said. 'When we get back . . .'

Father said, 'All I'm saying is *if*, Alma.'

A full minute while they ate. I could hear them washing it down with tea. I could smell Jamy cooking bread on the fire. My ear against the ground, the sound of the Earth rotating on its axis, grinding, as it had for billions of years; the bird still going who, who, and Jamy's cards as he put them down and said, 'I reckon I'm missing a Jack.'

'If it comes to that,' Father said, 'what about Benno? He's only fourteen. We should've gone back sooner.'

'How?'

'Made a way. Demanded. We should've. I think about it, Alma.'

'Well, don't.'

I wasn't sure whether it was better knowing or not knowing. When Father got better it'd just be a case of writing to the other kids, maybe not even mentioning it. But if he didn't . . . I imagined Opa gathering them and saying, 'We've had some bad news from Australia.'

Father said, 'Maybe we should've left him at Hermannsburg.'

'Just eat your food, Martin.'

'I'm allowed to say it, aren't I? We have to be practical, Alma. Look at our situation. A hundred and ninety back at the mission and Adelaide telling me to make do. I can't let those people down.'

'Enough!' Mother, in her pre-crying phase. 'You have to *attempt* to remain positive, Martin.' I heard her get up, walk into the bush, and I heard Bob saying, 'I reckon she's a bit raw, Martin.'

And Father agreeing. Mother calling, 'I'm fine.'

It was too hot. My face too sore against the ground. So I stirred, opened my eyes and said, 'What's the time?' I sat up, surveyed the scraps of bacon, the bits of egg. Bob said I was a lazy little bastard, but he guessed I needed my beauty sleep. Alf said, 'Leave the kid alone. He's only fourteen, isn't he, Martin?'

I said, 'I'm dying for a pee.' Jumped up, headed into the scrub. As I pissed I saw Mother further up the hill, adjusting her dress, but then sitting there thinking. I finished, and waited.

'But if so,' Bob's voice trailed up the hill, 'what can you do from six feet under, Pastor?'

Father said, 'Guess how many they've got in the seminary, Bob.'

A short pause.

'Three. So who's going to Hermannsburg?'

'What'll you care?' Alf said. 'You gotta think about getting to town. Just relax, have a bitta faith, Pastor.'

Mother was crying. Familiar. After an argument with Father, or Adele – in fact, it didn't take much to set her off. Although she mostly went to her room, or the toilet, to sook in secret. The sewing shed – that was her favourite crying place. But now she wiped her face, walked down the hill and saw me and said, 'You're awake?'

'You alright?'

'Fine.' In case I'd seen anything.

I followed her down the hill. 'How's Dad today?'

'Father? He's fine.'

'Are you worried?'

'No, of course not.' Stopping, looking back at me. 'Why would I be?'

When we got back, Silas was standing beside the fire, his arms raised. Mother sat in her spot, picked up her plate, sorted through the remains. Bob asked if she was okay and she said of course, why wouldn't I be? She said to Father, 'Benno wants to know how you're feeling, Martin?'

Another one of her ploys. Rub my nose in it. Father looked at me like, why, what's going on, and I realised he knew I'd heard, and he said, 'It's quite simple. I'm here, the Lord's here, we're all here, and we're having some breakfast, aren't we, Alf?'

'We are.'

'So help yourself, Benno.'

Mother glared at Father. Like she was angry with him – not for being sick, but for making the sickness difficult, involved, full of pointless detail. She could even be angry with him at a time like this.

'What's wrong?' Father said to me.

'Nothing.' I salvaged the last of the food from the pan, sat back and started eating.

'He's worried,' Mother said.

'I'm not! When did I say that?'

'You are. He is, Martin.'

'Well, he needn't be. All's good, Benno. I'm feeling better this morning.'

Silas was still waiting, his arms outstretched. Mother asked what he was doing.

'I was just telling Bob and Alf about that morning in the tree.'

'Christ! Martin, do we need to hear this again?'

'Go on,' Alf said to him, warming his hands on his tea mug.

Silas said, 'When I looked down I saw a woman in white, a boy by her side. And a big cross, with a lamb standing in front of it.'

Mother said, 'We better clean up. They'll be down with the animals soon.'

'So I climbed down from my tree, ran over to this lot (they were standing on the hill where Isaiah used to paint) and said, Who are you? But she wouldn't say who she was.'

'But she did tell you,' I began, a mouth full of bacon, 'that—'

'Shh, Benno. She said, Listen fella, I got a job for you.'

Mother started gathering dishes, but Father told her to wait. So she sat with the plates in her lap and said, 'Hurry up, Silas.'

'I said what job, and she said, This mob here is full of *venereal disease*. Your job is to preach to them, tell them they shouldn't be sleeping together, shouldn't be having sex.'

'Finished?' Mother said.

'Anyway,' Silas continued, 'I said what's venereal disease? She took her kiddy by the hand, covered his ears and said, It's when . . . you know, we're all grownups here, aren't we, Bob?'

'We are, Silas.'

'And when she finished I promised her, I said, I can do something about that. Then she told me a secret.'

'What's that?' Father asked.

Silas smiled. 'Ah, you won't get me that easy, Pastor. But she told me this secret and said I gotta keep it me whole life, till I die, never tell no one. And I haven't. And I won't.'

'So why bother telling us?' Mother said.

He ignored her. 'That's what she said. She wanted me to stop the clap, and I did, didn't I, Pastor?'

Father agreed, although he knew there was still plenty around. He knew Silas had tried, with graphic illustrations from the same Spanish company that'd made his Bible illustrations. He'd tried – he'd gathered everyone and told them how syphilis could make you blind, eat away your willy, big sores (illustrated), the lot. Then dead. And he had a picture of a corpse, too, although he didn't let the little ones see this.

'Is that it?' Mother said.

'I told them' – he pointed to his eyes. 'I told them this was because of venereal disease.'

'Wasn't it measles?' I asked.

'Yes, but I told the young fellas. You'll end up like me if you go around, you know . . .' And he giggled, and Bob said, 'No, I don't know, tell me, Silas,' and he said, 'If you have sex, yeah?' Thrusting his hips so we'd know.

Mother walked down to the river to wash the greasy plates as Bob and Alf helped Jamy load the tea chests, the swags, the tent onto the dray. Father called, 'Let me help,' but no one paid any attention. I walked him to his chariot, waited while he climbed up, one step at a time. Halfway up he said, 'I think I need to go.' So I helped him back down, into the bush, and waited, listening as he pissed, buttoned up and said, 'That'll do.'

Back to the dray, up, and I helped him settle in his chair, adjust his pillows. I found the towel for his forehead, filled his water and squeezed his Walter Scott between his leg and chair. Then I said, 'You ready, you reckon?'

'My hat.'

So I fetched that, too. Then he pulled me closer and said, 'Did you hear your mother this morning?'

'Yes.'

'That's what she went off to have a cry about, I guess. But you mustn't listen to that sort of stuff.'

'I know.'

'I'm perfectly fine. I'm not about to drop dead. Does it look like I'm about to die?'

'No.'

'She had a bad night. She didn't sleep. She's asking me, the whole time, you alright, Martin? I'm saying, I'm fine, get to sleep. But once she decides . . .'

'I know.'

'It's easier to fix a man than bury him, Benno.'

'Is it?'

'I believe so. But with women . . .' He shook his head. He picked up his Scott and said, 'Each chapter is part of the journey, isn't it?'

'I guess.'

'Therefore, one at a time. You can't read ahead.'

Ignatz, Ludwig, and six of the older boys arrived with the donkeys. Bob and Alf shouted orders, and they were harnessed. Ugly animals. They made a load of noise, jumped about, kicked the air. But ten minutes later they were ready – four on the dray, four on the cart, and two spares. They just stood there, waiting, an occasional whine, and Bob said, 'Don't be afraid to treat them rough. They're stupid, stupid animals.'

The dray was packed, me and Mother and Father, Ludwig driving, Silas in his usual spot. Jamy with the spares, and Ignatz on the cart. Bob said to Father, 'God bless you, Pastor.' Not an in-case-you-die God bless, but something left over from the Sunday roast, some sign of respect and civility. Bob was good at that. Alf said, 'We'll pick up your scent soon,' and Father said, 'Long as these donkeys keep going.'

They waved, and we set off along the Finke. The donkeys tried to stop and eat grass but Ludwig whipped them.

I looked back. 'See you, Bob, see you, Alf.'

But they just waved, watching. The few blacks picking over our old camp, and Elsie, up on the hill, looking at me going.

Goethe

Father stared out at the sparse woodland, scatterings of acacia and grass, a couple of ducks. 'Is it there?' he asked me.

I found his Goethe at the bottom of Oolong No. 29 and handed it to him.

'It's easy country,' Ignatz called.

Father turned to me and said, 'What did he say?'

'It's easy country.'

He shook his head, opened the book and began: '"Well, that's philosophy I've read, law and medicine and I fear,"' he laid it in his lap and recited from memory. '"Theology too from A to Z."'

Martin Gerlach, raging against the blue sky, the high clouds. '"Hard studies all that have cost me dear, and so I sit, poor silly man." You remember, Benno?'

And together: '"No wiser now than when I began."'

This reminded me – a few months before, both of us sitting in the study, Father trying to teach me vowels and diphthongs, the way Aranda words could be broken up and reassembled, before he set this aside, produced his half-morocco *Faust* and said, 'It's time for Goethe.'

Apparently, the time arrived for every German to read Goethe. A pilgrimage to the great man's Frankfurt house (Father had told me about his visits); to quote him at school, in mixed company; to scribble bad poetry and wander Europe in search of melancholy. And how better than memorising Faust's soliloquy? So we sat there, on maybe ten consecutive nights, seeing who could remember most. Father winning, of course, three pages in while I was marooned at "They call me Professor and Doctor forsooth . . ." And now all of it was coming back to him, floating across the plains, the donkeys singing Young Werther, the biting insects, Ludwig's whip, as Mother said, 'We've heard it before, Martin,' and Silas said, 'I wouldn't want to be reading about the devil,' and the dray rolled on, crushing rocks, sodium springs bubbling into the bleached light.

'"The last ten years now, I suppose . . ."'

It seemed familiar. Father standing at the front of the church – full robes and collar; Bible open in his hands; the same Faustian look, out of the glassless window at the back of the church. 'It is, of course, one of the commandments.'

This, in the early days, with my siblings. Perhaps I was two years old? But I remember, I swear. Sitting in shorts and pressed shirt and tie, swinging my sweaty legs on the hard pew, until Father glared at me. 'We need to get the simple things under control.'

The memory goes like this: a boy called Erwin, six or seven years old, standing at the front of the church holding a piece of bread covered with butter and jam – like a host, like he was offering it to someone. Father said, 'Should I continue?'

Silas (sitting behind us kids) told him he should.

'This is not about a piece of bread and jam. It's about a covenant between us and God, and the simple things he asks of us.'

Erwin was shaking, his legs trembling, his hands almost dropping the bread. Father said, 'I've talked with Erwin, he knows he's done wrong and he's promised not to do it again. The worst thing' – to the whole church now, because in those days it was full – 'is how he snuck into our kitchen at two in the morning so he wouldn't be heard, searched for the bread, sliced it, spooned on the jam. Is all of this correct, Erwin?'

He didn't answer.

'And how he wasn't thinking of others, just himself. Selfishly.'

I have a memory of this boy pissing himself. Maybe he did, maybe he didn't. But I can see this stream running down his leg, gathering in a pool at his bare feet, so he was standing in a little lake of piss, of shame. Father prayed for him, said he would learn, come to understand the things God asked. All of this in English, German, Aranda, just to make sure.

I'm more certain *this* happened. Father nodded to Ignatz, he came forward, pulled down Erwin's pants, leaned the boy forward, just so, just the right angle, before he started hitting his arse with his cane. I remember it clearly. The boy held onto the bread because he thought, I guess, if he didn't the punishment would be worse. The cane sliced air, and flesh; the look of determination on Ignatz's face; Father staring out of the window. And us kids, holding hands, terrified this was Father, the father of God and Love. Erwin dropped the bread and it fell, jam down, he knelt, the blacks' voices got louder and his mother came forward, pulled up his pants, led him out of the church. As we (especially Charlotte) sat horrified, Mother at the end of the row like nothing had happened, like these people had to be taught you couldn't just take other people's bread and jam, despite everything we'd taken from them.

There was a picture of Luther hanging at the front of our classroom. Miserable-looking cunt. Like Ignatz, Father, the Board, the Church were trying to convince us he was good for us. He was fruit, he was Psalms; he was government, he was Christ; he was doctor, and he was prime minister. But I never saw it that way. Looking up at him, all those years, I just imagined him making a list of the people who'd crossed him, whom he meant to punish, all in the name of a religion so wildly successful it'd made its way around the globe, as far as Hermannsburg, where we little Luthers got to continue his work.

Father ran out of memory. '"Robbed of all energy and zest . . ." What was after that, Benno?'

'I can't remember.'

'I thought I knew more but . . .' Staring down at the boards.

A scattering of casuarinas gave way to fallen rocks, and behind these, cliffs. There were paths up, and caves, and Ludwig said people used to live in them. Mother said, 'That was a lot of bother, I bet.'

And Father, 'What?'

'Getting all the way up there. What if you needed water?'

We approached the river, slowed, and stopped, and the donkeys found grass, sniffed the water, moved forward so they could drink. Ludwig said, 'It looks like there's no way round.'

'Should we get started?' I asked.

Someone had left a raft, of sorts. Eight kerosene drums supporting an old bed frame piled with salvaged floorboards, tyres, galvanised iron, all lashed with ropes to make a sort of ferry. I said, 'Will it get us across?'

'It's fine,' Ludwig said, getting down, stepping into the shallows and testing the ropes. 'Someone's done a good job.'

So that was the next hour. Unloading chests, pots and pans, the few cases and the food, all of it, onto the raft and across the Finke using a rope strung between two river reds. Unloading on the other side, going back for more. It was almost fun. By the second crossing I was soaked, so I took off my clothes and worked in my underwear. Wet hair and face, but cool! Looking up at Father and saying, 'You should come in.'

Just shaking his head, reading Goethe. We unlashed his throne, secured it to the raft and carefully settled him. Across, slowly, as the water came up over the edges, wet his shoes, his socks, his ankles, and he said, 'You're right, Benno.'

When the cart and dray were ready Ludwig and Jamy whipped the donkeys and, despite protesting, they entered the water, half-swimming, half-touching the bottom. I sat on the dray, legs dangling in the water, telling them to hurry.

Continuing into mid-morning, the donks settling into a rhythm of high ground, low ground, pull, wander, drift, as Father continued searching Goethe for clues: 'The question being *why*?'

'What?' Mother asked.

'Why was he willing?'

'What's it matter?'

And remembering: '"All that I now possess seems far away."'

I don't know what he was thinking. Maybe this would be a better story if Father had said more, made things clearer, explained his regrets, told me how much he loved me. But he didn't. All I divined were signs, sighs, muttered comments. So maybe I'll just *suggest* a few things he might have been thinking.

'"Seems far away . . ."'

Maybe now – as he was recalling Goethe's study, his bedroom, his kitchen with his couple of maids, his puppet show – he was standing at the window of our house, and the kids were being loaded onto the bus the government had brought, and he was trying to convince himself that the home *would* be good for them, they'd get a better education, prosper. Maybe he was thinking he'd done a good thing. But maybe it wasn't working. Maybe if I could talk to him now I'd say, *Do you know what happened to those kids?*

He'd say, *They were allowed to see their parents once every six months*, but that was impossible, because how were we meant to get them to Alice?

So why didn't you stop them?

Then he'd think about it and say, *I could've. It wasn't fair what happened.*

What?

Growing up without your mother and father. Your siblings. Your community and your school.

Then I might've said something about the irony, and he might've said he regretted that too, and if he could have his time again. All that mattered, really, was that people stuck together. But instead of all this, I just said, 'When we get back I can help you with your book.'

'Which one?'

'The stories. Better than Hans Christian Andersen. We can send it to a publisher. It'd be good for kids, wouldn't it?'

He just reached out, touched my shoulder, and continued reading.

'Isaiah could do some paintings for it?'

'He could.'

'And Ignatz could edit it. And we could go to town and . . .'

Maybe I had it wrong. Maybe Father was thinking about that Sunday morning, and what he'd done to Erwin, or maybe he was thinking of the day, a few weeks later, when Erwin's mother ran into our house holding her son, his head hanging low, his legs loose, his body limp, laying him on our couch and pointing to the bit of flesh between his ankle and foot and saying (in Aranda): 'Snake.' I remember this. I remember me and Anton and the others standing at the door, and Father kneeling, looking at the puncture wound and saying, 'Quick.' Leaning over, sucking and spitting the poison, as Erwin lay there, and his mother shouted, and Mother tried to shake the boy awake.

Maybe fifteen, twenty minutes, then Pauline came and took us out, told us to go play, but we just stood there saying (something like), 'Is he alive?'

Father came out a while later and sat on the porch, and us kids waited for Erwin to emerge, although he didn't, although his mum did, an hour later, crying. Anton said, 'What do you reckon?' Some kid appeared with a dead taipan. 'This is the one that got him.' Then Charlotte cried, Alwin asked if they could make him better, and Michael said probably not. Eventually, I reckon, we walked over to Father and asked what had happened, but he told us we shouldn't go inside. Pauline took us to church, and we had to listen to her praying, and Julius said, 'Did Erwin get bitten?' and she said yes, and he said, 'Is that why he's dead?' and she said yes, that's why he's dead. And when we went back to the house, and went inside, Erwin was gone.

That's all I remember. No funeral, no one talking about him, no one mentioning the church and the bread and the jam and the cane.

'We're making good time,' I said to Father.

'It's the donkeys,' he said, dropping Goethe onto the boards.

The Britannia Sandhills

Silas had collected some of Isaiah's paintings, put them in a biscuit box, brought them along. Now he took them out, flattened them, explained, 'This one here, just outside Alice Springs.'

'How do you know?' Mother said.

He didn't say. Just ran his hand over the watercolour, feeling the rough paper. 'Here's your ghost gum . . . canoe, see?'

Where the old people had gouged out a canoe, leaving a wound that'd healed hundreds of years ago. 'And a little one growing with it.' He indicated a smaller tree, a sapling at its feet.

Father said, 'He gave these to you?'

'All of them,' Silas said, producing a dozen paintings, sorting through them and saying where they were painted, when, how hot the day had been, Isaiah's mood. Father said, 'It's amazing how you can tell.'

We'd moved into the sandhills. Red to orange, powdered dust, as the dray dragged its tail, the wheels sank, the donkeys strained their shoulders, their legs, flicking flies as they groaned, but continued. Low hills getting steeper, Ludwig (and Ignatz, behind) having to work the animals to get the same effect. Input and output, as they sweated, heads down, walking into the morning sun.

'This country,' Silas said, indicating the hills, flattening another watercolour and comparing the two. 'Long way to go.'

'Britannia?' Father asked.

'See, here, that's in front of us.' Matching the swirls of watercolour with the distant sandhills, like paint equalled geography. 'Another hour or two and we'll be . . .' Tapping the paper again.

'It's a mystery to me,' Mother said.

'What?' Father asked her.

'How he can tell. How can you tell, Silas?'

But he just touched his eyes and said, 'I can see.'

Another painting, much like the others, the same view from the camp outside Alice. This is where Isaiah finished up, years later, penniless, proud and drunk. Living on his land, despite the council trying to take it back. Just him and his sons and his sister and a dozen people who came and went. This is what the whites hated – that they wouldn't settle down, build a house, plant lawn and grow vegetables. Just sitting there, all day every day, a board and a piece of paper in their lap, the same scene over and over, waiting for the dealers to arrive. Sometimes (this happened once when I was there) a white bloke would drive up in his car and say, 'Listen, Isaiah, I gave you thirty quid, and you only gave me ten pictures.'

'What do you want?'

'I gave you some drink, didn't I, and some food? So I reckon you owe me ten more pictures.'

Like this. Like the white bloke was determined to extract every cent. And this continued, years later, after Isaiah was long gone, his son, Micah, sitting under the same tree, some bloke pulling up in his Mercedes and asking for more pictures, and what did he want, five dollars, that'd do, wouldn't it? I remember seeing this and thinking it wasn't all that different to the way Father sent black girls to work in the station kitchens, and they'd return with money, and Mother would give them a few pennies and keep the pounds and say, 'For your board.' Or how the men would be sent to Henbury, and how Ted would arrive at Hermannsburg with the money and give it to Father, me standing there thinking, *But what about the blacks?* But Micah didn't get it. Isaiah didn't get it. Money meant nothing to them. I remember saying to one of these blokes, 'Listen, that's a terrible price, for all the work he's put into it.'

'And who are you?'

'Ben Gerlach. Patrol Officer.'

And this bloke said, 'Well, Ben, there's no one else offering them money for their pictures, is there?'

'But fair's fair.'

'They can buy some sugar and flour and feed their kids . . . if they insist on living in this shithole.'

Micah drank himself silly. He was dead at thirty-seven. I went to his funeral in Alice, and his son Blake gave me some of his pictures, but they weren't anywhere near as good as Isaiah's. Still, Blake sits in the same spot, painting the same views, full of the ghosts I couldn't see then, and can't see now. But he's got a Commodore, and his kids go to Alice High, so maybe it's just that things change slowly.

The hills were getting steeper, the donkeys slower, Ludwig and Ignatz kept whipping them, shouting at them to pull, pull, you rotten animals. I leaned over the side and watched the rims sink, lift, checked the country ahead, and wondered if we'd make it.

'Enough of that!' Jamy called to Ignatz.

Because Ignatz (alone on the cart) had called Jamy over, waited until he'd brought his donkeys forward, said something to him, and Jamy had shouted: 'You leave me alone!'

We turned to see. The dray slowed and sank and Father shouted at Ludwig to keep going for God's sake, so he did, but not enough to stop us sinking in the sand. 'Just what we need,' Father said.

But that didn't matter. Because now Jamy was running up a sandhill, sliding down a few feet, trying again, shouting back at Ignatz, 'Tell them then, tell them!' He eventually disappeared over the hill.

'What is it?' Mother called back to Ignatz.

He shrugged. 'I think he's tired.'

Unlikely. I knew. I jumped down, ran back to the cart, said, 'What is it?' Ignatz told me to mind my business, so I climbed the sandhill and called, 'Jamy?'

He was running. Down into a valley, turning and calling, 'Go back, Benno.'

I followed him up the next hill, caught up and grabbed his shirt and pulled him down. He just sat there, head between his knees, and I said, 'What did he say?'

'Nothing.'

I knew how Ignatz worked. I knew how he'd choose a kid he didn't like, say something to get his back up, wait for a bite, jump down his throat, then out with the cane. I could hear Mother in the distance: 'Benno? Come on, it's hot!'

I said to Jamy, 'He said to keep your mouth shut, didn't he?'

Jamy nodded.

'Is that all?'

'He says he could get the police onto me if I make up lies, and I could end up in prison for years, for me whole life.'

Jamy was nineteen at the time, but hardly an adult. Small frame, skeletal hands that shook (like now) when he was scared, moon face with brown eyes, head always lowered, like Himmel, like someone who'd had the life kicked out of him. The sum of all the cruelty that had been placed on his bone-sharp shoulders. I'll always remember the day the governor visited, looked around the stables, asked Jamy about his favourite mare, and Jamy just stared at the ground, up at me, and the governor said, 'Well, this is a man who knows about animals.' Jamy said, 'We got a foal out the back,' and the governor (who bred horses) asked about her, and they were both out there for an hour, more, chatting away. And when the governor came back, he leaned forward, pinched my chin and said, 'He might need someone to look out for him, Ben.'

'The foal?'

'No, Jamy. That's your job, right? By Royal decree.'

Jamy and I walked back over the hill to the cart. Mother, Father, Ludwig, Silas all watching. Ignatz just sat, reins in hand, staring at his feet. I stood in front of him and said, 'You told him to keep quiet.'

'Can we go?'

'And if he didn't he'd end up in prison.' And to Father, craning his head to see. 'That's what he said to Jamy. If he spoke up he'd go to prison.'

'Prison? For what?'

Ignatz called to him, 'Jamy's been complaining, Martin. I told him he should stop. We won't get to Horseshoe Bend by complaining, will we, Jamy?'

'That's not it,' I said.

'Can we go?'

I dragged Jamy along to Father and called up, 'You don't know what's been going on.'

'Benno. Enough!' Mother said.

'He . . .' I pointed, and my hand shook, and Father said, 'What's this all about?'

'Tell him,' I said to Jamy.

Father called, 'Ignatz?' He waited as Ignatz came forward, stood beside me and Jamy and said, 'We should keep going.'

'Benno . . . Jamy,' Father said. 'You better get those donks.'

I glared at Ignatz. I spat sand from my lips, tried to moisten them, but couldn't. I told Jamy to come with me and we gathered the donkeys, sat in a bit of shade and emptied sand from our shoes. We watched Father talking to Ignatz, and Ignatz using his hands to explain, like he did when he was telling us about Jesus or improper fractions. 'If he lies, I'll tell them,' I said to Jamy. 'You shouldn't let him talk to you that way.'

Nothing.

'Jamy?'

'He can't send me to prison, can he? I didn't do nothing.'

I watched as the meeting broke up, as Ignatz returned to the cart, got up and waited.

'What now?' Jamy asked me.

Then Mother waved for me to return. I went back and said, 'So?'

'We have to keep going.' Father.

'I saw what happened.' Pointing back, again. 'I know what he does and—'

'Enough!' Father shouted.

Mother called to Jamy to get on his donk, follow us. So he slipped into his saddle, moved the spare animals up past Ignatz, beside the dray, and said to me, 'We going?'

I dared not speak. When Father thundered, you stopped. Strange, from a man I always admired for his compassion and fairness. But this wasn't always so. Father, I was learning, was no David Copperfield, the hero of his own life. Whatever my fourteen-year-old sense of right and wrong said, the world didn't, couldn't always work this way.

I climbed up onto the dray, Ludwig whipped the donkeys, and they pulled and pulled, but we couldn't get out of the sand. So Mother, Silas and I stood behind the dray and pushed as the donks pulled. Rocking the boat, Father asking whether we wanted him to get down, Mother saying, 'We can manage.'

And we did. A few minutes later we were free.

Continuing again, as Silas put his paintings back into their biscuit box, closed it, dropped it into the tea chest. We descended, Ludwig rode the brake, and Silas said, 'It goes on like this for a long way.'

I watched Father's hands, all liver-pocked and shaky (though he was only fifty); the rolls of fat on his neck, his strong jaw, his red cheeks, his eyes. Then (so Jamy wouldn't hear) I whispered, 'I saw what Ignatz was doing.'

'It doesn't matter.'

'It does.'

'*You* can afford . . .' He looked back at me like I'd betrayed him – for all the thousands of hours of talking and singing and explaining, I'd betrayed him. But I didn't care. 'You shouldn't let him get away with it,' I said.

'What would you do?'

'Tell him to stop.'

'I have.'

A glimmer of truth. 'So?'

'Don't talk about what you don't know,' Mother said.

'But he said . . .'

'*He* is your father.'

What did that mean? 'But Ignatz . . . you know, don't you?'

'I've done my best,' Father said. 'I closed the dormitory, didn't I? I've explained, Benno, and that's that. I told Adelaide, but there was no one else to send, so if I insisted, I'd be left without a teacher. I'll talk with him again but . . . Jamy, are you listening?'

No reply.

'I've kept an eye on him, Benno. I always have.'

By way of an apology, or explanation? Either way. It seemed it would have to do. I called, 'You stay with me, Jamy.'

Idracowra

Half an hour at Five Mile Creek, Father resting against a desert oak, saying, 'They made Norman walk through sand, and after, they said his prints were the same as the ones they found.'

Mother, under her umbrella, eating a sandwich. 'Martin, don't go over that again.'

Father tried to sit up. 'We only had their word for it. Not so much as a photograph . . . and *that* was the evidence they used to convict him.'

'It was entirely their word, wasn't it, Martin?' Ignatz said.

'Yes. So it's not like it was a fair trial.'

'But he still *might've* done it?' Mother said.

I sat against a tree, hearing the same story again. Norman, and how he was innocent, surely? Nearby, Jamy played patience.

'But it was when we went to the prison that day, remember, Ignatz?' Father said.

'I do.'

'And we were led between the walls . . .'

'Martin,' Mother repeated.

'And there were markings where they'd buried the bodies. Where they'd covered them in lime so *nothing* would remain. Imagine doing that to a person.'

'They were murderers,' Ludwig said, sipping my hot tea.

'Still . . . just initials and a date, that's all. Then that guard, remember, Ignatz, asked if we wanted to see inside the hanging tower. I said no, but you wanted to look.'

Ignatz just waited, cup in hand.

'And it was dark and smelled like death. The big beam with the hook, the ropes ready on a table. I'm glad you insisted we look, Ignatz, because it was that, I think, that made up my mind.'

'What's that?' Ludwig asked.

'That no matter what ... this was no way for one person to treat another.'

We continued towards Idracowra. The donkeys seemed content, the occasional snort, as (at one point) Silas sang to them. Mother told him to be quiet but he said, 'It all helps, Alma.'

She didn't think so. Sitting at the front of the dray, arms crossed, asking me what I was doing, and Father said, 'My notes.'

'Is now the time?' she said to me.

'What else can I do?'

This shut her up. What else? The journey was long, slow, monotonous, like a Sunday afternoon at Hermannsburg where we weren't meant to work, play, anything. But we did. Me slipping out of the house, finding Oskar and pinching his arm. 'You.' Within a few minutes this would be me (in my best pants, shirt, tie, dressed for Jesus) and Oskar and a dozen other kids playing Silas. The game went like this – 'Silas' (the blind person, holding his eyes shut) calling 'Go!' and all of us scattering around the compound. 'Stop!' Silas stumbling around, using only his hands to find the next person. Once, Mother saw us playing, called me over and said, 'Why do you keep calling that boy Silas?'

Telling her what she needed to know, because she could be convinced. But she said, 'If you're making fun of him ...?'

'We're not.'

So the morning was Blind Silas Boring. I sat with a hundred pages of Father's trilingual dictionary in my lap. 'Altja, noun. Tinte. Ink.' I asked where he'd got the words, and he said, 'All over.'

'Altjira. Gott. God. But that's *their* god, isn't it?'

'It means he's not there yet,' Silas said.

'How?'

'*Unmade*,' Father said. 'Like he's being dreamt into existence, all around us.' Indicating with his hands; acres of bean trees, hills that went on forever – but apart from that, nothing, except a home for an unmade god. 'Hence Dreamtime,' Father said. 'God *coming* into being.'

I didn't get it.

'It's different to us.'

Like, *let's just leave it at that*. With the obvious questions – about which God he favoured, why he was promoting the opposition, how this made (for example) the night parrot real, but not real, how the laws were flexible, and changing, the spirits mobile, willing to become whatever they needed to be. Questions I've spent my life asking. Like the Pintupi, when was it, 1954? Standing in the middle of the Western Desert as the men painted their bodies, adjusted their headpieces – as I fed film into my Kodak Brownie, ran a few inches to test it and called, 'All ready.' The next hour, filming their ceremonies – the dances and singing and stories that should've remained private. But at the time I thought I was doing the right thing, continuing Father's work, calling out, 'Could we repeat that bit, thanks!' As they obliged, and we created a version of the Honey Ant song I wanted to show at a conference. And after, the men cleaning up and saying, 'This isn't where it's done.'

'It'll do. Who'll know? I'll explain to people.'

They weren't happy. I offered them money, but they didn't want it. I told them it would help white people learn about their culture, but they just said it was secret business, and I said, 'People will be interested.'

'For the men, yeah?'

'Yeah, the men. Wait till people know. This is fascinating. Colourful.'

We left it there – unresolved, uneasy, and I returned to town, developed the film, took it to this conference, showed it and felt bad, forever after, amen. That somehow I'd offended Altjira. But I had a career, people to impress, and when I was lecturing at university, research to be published.

'It's a polysemic term,' Father said.

'What's that?'

'Altjira means this person, this thing, this spirit didn't come from someone else. Like you came from your mother. Altjira doesn't have a beginning or end. No one created it.'

'Like the night parrot?'

'Like this country. God might've raised a hand and said, *Let there be desert*, but just as likely he might've sat there and looked at it and said, *That'll be fine as it is*.'

Packing my 8 mm, placing it on the back of my cart, setting off for Alice, a few men chasing after me saying, 'Where are you going now?'

'Alice Springs.'

'You taking us all in your machine?'

'My camera? Yes, I guess I am.'

They hadn't liked this idea at all – half paint, half feathers, they'd said, 'We did the dance for *you*.'

So there's me on the dray, trying to persuade Father I'd be his man; I'd finish and edit his dictionary. 'Altunta. White stone.'

He said, 'You're under no obligation, Benno.'

'What?'

'It's my work. I don't want you thinking you have to finish it.'

'I don't mind.'

'When I started,' he explained, clinging to his seat, 'I understood it might take so long that . . . I understood it was several lifetime's work. I didn't mean that to include you, or anyone, if you have other ideas.'

I didn't even know how I felt about it.

'Anyone that starts writing things down, stories . . . the risk is no one'll be interested, and even if they are for a while, what about afterwards?'

'I can do other things . . .' Bogging down in words. Like the cart, three inches in sand, although Ignatz whipped the donkeys until they got him out. 'I could be a detective and still . . . but by then you would've finished all of this, wouldn't you?'

We continued for half an hour, then the Britannia sandhills flattened and there was more grass, more cattle, purple ranges Isaiah had spent his life painting, so that (I thought then) the hills were more watercolour than real.

The Pintupi weren't my only regret. I've had plenty over the years. I might as well tell you about that Stern business now, because when you read this book you'll say, 'It was written by this fella called Gerlach.' If that person's old enough, they'll say, 'Oh, he was the one with all that magazine business, wasn't he?'

The magazine. *Stern*. German. This is what happened twenty years ago. Me and Kate had decided to quit the research council and make our own foundation to protect the artefacts Father had left me, years before. The headdresses, the tjurunga, the instruments, the hunting sticks, rooms full of it. To do this, we reasoned, we'd need money (after forty years in the desert, twenty years lecturing, my patrol officer days, there wasn't much left). So I decided to sell some photographs I'd taken (nothing to do with Father) to a German magazine called *Stern*. That'd be fine. Germans had an interest in Aboriginal people, and their ceremonies. Not sure why. Maybe it helped them forget, you know, the war? So they'd be published and it'd all be good because no one in Australia would know, no one offended, we'd get our money, start the foundation, rent somewhere dry and waterproof for all of our gear.

The photographs were published. I wrote the text to explain them. Western Desert. Honey Ant song. This is the meaning. This is how they see the world. And yes, there were a few pictures I shouldn't have published, but how was I to know that *Stern* had reciprocal rights with the *Women's Weekly*? And that they'd publish the images in Australia? Followed by the shock and horror, how dare he! Letters to the editor, an apology, all of the old people, the Western Desert people, writing me scribbled notes saying what right did I have, who did I think I was? Which hurt me. Because if there was one thing I wouldn't do, it was betray their trust.

It just kept coming. A news crew at my door, a federal member giving me a serve, and so many letters me and Kate burned them in the incinerator. Imagine if Martin Gerlach had been alive? As I wondered (during a few weeks of sleepless nights) whether he was drifting through the Dreamtime, cursing me.

So that's what happened with *Stern*. Eventually the German editor contacted me and apologised and said he'd had no idea how sensitive the material was, and he was sorry, and should he write to the black people? But I said no, I was the one who'd have to do the apologising.

So that's why people remember me as the *Stern* guy. But honestly, Martin and Benjamin Gerlach spent their lives trying to do the right thing by the Central Australian blacks. Maybe now the times have changed, people see things differently, but we only meant well.

Back on the dray, Father said, 'There are plenty of ways to live a life, Benno.'

But I just read: 'Amboa, old man, weary of life.'

Father smiled. 'You're not even through the A's.'

'It'll take a while, won't it?'

The hills returned. The sand deeper, the earth dryer, turpentine retreating towards the ranges; sun-bleached cattle bones, a hide lying open like a can of oysters. *Anbara. Weisse Stirn*. White forehead. The same spelling as moving forward, running past, going on, further away. All decided by one accent. I said to Father, 'I still need to learn how to use accents,' and he said, 'I've been meaning to teach you, haven't I?'

This seemed to concern him. Letters were one thing, but they hardly explained everything. 'Ignatz has some knowledge, don't you, Ignatz?'

'You teach me,' I said.

'But *he* knows.' The Gerlach pragmatism at work. 'I wrote a key to the accents, as an appendix, and if worst comes to worst you can study that.'

Worst comes to worst?

'You want to become a detective, don't you? Or what else did you used to say? You were going to be a fireman at one stage.'

'He never said that.' Mother.

'Oh, and a lion keeper. Remember when we went to Leipzig Zoo and you saw the lion and that's all you wanted to do?'

I said to Father, 'I could be running Hermannsburg one day.'

He laughed. 'You want to?'

'Over my dead body,' Mother said.

'Why not?' I asked. 'I believe in God.'

'If you want to go to the seminary, Benno, if you want to study, if you want to return to Hermannsburg, do so. But whatever you do, do it well, Benno.'

I was happy with this. I liked doing a good job. Maybe that came from years of Best in Class (not that it was much of a challenge). Even after I got to Immanuel, when Mother (I remember) marched me into the principal's office and said, 'Benno has very high standards.'

'Mother.'

'He likes to do things properly, like his father.'

'Pastor Gerlach?'

'Sometimes he sets himself unreasonable goals, don't you, Benno?'

'Yes, Mother.'

Like this. Half an hour of embarrassment because I liked to do things well. Match the German, the English, the Aranda, the right accents, dotted i's and crossed t's. Such a sin? Father saying, 'The main thing, Benno, is to do things with a certain . . . lightness. Something where you can laugh. Have fun. That's been lacking from our lives, hasn't it, Mother?'

The first thing I tried was teachers' college. Twelve months of basics, a letter from the Board, a one-teacher school at Bethany. Me, aged twenty-one, standing in front of sixty grim-faced, vacant-eyed Barossa Lutherans. 'Should we start with grammar?'

'No.'

'Who was that? Stand up, who?'

The whole class laughing.

'I won't put up with any of that. Who was it?'

The day going from bad to worse, someone's sandwich launched across the room, a pencil striking the back of my neck. And that night, writing home to Mother: 'I'm not sure I've made the right decision . . .'

But give it time, I thought. The next day I said, 'Your parents send you to school to get an education. Improve your prospects, so you don't have to spend your life picking grapes.'

Words to that effect. And the next morning, several irate parents at the front door saying, 'We've been picking grapes for thirty years, and we've turned out okay, haven't we?'

'That's not what I meant. I meant so your children have choices.'

Soon the kids hated me, the parents hated me, the Board sent an inspector to see what was happening. But I said to myself, Keep at it (as Father had, as Mother had). Until the morning I arrived at school, unlocked the door for the first students, and some kid said, 'Everyone reckons you're the worst teacher we've ever had.'

'They do, eh?'

'And if we can get rid of you they'll send someone nice. A lady teacher.'

I resigned, returned to university to study languages, to pick up where Father had left off.

Now, I dropped Father's dictionary into the tea chest and said, 'You don't want all that work to go to waste.'

And he just said, 'Worse things have happened.'

The camel pad

I'd stored some of Father's artefacts in my shed. Headgear, falling apart; an old woomera, broken into three; a didgeridoo. The notes I hadn't got to, and there, in a box, Father's dictionary. I took it out, blew away the dust, removed a few insect-eaten pages and decided to take it inside. Although what could I do? An eighty-year-old man with no connections in the publishing industry, no computer, no time, or will, perhaps?

'You ready?'

I turned and saw Jack standing at the door, and beside him, this boy – eleven or twelve, tall for his age, round face and shaggy, blond hair, dressed in soccer shorts and socks, a 'Vampires' shirt, looking me over. 'Dad, this is Tom.'

Tom stepped forward, offered his hand, and I shook it. 'My God, you've got your grandfather's nose.'

Tom didn't know what to say, so he looked at Jack, who smiled, but just said to me, 'Didn't think you'd see me again?'

'The soccer!' Looking my grandson over from top to bottom. 'You any good, Tom?'

He shrugged. 'I don't have to be a goalie anymore.'

'Good. That's good, isn't it? Who wants to be goalie? You want to be out running around, don't you?'

'I guess.'

Now, you're probably thinking I'm going to tell you I saw Jack in Tom, which was right. That I saw a bit of me in the boy, which was right. A bit of Martin, and Mother, all of them. But maybe that's me reading too much into it. After all, I'd never met the kid, but just the way he studied me, thinking; half-smiled, curious. Then he saw the didgeridoo, reached out and said, 'Is it okay?'

'Of course.'

He took it down, tried to play it, and Jack laughed. 'You better leave that, Tom, it's valuable, isn't it, Dad?'

'Well, it's meant to be played, although it's been a long time. I was given it by . . .' I realised I was starting a lecture they didn't want to hear. Jack said, 'All of this is . . .?'

'Martin's, and some of it's mine.'

Admiring it all, he said, 'Shouldn't it be in a museum?'

'I want to catalogue it properly, but I've got so much inside.'

Tom was making raspberries, and laughing. His father messed his hair and told him he was a natural. Tom said, 'Beats trumpet,' and Jack told me he learned trumpet at school, at Scotch College, and I said, 'That's pretty fancy, isn't it?'

'Nah.'

'The Gerlachs always went to Immanuel.'

'Not anymore.'

Tom just about shitting himself, long fingers grasping the rainbow serpent. My grandson, for God's sake. I said, 'You can borrow it if you want to.'

The boy's eyes all alight. 'Really?'

'Of course.'

'Dad . . . Society and Culture. This would be perfect!'

'I don't know,' Jack said. 'Looks valuable.'

'If you want to practice, Tom?' I said.

'Course. I'll look after it. Didgeridoo.' Trying again, this time producing something that sounded like music. Jack said, 'See, you've got it.'

'It's like the trumpet,' Tom said. 'You just buzz. Is that how you do it . . .?'

'*Grandpa*,' Jack told him.

'If I can use it for my project?'

He was a smart-looking kid, and I liked him straight away. No bullshit, no mucking around, no spoiled, smart-arse brat. Just another Gerlach. With the Gerlach nose and chin, the hint of indentation. He said, 'What should I call it?'

I pointed to the tag Father had written seventy years earlier. 'It's all there.'

'So you ready?' Jack said.

'Of course. Time got away. I didn't forget.'

'I'm sure you didn't. But we've got to go.' Checking his watch.

Tom didn't seem to care. He was admiring the other objects, picking them up, blowing the dust, reading the tags. A sacred stone, and I said, 'Your great-grandfather collected that in 1901.'

'No way!'

Jesus, the kid seemed interested. What twelve-year-old was interested in rocks? He wiped it on his top and asked about the markings, and I told him, but I said you didn't come for that, and Jack said we'll be late, so I said, 'Why don't you take that, too?'

'Really?'

'Go on. The tag'll tell the story. You might get an A-plus.'

And that's how it began. The story of Jack and Tom, the kid who liked everything, eternally curious, forgiving of an old fuck who'd let his father down thirty years before. He must've known the story, must've asked after his missing grandfather, but there was no hint of malice. Nothing. Just, 'I'll make sure I look after it.'

So we went out, and I locked the door and said to Jack, 'I need two minutes to get ready.'

Back to the desert. It's approaching four in the afternoon on Friday the thirteenth. The hottest part of the day, Father stretching back in his throne, wiping sweat from his face, Silas still at his feet, handing him water, Father drinking some, most of it spilling onto the shirt he'd opened to the belly. He said, 'There used to be a nurse, didn't there, Alma?'

'You know that, Martin. You gave her the job.'

'Of course.' Trying to remember. 'She cared for the kids for a few weeks.'

'Three years, Martin.'

'*No*. Not three years.' Trying to recall her face, perhaps, her voice, something about her. 'Three years?'

This was happening, too. The past falling away, the people and places, the endless Sunday services, all a fog. 'Her name was Schmidt?'

'Fielke.'

'Was it? Fielke?'

'Sarah Fielke. Remember? She came from Queensland. She lived in the spare room, next to Benno, didn't she, Benno?'

'Yes.'

I remembered. Like having an older sister, coming into my room at night, sitting on my bed, brushing her hair and saying, 'Do you ever stop reading?'

'Of course.'

'What's that?'

Showing her. 'Not much else to do.'

'You should go to boarding school.'

'Father needs my help.'

'I suppose he does.' Smiling and saying, 'You got a cowlick.'

'I know.' Spitting on my hand, plastering it down. 'It won't go away.'

'Leave it. It's funny.'

Like that. Like I was some toy, and she was deciding whether I was worth playing with. Either way, back beside the Finke, Father said, 'She was a good worker?'

'No. She was lazy.'

'Was she? Sarah . . .?'

'Fielke.'

'She was plump, wasn't she?'

'Not really.'

No, not really. Quite lean. The gap between the boards was enough. As I turned off my light, waited, watched her getting undressed. *Lean*. Her bra and panties, all of it. Sometimes she'd look at the wall, and I'd move away, the feeling she knew I was there. Mother coming in and switching on my light and saying, 'What are you doing in the dark?'

'You can't remember?' Mother said to Father.

'Course I can. She started the clinics, didn't she, so they'd bring their kids in from the desert to get shots . . . she did that, didn't she?'

'She did.'

'And she taught them about contraception?'

'She did.'

'See, I'm not stupid.'

'No one said you were.' She told Silas to adjust Father's hat, and he did, lowering it over his face and saying, 'She was a good nurse, wasn't she?'

'She was, Silas. Took care of you, didn't she?'

Mother was wrong. It'd only been eighteen months. I remembered. Believe me, I remembered. Discovering more about anatomy than Ignatz could ever teach me. Eventually telling Oskar about the motherlode, both of us in my room at night, lights out, standing, watching. Me whispering, 'Real thing's better.'

After those eighteen months, after an argument with Mother, when Sarah packed up and left, life was never the same for me and Oskar.

'It's a pity she had to go,' Father said.

'She *chose* to go,' Mother said.

'You made her,' I said.

'I did not. She wanted to go.'

'You told her to . . .' What was the point? Reminding her of the argument, Sarah Fielke calling her an old battleaxe, even a bit of pushing and shoving.

'She was very coarse, very rude,' Mother said.

She wasn't. She was fine. Mother brought out the worst in people.

'Sarah Schmidt?' Father said.

'Fielke.'

One point. It's not nice seeing your father, anyone, stripped back to basics, a sort of child, a state of innocence that had last occurred when they were one, two, three years old. Unaware of the world, what it held, the good, the bad and the unknown. This, in retrospect, was the bit I liked least. Father, of all people. Like I'd just left the shed open, and someone had come in the night and stolen everything.

Back in the car, Tom put his face between driver and passenger, me and Jack, father and grandfather, and said, 'Ben, isn't it?'

'Yes.'

'Dad told me about that time in the desert when you went with your dad cos he was sick, to try and get help from a hospital.'

I smiled at Jack and said, 'You remember?'

'When was that?' Tom asked.

'Nineteen twenty-two.'

'Whoa. That was so long ago. And you were like on a cart or something, and had to get through the desert?'

'The Finke Valley.'

'That must have been so cool.'

'Well . . . I'm not sure. But it was something I'll never forget.'

'Ten days, wasn't it?' Jack asked.

'Eight.'

'You must have been worried?'

'At fourteen . . .' And looking back. 'How old did you say you were, Tom?'

'Twelve. Grade seven.'

'And you like school?'

'It's okay.'

'For twelve grand a year it ought to be,' Jack said.

'And what's your favourite subject?' I asked.

'History.'

'No!' Beaming. I knew it! Another Gerlach, ready-made for the desert (despite skipping a generation). 'What sort of history, Tom?'

'Bushrangers.'

'Good. They're interesting. And settlement . . . the explorers?'

'They're interesting, too. Like that guy that went mad and walked around the desert for years and never came home.'

'Leichhardt?'

'That's him.'

'Well, your great grandfather was a sort of explorer.' Followed by a brief history of Martin Gerlach, before deciding I was boring him. 'So maybe,' I said, 'maybe you can help me with the Gerlach archives?'

'What are they?'

'Jesus,' Jack said, 'you've signed him up already?'

Bad idea. I was becoming my father too soon. 'Wouldn't you rather be a teacher like your dad?'

'And deal with people like me all day? But I could help with your archives, Grandpa.'

I couldn't help but smile. I tried to hide it from Jack, but I couldn't help it. 'No telling with kids, is there?'

'No.'

'Start off with the didgeridoo,' I said, looking back. 'I have photos, hundreds of them, and Ektachrome I took in the forties. It'll need conserving . . . it's in bad nick.' Stopping. Deciding. 'What's the other team like, Tom?

'Shit.'

Back in the dray, Mother squeezed a flannel, handed it to Silas, who placed it on Father's face and gently wiped him clean, and cool. Silas said, 'That better?'

'It all helps.'

'Once we get through these damn sandhills,' Ludwig said to Father. 'Hot, eh, Alma?'

'Yes.' Checking Father, as he started singing: '"Let the night parrots cover the edge of the world with their footprints . . ." Don't you reckon, Benno?'

'If we can find one.'

'We will. Given time. Nothing's surer. "*Lobe den Herren . . .*"'

'Martin,' Mother said.

But the hymn continued, and I wondered where my father was going. Back, into the sand, the water, the songs, the world he'd tried to tell us about. He just sang, and descended, and I knew he was off . . .

Five Mile Creek, sitting in his suit as me and Ludwig jumped in, as Jack and Sharon jumped in, and soon, Tom. What I'm trying to make clear, in my eightieth year. All of the borders, the lines on maps – imaginary. All of the cards to celebrate birthdays, marriages, christenings. People dissolving, disappearing into the unknown.

About then Ludwig pulled up. 'We gotta decide.'

There were two tracks. One, the wagon track. A few miles longer, but harder ground. Two, the camel pad, shorter, but sandier, tougher for the donkeys. Mother said, 'What did Alf reckon?'

'Short way,' Ludwig said.

'Martin?'

But he was just singing.

'Martin!'

'What?'

'Which way?'

He lifted his hand and indicated the camel pad, but Mother said, 'We'll end up bogged again.'

'We'll be fine.'

'Three miles we don't have to go,' Ludwig said.

'I reckon the long way,' Ignatz called, from the cart. 'We haven't seen the worst of the sand yet.'

I could've offered my opinion, but no one would've cared, but Jamy said, 'Camel.'

'We haven't got camels,' Ignatz called. 'And these donkeys have had it.'

Father sat up and said, 'We've always gone through the sandhills.'

So we veered onto the camel pad, and the donks complained, but pulled, and Ignatz said we'd regret it (and I said, 'We regret *you*, Herr Beck').

This was something new. Standing on the boundary, holding a latte or short something, I can't recall, finding myself, for the first time in my life, interested in sport. 'Come on, Tom, get it off him!' As Tom intercepted, captured the ball, lost it to another kid, turned to me and Jack and shrugged and smiled like it didn't matter. Laughing, playing around with his mates, as the coach called, 'Tom, stop fucking around!'

'He's about as good as you,' I said to Jack.

'What?'

'When you played for Nailsworth Primary.'

'I can't remember that.'

'You did. Me and your mother would go, Saturday morning. You did the same.'

'What?'

'Like you'd rather be somewhere else.'

'Bullshit.'

'Bullshit nothing. You did. Your mother thought it was important but . . .'

'You would've been out in the desert, dreaming, wouldn't you? Or in your study?'

'I guess I could be . . . preoccupied.'

He smiled. Wryly. 'Mum made it into a sewing room once you went.'

I knew he was right; I knew he remembered correctly. I was an absent father. 'One of the few games I saw, I guess . . . considering.'

Jack raised his hands defensively. 'I didn't invite you here to go over all of this old shit, Dad. Just so you could see your grandson.'

Watching Tom, trying for a goal, but not getting anywhere near.

'It's a decent school,' I said, admiring the sandstone buildings, the old chapel, a shiny new steel and glass block.

'We thought he'd be happy here, and he is. He went to Nailsworth Primary but there were some shitheads, bullies, and we told the school, and they said they'd do this and that, but they didn't do a thing, so we thought, screw it.'

Tom passed to another kid, and he scored a goal, but Tom ran around like it was him, so me and Jack clapped and called out, and Tom ran over to us, but instead of telling his father, he stopped next to me and said, 'Did you see that, Grandpa?'

Grandpa? Me. Taken out of that dirty old shed, dragged in luxury to Scotch College, given a coffee, and suddenly, this is life. This. Not the desert. Not the memories. Not the sticks and stones. This. I said, 'He wouldn't have got that unless you passed.'

'Exactly.'

'Your goal, really.'

Then he said to Jack, 'Did you see that?'

'I did.'

He lifted his hand, and Jack told me it was a high-five, so I high-fived, and Tom returned to the game (the coach telling him to get his arse back to work).

Jack said, 'You're quite a hit.'

'It was the didgeridoo.'

'No, not at all.'

I said, 'It's important you get these things right.'

'It is.' Without looking at me.

Tom returned again, another high-five, then the coach lost patience and took him off, and he stood with us. He said, 'We should take you to see Aunty Sharon.'

Jack smiled and said, 'Well, Tom, that might not be a good idea.'

'Why?'

I waited. I said to Jack, 'She had a son, didn't she?'

'She did.'

'But . . .?'

'Seventy-eight. The stone wall around the Botanic Gardens?'

I knew. I'd walked past plenty of times, looking where they'd replaced old stone with new.

Tom said, 'Aunty Sharon's got a pool. Gran comes over and . . .' He stopped. 'Oops. I wasn't meant to . . .'

But Jack just messed his hair, again.

Tom said, 'That's my classroom over there.' Indicating. 'Wanna see?'

He dragged me. I shuffled. We left Jack, or at least, he decided not to come.

The Baboons

Ignatz placed the book in front of me and said, 'Should we learn about baboons?'

'I guess.'

'Can you read aloud, Benno?'

'"Baboons travel along the ground, in trees, across rivers . . ."'

Meanwhile, the other kids had been given a piece of paper and pencil and told to draw a baboon. I showed them the cover of my book, and they drew long legs and arms, fat bellies and big ears. Although what did we know about primates? Our lives were a collection of guesses. Sometimes educated, sometimes not (especially when Ignatz was too tired, or ill, to 'teach'). A system devoid of critical thinking, ideas, or creativity. We were the baboons, sitting in that hot room scratching our arses, staring out of the window.

And here I was, with my baboon book, as we continued through the Britannia Sandhills. The sky had filled with low, grey cloud, but there was nothing in it. Just a few flashes of lightning, and distant thunder. Like we lived in a rain-shadow of misfortune, or at least rain. Always longing for the smell, the taste, puddles and wet hair, the way the boys found a piece of iron and surfed the sand before Mother came out and shouted at them to go home. The way the water tank filled, and all of us kids jumped in, and the way we ran, as fast as we could, to the waterhole.

'"Each baboon dies close to where it was born,"' I said. Looking around, trying to find baboons in our desert, one sandhill to the next, a teacher, preacher, wife and outcasts. 'Why's that, do you reckon?' I said.

'You'd have to ask the baboons,' Father said.

'It says here,' I added, '"they cannot talk, they cannot discuss what happened yesterday, or tomorrow. A baboon cannot add two plus two, or laugh at a joke."'

'We don't know that,' Father said.

I was sure if I looked long enough I'd see a baboon. Coming over a hill, running towards us, desperate for water or food or God. I said, 'Baboons have no name.'

'Why would they?' Father asked.

'We do.'

'We have identity, but baboons are ... baboons.' Smiling. 'Things cease being when they lose their name.'

'How's that?' I asked.

'You're Benno?'

And Mother: 'Martin. Must we?'

'But if you're not *Benno*, then who are you?'

The clouds were moving away from us, but I could still hear the crashing, the clapping, the bowel-rumbling music rolling across the desert. Ludwig slowed towards a hill and said, 'Should we let the donks rest?'

'No, get on with it,' Father said.

We made it to the top, pulled up and waited for Ignatz, who called, 'I'll lose the lot.'

'Try!' Father called, angrily. It was hot, and he'd had enough. 'Unless you want to stay here all night?'

Ignatz whipped the donkeys, they groaned, moved forward, pulled the cart up the incline. A crack, a splinter, then a wheel broke into pieces. The cart shifted, a few chests and cases fell to the ground, the whole thing upended; tight reins and tumbling donkeys, ending up on their water bellies, rolling with the cart until it reached the bottom of the hill. Ignatz jumped off just in time. The whole lot settled in soft sand. I jumped down, Silas felt his way, Ludwig, then Mother, Father shouting to help him down.

'Stay there,' Mother said.

The donkeys were going mad, kicking their legs, tails flicking sand everywhere.

'Let them loose,' Father called.

Ignatz tried to get to them, but they kicked him, and he retreated, cursed them and said, 'Because it's always me on the cart.'

Mother was shouting directions. No one was listening. Ludwig inspected the wheel and said, 'That's done, Pastor.' He walked back to the donks, released the harnesses, waited until they got up. Then he climbed onto the wreck, salvaged the first of the boxes and said, 'Stick them over there.' Five minutes later we had the cart unloaded, and Ludwig called to Father, 'What do you want to keep?'

'Just the food and water.'

So Ludwig found the boxes and canteens and handed them to me and Mother. 'Pop them on the back of the dray.'

'We're leaving all this?' Mother said.

She started sorting through a trunk she'd brought all the way from Germany – spare dresses, a few pairs of my pants, shoes, socks. Eventually she gave up and called to Father, 'What about these clothes?'

'We can get them on the way back.'

She wasn't happy, but the cart wasn't going anywhere. So she closed her trunk and said, 'Animals will get to them.'

'They don't want your petticoats,' Father said.

Jamy chose the four strongest donkeys, tied them to his saddle and said, 'What about the other ones, Pastor?'

'Let them go.'

'Bob won't be happy.'

'Bob's not here. They'll be okay.'

I doubted it. A few shrubs, no trees, no waterholes. I said, 'Should we leave them some water, Jamy?'

He just unharnessed the tired donkeys, and shouted at them to go. They took a few steps, waited, then walked off. We loaded our few things onto the dray, and continued. Looking back at the mess of boards and wheels, frame and harness, Ignatz said, 'That's a pity.'

'It can be repaired,' Father said.

It was never retrieved. It was never repaired. It was still there, thirty years later, when me and Terese and the kids pulled up, got out and walked around the rusted iron, hanging loose, the rotten boards, the leather, still good. When I climbed on top and said, 'I used to sit here with Ignatz. I told you about him, didn't I?'

Jack climbed up beside me and said, 'I can't believe you used to get around on one of these.'

'It's all we had.'

'You're from the stone age.'

And Sharon, arms crossed: 'If it was so dangerous, why did people come out here?'

'Why have we?'

'You wanted to.'

'I thought you might like to see where . . . people came to help the blacks. They were living primitive lives.'

'If they were happy . . .'

'They lived till thirty, if they were lucky. And we taught them about the world.'

'Did they want to know?'

'And God.'

'They already had one, didn't they?'

I said it was easy to say all of this now, but at the time people saw things differently. But she wasn't convinced. She just returned to the Land Rover and said, 'It's too hot out here.' I found Mother's trunk, although by now it was full of sand. I dug down, pulled out a pair of shoes and said, 'Jesus, these were mine.' Showing them to Terese, to Jack, who inspected them and said, 'They're made of canvas.'

Terese said, 'You're not keeping them, Benno.'

'They've been here thirty years.'

'Exactly.' Smiling, laughing, taking the shoes and throwing them away (before I told Jack to put them in the car).

After which we continued towards Hermannsburg.

But back then, towards Horseshoe Bend. I remember the stray donkeys following us, Ignatz marooned on the back of the dray, shouting at them to go away. Mother saying, 'It's cruel, just leaving them.'

And Father, 'What else can we do?'

'They'll starve to death.'

'We could eat one tonight,' Ludwig said, but Father said we had plenty of Henbury beef.

Like this, a troop of baboons, Ignatz on the outside, finding his place. Mother said he could ride one of the spare donkeys, but he said why him, why not me, or Silas? So she left it. Then Father said, 'I remember her now.'

'Who?' Mother asked.

'That Fielke woman. I never liked her much.'

'With the sand,' Ignatz said. 'Seventeen hours to Idracowra. If we can get going early tomorrow morning. Three or four, perhaps? I think we're in for a hot day.'

'I'm not sure what she was doing there,' Martin said. 'Something about her parents . . .'

'Four, should we say?' Ignatz asked.

I remember the canvas shoes on the front seat between me and Terese, and Sharon saying, 'Why did your dad come all the way out here? He could've gone somewhere closer to Adelaide.'

'He believed everyone deserved to know about the Bible.'

'Really?' Turning up her nose. 'Maybe he should've looked after his own kids.'

'Maybe.'

'I mean, it wasn't fair . . . with your brothers and sister and all.'

'You wouldn't mind if you never saw Jack again.'

She thought about this. 'It was pretty cruel, really. You were six, and they didn't see their own kids for years.'

Maybe she was right. Maybe it was cruel. But I told her, 'It's not like now, when kids are included. Mother didn't think they could get a decent education in Australia.'

'What about you?'

Continuing like this for another two days, arguing, bored, thirsty, until we pulled into Hermannsburg.

It was different by then. Still a mission, but only a few dozen blacks – the ones who hadn't given up on God, or wandered back to the desert, or gone to live in Alice. The same buildings, although most of them were run down, the church with its roof off, the sewing shed with a missing wall, the house unpainted and shabby, cracking walls and missing boards on the porch. Pulling up, parking and saying to Terese, 'Jesus, what's happened to the place?'

Getting out and telling Jack and Sharon, 'Well, this is it.'

'You grew up here?'

As they took a few tentative steps, Pauline came running out (fat-faced and slower, hair all grey, eyes red and rheumy). 'Benno!' Throwing her arms around me, a few people gathering, although I couldn't recognise anyone. I said, 'You're still here!'

'Where else could I go?'

'I just thought . . . I'm back! Remember, I said I would, and here I am.'

I introduced Terese and Jack and Sharon, and she felt them to make sure they were real. 'How long's it been?' she asked me.

'Years.' Studying the porch. 'I remember when we left for Horseshoe Bend and you and me and Adele sat there and you made me promise I'd come back.' Turning to my family, standing, stunned. 'Pauline was my mother, weren't you? She was . . . Jesus, I should've come sooner.'

Jack just said, 'I bet he was a pain in the arse.'

'No,' she said. 'He looked just like you,' and she took his head in her hands, like I remember her doing to me.

'And what about Adele?' I asked.

'She got sick and died. I wrote to you.'

'No . . . when?'

'Three years ago.'

'I never got the letter.'

She told me who was alive, and dead. She told me the new pastor was in town, but he was always in town, not with his heart in the place, like ingkata. No one, she said, had matched him. No one had done what he had. No one had been loved so much.

That's what it was like. Standing in the remains of my childhood. The buildings smaller and shabbier, minus the memories. The sheds where me and Oskar hid from Father and Ludwig. Gone. I said to her, 'It doesn't look the same.'

'No, it's not. Them days are gone, Benno.'

Then I heard Himmel. Quiet at first, then braying, her head over the fence, eyes wide open, teeth bared. 'Jesus,' I said. 'I don't believe it!' I walked over, took her muzzle in my hands and started stroking it, rubbing it hard, like I used to. 'Girl!'

'What's with the donkey?' Jack asked, above the noise.

'Himmel,' I said. 'She remembers me, doesn't she, Pauline?'

'I reckon. She hasn't made a sound for years . . . listen to her.'

Pauline walked us around the place. A few of the old people remembered me, talked about Mother, Father, Silas, Jamy. We returned to the house and Pauline showed me what remained, how Pastor Albrecht had kept it. I showed Jack and Sharon my room and they said how the hell had I lived there, no cooler, no fridge, no friends, for so many years. Pauline made tea, sugared it with half a spoon, and I said, 'You remember?' And she said, 'No time gone, Benno.'

When we left, when the kids were getting in the car, I returned to Himmel, stroked her face, wondered how I could leave again. As we drove off, I said to Terese, 'She won't be alive next time we visit.'

She smiled. 'She was waiting for you.'

'What?'

'For *you*? Maybe you read too much into things, Benno.'

But that was Terese: out of phase, a signal I could never quite tune on my radio.

I was telling you about that Friday, and how we lost the cart, but got as far as Ignatz said we should, made camp, drank more strong tea, ate salted beef, and listened as Father told us about Sarah Fielke and her father, her family. He remembered them now. He remembered she'd been sent to get her away from some bloke who'd got her pregnant. 'I reckon he was a teacher, wasn't he, Alma?'

'I can't remember.'

'And he'd made a bunch of promises but . . .'

'*Now* you remember!' Mother said.

'But then he'd just . . . pissed off. Just as well we helped her, I reckon.'

'You insisted,' Mother said.

'Did I?'

Sometime around eight, Ignatz said, 'Time we got to bed. I set my clock for four.'

'Five,' Father said.

As I lay, again, on my swag, taking in the universe, deciding that nothing we did, that happened, could make any difference.

Saturday 14 October (Day 5)

The Artificial Storm

I laid awake watching Father, propped up against a paperbark, lapsing in and out of sleep, Ludwig sprawled on the ground, Silas and Jamy deep inside their swags. The storm waited in the distance, rolling thunder, a few licks of lightning. Father woke, took a few moments to get his breath, gathered a handful of sand and let it empty. Perhaps he was praying for good health, making peace with God or the various spirits dragging chains through the sandhills, calling to him, asking him if he was ready. Or maybe he was adding the hours until Idracowra. Wondering how I'd cope; and the others, lost in a Leipzig autumn. Maybe, when I drifted off, they sang, '*If God himself be for me . . .*' Though I'll never know, because I fell asleep, and the next time I woke I heard someone in the camp. 'Who's there?'

Nothing. Father snoring, and these five bodies turning, sniffing, coughing.

'Hello?'

A few pots knocked over, but no one waking.

'Silas?'

I stood, and two donkeys ran towards the waterhole. Jamy stirred and said, 'They don't wanna go away.'

When I woke again a little after three, I smelt smoke. Sat up, looked around and saw a glow a hundred yards from the camp. As my eyes focused, this became fire – a long front burning spinifex, catching pine trees (flaring into the night), a wall of smoke rising, blowing across to the camp.

'Father!'

He stirred. 'What is it?'

A few whirly-whirlies lifting handfuls of fire and throwing them in our direction.

'Ludwig!' Father said, but he was already up, running over to the tethered donkeys, gathering the harnesses.

By now everyone was awake, Mother (for once) lost for words, Father telling her to gather our things. I threw the pans, the fire grate, the flour and damper into a box, onto the dray. The swags, but I didn't bother rolling them. Then Father, up, rung by rung, six steps onto his throne, calling, 'Come on, it's getting closer.'

The wide, white-hot front leaned into the wind as it moved towards us. And behind it, flashes, night made day, the rumble of earth, the skies, the ice women and God and Jesus. The crackling of grass that made a chorus, became a roar, as Jamy and Ludwig and Silas (hands out, searching the darkness) tried to gather the donkeys. One by one, harnessing them, Mother shouting to hurry as she got the last of the rugs, a book, canteens from around the camp.

I stood thinking what to do, but Father called, 'Forget it – come on.'

I went back, grabbed a donkey, pulled and shouted at it to move, and by now the fire was only ten, fifteen yards away, the heat on our faces, the pines catching like kerosene. I tried to gather the spares, but they bolted. Mother called: 'Benno, on the dray, now!'

I saw a burning donkey. I saw how it protested, and jumped about. I heard it complaining, a few groans, then silence.

The dray was ready. Ludwig got on, called for me to get away from the flames. I turned, and there was Silas, hands out, feeling for something, someone, before his pants caught and burned. I ran over, kicked sand on his legs, but then his jacket was alight, and he was asking what was happening. A vision, a flash, the colourised world of his Spanish pictures, again, before Ignatz pushed him over, kicked more sand on him.

'Hurry up!' Father said.

The front was burning the dray. Ludwig took the reins and headed up the hill, whipping the donks, as the spares followed close behind. Me and Jamy on either side of Silas, dragging him under the arms, tripping, continuing. Until we caught up with the others, and managed to climb aboard. Mother asked Silas if he was burnt, but he just laughed.

'Silas?' Trying to remove his jacket, although he pulled it on and said, 'I saw her again.'

'Who?' Mother asked.

'In white, with her son, and a lamb and a cross. I saw her again, Martin! In the fire.'

Mother pulled off his jacket and said, 'You were just about killed.'

When it was safe, we stopped. All of us except Father got down and looked back at the fire. Glowing, Silas smiling and saying he could feel her on his skin, Mother saying what were the chances? 'You saved us, Benno.' Two donkeys tried to find their way out of the fire. It seemed a shame, but Ignatz said they were stupid animals anyway, and wouldn't feel a thing. I disagreed. I said anyone (donkeys, baboons, horses) would know what was happening, wouldn't they? It seemed a strange time to lack compassion.

Mother inspected Silas's legs and said, 'See, you're burnt.' While we unloaded the dray, she laid Silas on the grass, removed his pants, threw them away (as he protested, saying he'd only brought one pair) and started rubbing snake-vine into his skin. 'Is it painful?'

'No.'

His arms, too, his left hand, a decent dose of calamine. 'You'll have to watch it.'

Half an hour later, and Father kept drifting off. We stopped again, made a rough bed of rugs and clothes beside his throne, and laid him down. Silas – wearing a pair of Father's pants, one of his shirts, three sizes too big – chose this time to start a sermon about the evils of the pox. 'The devil reaches out and says *she's* pretty nice, isn't she?'

Mother told him to shut up.

'Then she says, Come with me, fella, and she gives you plenty of sweet love!'

I laughed, we all did. Father said, 'What do you think that means, Benno?'

'Sex.'

A real belly laugh, but Silas wasn't put off. 'Next thing you know you've got a bit of an itch, eh, Pastor?'

'You do, Silas.'

Silas demonstrated – Mother turning up her nose, Jamy laughing, Ludwig shaking his head, Ignatz staring at the distant glow.

'Then you can't pee, and you go mad. Mad!' Shaking his head, tongue out, babbling. 'Then it gets worse. The sores, eh, Pastor?'

'That's right.'

'And there's no cure. You go blind, and run about naked.'

He gave this sermon twice a year. Generally there was a Bible story – someone who wouldn't listen to advice, coveted his neighbour's wife, laid his seed across the desert. All bad things. 'We did that, eh, Pastor? We taught them.'

'Eternally grateful,' Father said, rocking with the dray, mumbling something.

'What's that?' Mother asked.

But Father was asleep. And within half an hour, Mother too, head on her arm, arm on a box. Ludwig driving, Jamy checking the spare horses, and me, trying to stay awake. No good. So I got down, walked barefoot beside the dray, and Ludwig asked what I was doing. I said it was the only way I could stay awake.

After a time, Father said, 'Put something under my legs, Alma.'

She lifted his knees, filled the space with a jumper. 'Better?'

'Do you remember, Alma? What was it, 1917?'

'What's the point of going back over all that?'

The hills had flattened and there were decent plains, grassy, glowing green and grey in the full moon. Ignatz told me to watch for snakes, but I didn't. Off to our right, to the south, a forest of desert oaks, their needles straining the wind, smelling like the pines of Alster Radweg, me and the other kids running and climbing trees, sap on our hands, licking it, spitting it out. Michael and Alwin and the others were there, waiting for me. All I had to do was run after them, call to them, tell them to wait for me. Charlotte said, 'Where have you been all this time?'

'Teaching the blacks about syphilis.'

'What's that?'

Making my devil face a few inches from hers. 'It sends you mad, and blind, and covers your body with the pox, and you're always in pain, and screaming for help.'

Back on the dray, Mother said to Father, 'They were just protecting themselves.'

'We had naturalisation certificates. We were, we are as Australian as anyone. But that's what you get for giving up your life, your children. That's what you get, Alma.'

'We stopped the pox,' Silas said.

'We didn't.' And to Mother. 'We might have ended up in detention.'

Could I hear them? From the forest? Anton calling for me to hurry and join them. And when I arrived, 'Where have you been all this time?'

'I couldn't help it. Father thought I'd . . . it doesn't matter. Beat you up that tree!'

Oma and Opa calling for us to get down, because what if we fell, what if they had to write to Australia to tell Mother and Father we'd been killed in a forest?

Father wasn't through with regrets. 'The way they treated us that day.'

I remembered 1917. I was nine. We were summoned to Adelaide, three days in a cart, two days in a train, one night in a Grenfell Street hotel, then, the next day, a big room with green curtains, some man observing us like we were baboons. 'So, Pastor Gerlach, which part of Germany are you from?'

'We've been here for twenty-five years. We're naturalised.' Producing the certificates, flattening them on the desk. 'We came to help the black people. Twenty-three years at Hermannsburg, and before that . . .'

But none of this mattered. We were also German, and as this man explained, 'How are we to know your relationship with Germany? Your children live there?'

'Yes, for school. In Leipzig.'

He smiled and said, 'You can see how that complicates things?'

'No.'

'In Germany. You've been there, you're in contact with your parents, your children, and you, Mrs Gerlach, your parents in Breslau?'

Father had asked why it'd taken three years for them to mention this, and the man had said, 'All in good time,' and Father had said, 'You think, perhaps, we are spying for Germany?'

'I didn't say that.'

'How? Where? We live thousands of miles north, the middle of nowhere. What are we spying on? Who? This is . . . illogical.'

Back in the desert, Father said, 'Ungrateful.'

I just dragged my feet and listened.

'They had to do that, Martin.'

'They didn't. They never asked you, did they, Ignatz?'

'There was a letter asking questions, but by the time I returned it, it was all over.'

'Exactly, see,' Father said to Mother. 'What was I doing? Standing outside the army barracks and counting soldiers?'

'Nothing came from it. That's how things work in war time.'

'Stop making excuses for everyone, Alma. If I had my time over I'd stay in Germany, find a village in the mountains, write my sermons and leave it at that. Then I'd be happy.'

'Rubbish.'

'The way he made us write down everyone's name and address. And said they'd be checking. Like we were criminals. But it was us, wasn't it, Silas, up there teaching them, telling them about venereal disease?'

Nine, yes, I must've been nine. Looking up at a Union Jack, an Australian flag, this man saying to me, 'Benjamin, isn't it?'

'Yes.'

'It says here you've been learning German?'

'All of the children learn German,' Father said.

'Do you think that's a good idea, Pastor? With thousands of Australian boys being killed by *your* army?'

'It's not my army. I didn't start the war. I don't agree with it.'

'No?' Suddenly interested.

Mother warned him to keep quiet.

'As a Christian, I don't believe in this slaughter. I don't believe there's any need for it.'

'Despite your Kaiser starting the whole affair?'

'That's not what I mean.' But then he went quiet, guessing the secretary was taking notes.

Before we left they took our photos, and fingerprints. Father was furious, but Mother kept him calm until we were out on the street, and he said, 'That's it, we're going home!' Mother said how, with a war going on? Father, full of fury, pushing people aside, as we followed in his wake. 'I. Will. Not. Return. To. Hermannsburg.'

Back on the dray, Silas said, 'You've done a good job, Pastor. Those kids go blind with the syphilis. But not now. And they can read . . .'

'Some. Some can read.'

Maybe it was seven am, maybe earlier, when Ignatz said, 'This'll do.'

We stopped, and unpacked again, and I made damper and warmed the steak.

The murmuration

The birds stirred as we started again. As we placed the last boxes and stale clothes on the pile that had grown on the dray; as we found our spot (Ludwig driving, Ignatz beside him, Father on his throne between Silas and Mother, Jamy facing west, legs folded); as we lurched past a ruined cottage. A few curlews skimmed the water, rose, disappeared into the scrub. Father said, 'Proof, if it's needed.'

No one asked of what. We knew. The wandering emu, Jesus and his disciples, a collective world-brain that decided everything.

'Did you fill the canteens?' Father asked.

I told him I had, I always did.

'Ignatz, are we on time?'

'Mostly.'

Setting off. Mother had got to Silas with the calamine – cold, wet, sloppy and pink, smeared on like jam, as she told him he should've been more careful. 'And if it gets infected?'

'It won't. She won't let it.'

Father asked what she looked like.

'Like last time,' Silas said. 'All in white. She put out her hand and said I should follow her.'

'Into the fire?'

'*Away* from the fire. She tried to show me the way.'

'She wasn't doing much of a job,' Ignatz said, without looking back.

'I don't know what we should make of it,' Mother said.

'Whatever you want,' Father replied.

'It was the Virgin, was it?' she asked Silas.

He said he didn't know. Just a woman in white and a little boy holding her hand. Ignatz explained there was a tradition of this sort of thing, especially France, but Germany, Romania – no shortage of people having visions. 'Our Lady of Pontmain. The Golden Heart. Of course,' he said, 'people see what they want to see.'

'You shouldn't dismiss it,' I said to him.

He looked back. 'No?'

'If Silas says.'

The curlews returned. Father said it was a marvel. How God had come up with such a clever idea, and all we had to do was sit back and admire the result.

I remembered this country, too. Jack kicking Sharon, Terese telling him to grow up, telling me, 'This is the longest trip ever.'

I think I smiled and said, 'But did you see those budgies?'

'Very good. Budgies. We have one, remember?'

Back at Prospect, in a cage in the sunroom. 'But this is different,' I said.

'Jack, for god sake, stop it!'

Terese was Alma. Both along for the ride, but with deep reservations. And only at times like this did you hear what they were thinking. 'This is okay for you, but kids aren't interested in bulrushes and emu totems.'

'Yes, we are,' Jack said, still kicking his sister.

'Well, behave!'

He sat up and said, 'This place is great, isn't it, Dad?'

'It is.'

'Mum?'

'I would've preferred New Zealand.'

Even then, I could hear Mother. I could see it in her face, hear it in her voice, the way she looked at Father and sighed, horse lips, as loud as possible.

Anyway, the trip along these same banks, the rocks that had been sitting here for billions of years. Stopping, getting out and explaining to the kids, picking up a handful of dirt and letting it run through my fingers.

'You've gotta get the feel of the place.' Crushing a clump of grass, inhaling and saying, 'The smell of it.' Eating a bit. 'The taste of it.'

Terese standing with her arms crossed, Alma-style. 'Go on then, Jack, eat the grass.'

'I'm not a horse.'

'Sharon?'

Like she could make a point. I offered some to Sharon and she tasted it, spat it out and said, 'I have been filled with the spirit of the great emu.' Lifting her arms and flapping them and chasing Jack around the waterhole. Terese saying, 'Next year, Perth.'

Mother had cut Father's pants all the way up to his crotch, flaps of canvas and cotton hanging loose. Now she was rubbing gumbi-gumbi into his legs. Big, puffy watermelons; red and hot, heavy to lift and put down. His feet, especially, full of fluid. Father was cursing her, saying what difference would it make? Ignatz told her Father needed a diuretic; how the blood and lymph and will-to-live couldn't get back to his heart. Like this. Technical. I said to him, 'How does that help?'

'What would you have me do, Benno?'

'We just gotta be patient, don't we, Father?'

'You don't have to call me Father all the time. I'm your *dad*. Isn't that a different thing?'

I shrugged.

'Say Mum and Dad.'

And carefully: 'Dad.'

'Isn't that better? What do you think, Alma?'

'I like Mother.'

'Why?'

'Because I'm his mother.' Shaking her head, rubbing his legs, telling him to stop moving about.

I repeated: '*Dad*.'

'Nice,' he said. 'I always thought' – turning to me – 'I've had a distant relationship with my father, Benno.'

'Opa?'

'I remember the first time I met him,' Mother said. 'Three questions. Your name? Your family? Your church? And I thought, What am I in for?'

'That's what you saw,' Father said. 'But he can be compassionate. You kids have found that, Benno?'

'I remember the time,' Mother said, 'when we went to the theatre, and I looked back and there he was, with his chin whiskers, hands on his big belly' – she patted Father's swollen stomach – 'staring down at us, and I said to you, Martin, Is this what he does all the time? And you said, Mostly.'

'The Lutheran manner,' Father said. 'But there's someone different in there . . . as the kids have discovered.'

We passed another waterhole. Iltiriltutnama was long, deep, dark and promising. I just wanted to jump in, dive to the bottom, no matter how deep. I wanted to sit cross-legged until I ran out of air, and even then, hold onto the last gasp before I came up. I wanted to climb the box gum on the bank, the second, third, fourth branches, dive in, risk a broken neck (as Mother shouted at me to stop being so stupid). But Ignatz said, 'No time to stop.' So we just slowed past, peered at the little fish we could see, and continued.

'That looked nice,' I said, as Mother wiped her hands on a rag and said to Father, 'That'll have to do for now.'

'Say the word,' Father said to me.

'Dad.'

Smiling. 'There, that wasn't so hard. And your mother?'

'Mum.'

'And we must make the other kids . . .' Thinking. 'What time is it, Benno, in Leipzig?'

I knew. I could sense it, to the minute. 'Six twenty.'

'They'd be sitting down to dinner. Charlotte would be looking at the vegetables and saying, I can't eat pumpkin. Julius would be pushing his peas to the side of the plate.' Smiling.

'You'd tell him to eat them, but he never would, would he . . . Dad?'

'No. And veal. He hates veal. I remember him slipping it to Molly. Remember, Benno?'

'We all did. Every time we ate veal, we all gave it to her, and she wouldn't eat her dinner. She had a big belly.'

Father smiled at this thought. 'And then Oma, with dessert,' he said, 'and she's telling Alwin he isn't getting any because he's been . . . doing what, do you reckon, Benno?'

'Playing up. Somehow.'

Leaving the waterhole behind. Looking back, remembering the taste of sago, the freshest donks slowly pulling and Father rocking, smiling in the dappled light as we passed under more box gums. 'Benno, quick, let's write to them,' he said.

'But we don't have any paper.'

'Find it.' Waving his hand.

And eventually I did – under a few books. I found a fresh sheet, flattened it and said, 'To who?'

'*Whom*? All of them. *Greetings from our little dray as we journey towards Horseshoe Bend*.'

'Hold on.' I tried to write. 'Go on.'

'*Let me describe the scene. A single spoonbill, framed against a grey sky*.'

'It's blue,' I said.

'*Grey. Silas lapsing into sleep, Ludwig driving, Ignatz beside him, all of the survivors of a great fire, but I'll tell you about that when I see you soon*.'

'Wait,' I said, but he didn't.

'*I'm on my way to town. A minor medical issue, then we'll set sail, or steam, maybe even fly in an airplane. We'll be in Leipzig by year's end, then we can see you*.'

'You can't say that,' Mother said.

'Why not? It's where we should've been all these years. What's stopping us?'

'Your heart.'

'*The hope is that we can be home for Christmas. With Oma and Opa. And Benno playing up*.'

'You can't say what can't be,' Mother said.

'I can. I will. Benno, write it all down. I've decided. When this is all fixed. I can't even remember their faces. I can't recall Julius . . .'

Then Ungwatja. Twice the size, black in the middle and sandy on the edges. But again, Ignatz said we couldn't afford to stop, and Father agreed: 'We have to keep going, faster. We have to get to Horseshoe Bend. We have to fix my damn body. We have to see them, Alma.'

That's the last he said about it. 'You finish writing to them, Benno. But don't tell them about all this dropsy business. Just say how you and I and Mother can't wait to return.'

His second regret, I guess. It was one thing giving up other people's kids, but another of your own. I had no intention of finishing his letter. I folded it and put it in my pocket.

The last of Ungwatja. Narrowing to the remains of an ancient river, a scattered forest of white cypress spreading rheumatic arms across the water, dropping leaves, insect trails in fleshy, white wood, like someone was trying to explain what had happened here. To me, and my wife, and kids, Sharon saying, 'There are no fish here, are there, Dad?'

'Plenty.'

She peered in and said, 'I can't see any.'

'You're not looking hard enough.' Standing beside her, pointing. 'There.'

'Where?'

Jack just moving his line, gently, like he was holding the reins.

'There. See.'

'How could fish get into a waterhole? That doesn't make sense. It's not the sea.'

'It's connected to a river, idiot,' Jack said.

'Jack!' Terese.

'If there's fish, why can't you catch them?'

'Cos you're talking too much.'

Slowly, slowly, my children coming to understand all things happen, eventually, Sharon saying, 'What type of fish?'

'Sharks,' Jack said, grinning.

'Get lost, Jack.'

'The inner-Australian snuff-gobbler,' I said.

'That's not a fish.'

'Yes, it is.' Pushing her in, jumping in after her, Jack trying to save his line from the chaos, Terese shouting that we were all idiots.

Towards Idracowra

We stopped for lunch under box gums, canopies touching, offering shade. The birds were quiet. Just Mother, returning from a waterhole, hanging three of Father's freshly-washed handkerchiefs on a branch and saying, 'That'll have to do.'

She valued handkerchiefs. Especially in winter, when she'd boil dozens in a copper pot, hang them on the line to dry, gather them in, tell Pauline to iron them. But now she sat, poked the fire, started eating chalky damper and drinking rusty tea. In the near distance, Ludwig stood between us and thirty, maybe more shorthorns. 'All bones,' he said, watching them.

Father sat forward, coughed, and Mother patted him on the back. 'Clear it out.' He worked his ribs and diaphragm, spat and sucked and tried to get a lungful of air. We sat watching, feeling our little bit of hope dissolving.

The cattle had been left out to fatten, although there was hardly any grass. They just sniffed about, found what they could, came over to our small camp to investigate, and Ludwig told them to go away. Ignatz said, 'If that's the best they've got.'

They. Idracowra. But I knew they had better country.

'Plenty of cattle,' Father said, clearing his throat and spitting. 'Place that size . . . plenty, haven't they, Silas?'

'Plenty, Pastor.'

'No trouble making money.'

'No.'

Ludwig slapped a steer on the flank and it jumped, looked back in defiance. 'What, d'yer wanna bitta damper?' He offered some, the animal took a few steps, sniffed, returned to the grass.

'Always thought this was a nice spot,' Father said, reclining against a tree, holding his last clean handkerchief to his mouth, coughing again. 'Then you end up with some sort of infection.'

'You're fine,' Mother said.

'That's what finishes people.' He checked his mucus. 'I could always tell, the moment they came in – the old fellas, their wives – I could tell by their ribs, sucked in like . . .'

'You'll be fine,' Ignatz said, eating. 'No point worrying about what hasn't happened.'

'Exactly,' Mother said.

'Just saying . . . you could tell.'

'Most of them came good,' Mother said.

'Some.'

I knew he'd been in the hospital (years before Sarah), helping Mother lay sick blacks on stretchers, giving them whatever might help, but mostly, didn't. I remember. On top of everything else, Father had been a nurse, a doctor, a cleaner, an arse wiper. What we need to consider, when we think about the missionaries. They did everything. Father looked at some old bloke with bubbling lungs and said, 'Try taking deep breaths.' I remember standing at the door, watching these people struggling, arching their backs, clawing at their beds, shouting names, before settling. Father covered them and told Ludwig to get the family. Six, seven people arrived, the body was brought out on a stretcher. That's what my parents did. That's what civilisation meant to them (despite us having brought the bugs).

But now it was Father's turn. I remember sitting with the damper I couldn't eat – no hunger, no thirst, no concern for anything except his coughing, the hope he might stop, come good, get up and walk around. His swollen gut, the way he had to sit upright to breathe. Even then, struggling, sweat on his face, and this look of helplessness. Like he wanted

Oma to come in, kiss him on the forehead, stroke his face, and send him to sleep.

An old heifer appeared a few inches from my face. I pushed her away. 'Get your own lunch.'

Father panted, smiled across at me.

That autumn, 1957, there'd been cattle. The last of them. Walking around Hermannsburg, in and out of the old yards, Jack saying, 'They don't look so good.'

'No one's looking after them anymore,' I said to him, as we toured the compound.

All ribs, sharp shoulders, and no one had tailed or castrated them. Worthless rubbish cattle waiting to die, heavy heads and matted tails. Sharon said, 'Maybe someone should shoot them and eat them.'

'I don't think anyone could be bothered.'

I remember waving to Pauline, on the porch, in an apron. I remember Jack saying, 'This place is pretty shit.'

'Now . . . but it was different in our day. The roof there, we put that on, those out-buildings, Ignatz's place' – indicating the main buildings coming off the compound. 'The sewing shed, gone, the dorms, those water tanks caved in.'

'I thought what you meant,' Sharon said, 'was that you grew up on some big station, like a ranch in Texas.'

Pauline had gone in and we'd continued, back to the old iron and bed-frame camp that had grown up between the deserted cottages. The few people, some still in their white dresses, their calico pants, kids running about in a mess of empty bottles, bones and good intentions. One woman said, 'Benno!'

I wasn't sure who she was. But she looked familiar. I said, 'How have you been?'

She said, 'Long time, eh?'

Her husband, or some old bloke she was with, showed me a bad watercolour and asked if I wanted to buy it, but I just said, 'Been a long time.'

'He's gone for years,' she said. 'Sleeping.' And she demonstrated, and laughed, and said, 'Long time now.'

'Really?' Although I had no idea who.

'Seventeen years.' She checked with her bloke, who said yes, but he asked me again, maybe two pounds, one, whatever you've got.

'That one,' the woman said, indicating a tree.

'That tree?' I said.

As it slowly returned. Jamy's mother sitting in the same spot, telling me I should watch her son, make sure the others treated him properly. 'No good in school,' she said, with an angry face. 'No good. But you, Benno . . .'

How had she remembered me?

'That tree,' she said again. A big river red, with low-hanging branches. The same picture this man had painted. Not once, but over and over.

'That's where he did it,' she said.

'Who . . . Jamy?'

She smiled. 'Yeah, Jamy, that's where he did it. That teacher, he was a rotter, wasn't he, Benno?'

'He was.'

She slowed, and stopped, and I gave the man a pound for his painting, and gave it to Jack and said, 'I'll explain, later.'

Back beside the Finke, Father coughed again. Mother supported him, reminded him of big breaths, although how the hell was he meant to take any kind of breath? I was terrified. That we were close to some ending, and I'd have to face it.

Some idea, perhaps. As the bodies were removed from what we called a hospital, and the women flung themselves down in the dirt and screamed and punched the ground. Me, this kid, seeing it all. For all the talk; for all the plans; for all the consolations and she'll be fine, as long as we keep moving; for all the explanations and diagnoses from Father's book; for all my *dad's* looks, the way he (uncharacteristically) touched my hand – there was, in the end, no due preparation. No one I could reach out and touch, confide in, seek consolation from; no one who could say, Well, let me explain.

Coughing, again, all of us sitting, concerned, Ignatz saying, 'Get it all up, Pastor,' and Jamy saying, 'Get rid of the muck.' Father looked at me and Mother and Silas with child eyes. He checked his handkerchief again, showed Mother, but I could see, we could all see the blood. Mother said, 'That'll clear up, later.'

'I gotta go to the toilet,' I said, and walked towards a stand of old trees, into the shade, darker and darker, until it was night in the collective canopy. I looked back. I could see them. I moved. I squatted, closed my eyes. '"The Lord is my shepherd I shall not want . . ."'

Then Ludwig was there, and he said, 'You alright?'

'Fine.'

He squatted beside me. 'You come back, for your dad, see?'

'Yeah . . . I know.'

'Cos it's time, Benno.'

'What is?'

He thought and said, 'Twenty years before you were born, before I'm married by the pastor, before Oskar, any of that . . .'

'What?'

'I'm out hunting, and Dietrick, you know Dietrick?'

'I've heard of him.'

'He comes along with his horse and gun and Remington, and he says, You're the one, eh?'

I just waited.

'The horses,' he said. 'You know what I mean. And he calls me all these names. Black bastard. Like that. Then he raises his rifle and says, We've got laws about that sort of thing. I say, I didn't take no horses, and he says, You're a lying bastard, too. And he was ready to shoot me.'

'What happened?'

'Remington says, Go on, shoot the filthy bastard, and Dietrick laughs, then your dad comes out of the bush doing up his fly. Plain as day, he says, So, what's going on here? You've already had the trial, Dietrick? Then Dietrick lowers his gun and says, I reckon he's the one, Pastor Gerlach. The pastor says, I reckon he's not. We're headed for Idracowra. Old

Blake, remember him? Apparently he's nearly dead, and he wants me to introduce him to God. And I say, Last rites, eh, Pastor? And ingkata says, Yes, that's right, Ludwig. Last rites. And we've been riding, haven't we, Ludwig, for four days, and we're pretty hungry and thirsty and tired, and I can't see how, Constable, me or Ludwig or any mad bastard could've stolen anyone's horses.'

By now I'd forgotten what was going on under the gums.

'So your dad says we're off, and we got on our horses, and we say goodbye to Dietrick, and the pastor says, You might ask a person first, Constable. Then we rode off, and we talked about that day for years.'

It wasn't the first time I'd heard the story. There were other versions, tailored for other times, but this one worked for now. I knew it was true, mostly, because when Father listened he never corrected any of Ludwig's facts. Even if they were different from last time.

'What I'm saying,' Ludwig said, 'is that it's time, eh?'

I listened, and I said, 'Has he stopped coughing?'

'For now,' he said, 'but he'll start again.'

'I guess.'

'He saved my life, Benno. And years later, Oskar saved yours (bloody idiot, jumping into that waterhole). So I'd say it's even.'

'I reckon. But the blood . . . that can't be good,' I said.

When we went back, Father said, 'I'm fine, Benno.' Folding the handkerchief, stuffing it in his pocket. 'A bug, isn't it, Alma?'

'Yes. It is. A bug, Benno.'

'Come on,' Father said. 'No point hanging around here. Let's get to Idracowra.' Trying to push himself up against the tree. 'Benno?'

Me on one side, Jamy on the other, raising him from the ground, leading him towards the dray, as he said, 'Easy to knock a bug on the head. You can't worry about a bit of a cough, Benno.'

'I know.'

'I'm a tough old bastard, aren't I? Haven't I got through worse, Alma? A pick through my foot, but that didn't stop me, did it?'

'When did that happen?'

'After Alwin, before you came along. Compared to that, bit of a puffy leg, eh, Ludwig?'

'Too right.'

Maybe he convinced me, maybe he didn't. I can't remember. But I knew we had to keep going, move slowly, on the dray the blacks had built for us.

Ignatz Beck

'Because we should,' I said to Terese.

'We haven't got that sort of money.'

'Soon . . . when I'm Level Two.'

She smiled and said, 'You'd make more lecturing.' She stroked her belly (a habit she'd had since the beginning) and lifted herself by pushing against a tree. 'I need to pee.'

'There are places at Prospect,' I called, as she walked off.

I sat poking the fire, feeding sticks into the flames, imagining the house I'd seen in the brochure – the generous living room, three bedrooms, a carport and a big shed to store Father's boxes. 'It's a good area,' I called.

It was 1936. My second trip north as a newly-minted patrol officer (a degree in Classics, a near-native grasp of Aranda, and the only person who'd applied for the job). Terese, young and beautiful and smart, a foil for my sarcasm, my complaining, my bitter view of the world – my new wife, four months pregnant, calling, 'Benno . . .'

'What?'

No reply.

My reluctant wife. Asking why I had to work in the middle of nowhere when I could get a perfectly good job tutoring at Adelaide University; why I'd want to leave her, and the boy; why I wanted to make life difficult, when all she wanted was for us to be together. The average conversation running something like, 'No place to live.'

'Plenty of places – billions, under the stars, along the Finke – who'd wanna be anywhere else?'

'No place to buy food.'

'If you know where to look . . .'

'Stuck out there, isolated, with *those* people.'

'What people?'

At which point I'd remind her of my fourteen years living at Hermannsburg, of Ludwig and Oskar and Silas and Jamy, and she'd say, 'Yes, I know all that' (I'd told her many, many times) 'but all I'm saying is when the boy comes along *he'll* need you, Benno.'

Trying to explain, again, this force pulling me back to the desert. 'I think it's . . . unfinished business.'

'Your father's business?'

'No. I *want* to go, I *want* to continue . . . you get it, don't you?'

'You're just like him.'

'You're just like your mother.'

'No, I mean it, you're just like him.'

I wasn't sure how I should take this. It was a veiled criticism, but at the time . . . and she was pregnant and beautiful and wanted to live with me in the Prospect IV for the rest of my (when-I'm-home-from-the-desert) life.

A whimper, a cry, and I went running. Through the grass, a few saplings, the ruins of an outstation we'd been using as a toilet. And Terese, squatting, holding her hand up to me – blood dripping between her fingers, down her legs. I took a few steps, squatted beside her and said, 'What should we do?'

She said (I remember this clearly), 'Well, it's not like we can get to a hospital, is it?'

Putting this together with Father, the trip to Horseshoe Bend, the regrets that we (Mother, Father, mostly) had ended up in the middle of nowhere, far from people, hospitals, help – and somehow, we were paying the price. Over and over.

'Wait.' I ran back to our car, sorted through the clothes, found a towel and returned and said, 'If we can stop the bleeding . . .'

She wiped her legs, sat back on the rubble and said, 'That's the end of that.'

'No.'

I sat beside her, avoiding the blood, dry, pink and brown on her legs and the rocks and in the dirt. 'We can try and drive to . . .'

By then I worked it out. How she was crying, her head hanging low, turning and punching me and saying, 'Do you still think this was a good idea?'

It was no time to defend myself – just to sit and take whatever she had. Maybe she was right. Maybe I was selfish. Leading from that outstation, to Prospect, to Jack and Sharon and me packing my bags. See, I'm not beyond self-reflection or criticism. That I gave too much to the desert, its people, when I should've been home making porridge.

Now (14 October 1922), I walked through the bush towards the same outstation, into a room with its boards intact, a rough canvas curtain someone had strung up to keep out the heat, the flies. And on the window ledge, a jam tin with a picture of a plum, still glowing in the bit of moonlight.

'Watch for snakes!' Mother called.

'For Christ's sake.' I kicked stones, a few crumbling bricks, a doll's head. Kneeling, I searched for the body, arms, legs, then studied her porcelain grin, red cheeks, and hair that had frizzed, electrically, like Shock-Headed Peter. Oma gathering us in her bedroom (in our night clothes) and reading the story of the inky boys. Edward teasing the African (although, to me, one of Father's blacks) with the green umbrella. As he (Oma read) '"kept on singing – only think! – Oh Blacky, you're as black as ink!"'

There was a moral, of course. Dr Hoffmann always had a moral. Agrippa gathering the bullies and dunking them in a pot of Indian ink, like this was the worst punishment any boy might suffer. Running around, for the rest of his life, being teased.

Oma said (something like) let that be a lesson to you all.

Julius asked, 'Why?'

'If people are different you should never tease them.' Although, years later, I'd discover the irony of this – but that's another story.

Charlotte said, 'Even Torsten?'

'Who's he?'

'He's retarded,' Alwin explained.

Oma thought for a moment, but returned to Peter's next adventure. I said, 'They're a bit like Father's blacks, aren't they, Oma?'

'I suppose they are.'

'Maybe that's how black people are made?' Smiling, as the other kids laughed, and she looked like she was about to slap me.

I went into the room where, fourteen years later, Terese and I would lose our first son (we'd already bought his clothes, his bedding, his cot). I gazed out of the window at the distant lights and campfires of Idracowra. Reassuring, somehow. It wasn't like we were in the middle of the Sahara, or Great Sandy Desert. As I pissed I imagined the blacks, the singing, the smell of damper, the taste of what passed for civilisation. Then I heard footsteps – through the bush, into the front room, Ignatz unzipping and saying, 'That you, Benno?'

Waiting, as I wondered what he was doing.

'I was going to have a quick word about Jamy.'

My waterworks had frozen, but I just stood listening to him pissing against a wall.

'He's just a child, isn't he? You know, mentally.'

As the stream stopped, a moment passed, and he came in and said, 'All done?'

'I better get back.'

'One minute.' He put out a hand, stopped me, sat on a pile of rubble. 'You understand, Benno, don't you, that the blacks are different? The only stone age people left in the world. Even the Africans have some sort of civilisation, but our blacks . . .'

'What?'

'I know what your father says, but here's a people without writing, culture, who haven't managed to cultivate food, selective breeding . . . *stone age*. Which is why we must help them.'

Mother called again. I wondered what Ignatz Beck wanted from me. He said, 'Really, they're just one rung up from the apes.'

'That's not fair.'

'But it's true.' Smiling. 'They reckon they've been here forty thousand years, but what's there to show for it? And us, a hundred or so, and look' – indicating the half-ruin.

'I gotta make tea.'

But he stopped me again and said, 'So, Jamy, seeing how he's slow . . .'

I tried to move, but by now he was holding my shirt.

'Compared to someone . . . like you.'

I waited. I said, 'I saw.'

'I was helping him. He was having trouble. They're not the same as us, Benno.'

It made sense. The colouring-in, the simple sums, the way he lined kids up and inspected their hands, the way he said, 'Who's shit themselves?' Checking pants, finding the culprit and calling him disgusting.

'Well, if you hate them so much . . .'

'I didn't say I hate them. I said they're different. They can't do things, mentally. They can't see things like we do. They *misinterpret*, Benno.'

I said, 'Let go.' And he did. I said, 'Oskar's as smart me. And Jamy might be . . .' Maybe I was listening to Oma, studying the pictures of the inky boys. Maybe I was working it out for myself. Maybe I was sitting at my bedroom window watching the men dance, trying to figure out how they were different from Oma and Opa, practising a waltz in their sitting room.

'All I'm saying,' Ignatz said, 'is they're not reliable. And anyway, we have to stick together, don't we?' He put out his hand to shake. 'You and me, Benno. You're the special one, aren't you?'

'No.'

'Your father's always saying you are.'

'So?'

'All this time, I've only been teaching *you*.'

'Not just me.'

'I've been trying to civilise them, Benno. What's right, what's wrong, how to keep clean, write their name, add a few numbers, not to steal, because we can't have the girls stealing from the stations, can we?'

I stormed out, crushing the porcelain head as I went. I walked through the saplings, and Father was struggling towards me. 'Where have you been?'

I said, 'He reckons the blacks are apes.'

Father continued through the grass towards Ignatz. I returned to the camp we'd set up, sat on the ground, knees up, head down, although I kept glancing up, watching Father and Ignatz talk, then Father shout something. Mother said, 'What's that all about?'

'Nothing.'

'Lot of noise about nothing.' Calling: 'Martin, come and sit down.'

Jamy watching, Ludwig, and Silas saying, 'Ignatz, is it?'

'Yes.'

'What'd he say?'

I didn't want to tell them. Couldn't. Father shouted, 'What gives you the right?' Ignatz said something about advice, and Benno should understand, Martin. Then Ignatz walked off towards the lights of Idracowra. Father just watched him go. Didn't say a word. Wobbled about a bit, then headed back to camp. As he attempted to settle on his throne (Jamy and Ludwig had set him up beside the fire) he said, 'Second biggest regret.'

'What?' Mother said.

'If I'd had any choice . . . it all gets back to the Board, doesn't it, Alma?'

'It does.'

As we all watched Ignatz go, using his hand to fell the long grass.

'What did he say?' Father asked me.

'That as long as they could add up . . .' And to Jamy. 'You okay?'

He raised his head. He tried to smile, but then said, 'Maybe he gets lost?'

'We can only hope,' Father said, wiping his forehead with his handkerchief, coughing up more blood, spitting it into the dirt. As it sat there, looking back at me, as Terese said, 'I don't want any more of this, Benno.'

'But we agreed I'd take the job.'

'Get another one.'

That didn't happen. I was in the desert for another twenty years. I always regretted it. I always felt bad, kids at home, wondering if I was any better than Martin and Alma, depositing their children in Leipzig.

Anyway, that's what happened, six miles from Idracowra. 1922 and 1936. The same thing repeating, over and over.

The Harmstorfs

Six miles in the dusk, then dark, a track leading down a hill, across a valley full of cattle, closer to the house lights, the campfires, men shouting and singing as I tried to stay awake. The donkeys pulled dutifully, although Number Three (as Jamy had named her) had a sore on her shoulder, weeping, aggravated by the harness. Rocking, drifting off, *Daisy, Daisy, give me your answer do*, a didgeridoo (destined for Tom's show and tell), Mother asking Father how he was, perfectly fine, stop asking, Alma. She said, 'I remember you riding here, when his first wife was sick, but you didn't arrive in time, did you?'

'But I helped bury her.'

Something about this rhythm. Something about the thought, making its way into my head like an earworm. Something about the Harmstorf's daughter, twelve or thirteen when I'd last seen her. But I gave up on whoever she was, how old she was, and thought of Elsie. I looked into the sewing shed, and inside, twelve Singers lined up in four rows of three, eleven girls on wooden stools pumping their pedals, threading their needles, running garments over the strike-plate, as Mother (standing at the front) said, 'A is for Admiration. Has everyone got that?'

Walking around, checking they'd sewn A in the way she'd taught them, stopping and correcting some girl, making her unpick the mess. I said to Mother, 'Molly reckons Elsie should come home.'

'. . . *says* she should come home.'

Shrugging.

'Well, she's busy, so tell her she can't. Girls: B is for Benevolence.'

'She said.'

'Why?'

'Your grannie's sick, Elsie.'

And Elsie: 'I better go then.'

No one was sick, and Elsie wasn't wanted, but that didn't matter. Both of us, half an hour later, walking around Manangananga, Elsie saying, 'Your Mumma's gonna get you.'

'Don't worry about her. You wanna swim?'

'Okay.'

She was off in the reeds, removing her dress, saying I shouldn't look, and wasn't I coming in? 'Okay, I guess.' Although I didn't need any reeds. Shoes, socks, pants, shirt, all in the dirt, standing in my underpants, watching, as she slipped in (her sewing dress blowing in the breeze), one foot, the other, calf then leg then panties, all wet. She said, 'You shouldn't have lied to your Mumma.'

'She won't know.' Walking into the water – hips, belly, chest.

'She'll check.'

'Do you care?' Now, a few inches away, and the rest, I guess, I've invented. Holding her tightly, putting my lips on hers, then the tongue (Oskar had told me about it). One thing leading to another. Wandering hands, and her saying, 'We can't do none of that.'

'Why?'

'You're just a kid.'

'I'm thirteen. All my bits work.'

Back on the dray, Mother stood and called to the local blacks. 'You men go tell the boss we're coming.' A few of them ran up the hill, shouting. I tried to get back to Elsie, to the waterhole, to our swim, but I couldn't. Half-delirious, Father said, 'Wasn't Allen the head of the Roman guard, Silas?'

'Nah. He never was.'

'I remember. Didn't his sister have a shop in town selling, what was it . . . she was a hairdresser?'

'There was no hairdresser,' Mother said. 'He doesn't have a sister.'

Anyway, it got worse. Because as we arrived, as we tackled the big turn-around, as the donkeys stopped and spat phlegm, as Allen Harmstorf's kids came out, I thought, *Damn*. There was the daughter, fourteen or fifteen, a long giraffe neck, a hard face with pimples, wire-framed glasses. Perhaps the dim oil lamps burning on the porch? But as we stopped, got down, I could see that she was no Elsie. There wouldn't be any love, imagined or otherwise, beside the dam tonight. Long arms that seemed to reach the ground, dressed in what might've been a curtain. But she smiled at me. I noticed her brother, Kurt, and waved.

It didn't take long to get organised. Allen Harmstorf (with his infamous chin whiskers) came out, stood with his hands on his hips and called for the blacks to unharness the donkeys, take them and the spares to the long paddock. Trish, his second wife, stood with a flyswat in her hand and said, 'We got scones on. You want scones?'

'That'd be a treat,' Mother said, climbing down, gathering her dress, awkwardly hugging the farmer's wife. 'After what we've been eating these last few days.'

What did that mean? I'd been working my arse off – for everyone, every day, without resorting to fly biscuits. But no, that'll do, Mother: *after what we've been eating*. I said, 'I did a good stew, didn't I?' But she just ignored me.

Silas sat on the porch, and Gale, the Frankenstein daughter, said to him, 'You Blind Silas?'

Her mother told her not to be so rude. Allen was busy helping Father, the last few steps, across the rough porch, and inside.

I waited. Kurt said to me: 'Your dad pretty crook, is he?'

'Yes.'

Gale turned and said, 'You oughta hear what they been saying.'

'Who?' I said. About what? What an enormous disappointment.

'About your dad. That he's gonna die.'

'Gale!' Kurt.

'He is not,' I said. 'Who said that?'

Inside, the adults knocked over chairs, made small talk. I heard Mother saying, 'This is all very civilised,' and Allen: 'Nothing the doctor can't fix, quick smart, eh, Martin?'

Gale warmed quickly. 'I got the scones on when I heard.' She took my arm, dragged me inside, pulled up a chair and told me to sit. 'Last time I saw you, Benno, you were this tall.' Indicating.

'No, it was only twelve months ago,' her mother said.

'But he was a little thing.'

'Not that little.'

Gale went out to the kitchen. Kurt sat next to me and said, 'We've got plenty of calves this year.'

'Really?'

'Considering how dry it's been, hasn't it, Dad?'

But Allen Harmstorf waved him away, leaned towards Father and said, 'When I heard you were coming . . . but I guess there was no choice, was there?'

Mother took over. She explained how, at first, she hadn't agreed with coming; then, when things got worse, saw the necessity; how it'd been a hard slog, and we were all tired. A collection of woodfired aphorisms and niceties. She said how Bob and Alf had given us donkeys, but they were past it, too, so maybe if we could just rest in the morning? A day?

Trish said, 'What about Ignatz?'

Everyone fell silent.

'He was at the doorstep, an hour ago, saying he came ahead.'

Mother turned to Father, who said, 'Where is he?'

'On the back porch, with Ted.'

Mother started again. What Ignatz had said to me, the argument with Father, the tantrum. 'All this time, you know, people's patience has been tested.'

This was interrupted by Gale, the scones, the jam they'd made from strawberries growing in their backyard. Gale sat beside me and asked if I'd seen Elsie and Ettie lately. I told her, back at Henbury, and she told me they were horrors. But that was what happened when you had one of each.

'One of each what?'

She wouldn't say.

Allen Harmstorf said grace, asked the Lord to bless our scones, our journey towards Horseshoe Bend, Father and Silas and the boy (me). Then we ate. After a few minutes, Ignatz came in from the back porch. 'I didn't know we'd started.' He sat at the far end of the table. 'I've been doing the sums, Martin.'

Who glared at him, struggled with a scone, crumbling down his front, cream all over his mouth (as Mother wiped it).

'If we can start early?'

'No, we can't,' Mother said. 'We need to rest.'

'Quicker we're off.'

He looked at me, but I avoided him. He asked if I was okay. He said when you put a group of people together everyone has to try their best to get along. I said *I* tried.

'But there are limits to that, aren't there?' Allen Harmstorf said to Ignatz.

Allen was a big man – across the front, a sort of Goodyear belly and sumo wrestler boobs, a giblet effect on his neck and bloodhound cheeks. He had tanned arms, covered in a forest of white hair. 'Been plenty of dramas, Herr Beck?'

Piling on the jam, Ignatz said, 'How's that?' Glancing at me.

'You people got to stick together, I reckon.' But he left it at that. 'That's a disgrace about the Board, Martin.'

'I wrote to them.'

'So did I.' He took a letter from his pocket, flattened it on the table and read: '"Written on behalf of Pastor Martin Gerlach."' Explaining how, at this very moment, he was busy helping the Gerlach family, on route to Horseshoe Bend. How, as an elder of the Lutheran Church, he found it unacceptable that Pastor Gerlach should be treated like this.

Ignatz stared at me and I said, 'What?'

'You feeling better?' he asked.

'"I know for a fact that funds are available and several cars are already in use in Adelaide. If the church expects good people to minister to the natives then maybe it should stop and think."' He said how this would be taken further, once things had settled. When the pastor was home or (who could blame him?) on his way to Germany to see his children.

By the time we'd finished, by the time I helped Gale clean up, wash the dishes, it was after ten. Mother and Father were given the Harmstorf's bedroom, and Allen and Trish slept in their daughter's room. Me, Jamy and Ludwig unrolled our swags and settled on the front porch. It was too hard, and I went down into the garden, between a few roses Mrs H. kept watered. Some *californica* Mother had given her years before. Ignatz swung on a chair, hitched to the other side of the porch. He said he'd sleep there. Kurt pulled a mattress from his room, dragged it beside my swag, and said he preferred it under the stars.

The place settled. The lamps ran out of oil and died. A single candle from the Harmstorf's room made shadows across the porch, the front garden, the rosemary and canna lilies that survived in the sand. And somewhere, mock orange, taking me back to our own back porch, Mother standing saying, 'You made a decision. He did, didn't he, Martin?'

'I guess. But that's the sort of stupid thing you do at thirteen.'

'Stop making excuses for him. He' – returning to me – 'made a decision to lie to me, to your own mother.'

C is for Carnations, but it was too late now, the twelfth girl having arrived just after me and Elsie had left, telling Mother no one had asked for anyone.

'What have you got to say for yourself, Benno?'

'Sorry.'

'And what did you get up to?'

I shrugged.

'Stop lying!'

I thought about it. There was no use. D was not for dahlias. Father looked at me like he wanted to understand, but couldn't.

'We went for a swim.'

'Why?'

'To cool down.'

'You like her?'

'I guess. I thought, since it's hot . . .'

'You'd make up some story?'

'No . . . I didn't mean to . . .'

Mother said to Father, 'What are you going to do?'

He just said, 'You shouldn't lie, Benno.'

'Is that it? Punish him. He lied to me.'

'Benno?' Thinking for a moment. 'No dinner tonight.'

She wasn't happy. She went in, returned with a wooden spoon, handed it to Father and said, 'Go on.'

It looked nasty. But Father put it down and said, 'Reason is preferable.'

'*Reason*?' She shook her head, said (something like), 'This is pathetic,' and went inside. Father said, 'Sit down.'

I did as I was told.

'By doing . . . *that*, you put your needs before anyone else, didn't you?'

'Yes.'

'Can *I* afford to do that?'

'You should. More often. We should just pack up, go back to Leipzig.'

'And who'd take over?'

'You can't worry about other people *all* the time. Or else you'll end up . . .'

'What?'

Taking a moment. Choosing my words carefully. 'Stuck here forever.'

Father thought for a moment then said, 'You best go in to bed.'

'But it's only four.'

Ending like this, as I lay smelling the mock orange on the Harmstorf's porch, hearing my father say, 'Then there's the account in Leipzig.'

'Martin . . .'

'I think there's two thousand in it. But leave it there and maybe . . . what'd be best is some sort of trust fund for the children, to finish school and go to university. But only if they'd like. Benno, especially. I have no doubt he will. The question is,' he said, 'how much the Board will think a life's worth.'

Mother was silent. She did this when she sensed there was no use arguing.

'Enough, I'd hope, to settle a mortgage.'

'Get to sleep.'

'What's the point? I haven't slept for two days.'

'I'll get you some more laudanum.'

'I've had enough.'

Then Kurt leaned over and whispered, 'What's laudanum?'

'It helps him sleep.'

Father said, 'I'd like Benno to keep all the notes. He can have my desk, too. Charlotte can have the dresser, if it's worth anything.'

A few hours after the incident at the waterhole, Father had come into my room, sat beside me and said, 'A small, short tail. Yellowish-green. Mottled brown and black. It'll only fly when it really has to, when it's in danger.'

'The parrot?'

'*Pezoporus occidentalis*. Although there was some debate, at the beginning. Gould suggested it was a ground parrot. But it wasn't. It isn't. It's something special. Highly secretive. It hides in the spinifex, never goes far from water. Has this strange whistle.' He tried to demonstrate. Mother called out, asking what he was doing, but he tried again. 'Or a more drawn out whistle, like this.' A long, slow sound. 'A contact whistle . . . when it's trying to find another night parrot. In the dark. All alone. A bit like us, eh, Benno?' He smiled. 'Dozens of ornithologists are looking for one, but they always turn out to be a zebra finch, corella, something . . . So maybe they don't even exist.'

'I reckon they do.'

'Why?'

'They have to.'

Now, back at Idracowra, he tried the calls again. Out of the bedroom, across the yard. Ding-dong. Then louder, longer, sweeter. 'That's the night parrot,' I said.

'No such thing,' Kurt said.

Sunday 15 October (Day 6)

The next morning, Father stayed in bed. Me, Kurt, Gale, the strange mother and Allen Harmstorf around the table, Ignatz, Jamy, Ludwig and Silas, all crowded into the dining room – Mother calling, 'Would you like some bacon, Martin?'

'No.'

'How about an egg?' Trish asked. 'That can't hurt.'

'I'm not hungry.'

And Mother: 'You've got to eat.' Sitting forward, whispering, 'He's barely had a thing in days.'

Allen Harmstorf was having none of it. It didn't matter how sick you were, you ate. So he took his own meal, went into his bedroom and said, 'Maybe you should try, Pastor?'

'Just makes me feel ill.'

Then he must have sat beside Father, and tried to talk him into it, because Mother leaned forward again (so we kids wouldn't hear) and said to Trish, 'This is what I was worried about.'

'What?'

'Him getting sick along the way.'

'We're nearly there,' I said to her.

'Much further,' she said to me. 'If we'd stayed, and had the opportunity . . . all this travel has probably set him off.'

'It's the illness,' Ignatz said. 'The journey doesn't matter. It's still' – he dropped his voice – 'our best chance.'

Mother whispered to Trish: 'Yesterday he thought he was' – looking around to scare us off – 'he thought it was last century and he was in the snow with his brother and he was saying the paths were blocked and they couldn't get home and his parents would be out searching and they'd thrash them.'

'He was confused?'

'More than that. He didn't know where he was . . . or who he was.'

'That happens sometimes,' I said.

'When? When does it happen?' Mother asked.

She'd had enough of me, so she just mouthed a few words to Trish. She checked we weren't listening, continued, and I said, 'I can't see how that helps.'

'What?'

'When I do that, you say it's rude.'

So she sat up, and again, to Trish, 'Maybe I'm reading too much into it?'

Then Father called, 'Everyone's very quiet.'

All of us sitting eating our eggs and bacon, sometimes a comment, but mainly just silence.

Trish didn't like it at all. 'Gale, go get your dress.'

'Do I have to?'

'Go on.'

So Gale left the room, and Trish said, 'She's good with a needle, Alma. Cosa what you taught her.'

Gale returned, said to her mother, 'This is embarrassing,' but was put in her place. So she held up a dress, we admired it, and Ignatz said, 'Fine craftmanship.' Her mother made her show everyone, let us feel the fabric, admire the stitchwork, the embroidered collar. Trish said, 'She's been working on that for months, haven't you, Gale?'

'I suppose.'

'No supposing. You have. And there are others. She's made a nice jacket for the cold, not that we get much of a chance to wear jackets out here.'

A light cotton dress with edelweiss motifs, like we were in Bavaria. Silas reached out, rubbed the fabric between his fingers, smelt it, said he could just imagine; Jamy, telling her she was clever; Ludwig asking if he could try it on, Mother telling him to stop being silly; and Kurt, saying it was stupid making things you couldn't wear. Gale just scowled at him. 'That's not the point.'

'Yes, it is. Why make something—'

And from the bedroom, Allen Harmstorf: 'Kurt, enough of that.'

I felt it. It was just a dress. If that's all you had to show for sitting around all day. But I said, 'You must have a steady hand.'

And she glowed, like I'd proposed marriage. 'The more you do it the better you get.'

Allen agreed – appearing from his room with the uneaten food, admiring the dress and saying, 'She's pretty clever, isn't she, this girl?' Putting his arm around her and kissing her on the head. As Father called, 'Alma?'

And she went in to him.

But Gale had more. She went back to her room, returned with a few dolls, told us their names, their family history, handed them around. 'This one' – showing us a golliwog – 'would eat scones all day if you let him.'

Kurt stopped himself from laughing.

'Kurt!' his mother growled.

'Last week he went to Capri, in France,' Gale said, waving him about, his head half off. 'He went with Dolly, she's in my room, and they spent the week on the beach sunbathing.'

'Is that why he's black?' Kurt asked her.

'Don't be smart. And next week they're both going to Perth for a few days.'

Silence. As we all thought the same thing. Although not Allen. He said, 'Each one. Hand-sewn. Marvellous what she can do.'

Kurt grinned at me again.

The next few minutes – porcelain dolls, rag dolls, tin dolls, man, woman and child, an array of hand-stitched clothing and an explanation of how her bubbas liked to go on holiday, because it was a bit tedious, wasn't it, Mumma, being at Idracowra all day with nothing to do. I felt like asking the obvious question. But Mother was glaring at me.

'Show Pastor Gerlach,' Trish said to her, and she took her dolls into the bedroom, and we listened as she started explaining to Father. Mother said, 'She's growing up, isn't she, Trish?' Kurt said, 'Do you reckon?' Trish told him to stop being so rude, was he perfect? He said, 'I'm not perfect, but I don't actually . . .' Turning to me. 'We went to Adelaide and she got her picture taken in front of the war memorial with them and . . .'

He realised his father was watching him.

'Just saying. You don't take your dolls on a holiday. To the zoo. Her and Etsy in front of the lions.'

Allen just said, 'One day you might realise . . .'

Kurt just waited.

'God made us all different, Kurt.'

Glancing at me again, this time without a grin.

'Extraordinary amount of detail,' Father said to her. 'Trish, you've got a real artist here.' And to Gale: 'Maybe this could lead to something along the lines of . . . a costume designer, for the theatre. Or a fashion designer in Paris, imagine that?'

As Allen just glared at his son.

And Gale: 'I made this one from an old pillow.'

'No?'

'She's called Gale, like me, because she makes her own dolls. And she always comes with me, wherever I go, and sleeps with me.'

I watched how Allen ate his bacon, his eggs, slowly pulling them apart, joining the bits and pieces, loading them into his mouth. It wasn't shame, I don't think. He wasn't even uncomfortable. Like someone had chopped off his feet, and hands, but he just got on with it. Later, years later, I'd know the name of this thing. But then, sitting at this table, it confused me.

Gale re-emerged, and Allen stood, hugged her again and said how clever she was. Mother agreed, there was something in it, a future career, a useful occupation. Kurt just ate his eggs. But I knew what he was thinking.

I wasn't sure, at fourteen, how this form of parenting differed from the one I'd experienced. I can't remember Father looking at something

I'd done, gushing over it. Mother, too. Barely a 'Very good, Benno,' or a 'Should suffice, if you ever finish it.' Parents were variable, depending on the weather.

Gale put away her dolls but returned with her photos, and started handing them around. Ludwig told Silas what he was looking at: Gale, her dolls, Hermannsburg, Horseshoe Bend, Alice, Katherine, Darwin, Adelaide from the hills, highlights of the Barossa, her father standing in front of Langmeil Lutheran with the other elders, her, and Etsy.

'She's got around, hasn't she?' Trish said to Mother.

'My word she has.'

My word? When had she ever used that expression? And why was this girl, this retard, more impressive than me?

Kurt stood and said, 'Should I help with the dishes?' But Trish, I think, just wanted to get rid of him. 'No. Go on.'

'Benno? Come on.'

So we left Mother, glaring at me, and Trish, shaking her head, but then saying to Mother, 'We could always try a sitz bath?'

Into Kurt's room, where he sat on his unmade bed and said, 'Dolls!' Laughing. And Allen called, 'We can hear you.' So he closed his door and said, 'She fell off a horse, or hit her head or something happened, they wouldn't tell me.' But he didn't seem fussed. He took a cigar box from under his bed, opened it and said, 'My uncle, Dad's brother, sent me these.' Producing an Iron Cross, 1914–1918, handing it to me. 'Second Class. Real thing.'

'Nice.' Feeling it, admiring its markings. 'Whose was it?'

'This bloke next to him, a bullet through the head, he said, so he took his medals.'

There were more. An Honour Cross. Brass. Heavier. 'You get this one for killing people. He woulda got that for shooting one of ours. Sort of.'

Sort of. Because we were Australian, really. But German. We were having a bet both ways. Allen, with his colourised portrait of the King hanging above the phonograph, but in his bedroom, the Kaiser. A Kentish landscape; the Herz Mountains. But really, it was irrelevant – we were stuck in Australia, in the middle of nowhere, neutering cattle and praising the Lord.

Kurt said, 'How's your dad going to get to Horseshoe Bend if he can't get out of bed?'

'He can. He's resting.'

'Mum says he can't. Says it'll kill him if he goes.'

'Rubbish. We've come this far.' *And anyway, why do you keep having to say this shit*, I thought. 'My dad's tough.'

'He's pretty sick. What is it?'

'Dropsy.'

But he didn't care. 'And this one's *really* old, 1890. Service Cross. Uncle said he got it off a bloke he was burying, and his head was all caved in. How good's that?' Grinning, again. 'He was wearing this at the time. Imagine!' He held it against his pyjamas, pretended half his head was missing.

'We got in trouble,' I said.

'What?'

'We had to go to town and some government bloke interviewed Father, all of us, and asked about my brothers and sister in Leipzig. I reckon they thought we were spies.'

'Were you arrested?'

'No, they let us go.'

Strange, but when I was summoned back in 1942, the same man was there. He said to me, 'You were the boy . . . Benno?'

The same secretary taking notes, sitting in the same room. Like this happened every time there was a war with Germany. The same curtains, the same floor polish. I said, 'So what do you think's happened since then?'

'Probably nothing. But it has to be done, yes, Herr Benjamin Gerlach?'

'Mister.'

'Just saying. In some people's eyes, once a German, always a German.'

'I was born here.'

'I know.'

'I'm a citizen. I'm married to an Australian and I spend my life (before you made me return to Adelaide) researching Aboriginal culture. I'm not sure how much *more* Australian you need me to be.'

'*Some people* think, Mr Gerlach. Because there are, you know, societies.' He showed me a photo of a dozen men standing under a gum tree in the Barossa Valley, saluting a swastika. 'They claim to be Australian, too.'

'I don't have one of those flags.'

'Good.'

'I think you're confusing me with someone else.'

But he said, 'A list of questions. I ask, you answer, then we can all go home.'

I agreed. I just wanted to leave. Seething with anger, that my work, my ties with the land, the blacks, meant nothing. Like no one had bothered checking my research, asking the other professors about me. And who was this man? Licking the tip of his pencil.

'Your relatives?'

'My mother returned to Germany in 1931. I haven't seen her since.'

He wrote.

'Your siblings?'

'Let me think. Michael. Leipzig. Married to Annalise. Works as an accountant.'

'He was never drafted?'

'No. His eyes. He can't tell . . . really, I have to go through all of this?'

'If you would.'

That's how I remember it. Finishing what Father had begun in 1917, this boy in short pants, his legs barely touching the floor, listening to his father justify his Australian-ness. Me, saying, 'This is no way to treat people who have come here, made a commitment to Australia.'

'I suppose *we* get to decide that.'

I sat and remembered what I could, and said my wife Terese and I are planning on children soon, and I want them to be raised in a free country, and he seemed impressed with this. I said, 'Does this mean, when my son is my age, he gets to return and do all of this over again?'

He smiled. 'I'm fairly certain I should be retired by then.'

Back in his bedroom, Kurt said, 'This is the best of all.' He reached under his bed, produced a hunting knife, removed it from its scabbard and showed me the markings. 'Real thing.' I took it, examined it, ran a finger along the blade, the deer-antler handle.

'The same bloke with his head blown away used this to cut a Tommy's throat. Imagine!' Again, he demonstrated.

'True?'

'That's what he said. But they got all the blood off, didn't they?'

Anything, I guessed, examining the last of Kurt's medals, so you weren't sitting in a house in a desert wondering about what you'd do tomorrow, the day after, the week, the month, the year, the life. Anything to take you somewhere more interesting.

Allen called for us to come out for a photo, and Kurt said, 'Do we gotta be in it?'

'Yes. Now!'

Kurt packed away his medals, his knife. 'Let's get it over with.'

When we emerged, Father was up, sitting at the table, sipping cocoa. He said, 'Where have you two been?'

'Talking about girls, no doubt,' Allen said, ruffling his son's hair. Hugging him. They were like that. They were close. It seemed strange. If I remember one thing about my father, it was the distance. Physically, of course, but in other ways. Almost like there were rules. Good, strong, Prussian rules that said fathers and sons needed space. Allen lined up his son and daughter, manhandled them into position, placed Etsy in Gale's hands, Trish, then Ignatz, Ludwig, Silas at the front, his suit all brown and burned. Then me, Mother, Father. As Allen stood, focusing his Brownie, and said, 'This is one for the ages.'

Then later, in the sitting room, Allen in an old recliner, Gale at his side. He stroked her hair and told her she was marvellous. Father, across from him, in a borrowed dressing gown, but I knew I couldn't get that close. Perhaps I wanted to feel his hand in my hair and hear him say, 'Benno's pretty marvellous, too, aren't you son?'

I'd say: 'Why?'

And he'd tell them. How I could spell any word, cook any meal, talk to the blacks in their own language, German, English, how I was the son of many mothers, and a good one at that, how I was destined to be the global authority on everything Aranda. Like that. But I realised that could never be. So how was I meant to ask him how he was feeling (and get an honest answer); if he was afraid of dying; what he'd say to me, if we only had ten minutes left.

Etsy, again

Father sat on the porch in his shorts, shirt open to the breastbone, a rug over his legs. Comfortable in the shade, the Harmstorf's phonograph playing Schubert through the window, the curtain blowing in and out, Father calling across to the yards: 'I tell you, Allen, it was a marvel. He ran all the way to Alice, didn't you, Ludwig?'

'Bitta walking too,' Ludwig said.

'Ran. Must've, to do it in three days.'

We sat waiting outside the yards – me and Kurt, Ludwig and Jamy, Allen Harmstorf and a few of his blacks. On a long log, as the fire burned in the furnace, heating the two IDR brands.

'And what did they say to you, Ludwig?' Father said, cooling his head with one of Mother's fans, sipping barley water.

'They said no one could come.'

'Exactly! See, Allen. A reply, straight away. Nothing like give us a few days and we'll see what we can do. Just no, no one can help. And poor old Ludwig running all the way back, didn't you, Ludwig?'

'Yes, Pastor.'

'Just about killed him, didn't it, Ludwig?' Mumbling about the Board always letting him down, treating him like a joke for so many years, how stupid could a man be?

Allen moved the brands in the coals and said, 'He needs to rest.'

'He wants to get going,' I said.

The calves continued pushing and shoving each other in the yards, watching us with big, brown eyes, shitting and stepping in it, like they sensed, like someone had told them something unpleasant was approaching.

'When I get to town, when I talk to them,' Father said, lifting the rug from his legs. 'Someone's going to be made to explain.' He got up, took a few steps, and Allen said, 'You stay there, Pastor. Stay and rest.'

'There's nothing wrong with me. I can help.' Managing the few steps, his big, red legs plodding the fifty feet to where we sat. 'Let's get on with it.'

'You got to rest.' Allen.

'Rubbish. Come on.' Grabbing one of the brands and checking if it was glowing.

'You need pants, Pastor,' Ludwig said.

Allen took the brand from Father, returned it to the coals and walked him back to the porch. 'If you wanna get better, if you wanna get to Horseshoe Bend, you have to rest, Pastor.' He helped him up the front steps, and Mother came out and said, 'What are you doing, Martin?' Doing up his buttons, leading him back to his seat, to Schubert, to barley water.

'Is he a bit dotty?' Kurt asked me.

'He's not . . . dotty. Your sister's dotty.'

'I know that but . . .' Watching Father settle. 'Does he even know where he is?'

'Of course.'

'What's happening?'

'If you don't understand,' I said to him. 'You shouldn't talk about what you don't understand.'

'Suit yourself.' Shrugging.

But then Father mumbled, 'He did, didn't he, Alma? Tell them. Eighty miles. That's more than an Olympic marathon.' Calling: 'Isn't it, Benno?'

'I reckon.'

'Allen? A marathon.'

'Settle in there, Pastor, and try to rest.' Squeezing my father's shoulder, like he did his son's, his daughter's, his wife's. Then he pulled my mother aside and started talking to her. I watched, trying to get some idea. I knew, anyway. I knew every word they were saying.

A few calves, heads between bars, eyes popping out, snot across their faces. Kurt threw a branch to scare them off, then said, 'I told you about Elsie.'

'Bullshit.'

'Don't believe me then, I don't care.'

Father shouted, 'Just finish those calves, men. We haven't got all day. Ludwig. You take charge. Let me know when you're done.' And quietly. 'I'll be inside with my books . . . you can find me there . . . can't he, Benno?' Running out of puff, closing his eyes, shouting, 'I'm all-bloody-right, so let's get moving. How far to Horseshoe, Ignatz?' Looking around. 'Where's Ignatz?'

Mother and Allen still talking, and Kurt said, 'I tell you, she did.'

'Bullshit.'

'In her room. I'm telling you exactly what happened. We were at Henbury a month ago, we stayed for a week, and she kept coming up to me and . . .' Smiling.

Then Allen decided, went over to Father and said, 'You're too sick to leave, Martin.'

Father didn't hear him. Didn't respond. Just sang along with the music.

'Did you hear me, Martin?'

'Are you listening, Martin?' Mother said.

'As long as we're gone by lunch,' he replied.

'No, not lunch,' Allen said. 'A few days, perhaps, until you're better.'

'No, no.'

'You have to listen.' Trish, standing at the front door.

'What do you know?' Father said to her. 'Nothing. Who are you, anyway? Some sort of . . . Alma, who the hell is she?'

'You know.'

Father just glared at Trish, and shook his head.

Allen came down to the yards, checked the brands and said, 'Let's go.'

I drafted the calves, Ludwig, Jamy and the others removed balls, tagged ears, and vaccinated. Father and son (Harmstorf) pulled them over, Kurt held them down and Allen branded them. Father called from the porch, 'We gotta get them done by lunch . . . there's more to bring in, isn't there, Ludwig?'

'This is it, Pastor.'

Until we had a pattern. Until we settled into the monotony. After a while Kurt said to me, 'She isn't half off.'

I glared back, and Allen said to his son, 'Who?'

Kurt blew me a kiss and said, 'They need to keep her in a cage, I reckon.'

'*Who?*' his father asked.

'Elsie. She's keen on Benno.'

Allen put his brand in the coals, took the hot one, said to me, 'Elsie?'

'He's making it up. We're friends.'

Allen said, 'Keep them coming, Benno. You and Elsie? I'm not sure anyone'd be happy about that.'

'Why?'

'*Why?*' Raising an eyebrow. 'If you gotta ask . . . I wouldn't let your mother know.'

'She doesn't . . . it doesn't matter. That's a load of shit, Kurt.'

Father stood again, unbuttoned his shirt and said, 'See, nothing wrong with me.' Mother came out and settled him.

Allen said, 'What do you think's going to happen to your father, Benno?'

'Don't know.'

'Long way yet.' Another calf, then another, so it was a minute, more, between comments. 'And if he gets worse . . .'

'What can I do?'

'Not much. Pray. You pray?'

'Yes.'

'That helps. But with his heart . . . You either run for the line, or wait it out, Benno. And who's to say what makes more sense?'

'He wants to get to Horseshoe Bend.'

'Well, that's good thinking. Positive.' Stopping, sizing me up. 'It's important, if he thinks he can make it. He's certainly done a lot for people, and he should expect better . . . You gotta help him, Benno.'

'Mother reckons he's as strong as a bullock.'

'He is. I know. Twenty-eight years at that place, doing what he's been doing. A bullock. You've got reason to be proud of him.'

I didn't reply.

'And you should tell him at some point. You're proud of him.'

'He's not gonna die!' I slammed the gate on a calf, halfway through, and Allen told me to be careful.

At that stage, that day in the yards, there were things I did and didn't want to hear. How did you tell your father you were grateful? That was sentimental. Awkward. Then Kurt chose the wrong moment to say, 'She's like one of those cats, Benno.'

'Who?'

'Elsie. You know. No one's neutered them, eh, Ludwig?'

'No more babies,' Ludwig said, smiling, holding up a bloody set of balls.

'Just saying, like a cat, running about sniffing everything she finds.'

I jumped down, walked across to him, pushed him into the sand. He said, 'What was that for?' He tried to get up, but I kicked him back down, and Allen said, 'What's all this about?'

'Nothing,' Kurt said.

'Benno?'

'Nothing.'

'None of that,' Father called. 'I'm not paying you to play around.'

'Back to it,' Allen said, and after a few more calves: 'What's wrong with you two?'

'He was talking about Elsie,' I said.

'What about her, Kurt?'

'Nothing.'

'Benno?'

'Nothing.'

Now, the yard was half full of calves, the smell of burned flesh and hair, blood from the ears, from the balls, all over the ground.

'Elsie's one of my *friends*,' I said.

Allen wasn't listening. 'Doesn't hurt to tell people you appreciate them now and again, eh, Kurt?'

'I reckon.'

'There's a . . . we need a verse about that. I'll look one up. We'll share it. We'll discuss it.' Raising his voice. 'Won't we, Martin?'

'What?'

'Telling people how much you appreciate their efforts.'

Father'd had enough. He stood, tried to pull on his pants, failed, and wandered down again. Allen called, 'Trish, you there? Alma?'

No reply.

'Shit.' Throwing his brand aside, telling us to stop and wait, jumping over the fence and saying, 'Where are you going, Pastor?'

'You'll help us get ready? Ludwig, Jamy, you get those donks.'

Allen took Father's arm and led him towards the horses. One slow, shuffling step at a time, calling, 'Alma?' I followed. Kurt behind me. Ludwig and Jamy further back. When we arrived at the yards, Allen pointed to the donkeys and said, 'See, they're in no state to travel.'

'They'll do.'

'All bones. Look, half of them have got sores.' Indicating where he'd treated them. 'And they were dehydrated. You can't keep pushing them.'

'They're donkeys, they're stupid animals,' he said.

'Maybe so, but they can't keep pulling that.' Indicating the dray. He took us over, showed us the wheel someone had started fixing. 'I've got a few men onto it, Martin. Like you said, Mr Wurst would be at Oodnadatta by now, wouldn't he?'

A glimmer of recognition. 'Wurst. Of course!'

'So this morning I sent two men on my best horses to Horseshoe Bend.'

'You did? When?'

'When you lot were all asleep. Charlie and Brian. To Horseshoe Bend, Martin. I told them, I said to find Gus Elliot and give him this letter I wrote.'

'A letter. About what?'

'Simple. Send Mr Wurst's car. Send a couple of donks, too, because there's no way they'd get through otherwise.'

'Good. A letter. You're right. He'd have to be at Oodnadatta by now.'

Then Mother was at the door, wiping her hands in a tea towel. 'Martin. What the hell are you doing?'

Father said, 'Gotthold. Allen remembered. He's sent some men.'

'I know.'

'That's good news, Alma. So we can wait for a reply . . . or better, we can fix the dray, the donkeys, we can get going, we can meet them half-way. Then it'll be fine, won't it, Alma?'

Mother came down, took his arm again, led him back to the porch and settled him in the cane chair. 'Time to rest, and wait. It's been a long trip, hasn't it?'

Gale came out with Etsy, Silas with the golliwog. Trish said they should sit with Father and tell him about the doll's holidays. Gale started off with the story of Etsy in Sorrento, in Victoria, which is the nicest place, isn't it, Father, you could ever go for a holiday?

Father said, 'They've got good horses, have they, Allen?'

'My best.'

'Wouldn't take them more than a day, would it?'

'Bit longer. But they'll go like the clappers, Martin, I promise.'

Seven Last Words

Father sat on the porch with his uneaten lunch (pork sausage, pickles, sauerkraut and bread), saying, 'He was the only one suitable, weren't you, Benno?'

'I guess.'

I'd finished most of it, except the pickles, decomposing in brine. Trish said, 'What, you don't like pickles? A good German boy like you?'

Father was insisting to Allen: 'With an interest in this sort of work . . .' Rubbing his eyes, trying to focus on the calves, still complaining in the mid-distance.

'Is that right?' Allen asked me.

'Yes.' What else could I say? I couldn't argue, I couldn't ask what Father meant, or intended. I couldn't say, I never remember showing any interest in spear throwers and dilly bags. Maybe I should've been flattered? Maybe this was the closest I'd ever get to approval?

'In fact,' Mother added, 'Benno's the reader of the family, aren't you, Benno?'

Again, should I tell them there wasn't much choice? Just then Trish said, 'We've got boxes of books in the shed, haven't we, Allen?'

'Plenty.'

'Novels, all sorts. You like novels, Benno?'

'Course he does,' Mother said. 'If you let him, he'd sit there all day reading, never get anything done.'

Great. Only Mother.

'Go on,' Trish said to Kurt. 'Go show Benno.'

So Kurt put down his plate, led me across to the shed, opened the door and said, 'You better watch for snakes.' Past old fences and gates, a cart with its wheels removed, the various spokes and rims in pieces on a bench covered in old tools. Kurt said, 'What's the point of reading stuff?'

'Improves your brain.'

Slats from some long-dead bed, a collection of springs, hanging loose. Strange how the books were under all of this. Kurt moved an old scythe, some sort of motor, a collection of broken lamps and, finally, a box with the word BÜCHER.

'Here they are. Help yerself.'

I opened the box and started searching: a German primer, technical manuals (a seeder, a water pump), kids' books with the pages eaten away.

'I was only joking about Elsie,' he said.

'Didn't sound like you were joking.'

Nothing in that box, so he found a second, and plenty of novels, but all in German. I told him I'd prefer English but he said, 'Your dad'd kill you anyway. An Aborigine.'

I didn't know any of the authors. I asked if he'd read any, but he just laughed and said, 'You can't actually marry them or anything.'

'What about Bob and Alf, and the Mollys?'

'Dad reckons they're a disgrace.' He picked up a book, blew off the dust, read the title and threw it back in the box. 'Anyway, wouldn't you prefer someone *white*?'

I shrugged. Mann. I'd heard of him, so I put him aside. 'They're not animals. They're people.'

'Not *real* people.'

I didn't get it. 'What are they then?'

'They're good on a horse. And they're good in the kitchen, if you train them up proper, but to marry them, Jesus. I wouldn't have done anything with Elsie, not in a million years.'

'She's nice.'

But he just shook his head. 'If you let them be, they just sit under a tree and sleep.'

Maybe somewhere around then I worked out the importance of books. About reading my way out of this world, away from these people. Maybe that's what Father was doing, and hoped for me. 'Anyway, I'm not marrying anyone,' I said.

'What are you doing then?'

'I want to go to university. Don't you?'

'Why?'

'Learn about stuff. The world. Plenty outside of here.'

'A bit. But like Dad says, People gotta eat, so someone's gotta farm cattle.'

'Don't you want to see the pyramids?'

'Not really.'

Shakespeare, collected plays, in German, so I put it on the pile.

'So, what'd you be, some professor?' he asked.

'Perhaps.'

'What of?'

'Languages. Something to do with language.' Holding up a book to make it clear.

'But you can already speak English, German, Abo.'

'Aranda.' I gave him a few phrases, and he said, 'Well, maybe you oughta marry Elsie then?'

'Plenty of world outside Idracowra,' I said, placing something by Marx on the pile.

Then a script, of sorts. It looked familiar. Typed up, but covered in handwritten notes. 'The Passion of our Lord Jesus Christ. Completed by Pastor Martin Gerlach. 1909.' Fourteen scenes from fourteen stations. Again, comparative, English and Aranda. Dialogue on one side, directions on the other. And in Father's hand: 'Jamy moves UC before saying . . .' Inside the front, rat-eaten cover – the main players:

Jesus: Silas

Mary: Trude

Captain of the Guard: Ludwig

'"Forgive them, Father, for they know not what they do,"' I read.

Kurt stood beside me, reading. 'That's what they used to put on, didn't they?'

'Every year, but they stopped for some reason.'

I flicked through Father's small writing, a palimpsest of who goes where, when, how they say a line, even expressions, sigh here, laugh there.

'"Truly, I say to you,"' Kurt said to me, '"today you will be in Paradise." There you go, Benno. Bitta light reading.'

I've been thinking of giving it to the museum. This script. But what would they make of it? It's nothing authentic. It doesn't describe some traditional ceremony, or object. It tells us nothing about the Aranda way of life, beliefs, tens of thousands of years in the desert. In fact, it's more a corruption, a diluting, white man marries black girl and makes grey babies. Maybe, if it were put on display, people would refuse to look at it, boycott it, or maybe they *would* understand?

This is what I was trying to tell my grandson, on a hot summer's day in 1988. Out in the shed, again. Jack had dropped him at the door, said, 'As promised.'

I said, 'Nah, you don't wanna see all that old rubbish, do you, Tom?'

'Yeah.'

So Jack had pissed off somewhere, some sport practice with his old school mates, and I'd brought Tom into my house, cleared a spot for him at the table, made him a ham and cheese sandwich. He'd tried to eat it, but he was the pickle boy, being nice, and I said, 'Would you prefer some fish fingers?'

'I love fish fingers.'

Following me out to the kitchen while I got them out of the freezer. 'You live here alone?'

'I do.'

'Where's your wife?'

'She died. A couple of years back.'

'That's bad.'

'Yeah. Bad.' Placing the fish fingers on a tray, slipping them in the oven and explaining I didn't always eat like this.

'You should've stayed with Grandma,' he said.

'Quite possibly,' I agreed, ruffling his hair. 'But that's easy to say now.'

'Go back and see her.'

'I don't think she'd want to see me.'

'She might. Should I ask?'

'No, don't ask. That was too long ago.'

'When?'

'Jeez, you ask a lot of questions.'

'Sorry.'

'No. Ask away. A kid should be curious, shouldn't he?'

'I guess. She might want to see you.'

'Not after what I did. D'yer want a Coke?'

'Dad reckons it rots your teeth.'

'Dad's not here.'

So I poured us both a Coke. We sat at the table, and I said, 'It was 1955.'

'What?'

'You asked when I last saw your gran.'

'That's *so* long ago.'

'That's what I told you. So it's best to let sleeping dogs lie.'

'What's that mean?'

'Let it go.'

'But she might say, Oh, Benjamin, oh, Benno, where have you been all these years, my darling!' Laughing.

May I say (though I'm biased), you can't not like Thomas Gerlach. You can try, but it won't work.

'You could talk her around.'

'What, are you trying to get us together?'

The Gerlach shrug.

'Do you know what I did?' I asked.

'Yes. You walked out on Grandma and Dad and Aunty Sharon.'

'That was a terrible thing to do, wasn't it, Tom?'

'But if you're just gonna sit here and . . . Dad reckons you gotta try to make things right. That's why he said he followed you home that day.'

'Well, I'm glad he did. I'm very glad to meet you, young Gerlach.' I offered him my hand, and he shook it, and said, 'I think people aren't as shitty about things as you think they are.'

'No?'

'You think like, this teacher hates me, but then you get talking.'

'You're wise for your years.'

'Not really. It's just common sense. Like Dad says, you can't write people off.'

So we ate fish fingers, drank Coke and eventually took the bottle and sat out in the shed. I said, 'It's old stuff, Tom. We could start by writing labels for some of these stones. See. They're called tjurunga.' Opening a box that hadn't been touched for thirty years. 'You got good handwriting?'

'Pretty.'

'Right, that's your job.'

Ten minutes later I said, 'This one's from the MacDonnell Ranges. South of Alice Springs. Write that down.'

I watched as he worked. Resting the new labels on a book, biting his lip, clutching his pen like it might run away, pressing down hard, too hard, and I took his hand and showed him, soft, like this, and he tried again. 'MacDonnell Ranges. South of Alice Springs.'

'Sacred stone, and in brackets, emu totem. Collected around, what, 1937, 38.'

And he continued.

It was hot in the shed, but Tom didn't care. Bony fingers and awkward hands, long arms dangling down to the ground; broad shoulders and a long neck, with a little artery (I watched it) pumping blood to his precocious brain. Sweat on his face, in his eyes, but he just wiped them then showed me the label and said, 'Is that okay?'

'Good.'

I showed him how to attach the label, and where to put the stone. Then, the next one (of dozens). I said, 'Say when you want to stop for a break.'

'We've just started.' Biting his lip, looking up and asking, 'Same as before?'

'No. This one, as I remember' – examining it – 'was from around Idracowra.'

'How do you spell that?'

Back in the shed at Idracowra, another box beside the books contained bark paintings, digging sticks, stone axes and a coolamon. I said to Kurt, 'Where are these from?'

He shrugged. 'Dad used to collect them.'

Examining them. 'These are special to the blacks.'

'Said he might be able to get some money for them.'

'You gotta ask the old people about that.'

'Your dad does it.'

'He asks. And it's for study. He writes it all down.'

'Just a loada old shit.' Going through the box, throwing shields, necklaces on the ground. 'Crap.' He threw a carved stone across the shed, and it made a clatter on the iron, and Allen called, 'What are you doing?' Kurt said: 'Wouldn't get anything for them anyway. Loada rubbish.'

Back at Hillcrest, I said to Tom, 'Got that one at Idracowra, 1922, on the way to Horseshoe Bend.' I told him how I waited until Kurt was busy looking through some boxes, then grabbed a handful of stones, put them in my pocket. 'He never knew.' And later that night when I showed Father (in secret), he said, 'Pack them away good and proper, Benno. We'll find out about them later.'

Eventually, we got sick of stones, and Tom, like his grandfather, started searching through boxes of books, notes, documents, and found the script, read the names and said, 'What was this all about?'

I told him it was the Passion, but he didn't get this, so I described the crucifixion (he'd heard of it in RE) and explained there were fourteen stations, and years ago people used to put on a sort of theatrical production, and he said, 'Like *Les Mis*?' I said, 'Yes, sort of.' Eventually, he understood and sat reading the stage directions, the dialogue. 'We did some drama, and Mr Goodburn said each character's gotta have some sort of motivation.'

'Well, I don't know if you'd call it that. Just Father telling people what to say.'

'That's strange.' Searching through, smelling the paper, flicking the rat shit. 'Like a TV ad.'

'How?'

'You know, people pretending to like burgers, and the whole family is eating chips, but you know it's not real.' Reading: '"Woman, behold your son. Son, behold your mother."' He wiped his face with his sleeve. 'So you were like, *really* religious?'

'Your grandfather was a Lutheran missionary. It doesn't get more religious than that. Although, in the end, he was more interested in the blacks and what *they* believed.'

'So it was like *he* was converted?'

'I guess he was. Although he never stopped believing in God.'

'But they can't both be true.'

'Why not?'

'Because either . . .' I watched him try to make sense of it. It was important to Tom to understand.

'Father was very straight-laced, but that was the world he was brought up in.'

'Father?'

'Dad.'

'Couldn't you call him Dad?'

'I tried. Several times. But it never worked.'

Tom smiled and said, 'It's good we found you, Grandpa. Before you got too old, or died or anything. It's funny to think you're Dad's dad.'

'Why?'

'You're not like him, or anyone I've met.'

Kurt wiped the dust on his pants and said, 'I don't know what I'd do if I was you.'

'What?'

'If my dad was that sick.'

At that age a dad was necessary. Despite their smells, their embarrassing comments, their weight, their plain stupidity and ignorance, you needed one, at least one, to get by.

'He's fine.'

He picked up a book, placed it on my pile and said, 'Mum'd have no idea how to run this place. We'd have to sell it.'

'So what? You'd sell it. Go somewhere else. Continue. Things'd change. How's this help?' And I threw the script on the pile.

An hour later, Tom and I had given up. We'd locked the shed. We'd walked around the block to the fish shop, ordered potato cakes and pineapple fritters and minimum chips, with plenty of vinegar. I'd bought him mixed lollies, and Don had tried to give him a pre-packed version, but no, Tom insisted on choosing every lolly himself. Then, as we waited, he said, 'Dad told Grandma about you.'

'Really?'

'She just sat there like, you know, blank face, and Dad said we can take you to see him, and she said, What makes you think I'd want to see him?'

'Not good,' I said, stealing a milk bottle. 'How did she seem?'

Shrug. Chico. Don watching (but not watching) the cricket on the telly on top of the fridge.

'She didn't seem too excited. But Dad kept asking, and she said, He's the one who left us.'

I let out a deep breath. 'What do you think my chances are, Tom?'

'She didn't say no. And I bet she'd like to see you as much as you'd like to see her.'

Don gave us our food and we walked home around the block. Tom told me he was meant to be at cricket, but cricket was shit, so boring, wasn't it, and he'd told his dad he'd rather come and do my labels.

'I don't lead the most exciting life,' I said.

'Are you kidding?'

'You could be out on your power boat. Didn't your dad say you had a boat?'

'Not a power boat, Grandpa. A ski boat.'

'A ski boat. A Gerlach with a ski boat. You go skiing?'

'Of course.' Taken with the idea. 'You have to come, Grandpa. It's so much fun.' Grabbing my arm, pulling it, to persuade me. 'Yeah?'

I laughed. 'Me? Skiing?' But even then, I knew, once Tom had decided. 'Maybe, once we finish the labels.'

'Can we do some tomorrow?'

'You got school.'

'After?'

'Homework?'

'I do it all at school.'

When we arrived back in front of 31 Ramsay Avenue, Jack was waiting. Resting against his car. 'Healthy eating, is it?'

Tom offered him some chips, and when this didn't work, the sweaty remains of the lollies. He said, 'Grandpa wants to come skiing.'

Ereakura

After lunch, the place settled. Father and Mother rested in the Harmstorf's bed, Father lapsing in and out of sleep, of dreams of white frocks and Singer strike-plates, drench running down ribs and flanks, a well-oiled mission at its peak, 1912, or earlier? Perhaps he was dreaming – perhaps he was floating through the bush on a summer's day; perhaps he was smelling eucalyptus, listening for the night parrots; perhaps he was rising, leaving all of this behind; perhaps he was looking back, seeing Mother, calling for her to help him. I don't know. Ignatz was in the sitting room, deep in a couch, reading about Dutch weirs. Kurt and his sister, helping in the kitchen.

I walked across to the calves in the long paddock. Stopped and watched them, and thought: option one. He'd have to be buried at Horseshoe Bend, then me and Mother on a train to town, a telegram to Germany, then we'd go, or they'd come, and a few weeks later, all of us would return to Hermannsburg to pack up and put things on a cart, wait for someone to replace us.

Continuing down a hill, wave-top weeds, grass moving in the breeze, as it was. Option two. We get to Horseshoe Bend. Gus'll be there, and his wife, and she's a nurse, isn't she? Then there's a solution, something simple, something we haven't thought of, and Father takes it and feels better, good enough to get on the train at the railhead. Then to the hospital, and some doctor says, 'No great drama. A few days we'll have you back on your feet, Pastor.'

This hill settled in a dry creek, some tributary of a tributary of the Finke. A row of river reds leaning in towards the middle, hoping for rain.

And Silas, sitting on his haunches, looking at where the water should be. I stood next to him and said, 'What are you up to?'

'Benno?'

His suit was singed, covered in mud stains. But he wore it proudly, belt tight, no socks with his leather shoes. A small cross around his neck (given to him by Mother and Father for his twelfth birthday). He said, 'Smell that.' Taking a deep breath.

'What?'

But he didn't say. I sat beside him and said, 'What are you doing down here?'

'Get away from that lot.' Indicating.

Option three: we wake tomorrow morning and Mother calls, 'Benno, come look!' I run into their room and there's Father, stick-legged and flat-bellied (as much as could be expected), jumping about, saying something about a miracle, all we needed was patience, a bit of faith. I took the chance and said, 'What do you reckon about Father?'

'Everyone's doing everything they can. Plenty of people want him to get better, Benno.'

I didn't reply.

'Don't worry. I know what you're thinking.'

'What?'

He didn't say. But I guess he knew I was worried about Father, how it might end. Option four: on the way to Horseshoe Bend, and Father has to lie down, in pain, lots of pain, and everyone *is* trying to help him, but it doesn't matter. He closes his eyes, and it's like he goes to sleep, and Mother's shaking him, and Ignatz is saying, 'There's nothing we can do, Alma,' and I'm thinking, *It can't happen like this* . . .

'No more worrying, right?' Silas said, sitting and taking off his shoes, letting his feet sink into the sand.

'It's taking forever to get there, isn't it?'

He nodded.

'And he seems to be getting worse?'

'Perhaps.'

'And we've still got a way to go, and the donkeys and the cart and the condition Father's in . . . if we were at Horseshoe Bend now but—'

'Stop.'

He was forbidding me to go down that path. Instead, he took out his favourite watercolour, flatted it in his lap and said, 'Does it look like this?' Indicating the land in front of him.

'A bit.'

'Go on then – paint the picture for me.'

'Well, there's a creek, like this one, but there's no water in it. There are some hills in the distance, and they're purple and blue and . . . a mix of colours.' I seemed to be getting it right. 'There are cliffs, and they're falling apart, and it looks like there's been some sort of pump house, or maybe where someone lived. And that's about it.'

'No,' he said. 'Plenty more. You're not looking, Benno.'

'There are some wattles or pines, I'm not sure, halfway between here and the hills.'

He placed his hands above his head, like he was holding something, and he pretended to shake whatever it was. 'Ereakura.'

'The plant?'

Moving the basket above his head, winnowing bulbs from roots, like the old women, before we made them use flour instead.

'That's about all,' I repeated.

'Isaiah tried to teach me,' he explained. 'He put a brush in my hand and said, Paint what you see. I said, I can't see nothing, but he said, That's not true, is it, Silas?'

'What'd he mean?'

'He meant I wasn't looking careful enough. And he was right. Because there I was, an hour later, painting this picture (I lost it now), and he comes up to me and says, That's real good, Silas.'

'Was it any good?'

He shrugged. 'How do I know . . . Jesus, Benno.' He smiled, and reached out and pushed me.

'So he meant what you *reckon* might be there?'

'No. What *is* there.'

We sat there for five minutes. Silas sang about the old people, winnowing ereakura, and I thought about Father. It was nice beside the dry creek. I guessed there was never much water in it, but when there was, things came alive. I could see it, the start of it, the possibility of it, the parrots and the moles, the wallabies in groups of three or four coming down to drink.

All life was new life. That's what I wanted Tom to know, years later. And what he wanted me to know, I guess.

Then he got an idea (Silas, I should've told you, was always a bit frisky) and smiled and punched me on the arm and said, 'You gotta show people, Benno.'

'What?'

He stood, took more paintings from his pocket, checked for the right one (don't ask), and said, 'Isaiah helped me with this one, too.'

I'd seen it. I'd been shocked by it (years ago, when I was ten, when he first showed us, when Mother and Father told him to put it away). A woman on her back, and some fella with a big knob dripping syphilis, the woman saying: 'None of that thank you very much!'

I laughed then, and I laughed now. These two figures with cartoon genitalia, discussing the dangers of venereal disease.

Silas said, 'Listen to me, ladies and folks, this bloke's full of the clap, eh, Benno?'

'He is.'

'And now he goes and makes love to her, and she's full of it, and she meets some other bloke, then everyone's got it.' He sat, and handed me the cartoon. 'Isaiah taught me how to paint this, Benno. He held my hand and guided it, till I got the idea.'

I got the idea. There were plenty more of these paintings. He said he preferred them to the ones he bought, or the ones Oskar's brother kept under his bed (and Oskar stole). These ones made it clear. 'Kissy-kissy,' he said. Some quite graphic. Some bloke with his ears and nose eaten away, because this is what happened, in the end.

He wanted to stay, so I left him beside the creek, watching the landscape I'd painted for him. I went up the hill, towards the house. Nothing except a dog, scratching its leg on a fence post. It looked bad, red raw, weeping. I wondered whether it mightn't have been kinder to shoot him. There were no vets. If you got sick, you died. Back, onto the porch, I sat on the cane chair and surveyed the station. The whole place, an afternoon of sleep and dreaming, half-read paragraphs of never-finished books, the smell of roast from the cookhouse, someone flicking a tablecloth somewhere. And under all of this, the same Schubert on the same gramophone.

Mother said, 'I don't know why I did it.'

'What?' Father.

'Why I did it . . .'

The same bird: who, who, who. I looked around but couldn't see it but wondered why it was everywhere I went. The sound of a hammer on iron, as a few of the blacks finished repairing our wheel. And Mother: 'I sometimes think how it might have ended.'

Father didn't reply. The curtain blew out of the window, and I thought she'd see me, but she didn't stop.

'I could've. I topped the year in science, in chemistry, especially.'

'You chose,' Father said. 'We all chose.'

'You did. I've just been along for the ride. There was that scholarship, because they wanted women to study science.'

'You've told me. A hundred times. What do you want me to say?'

'Just saying . . .'

Mother could do this. Off on some tangent, with no idea where she was, what she was saying, how anyone else might take it.

'You shouldn't have married me,' Father said.

'But you were there on our doorstep that night . . . bugger you, Martin Gerlach.'

'I had no interest in women. I'd finish seminary and go to Australia. *You* inserted yourself into *my* life, Alma. You had no interest in becoming a chemist or metallurgist, despite what you've been saying for forty years.'

'I did. I had real potential.'

Allen Harmstorf appeared from the yards, climbed the few steps to the porch and said, 'What are you up to, young Gerlach?'

'That you?' Father called.

Allen went into his room, stood in the doorway and said, 'Those donks, Martin . . . forget it.'

I waited. As Father sat up (or Mother helped him). 'What do you mean?'

'They're knackered. They won't get you far.'

'They have to,' Mother said.

'They won't. Donks can't keep going like horses. Sores. All hunched over. Few of them have stopped eating. They're a mess, Martin. I reckon you wait a few days. Gus'll send horses. I asked him.'

'They're gonna have to do it,' Father said. 'We gotta get going.'

'Well, if you want to pull your own dray.' He went out to the kitchen, and Mother followed. She said: 'By tonight perhaps?'

I went into the hallway, past the bedroom, and saw her, arms crossed, pleading. 'Once they get moving . . .'

'Then you're stuck out there, God knows where, and we've gotta find some way . . . no.'

'Well, we're going.'

'You're not.'

'Stop us.'

Silence. I retreated. Back to the porch, down the front steps. Jamy went past and asked when we were leaving and I said when Mother finishes arguing with Mr Harmstorf. He sat with me. After a few minutes of silence, we heard Mother returning to the bedroom, and saying, 'He thinks he knows best.'

Red Rover

The smell of roast beef and Yorkshire pudding saturating a Sunday afternoon with what had always been, and always would be. Me and Terese and the kids standing on the same porch, the same curtain blowing out of the window. Gale saying, 'I remember you, Benno.' And me: 'This is my wife, Terese, and my kids, Jack and Sharon.' Gale with Etsy's baby, a forty-year-old woman with rags in her hair, a few bad teeth, wiping her nose on her arm and saying, 'What brings you back?'

'I came to show my kids the place.'

And Allen, this hunched-over old man with sunken cheeks and a few tufts of silver hair: 'You working with the blacks again, I hear?'

'I've got a scholarship. National Research Council.'

'What are you researching?'

'Aranda language.'

Lighting up. 'Like your dad did?'

'I'm sort of . . . continuing.'

Then I said, 'How's Kurt been keeping?' They fell silent. Because he'd stayed, but not stayed. Done as expected, but surprised everyone. Gone out to the machinery shed (Pauline had told me, days later, when we'd arrived at Hermannsburg) and put a rope over a rafter and decided (I guess) enough was enough.

'Anyway, d'yer mind if I show the kids around? I was just telling them about that time in 1922 when we stopped here, remember, with Father, and we played Red Rover?'

'I remember,' Allen said.

'And we branded those calves.' Pointing to where the yards used to be – the cattle, animals, everything gone. Because what was the point if there was no one to take it on?

Remembering. Kurt standing in the middle of the compound, spitting on his hands, kicking the station dogs away and saying, 'Carn then, who's game?' Me and Ludwig and a few of the station boys. Jamy standing on the side, half-interested. And on the porch, the Harmstorfs, Mother and Father and Ignatz.

'Go!'

We took a few steps, watched Kurt, sniffed out a likely path, left, right, and he decided on me. The others sprinted, made it to the other side of the compound, then it was just us, facing off, and Allen calling, 'You're not gonna let him, are you, Benno?'

No way. Because Kurt was, after all, a farmer; he was solid and stolid, built like a brick shithouse, moving in the breeze like a bullock with a broken leg. 'Just you and me, Gerlach.'

'Suits me.'

His squashed-in nose, prominent brow and spinifex hair. If Red Rover was a slimmed-down Etsy-version of real life, if it was survival of the fittest, or least stupid, then there was no way I was going to lose. One foot forward, another, dash, back, but then he misstepped and I chose my moment and flew out. He pivoted, jumped, dragged me down and I heard them clap, and Allen say, 'You got the Harmstorf spirit, boy.'

Apparently not. According to Pauline he'd become a different version of himself. He'd withdrawn, stopped talking, stayed in his room, wouldn't come out and help with the muster, the fences, peel a few spuds. He came to the mission once, and the whole time Trish kept saying to him, 'What do you think about that, Kurt?' But he just shrugged, not even that.

Later, much later. But for now, I stood and waited and said, 'Red Rover all over.' They tried again. Mother called, 'Don't hurt yourself, Benno.' Mumbling: 'That's the last thing we need, isn't it, Trish?'

Ignatz jumped out of his chair, said, 'This looks easy,' bounced down the steps and joined the all-over. Waiting, staring at me, grinning, a few tentative steps. This time, I chose him. I could, I thought, bring him down. He ran, I ran, reached out, touched his arm and said, 'Got you!' He just smiled at me. 'You got lucky.'

'It's not luck. You're not fast enough, old man.'

'Old man? Did you hear that, Martin? He called his teacher an old man.'

'He's faster than you,' Father called.

'You'll have to try better next time, won't you?' I said to him, but he didn't like it, and mumbled, 'You've gotta learn the boundaries, Mr Gerlach.'

'Do I? Really?' Like two things had blurred, and what had been fun wasn't, and what had been physical was all in the head.

Later, at tea, I asked this older, broken version of Trish Harmstorf about her son, and she took a moment then said, 'He went away.'

'Where to?'

'Some woman. Musta been good, because we haven't seen him . . .' Deciding if the lie was believable. 'Allen doesn't like to talk about him. Makes him upset, so maybe if you don't say anything?' Helping Jack mix this or that, I can't remember. Then she said, 'I don't know what I did to cause . . . I still remember that time.'

'With Father?'

'They were frightening days. And you, weren't you, you were terrified?'

'I think so.'

And Jack: 'About what?'

'Father's health.'

'See,' she said, 'as much as you want to be in control of a thing . . .'

But for now, it was Ignatz. 'Red Rover all over.' He started off with me, a sort of grin, but something else; hands out, jumping: 'Boo!' I told him to pick on someone his own size, but he said there wasn't, so I'd have to do. I ran, Jamy, Ludwig, all of us. Ignatz realised I was too fast, tackled Jamy and brought him down. A few moments in the dust, we all got over, then looked back, and Jamy kicked him off and said, 'I know why you wanted to play.'

'What is it?' Father called.

They waited for what came next, a tumble towards an infinity of days that repeated, wafer-thin-worse than yesterday, the day before, retreating into an already-written history of how shit life was. Like Kurt (I'd often imagine, in the following years), lying on his bed, thinking that's enough, walking out and saying, 'That wood needs chopping.' Excusing himself from his family's life. Going out and finding a rope and doing what he'd already done, in his head, a thousand times. The act was nothing. Just a way of making the thought go away.

Ignatz extended his hand to help Jamy up, but he didn't take it. He just stood, brushed himself off and said to Ignatz, 'You coulda got any of them.'

Father watched the scene develop. Mother said, 'Maybe that's enough games, you boys. Ignatz, don't encourage them. What about cards? Jamy? Show them how to play twenty-one.'

'I don't feel like cards.'

'Well, just make yourselves scarce.'

One of her sayings, when nothing else worked, when we persisted, and she wanted peace. Allen helped Father up, across the porch, around the house to the yards. I followed, six, seven steps, but miles, really. Allen got in with the donkeys, held one or two, showed Father the ribs, the sores. 'They're not going anywhere.'

'What do you suggest?'

'See what happens tomorrow. But Alf should've known better.'

'He was only trying to help.'

Coming out and saying, 'I got three horses I could give you, but the others need shoes. No spares.' Then: 'You feeling any better?'

'There's nothing wrong with me.'

Allen in a Sunday suit, although it wasn't much – old pants with patched knees, a woollen vest with holes, a tie he was still wearing, years later, when the Gerlachs arrived. And Father in his white shirt, most of the buttons undone to allow his belly to sit, comfortably, above a leather belt Ludwig had made him. Like the donkeys, past their prime.

'Well, there's *something* wrong,' Allen said. 'Or else you wouldn't have got on that cart and come all this way.'

Father stared at me, as though what needed saying couldn't be said now. 'Benno's got it under control, haven't you, son?'

I shrugged.

'We'll pray, eh, Allen?' Smiling.

But Allen wasn't having any of it. 'You told the boy what might happen?'

Like I wasn't there, or couldn't hear. Father said, 'He's not stupid, are you, Benno?'

'He needs to understand,' Allen said, 'that—'

Father just turned and started walking back to the porch. Allen said, 'You gotta be practical out here, don't you, Martin?'

'Me? Practical?' Looking back. 'Jesus, who built a mission, Allen?' Continuing. When he was out of earshot, Allen said to me, 'Not getting much out of him, eh?'

'I guess not.'

'You got some sense of what might happen though?

'Probably won't.'

Allen didn't bother with consolations. 'Things'll become clearer in the next few days. But you know . . . how old are you?'

'Fourteen.'

'That might have to be old enough.'

'For what?'

But he just shook his head, surprised I couldn't see it. 'To take over.'

'The mission?'

'Everything. You might have to grow up quickly, Benno.'

And that was it. He squeezed my shoulder and said, 'Hope for the best, plan for the worst. I was running my dad's farm at thirteen. Had to. He fell under a harvester. It can be done. If need be.'

I didn't want to grow up, or run a mission, or fix cows. Not then, not now. I didn't want to listen to what he had to say. So I followed Father, but Allen called after me, 'If ever I've met a kid with a good head on his shoulders . . .'

Stopping, looking back. 'Sorry?'

'A good head. You. You just need to accept it, Benno.'

'Allen, carve the meat, will you?' his wife called.

So there we were, fifteen minutes later, gathered around the table for our Sunday roast – Allen cutting and serving, Trish with the brussel sprouts, potatoes, turnips curled up beside burnt carrots. Allen said, 'I hope this meat's nice. I had some trouble.'

'How's that?' Mother asked.

'You don't want them knowing what's coming. It's the adrenaline, eh?' Laying four slices on his daughter's plate, as Trish claimed Etsy and threw her on the sideboard.

'But there's not much grass for them anyway, is there, Martin?'

'No.'

'Place has dried out.' Checking everyone's plate, deciding we all had enough, sitting down to pray. 'Dear Lord – bless this beastie, and what's he done for us. And bless Pastor Gerlach, busy doing your work, saving souls.'

'Not too long,' Trish said.

'It's not going anywhere, dear. Bless the Gerlach's journey. Get them to Horseshoe Bend quick smart. And Lord, give the Board a kick up the . . . you know, make them see a bit of sense, while there's still time.'

'Amen,' Father said.

A few minutes eating in silence, then Trish wiped her mouth with a napkin, chewed the tough meat and said, 'I think, when you get to town, you should have a rest, Martin.'

'I can't swallow it,' Gale said.

'Just eat. Martin?'

She was right. It was rubbish. Belt leather. But I knew the trick (from some of Pauline's failures). Deep breath, swallow, continue.

'I'll be looking forward to that,' Mother said. 'Relaxing a bit. Before we have to start organising everything.'

Allen said, 'You've made great progress out there, Martin.'

'Not so much.' He took a bolus from his mouth and gave it to one of the dogs.

'If any of them lot in Adelaide got off their arse and went up there and saw. Most of those buildings . . .' The meat didn't seem to bother him. A couple of quick chews, and down. 'Where'd the money come from?'

'There was no money. Just stuff I salvaged. Or donations, weren't they, Ignatz?'

'By and large.' Sitting in a corner, eating in silence.

'What was your greatest achievement, Martin?' Trish asked.

Father thought about it. 'Convincing myself to get up every morning.'

'It wasn't like that,' Mother said.

'And your greatest regret?'

'Well . . .' Looking at me. 'That day I took you to St John's, remember, Benno?'

Like this. Ever since they'd taken the mixed race kids, Father had said, 'I hope they're looking out for them.' Because that was his only consolation – they'd be looked after, schooled, kept away from a black world that didn't want them, a white world that couldn't stand them. Leading here, St John's, and the day me and Father went to town, caught a train to Semaphore, walked the two miles to the home *his* kids had been sent, knocked on the door, waited for a nun, went in and said, 'How are they coping?'

A dozen, more, sitting in classrooms, and when he stuck his head through the door they waved and called his name and said, 'Eh, Benno, you coming here, too?'

Like that. Like pigeons, plucked and stored in an icebox, ready for cooking. One girl, busy with a mop, said, 'That you, Pastor Gerlach?'

'How you been keeping, Annie?'

'See me mum next week.'

'I know. They told me. Are you looking forward to that?'

'We get the whole day.'

Two boys, working a wringer, and one said, 'When do we get to come home, Pastor?'

'Well, the thing is, they're teaching you . . .' Unable to explain this in-between world was their world now. 'But you saw your dad the other day?'

'Nah, he didn't come. Can you tell him we want him to come? Can you tell him that, Pastor?'

Later, when we got back to the mission, the parents were waiting to hear about their kids. Father told them how happy they were, how they were prospering, learning everything, ready for high school, university, all the stuff they never would've got at Hermannsburg. But I could see it in his face.

'We shouldn't have let the mixed kids go,' he said to Trish.

'That was the right thing to do,' Allen said.

'I'm not so sure.'

'The blacks didn't want a bar of them. And would you, Martin, have them in your home?'

Father lost, wondering what else he might've done. 'I know the situation was . . . but we created the problem, didn't we, Allen?'

'We saved them from themselves,' Allen said. 'Just remember that, Martin. The love of God. Maybe that's our biggest achievement. Introducing them to God.'

'I'm not sure.'

'Why?'

'If a child hasn't got his mother or father or brothers or sisters . . .'

Regrets. Plenty of those about that time, as I remember. But I'd just like to say one thing. Regrets serve a purpose. So there's me, twenty years later, out around Macumba somewhere, and the government was still at it. There was a camp, and plenty of white ringers and travelling people had stopped there over the years, so there were lots of mixed race kids. And one day, I get this letter telling me about this camp and these kids and how they would be taken and cleaned up, educated. I wrote back, I said, Not a good idea. They wrote back saying it's been decided, and it'll happen on such and such a day. So I was there, waiting, and they came with this van, and when they pulled up and said it was time, I said, Look, too late. No kids. They're gone. These people asked the blacks: Where are your kids? But they (I'd even told them what to say) said, 'Gone away to school.'

'Where?'

'The moon. The stars, wasn't it?' Laughing between themselves.

Like this, plenty of times. Burning letters. Arriving ahead of time, organising cars, trucks, whatever was available at the mission, finding beds, for days, weeks, until things blew over. Not that I stopped it all. Or avoided many going. The government was too determined. But I tried.

'You did the right thing,' Allen said to Father. 'One day people'll thank you. You gave them some hope. Look at Isaiah. His paintings fetch hundreds now, eh? But if he hada stayed on the mission . . .'

'He didn't see Micah for years,' I said.

'That's the price they gotta pay.'

'For what?'

'For rooting around.'

Father was too decent, or timid, to say anything more.

In the end, there were seven or eight plates, still with their meat, and Allen Harmstorf said, 'I'm sorry about that, Pastor. I was hoping we could make a decent roast.'

'It was, Allen.'

The Book of Job

Father placed his hand on Silas's head and said, 'I think I can remember.'

'It's quite alright,' Trish said.

'I'd like to, if I may?'

'If you want,' Allen said. 'But you seem tired, Martin.'

'I'm fine.' And again, to Silas. 'We won't worry about the processional or invocation. Let's just get to it.' He made the sign of the cross, and began. '"We humbly kneel before our God, acknowledging our sins."'

Sunday evening, seven, eight, I can't remember. Father set up on the porch, Silas at his feet, the rest of us in chairs moved down from the dining room, a little semicircle, ready for divine service. Me and Mother at the front, Allen and Trish, Gale and Kurt behind them, and further back, Ludwig, Jamy, Ignatz, a few blacks who'd come up from the camp to see what was happening.

'"If we say we have no sin we deceive ourselves, and the truth is not in us,"' Father said, and we replied, '"But if we confess our sins, God who is faithful and just will forgive our sins."'

Father was tired, his eyes opening and closing, his body rocking back and forth. '"Let us then confess our sins to God our Father."' Trying to think of the words he'd said a thousand times in his small, whitewashed church, the dozens of faces watching and listening. But now it was beyond him; like he was blind, reaching out and grasping for each word, and sometimes they were there, sometimes not. '"Almighty God has given his son to die for you."' Smiling, saying, 'Remember, Benno?' Although he wasn't looking at me. 'I was standing waiting when Pauline brought you in, and you were wrinkly and . . . wasn't he Mother?'

'Maybe that's enough?' Mother said.

'Little red fish, looking up and crying. Like all of them. Remember Julius, Mother?'

Silas said, 'He was a fat one.'

'He was, wasn't he?' Father said, laughing. 'But you, Benno. Your mother telling me to hurry up because everyone thought you were going to die. But you proved them all wrong, didn't you? "As a called an ordained servant of Christ . . ."'

There was some chance he'd entered Mananganganga, dragging his puffy feet in the soft sand, some of the old people explaining the paintings. He was saying, 'I sinned, perhaps? I brought my son here, despite knowing.'

Now, he was forgetting. 'The entrance, or the Kyrie?' he said to Silas.

'You gotta forgive our sins.'

'Of course. "I therefore forgive you all your sins." Bob, when he married Molly that time. A decent crowd. Do you remember, Alma? She had that dress. You helped her, remember, took weeks, and I think the other Molly used it when Alf . . . I married him, too, didn't I?'

'Come on,' Mother said, standing, but he said, 'I still don't understand . . .'

We waited.

His head raised: 'I bet you can still feel the water on your head, can't you, Benno?' Smiling at me. '"May God above not care about it . . . light shine above it."'

A divine service was about bringing structure to the diffuse, the scattered, the bits and pieces of life and love and universe that made sense of God and the strange act of being. If all of this fell away it was just *things*, places, people. Father was writing small, mental notes, and nailing them to his own church door (made from rough beams by Ludwig and a few of the men). He was remembering every verse, every quote, every transcribed sermon in an attempt to define the extent of his understanding of this hot, dusty world.

'"May a cloud settle over it . . ." Straight on to the homily, I think, Silas. Allen, is everyone comfortable?'

'Yes, Pastor.'

'Let me explain. People thought they knew about Job, but they didn't. Everyone had an opinion. Some people, that he was a servant of God, others, that he was smug and comfortable and religion was just so much . . .'

Night. The last of the pots and pans washed, put out to dry; a few crows settling; ghosting smoke from extinguished candles, insect chatter from the bit of garden they kept watered. Three types of ephedra (Mother had already pruned) and the occasional flutter of pages from a book left open on the porch. Terese, Kate always asked why I felt the need to return to the desert, and I could never explain. This was about as close as I got – the smell of porcupine grass, cassia, wattle flowers as the day drifted into dusk.

'One day,' Father said, 'Satan appears to God and says, You know this Job character, he doesn't care about you. And God says, What would you know? And Satan says, He's had it too good for too long. You think he worships you, but it's not you, it's not about *you* . . .'

Now he was more comfortable. Now, we were arriving in Leipzig, the biggest railway station in Europe, and Michael and Alwin and Julius and Charlotte were carrying their cases, staring up at the grand hall and saying, 'This place is *so* big.'

Father beside me, saying, 'I just had to tell you one thing, Benno.'

I wasn't listening. This place beat Hamburg, Berlin, all of them. The shops and cafes, a woman holding a small dog as she sang in French, as we colonials dragged our cases towards the entrance. I can remember someone (probably Julius) calling out, the words amplifying, echoing, a few people glaring at us, Mother saying, 'We're not in the outback now.' And thinking, I know. An aniseed-smelling lolly shop, a man in a bowtie emptying humbugs into a bag. As us kids gathered around and waited for Father to take out his wallet.

Afterwards, Father said to me: 'The others will be staying here in Leipzig.' Choosing the right words, calling for Anton to climb another set of stairs. 'But you'll be coming with us.'

'Back to Hermannsburg?'

'Yes.'

'Just me?'

'Yes.'

'Why?'

Back at our outdoor mass, Father said, 'Satan was so convincing, he is, isn't he, Benno?'

'I guess.'

'I guess!' Shaking his head. 'What do you think, Kurt?'

'He's pretty convincing.'

'Exactly! So he says to God, I have an idea. We'll test this Job character. We'll make all of his children die, then see if he still loves you. God thought about this and said, I'm not sure. That's pretty rough. Ten kids. But Satan insisted. If you don't test him, you'll never know if he *really* loves you.'

Love is a slippery bugger. You've got to understand, I didn't walk out on my family for convenience's sake, because I was tired of them, because I couldn't be bothered. It was because I loved Kate more. I've been vague with the details, but I was tested, too. 1982. There I am beside Kate's bed at Memorial Hospital, the smell of cassia and citrus from the bathroom, pumpkin and mint peas from her uneaten meal. I could turn my head and look out across Pennington Gardens, the rows of hedges and just-pruned roses. Thinking how difficult it was to give life this sort of order. The double-glazed windows that wouldn't open. That was the worst. For the whole thing to play out minus a breath of fresh air, a hint of wet wood.

Kate tells me she can't see anymore, but if the optometrist came she could get new glasses. But it wasn't about new glasses. It was about this fist-sized lump behind her eyes. And me saying, 'You should just rest. Sleep. Don't worry about reading,' (she loved to read, anything about science, about the blacks, about the Centre). Me sitting back, reading to her, but stopping every now and then to think, *Why?* '"The geology of the MacDonnell Ranges is still little understood . . ."'

'Keep going.'

'You're tired.'

'I'm fine.'

Kate was a smart woman, considered each thought and word, never spoke harshly of anyone, especially Terese and the kids. A sort of peace I'd never found with Terese; a sort of understanding of the boy Benno. But in the end, all that remained was a woman afraid of opening her eyes, of seeing the end approaching.

Like now, the billions of stars going in and out of phase, as Father said, 'So God agreed. But . . . you've all heard this before, haven't you?'

'Go on,' Allen said. 'We've forgotten, haven't we, Trish?'

'Yes, I can't recall. Something about the devil.'

'So God agrees, and next thing you know, all ten kids. Horrible, really. Poor old Job gets this skin disease and he's sitting there scratching himself all day and he's saying, Why me, God? Why me? "Let me die, without wisdom . . ." Then God says to the devil, There you have it. I shouldn't have doubted.'

We emerged from the station to a big, blue sky, Opa trying to find somewhere for the cart, the other kids running about, climbing some statue, Mother telling them to behave, Father sitting beside me and saying, 'Your mother and I have talked about it, and we've decided, Benno.'

'For how long?'

'A year. A few.'

'But couldn't Anton come, too?'

'He needs to look out for the others.'

'This place looks pretty good,' (although it had already started to snow).

That's how it was. As Father went off to gather the others, Mother tried to organise the cases, I stood, the cold on my face, wondering why it had to be me. Wanting some sort of explanation. Slumping forward, Charlotte coming over and asking what was wrong, wasn't I happy to be in Leipzig, didn't I want to say hello to Oma and Opa, and could we make a man if there was enough snow tonight?

'Job curses God,' Father said, 'and finds him to be unjust. "Whoever perished, being innocent . . ."' He sat for a minute thinking about Job's words and God's reactions, and his old body (though he wasn't old), and his heart, his legs.

'I'm not sure the optometrist has my prescription,' Kate said to me. 'Maybe you could give him a call, Benno?'

'I will.'

'I know I have a spare pair somewhere.' Trying to read the hospital menu. 'What's it say, roast beef?'

I checked. 'Beef or lamb.'

'I'd rather the beef, I think. What about you?'

'They won't feed me.'

'I can get a spare. If you need to stay. You're going to stay, aren't you, Benno?'

'Of course.'

'That old battleaxe nurse said she wasn't paid to read to me . . . But you know what I'd really like?'

I knew. I'd introduced her to Dickens, and she'd grown to love him, as we sat around the fire contemplating the same stars. So now, I picked up my old copy and read: '"Chapter Fifteen. I make another beginning." That was it, wasn't it?'

'Yes. Fifteen. Go on. If he gets me some new specs I can read myself.'

But he wasn't coming, and she had glasses in the drawer beside her bed. Way too late for that. Just a few days, less, before she fell asleep. And then two weeks in a coma before she died. Me sitting there, the whole time, reading *David Copperfield*.

Father said, 'But then Elihu enters the scene, eh, Silas?'

'He does.'

'And . . . you don't want to hear the speech, but he says what the hell is it our business? Why does God need to explain what he does?'

Back at the station, Father sat beside me and said, 'What, you're angry with me now?'

'No.' Glancing at him.

'I need your help, Benno.'

'Why?'

'You can stick to a thing, and finish it, but this lot' – and he indicated, jumping on and off of Opa's cart, scraping snow from the ground and throwing it at each other. 'You'll have to trust me, Benno. I'll need help with the blacks, and with my writing.'

Just then Oma called for him, and he stood and walked off, and I was no closer to understanding.

Like Father, on the porch, holding out his hand, looking for the same answer. 'Not only that God was always right, but he was merciful, and whatever happened was for the best.'

I wasn't sure if Father really believed this. He'd spent his life repeating this story, but got no closer to understanding it. Where was the grace in dropsy? In a brain tumour? In the thousand things he'd endured at Hermannsburg? 'How long did Job live, Silas?'

'A hundred and forty years.'

'Exactly! A hundred and forty, and he had ten more children (imagine his poor wife). God told Satan to go away and made everyone apologise to Job, and there was justice.'

That's how the story ended. Things made right. Kate drifting off to sleep and me saying, 'He did go on a bit, Dickens, didn't he?' Touching her arm, shaking it a little, but she wouldn't wake. Then the nurse came in and checked and said, 'We won't know what's happening . . . if she's okay in the morning.'

The next morning there was cereal, and tea and toast, and orange juice, but Kate just slept. I waited. Hours. I read. Chapters. But all she did was sleep. And maybe, maybe I was back in Leipzig, beside the station, waiting for my father to explain.

Monday 16 October (Day 7)

I woke at six-thirty in my swag on the floor of Kurt's bedroom. Kurt was still asleep. Sun through the blinds, the clang of pans and the smell of cooking bacon, someone saying, 'You better bring in my water.' I slipped on my pants, my shirt, my socks and shoes, went out to the kitchen and one of the girls said, 'Where are you making it?' Pointing at me and laughing.

'Sorry?'

'Making it? Where are you making it?'

'Making what?'

But they both laughed again, checked the bacon, lined up the eggs, spooned tea into the pot.

I went outside, dogs sniffing each other, birds waiting on an empty feeder, a few of Gale's dolls left on the lawn. The sun was already hot on my arms and face, and I knew it was going to be a stinker. I went around to the front of the house and saw Ludwig and Jamy asleep next to each other, Ignatz off under an arbour covered with jasmine. Apart from that, nothing. I heard a didgeridoo, and stopped and listened. The drone through the warm air, and a voice, a small variation on the single note – although I couldn't work out what he was singing about. So I walked around the house, down the hill to the blacks' camp, and there, six or seven men gathered listening to a teenager playing. They just watched me. Didn't say a thing. I sat and said, 'I'm Benno.' They didn't care.

This Isaiah moment, this Micah moment, as I drove into his camp near Alice Springs (1950, perhaps), got out and said to him, 'Your dad around?'

He just shook his head. So I studied his paintings, which were all the same painting, and said, 'Selling many?'

'Couple.'

'How much are you getting?'

'Two quid.' Showing me with his fingers.

'You shouldn't be selling them for two, Micah. What about your dad?'

'He's gone into the dealer. Gives him five.' Again, showing his fingers. 'Says he can get him a drink.'

'Who?'

'The bloke with the picture shop. Drink, and some flour, and when the boys come from Hermannsburg we can have damper and grog.'

'You gotta ask for more money, Micah. I saw them in his shop. Twenty, thirty quid. He keeps it all for himself.'

'Nah.' Shaking his head. 'Treats Dad good.'

'No, he treats him rubbish. Isaiah's too good for that, Micah. You're too good. Ask ten, at least.'

Looking around this camp. The huts full of stirring bodies, dogs – one with no back legs, dragging its body – kids playing in the muck. I asked him if he wanted me to take them, but he said they weren't interested. 'But they gotta learn, Micah.'

'We'll teach them.'

'They gotta learn to add up and write.'

'Why?'

'So they can get some sort of job, eh?'

'Who's gonna give them a job, Benno?'

He had a point. This was no Hermannsburg schoolroom, no washed pants and shirts, no brilliantine hair. I said, 'If they can't do maths, how are they gonna know how much money they're due?'

'You wanna buy this one?' Showing me a picture he'd barely begun. 'I can finish it while you wait. The pastor liked them like this, eh? Dad said so. He had a few. And poor old Silas, he had plenty, didn't he? He paid us good for them.'

'He did?'

'Yeah, plenty. Mad bastard, wasn't he?'

Each time I went back, a month, a year later, it was always the same.

One time I went and saw this dealer, Volker or something, and I told him he should be paying them better. He said why, they just drink it all. I said he should start a bank account and put some aside for them for when they're old and need some place to stay, or want their kids to go town to school. But again, he just laughed and said that would never happen. I said, You giving them two quid doesn't make it right. And he said, Well, the government doesn't give them anything. Which was right. 'Compared to what your lot did to them, Mr Gerlach, I reckon I'm helping.'

'My lot?'

'Teaching them to depend on others. They used to be able to look after themselves. Forty thousand years, until your dad taught them they gotta sew some old girl's frocks, or muster some bloke's cows. So I'm not sure *I'm* the problem, eh?'

'My dad did a lot for them.'

'He did. He helped them. But he also made the problem worse.'

The young bloke finished playing the didgeridoo, handed it to me and said, 'Have a go.'

'I can't.'

'Go on.'

They all insisted, laughed, and the young man showed me how to hold it: 'Blow good and hard.'

So I tried, but it was just a buzz, and they laughed even harder. One of the old fellas fell off his log and said it was like something coming out of his arse, and demonstrated, and they cackled some more, and I tried again, and they laughed again.

Like Tom, standing in front of his class, saying, 'This is a traditional Aboriginal instrument, but I don't think it's played much anymore, is it, Grandpa?' Checking with me, standing at the back of the room, ironed pants and shirt. I said, 'Hardly ever these days, Tom,' and he told his class, 'They didn't have stuff like we do, like a piano or anything. They couldn't carry that around in the outback, I suppose.' Some smart-arse asked if they had violins, and Tom said, 'That wouldn't make much sense either, would it?'

Me, Jack and maybe twenty other parents listening to our kids and grandkids showing and telling the thing 'That Makes Me Special'. Tom. A didgeridoo. We'd just sat through some Italian kid showing us pictures of the car he was fixing up with his father; and a girl with a hockey stick saying she'd been selected for the state team, and hardly anyone got in, so it was quite an achievement, wasn't it, Mum? As the old girl (in a pricey frock, pearl necklace and a blue bob) nodded and said, 'Yes, only two per cent of kids make it.' Cow.

I won't get started on class or anything, but just to mention, the kids in their blazers and pressed pants and ties and badges saying they were vice-president of this and that, head prefect, lacrosse club, you get the picture. A bunch of little misters and misses. Winners, I think they're called these days. Even Jack, looking like George Bush in some silk suit, and me, like something the cat had dragged in. But I didn't care. Tom certainly didn't care. He just said, 'So this didgeridoo is from Arnhem Land, and it isn't just for them to blow in. It's not a toy. It's important to these people because it's how they tell their stories.'

One boy said, 'They don't do that now, do they?'

'Yeah,' Tom said.

'But don't they just watch television and . . .' Smiling, looking around, but deciding he didn't have the numbers.

'My Grandpa, there' – Tom pointed, and they all turned their heads to see – 'was born on a mission in the desert, and when he was fourteen his dad got sick and they had to get him to this place called Horseshoe Bend, to get help. Right through the desert. Like some film or something. Then when he was older he was a . . . what was it, Grandpa?'

'A patrol officer.'

'That's right, and he had to take care of the *Indigenous* people to make sure they were okay. He did that for like, thirty years or something.'

Maybe that was the best I'd ever felt. Maybe that one moment made it all worthwhile. I think. Some kid (who'd just told us he could ski barefoot) said, 'Where did he get the didgeridoo?'

I said, 'Some old blokes gave it to me as a present.'

Now's the bit where I could write an essay about ownership, people having their own stuff, protecting it, value-adding, making money, personal wealth, investments, fancy cars (like the ones I saw in the car park that morning at Scotch College). But I won't. You do the research. Find out. They didn't see things that way. Never had, would or will. Which was part of the problem, perhaps. They didn't want to play our game. They didn't want to get ahead, do better, compete, send their kids to Scotch. They didn't want to import coffee machines and sell them with a mark-up and think they were doing something clever.

'And these paintings,' the teacher, a forty-something man-boy, asked, 'have some sort of spiritual significance?'

'Yes,' Tom said (I'd explained it to him). 'There's a story about three caterpillars . . .' He took a minute to give them the condensed version. 'And that's how they think things were made, don't they, Grandpa?'

'They do.'

'Compared to science or geology, which they still understand . . . but they like to believe, I guess, sort of like we believe in God and stuff.'

And some kid (who'd told us about his trips to Paris) said, 'But didn't you say there was a mission?' Turning to me. I said, 'The Lutherans thought people should be taught about . . . they were complex times.'

'So they were *made* to believe?'

'No one made them believe anything. But you're right, we saw things differently back then.'

'Wasn't it like a genocide?' the hockey girl said.

'No, it wasn't.'

'But didn't the white people go around shooting the black people?'

'No, that never happened.'

'It did.'

'Well, a few bad ones. There was a bloke called Dietrick, for example, but . . . for everyone like him there were a hundred others trying to do good. Like my father. And me.'

Tom sat, put the didgeridoo to his lips, made a nice drone, stopped and said, 'The hard part's circular breathing, so you don't stop.' He tried again, and breathed and blew at the same time, as good as any of the blacks I'd seen, and the kids were all surprised, and excited, and tried to do the same.

Jack poked my arm and said, 'Quite the hit.'

But it was all about Tom – adding a rhythm, short and sharp notes, long and dramatic. Eventually he placed the didgeridoo in the coat rack, sat down, turned back to me and mouthed, 'Was that okay?'

I gave him the thumbs up. *Beautiful*. Jack said, 'I think I'm becoming surplus to need.'

'You're the one knocked on my door.'

On the way home, Jack said to me, 'You should come for tea one night. Steph'd like to meet you.'

I felt myself slipping into their lives, like pulling on a pair of old pants. I said, 'It's remarkable what Tom can do.' Maybe there was something in my voice. I'm not sure. I'd always been taught to hide emotions. It wasn't a habit you could break. But Jack squeezed my arm and said, 'It's good, Dad, isn't it?'

'What?'

He didn't say. Just lifted his hands from the wheel, looked at me, like there was some question I should answer.

'It's good.'

Imagine me sitting with my dad, and him saying, 'It's pretty remarkable what you can do.' Squeezing my arm. Although that's what I was hoping for in the Hermannsburg days, watching Father, waiting for a way in, somewhere I might meet him, halfway through the long paddock of things-better-left-unsaid. Sometimes I tried. I said, 'How many years have you been out here?' And he said nearly thirty, and I said, 'I bet no one else has stuck it out as long as you.' And maybe he said, 'It's what I chose to do, Benno.' Theory being, whatever I gave I'd get back. But that's not how I remember it. 'I reckon all the blacks look up to you, Father.'

'How?'

'Respect you. A father. Ingkata, isn't it? Isn't that where it comes from?'

'Just the way they say it.'

'But they mean it. The way they line up and wait for you and do what you say and always come to the door asking for advice. *Ingkata*?'

Nothing seemed to work. Nothing I gave ever came back. All I heard about was plans, succession, what might happen *if*, *after*. That was it. What did I care about a will? About comparative dictionaries, the fate of Hermannsburg? I just wanted to know the feeling of Room 6B, Scotch College, 17 October 1988.

Back at Idracowra, I could smell bacon and eggs. I said, 'I'll be back,' and they said good luck with ingkata (they all knew someone who'd been baptised, confirmed, married, educated or buried). I ran up the hill, onto the back porch, leaving the didgeridoo with the spades and shovels. Mother came out and said, 'Where have you been?' She told me to wash my hands, find Father, God knows what he's doing out in his condition. So I went around to the water tank and saw Father standing with his Box Brownie, pointing it at the distant ranges. 'Mother says come in.' He looked up, down, into his camera. 'Lot of good, this.'

'What?'

He motioned to me to come over. So I joined him, took the camera, peered through the cracked lens. 'You can still take pictures.'

But he shook his head, reclaimed the camera and threw it into a pile of old steel and iron, a bed with a broken back. 'Had that forty years.'

'We'll get you another one in town.'

'Perhaps.'

When we went in for breakfast, Ignatz was already buttering toast, piling on the bacon, eggs. He said, 'I won't bother you then.'

'What?' Father asked.

He went out the back door, sat on a pile of clothes beside the didgeridoo.

Then we ate, all in a circle, Allen and Trish, Kurt and Gale, nothing said, a grunt here, pass the salt, if you would, like the hospitality, or at least patience had worn out. Allen whispered, 'So what are you going to do about Ignatz, Martin?' (the stories, I'd assumed, had leaked). 'He can stay here with us. You've got too many on that dray anyway.'

'He can come.'

Jamy looked up from his food. Ludwig said, 'Maybe, considering . . .'

'He can come!'

Mother said, 'It's not like we're going back there, and starting again, with him hanging around. Not a hope.'

'You don't know the full story, Alma.'

'What?'

'If you'd had an upbringing like his . . .' Watching her pleadingly, but returning to his food.

'What?' Mother asked.

'Thrown into a bloody home by his hopeless mother. And what they did to him.' He realised he'd said too much. 'He can come, and we can sort it out. I'm meant to be getting better. Apparently.'

Mrs Gus Elliot

Kurt led me down the hallway, turned and said, 'Shh.' Took a few steps, waited outside his sister's room, listening. 'Do you know how old she is?'

I shrugged.

He didn't tell me. Just waited, grinning, and Gale said, 'Let me do your hair. Do you want me to put it up in a bun?'

Kurt nearly laughed. He played with his hair, pulled a face that was his sister's face, I suppose.

'Or like this . . . have you had a bath today, Etsy?'

'Fourteen,' he whispered to me. 'Fourteen.'

'I bet that's nice and cool, Etsy. With this hot weather, and there's a lot more to come . . . Yes, I know, but what can you do? Terribly vulgar, aren't they, but we have to, I suppose.'

I could hear water splashing as, I supposed, she bathed Etsy. 'There, and some soap . . . I know, I know, but if I don't wash your hair it'll get all hard and scaly.'

Kurt said, 'Mum reckons it's normal, but it's not normal, is it, Benno?'

'I guess she's not hurting anyone.'

He didn't like this. Of course she was hurting someone. Him. And who talked to a doll when they were fourteen?

'Now, let me dry you off properly, Etsy. Under the arms . . . you know what happened to Mum because she didn't dry herself properly.'

Kurt turned into her doorway, stood watching, then said, 'What are you up to?'

I couldn't see her; I didn't hear her response.

'And that's her boyfriend, isn't it?'

No reply.

'You don't want to dress her in that, it's way too hot.'

And angrily: 'It's not too hot for her. She doesn't feel the heat like we do.'

Kurt pulled me into the room and said, 'See, this is what she does all day.'

'Not all day,' Gale said, placing the fully-dressed Etsy into a miniature wicker chair.

Kurt stepped forward, took a similar boy doll, held it up and said, 'This is . . . what's his name?'

'Errol.'

'*Errol.*'

'Give it back.' Reaching out, grabbing, but Kurt held it higher.

'Errol and Etsy are in love,' Kurt said. 'And they like to . . .' He picked up Etsy, held her against Errol, and rubbed them together. 'They like to make love, don't they, Gale?'

She moved around him, tried to grab her dolls, but he was too quick. 'They like to go all night. I hear them, Benno!' Laughing. 'Etsy says, Oh, Errol, that feels so good.'

Gale reclaimed the dolls, but Kurt picked up a big, porcelain baby and said, 'This is Leo. He's their first child. Conceived under Gale's bed. And there are others, aren't there, Gale?'

She grabbed Leo and said, 'No.'

Kurt wasn't happy. 'But you don't think they're real, do you? A person your age doesn't think dolls are people and can talk and need a bath, because that would be completely retarded, wouldn't it, Benno?'

'Shut up. Get out!' Punching him to go. 'I hate you!' She ran from her room, from the house, and Trish called down the hallway, 'What's all that about?'

'She's got the shits on.'

I could see her go, across the yard, into the scrub. I could hear Trish on the porch, calling for her to come back, giving up and storming down the hallway. 'You been giving her a hard time?'

Kurt just stood, Etsy in hand. 'No.'

Then Allen, calling from the front of the house. 'Trish, they're here.'

We left the room, down the hall, out the front door. Allen and Silas were waiting on the porch, watching the approaching cloud of dust. Allen said, 'They made good time.'

'How many horses they got?' Trish asked.

Mother helped Father come out, and he said, 'Four, and some spares. Praise the bloody Lord, Alma, we're back in business!'

Four horses, two spares – loose, frisky, jumping about, Allen's men on their Idracowra horses. And at the rear, Mrs Gus Elliot. 'Martin . . . Allen.' Jumping down, coming over and spitting dirt and saying, 'You lot are the welcome, are you?'

'We'll have to do,' Allen said, attempting a half-hug. 'I wasn't expecting you till later tonight.'

'No point fluffing about, is there, Benno?' She messed my hair. Everyone did. God I hated that. I wasn't six anymore, and I certainly didn't play with dolls.

We went in, settled in the sitting room, and Father wanted to know the whole story. When did you hear? So you must've come straight away? You must've ridden all night? But she just said, 'No, we stopped and slept for a bit.'

'You must've gone quick, I mean, what is it?' Checking his watch.

'We don't muck around, Martin.' She drank some barley water, wiped her mouth, mud across her face. 'You know we don't muck around. Specially when it comes to someone's health. And you've been okay then, yesterday?' Studying his naked legs, his big feet, his Father Christmas belly, let out for air.

'Don't worry about me, Lou. I'm alright. It's just the donks gave up. We've been stuck here, well, not stuck, I mean, we've had to stay, with the very best hospitality.'

Trish motioned to Kurt and said, 'Tell Gale to come in and say hello to Lou.'

'I don't know where she is.'

'Just do what you're told.'

So he went out, and Lou Elliot said, 'Jack's been telling us all about yers.'

'He's at Horseshoe Bend?'

'Coupla days ago. Said you were up on a chair on the dray, the only way you could sit.'

'But it's worked, hasn't it, Ludwig?'

Standing at the door, shaking his head. 'So far.'

Like this, like a coffee clutch, one of the girls refilling Lou's drink, Ludwig standing back, Jamy peering in from further down the hallway, even Ignatz, leaning on the front door jamb.

'These are good horses, Martin,' Lou said. 'They'll get you there. If we leave tomorrow.'

'Tomorrow?'

'We gotta rest them.'

'What about tonight, when it cools down?'

'And I reckon it might,' Allen said. 'According to the barometer. At least a few degrees.'

So Lou agreed. Tonight. As long as the horses were okay. She said, 'There's good and bad news, I guess.'

'How's that?' Father asked.

'I saw Pastor Stolz and that Wurst fella, what's his name?'

'Gotthold.'

'. . . at Stevenson Crossing. Wurst's car was a mess. They were trying to fix it, but they couldn't. Wurst said to tell you sorry.'

'He got that far?' Father said.

'All the way from Oodnadatta. Couple of hours. Decent job, I reckon, but a car like that was never up to it. He shoulda known. Shoulda had some common sense. Or the pastor shoulda told him.'

'But he *tried*,' Father said. 'He got that far?'

'Lucky for him it happened at the crossing. Lucky it wasn't out in the middle of nowhere. They coulda died out there, this weather. They didn't think.'

Trish insisted that Lou rest, and she went and laid on their bed, fell asleep straight away. Half-snoring, as we sat and discussed the good news, and Father said, 'See, bitta faith. That's all we needed.'

'No, we needed Lou,' Mother said.

'We did. Lou. And those horses. They'll get us there, won't they, Allen?'

He'd been out. He'd put them in the stables. He'd given them his best feed, and fresh water. He'd checked them over, and said to me, 'She's picked some good ones.' Running his hand over twitching flanks, strong calves. 'You might be okay after all, Benno.'

Horseshoe Bend tomorrow, the train, a hospital smelling of ether. Father would come good, but he'd learn his lesson, and he'd say, 'Never again, Benno,' and we'd flee this inferno of hot sand and fires.

When we went back in, Trish was talking to Kurt, her face an inch from his. 'She can'tve just gone nowhere.'

'I don't know.'

'What was all that business about?'

He shrugged.

'Go look again. Get the blacks to help you. She can'tve gone far.'

'What, no sign?' Mother asked.

Trish just said, 'Don't worry, it happens. She always comes home, eventually.'

I went out with Kurt. We walked back to the blacks' camp, told them they better help us look for Gale, and they said, 'Again?' But agreed, and spread out, started searching. We sat on a log in front of their fire and Kurt said, 'At least you're getting out of the place.'

'You can, too.'

'How?'

'Plenty of things. Go to uni.'

'With six years of school?'

'Drive a train?'

'That'd be okay, eh?' Then he flicked a bug with a stick, looked up, said, 'If you had parents like mine . . .'

'I do.'

'Nah . . .' Shouting. 'Gale!' Returning to the beetle. 'Or a sister like mine.'

That was Kurt, as I remember him now. This little cloud of dust, whipping himself into a frenzy, losing energy, settling.

'Maybe if I'd had a brother,' he said, 'instead of a . . . retard.'

We sat there for half an hour, talking, when we should've been searching. I said, 'If she tells your parents . . .?'

'So what?'

'Should we look?'

'Why? I might find her.'

Eventually the blacks returned and said they couldn't find her, so we went back to the house. Into the kitchen, and we heard Lou, freshly-bathed, saying, 'All of that aside, he's a bloody good doctor.'

'He's at Oodnadatta?' Father asked.

'Yes.'

'And you reckon he could make it to Horseshoe Bend?'

'He said if you can get there, phone him, he'll tell you what to do. He's from Marree, and he'll have to get back, but he says, if need be, he'll try to get to us.'

'That's even better, isn't it?' Mother said to Father, but he just said to Lou, 'We're getting closer, aren't we?'

Ludwig came in and motioned to Trish, and she went over and he whispered, then she said, 'There's no sign of her.'

Kurt looked at me. Nothing in his face. Trish asked him what he'd said to her.

'Nothing. Why's it my fault?'

The search went like this. Me and Kurt heading towards the low hills that led, eventually, to the ranges; Lou and Allen out back, past the blacks' camp, the dry creek, across salty country with no trees; Ludwig and Jamy, even Ignatz, searching the sheds. The rest of the blacks looking for tracks. I said to Kurt, 'What if she just kept walking?'

'She wouldn't do something that dumb.'

After an hour, Kurt stopped and said, 'She wouldn't have come this far.'

So we headed back. We retraced our steps. As we approached the house we saw Mother, Trish, Ludwig on the porch, and I called, 'Has anyone found her?'

Before they could answer, Allen stormed from the house, half-ran towards his son, and when he got to him he raised his hand, went to strike him, but Kurt moved away. Allen reached for him, grabbed him, struck him across the face, and again, and now Trish came running down from the house and said, 'Allen, stop it.'

Father and son stood a few feet apart, waiting. Lou came out of the house and called, 'She'll be fine, Allen.'

Anyway, that's how I remember that morning. I remember Kurt sitting on the porch as we sat at the table eating cold beef. And later, when Mother and Father were back on their bed, and Lou was asleep again, and things had settled (Allen out fitting the wheels on the dray), I went down the hall, stopped at Gale's door, peered in. Lying in her bra and underwear, her body red, burnt, fine scars from thorns – across her face, her neck, her chest. Dried, already. Etsy and Errol asleep beside her.

Kurt came up behind me and I said, 'She's crook.'

He stepped into her room and said, 'Gale, you awake?'

She opened her eyes, turned away from him, but he said, 'I'm an idiot.'

She spoke with dry lips. 'You wouldn't have said it if he wasn't here.' Pointing at me.

'I guess. D'yer need a drink?' He didn't wait for a reply. He picked up her water, held it to her lips, lifted her head, waiting as she drank. 'I'm an idiot,' he repeated.

The Spanish Flu

Thomas, Caleb and Ezekiel. Eight, nine years old, all spindly and dusty, telling me to hurry up. I tried to work out who'd be easiest, clumsiest, but they were little rabbits, jumping about in the sun. Mother came out with a basket and started hanging clothes on the line. 'Want to join in?' I asked her.

'I haven't got time for that sort of thing.'

Caleb said, 'This is getting boring.'

'Red Rover all over!' They shot across the compound, I threw myself at Ezekiel (the smallest) but he was gone, all of them, gone, and I was left standing, and they were laughing, and Mother said, 'You'll have to do better than that, Benno.'

Kurt watched from the side of the house. He'd been forbidden to come out of his room, but he'd climbed out his window anyway. And Gale, at her window, watching us, but when I waved she pulled the curtain across.

'How's ingkata?' Caleb called to Mother.

'Fine,' Mother said. She didn't spend much time talking to the blacks. Just fine. That's all they needed to know.

'Come on!' Ezekiel said, but Thomas wanted to know: 'Benno, is your dad gonna make it to Horseshoe Bend?'

'Of course. Why wouldn't he?' More, perhaps, for my mother's benefit.

'It'd be bad if he died.'

'He's not going to die!' Mother said.

'Looks like it. Dad reckons he will.'

'Who's your dad?' Mother asked, furious, holding a pair of socks.

Thomas just shrugged.

'Well, you tell him to mind his own business, and not talk about people behind their backs.'

'Sorry.'

'You should be. That sort of thing very definitely doesn't help.'

Kurt laughed, and Mother asked him what was so funny, but he just said, 'Nothing.'

'Red Rover all over!' They went again, but I had no hope. Caleb said, 'You gotta try get us, Benno.'

'I know how to play.'

'You're slow!' They all laughed.

Caleb said, 'You better get a doctor quick.'

I didn't reply; neither did Mother.

'If yer heart stops.' He stuck out his tongue, pretended to faint, and lay in the dust. Mother stormed over, flicked him with a singlet and said, 'Get up!'

So he got up, laughing, and they all laughed, and she said, 'Do you think that's a nice thing to do, what's your name?'

'Caleb.'

'Silly little boy. Think about others, perhaps. Who's your father?'

'Benny.'

'Well, I'll be having a word to him, believe me.'

And from the side of the house: '*Believe me . . .*'

'Sorry?' Mother called to Kurt, but he just smiled.

She'd had enough. She'd blown her steam, I could tell. She returned to the line, and the washing, muttering under her breath, shaking her head.

'You get one more go, then I'm it,' Caleb said.

'It's my turn. Until I get someone.'

Just what I said to Jack and Sharon, as we stood in the park opposite our house in Prospect. 'Don't worry, I'll get you.'

And Jack. 'Unlikely.'

'I bet she's been cursing me?' I asked.

'Sort of.'

'She has? When?'

But he just shrugged, lifted his hands in the air so I'd be sure.

It was 1956, and I'd popped by to visit. Terese had greeted me at the front door and said, 'What do you want?' I'd replied, 'I thought I could say hello to the kids.'

'Why?'

'Because they're my kids.'

Eventually she'd agreed. 'You can have fifteen minutes . . . over there, in the park.'

'I was thinking of taking them to the movies.'

'You didn't phone ahead.'

'I just thought of it.'

She stood with her hands on her hips. 'It's not a good time. Sharon's got ballet at two. Half an hour. The park. Next time, call ahead.'

I was it, and the kids stood waiting for me, but there wasn't much spirit, much fun in it. I said to Jack, 'Just cos it's changed doesn't mean I can't come and see you two.'

Sharon said, 'If you wanted to see us why did you piss off?'

Instead of arguing, I said, 'Red Rover all over.' Jack took a few steps, waited, said, 'You can get me now.'

'You gotta try.'

'*Really*?'

Sharon didn't move. Just stood there, arms crossed. I told her to try, but she checked her watch and said she had ballet. I said to Jack, 'Is there any point?' He walked around me, kept going, to the other side of the park, then waved his hands in the air. 'Oh, look, I made it!'

Thomas and the others weren't so easy. Across again, diving and darting, Caleb rolling on the ground, back up, to the other side. Mother laughed and said, 'Goodness, Benno, you don't seem to be doing too well.'

'They're fast.'

'You're slow,' Kurt called.

'Aren't you meant to be in your room?' I said to him, and he shrugged.

Mother said, 'You're never going to get anywhere like that.'

'You couldn't do any better.'

'You think?' She threw a pair of knickers in the basket, stormed to the middle of the compound, indicated for me to join the others, and said out loud, 'Which of you kids runs the best?'

Thomas said he did.

'Right, let's have you.' Rubbing her hands, leaning forward, like she was determined to forget where she was, what was happening.

All of this, like Terese, storming across from the house and saying, 'That's your time, Benno.'

'It hasn't been half an hour.'

'Close enough.'

The kids didn't need any encouragement. They walked across the park, back to the house, and I called, 'Maybe we could go see a film?' But neither replied. Terese said, 'Wasn't such a success then?'

'What have you been telling them?'

She came closer, right in my face, and said, 'Nothing. I've been telling them nothing. I've been careful not to. That' – indicating – 'is entirely their own choice, Benno, so don't give me any shit about brainwashing them.' She turned and walked back to the house, and I knew I had problems. I knew there was no going back, no more Red Rover, no more *Tarzan*.

How it was. For thirty-odd years. Until Jack knocked on my door and said hello.

So there was Mother, waiting, and she said, 'Red Rover all over!' We all sprinted past her. Not so much sprinted as ran, walked, teased her by dragging our feet in the sand, saying, 'Oh, no, I think she's going to get me!' I said to her, 'You gotta try harder, Mother.'

'I don't need your advice.'

'Yes, you do,' Kurt said, and she turned and glared at him. 'I would've thought, considering . . .' And then from Gale's room, a muffled, 'Me too.'

'Red Rover!' she called, and we ran, and she reached to touch us, but couldn't get close. Then she said, 'I've got better things to do,' and returned to the washing. Caleb said, 'You gotta keep going till you get someone.'

'Benno, take over.'

So I went into the middle. 'This isn't fair. You kids are faster than me.'

'Don't make excuses,' Mother said.

'*Me*?'

Kurt laughed.

'You get back into your room!' Mother said to him, pointing.

'Why? You're not my mother.'

Trish came out and said, 'What's all this about?'

Mother explained, and Trish shouted at her son to get back to his room, and he went, half-grinning at me, up the back stairs, and inside.

'I've had enough,' I said, and the boys said no, we had to finish what we'd begun, but I just said, 'What's the point? You win. I gotta see how Father is.'

Twenty minutes later, I sat watching Mother rubbing ointment onto Father's legs. 'Just keep still, Martin.' Father face down on the day lounge. Trish sat across the room, watching. 'It's that attitude of his that gets to me, Alma.'

Father groaned. 'Go easy, Alma.'

'I gotta get it in deep.' As she examined the weeping sores, the pussy skin she kept bandaged. 'Maybe you should sit differently?'

'How?'

'Take the pressure off.'

I knew why. I had my own sore arse. Sitting on the same spot for days, trying to shift, to keep comfortable, as the dray rocked back and forth. Father said, 'He's doing it on purpose.'

'Who?'

'Him! God. Gott. Altjira.'

'Don't be so dramatic.'

And from his muffled mouth. 'Seven days. Stinking hot every day. *He* could've done something about it.'

'I'm not sure he's interested in the weather.'

Trish said, 'Nothing bothers Kurt. He doesn't care.'

'Jesus, Alma, that hurts!'

'The things he says. Right to your face. You're lucky you're not dealing with that, Alma.'

Mother turned to me. 'He's no angel.'

'What?' I asked.

And Father: 'Every day. Stinking hot. Then the horses, the donks, like someone's got it all planned for me.'

Mother made him turn over so she could get to his other leg. 'So God's got it all worked out? Torture Pastor Gerlach?'

'If it wasn't for people like you, Trish, and others . . .'

Silas rose from his spot in the shadows, approached Father and said, 'We can get them better, eh, Missus Gerlach?'

'Of course.'

He knelt beside the day bed. 'He's testing you, I reckon, Pastor.'

'Don't start all that rubbish, Silas. I've been tested enough. There's no God. I know it. I saw it. We did, didn't we, Silas?'

'When?'

'That Trevor boy.'

'That was years ago.'

'Who was he?' Trish asked.

'During the flu epidemic,' Father said, 'those couple of years back. Place was full of it, remember, Alma?'

'Yes.'

'God'd forgotten Hermannsburg, apparently. There was this one boy, Trevor, and he had it. He coughed and spewed and he was hot and stiff and we had him in the hospital, remember, Alma? I think that Fielke woman was there at the time.'

'She was long gone by then.'

'Either way. This boy's mother comes in during the night and gets him and takes him somewhere, miles out in the desert, and leaves him there. Then she comes back and we're asking, *What did you do with him?* But she wouldn't say. Just, *He's better off*, or something like that. Can you imagine, Trish? This little boy sitting out in the middle of nowhere till he's dead. With God watching!' He tried to sit up, to see what she'd make of it.

Mother was wrapping Father's sores with bandages. She said, 'You get like this.'

'What?'

'When things are . . . you always tell that story about the boy in the desert.'

Father wasn't finished with Trish. 'Me and Silas, didn't we, Silas, we got on our horses and rode around the mission, way out, for days, looking for Trevor, but we couldn't find him.' So tired he let his face sink into the cushion, closed his eyes, waited as Mother finished the bandages.

But there was more to the story. About how, a few months later, some of the men came back from the desert and presented this mother with her son – a small, black parcel with no arms, where the dogs and birds had got to him. Father gave him a funeral and he was buried in the graveyard beside the church, along with all the other kids that God had killed. Sometimes, when Father was dark, it was all God's fault; other times, just kiddies He'd *allowed* to die (apparently not as bad); other times, He had nothing to do with it at all. Sometimes, of a night, Father would say he was never the same after wrapping this little body in cloth, and sealing the coffin. That was one cure for the flu. God's cure. But now, I guess, he was too tired to finish the story.

I said to Trish, 'I agree with Father.'

'What?' Mother asked.

'God.'

'Don't talk about what you don't know.'

But I did know. I knew then, and I know now. 'God's *shit*!' I said to them.

'Benno!'

'What's he ever done for me, or anyone?' For the half-castes, for Jamy, for Father, for Anton, for Alwin, Michael, Julius, Charlotte, for the millions dead in the trenches and from the flu, for Ignatz, even (I knew how he was taken by the hand, walked to the wash-house). 'He's shit.'

Mother and Trish stared at me.

'Don't you understand? *Es gibt keinen Gott*!'

'Benno!'

'*Niemand kommt*! Can't you see? *Niemand*. No one. *No one's coming*.'

I ran out to the side of the house, to Thomas and Ezekiel and Caleb, and I called, '*Es gibt keinen Gott*!'

They didn't understand.

'*Voller Krankheit*! Mendabatanga, you idiots!'

Rebecca Lee

Father slowed across the compound, noticed one of Gale's dolls in the sand, steadied himself and picked it up. He examined it, then continued to the front porch, saw me and said, 'Helping your mother?'

'Yep.'

He went in and called, 'Gale, is this yours?'

'Benno!' Mother. I ran around to the back door and she was waiting, holding a Lux box full of food. 'Put it in nice and tight.' I returned to the newly-repaired dray and handed the supplies to Lou. She packed them beside Kangkaita and Oolong No. 29. 'Any more?'

Back to the porch, and I said hello to Gale, sitting watching me. She said, 'What time are you going?'

I shrugged.

'You could stay here. Wait till they come back.'

'Father needs me.'

Mother came out and handed me another box. 'Make sure it doesn't move about.' She went in and I said to Gale, 'Anyway, we might not come back.'

'Why?'

'When Father gets better. I got school.'

'Where?'

'Immanuel.'

She seemed disappointed. 'Dad reckons I don't need no more school.'

'It's heavy.' I carried the box around to Lou, returned, and Gale said, 'Once you go to school – you coming back?'

'Maybe.'

'You'll go away. They all go away.'

'Sometimes people need to . . . you could go to Immanuel. Your dad's an elder.'

But she just shrugged, and stroked her doll.

'You'd be a good . . . like a governess, or maybe a teacher. You're good with kids.'

She gazed at the distant pink hills. 'Who's gonna trust me with their kids?'

'Benno!'

I went in and Mother was packing another box with salt, sugar, bread, fresh from the oven; a leg of lamb, wrapped in cloth, bleeding fat and blood; bush biscuits, a few apples and oranges. She said to Trish, 'Listen, keep these' – putting them back on the table – 'we can get more at Horseshoe Bend, and you're short on fruit, aren't you?'

'We got plenty.' Putting them back in the box.

'It's only a day.' Taking them out. But Trish won. She returned them and said, 'You need to make sure Martin's eating proper.'

'Just a bit of bread,' Father called from the sitting room, before appearing, smelling a lemon, saying, 'We're not sailing to England.'

Then, with the box packed, Trish moved closer to Father. 'Me and Alma were having a word about Ignatz.'

'Don't worry about him.'

'He's fine to stay here. He can help out, and he can wait till you return. He doesn't serve any purpose, Martin. I'm not even sure why you brought him.'

Father thought for a moment, then said, 'I need someone . . . sensible.'

'What about me?' Mother said, placing a banana in the box, a jar of oats.

'I'll tell him, if you're worried,' Trish said.

'*No.*'

'Martin!' Mother growled. 'He meant every word of it, you know.'

'He wrote it in anger.'

'Don't be soft. *Reprehensible actions?* Unfit for the service, the duty he's been given.'

Father sat on a wobbly chair, steadied himself. 'I've said worse.'

'Christ, Martin!' She spread a tea towel over the food, slid the box across the table and told me to take it out. The back porch, Gale ('You coming back, Benno?'), Lou, who said, 'Tell her that'll do. Day's trip. No one's about to starve, eh, Benno?'

I darted back to the porch ('Gonna sit and talk to me, Benno?'), into the kitchen, and Mother standing with a letter in her hand. 'Listen to this, Trish. "Having been over both accounts it's apparent there are inconsistencies in the ledger. I have included a copy herein." See, that's what he's been doing, hasn't he, Martin, behind our backs, for years.'

'I wouldn't have a bar of it,' Trish said. 'Leave him here. Allen will sort him out.'

'"No real understanding of where this money has gone, so I thought it my duty to alert you to the fact . . ." And what I don't get, Trish, is how he's lived with us for so long, close, hasn't he, Martin, sharing food with us, our kids, Benno, he's been like a second son to him, haven't you?'

'Not really.'

'What do *you* make of him?' Trish asked me.

I shrugged. 'Most of the time he's a good teacher and knows what he's talking about, but other times—'

'Enough!' Father said.

'Well, I'm not taking him,' Mother said to Father, shaking the letter in his face.

'We started together and we'll finish together,' Father said.

'Why don't you get a bit angry once in a while?' Mother asked him.

'Because I'm just about dead, that's why, and all you go on about is some letter you dug up.' Settling. 'He's not that bad, is he, Benno?'

'He can be decent, I reckon.'

'Yeah, right,' Mother said. 'Decent with his—'

'Don't you start that,' Father said.

Gale put her head in and said, 'Benno, you wanna come out?'

'In a minute.'

'Go on,' Mother said.

So I went out. But I kept listening. I heard everything Mother told Trish, and I heard Father protesting, but Mother wouldn't stop: 'We're not taking him one inch further, Martin.'

Strange, because Ignatz was sitting fifteen, twenty yards away, under a pepper tree, reading. Taking his pen and scribbling something in the book.

'Mostly,' Gale said, 'I like reading books about history. I like Arthur and the knights at the round table. You like them?'

'Yes.'

'I thought if I could study history I could teach little kids. Not the old ones, not the ones that know more than me, but the little kids.'

Mother said it was out of the question. She said she didn't want to talk to him again after his latest letter, and he certainly wasn't coming to Horseshoe Bend. But again, Father said, 'Go on all you want . . . he's coming.'

I never got it then. I never got it, for years. I never understood what it had to do with Rebecca Lee, and the Todd River, and the doll they found in the sand.

By way of an explanation, let me tell you about this little girl from Alice Springs, wandering off from her house on a Sunday night. That's what the papers said, and what everyone knew, and what we, at Hermannsburg, were always told by Father. *Mostly*. It'd come up at tea, and Father would say, 'That was then, let's leave it.' I'd say, 'But you got him off, didn't you?' And Father would say, 'It wasn't me. He didn't do it.' Mother would say (something like), 'Bullshit he didn't.' Rebecca Lee, found dead on Monday morning when she should've been getting ready for school. Her Raggedy Ann body under a bridge. Legs splayed, because Norman Rennie had begun, she'd screamed, he'd covered her mouth (the police had found bruises on her lips) so hard, so long he'd suffocated her. But then he'd finished what he'd started.

Norman Rennie. Perhaps. Although to this day no one knows if it was him, or someone else. But let's assume it was Norman. Let's assume, as the detectives did, that he saw Rebecca heading for the shop, a fistful of change, and followed her, and said he had lollies in his camp under the bridge. Let's assume he saw her, in the half-light, and couldn't control himself. Let's assume he was arrested, movements tracked, witnesses found, charged with murder. Let's assume a copy of his confession was given to the judge and . . . but that's where it all breaks down. The confession. Detective X saying to Norman: 'So let's have the truth, boy.' Norman saying, 'I told you that, eh?' X saying, 'Or we could start again?'

The length of hose, the laundry trough full of water they'd used to persuade him. The stick across his soles, the twelve volts up his old fella.

'Right, get this down, Constable. "I, Norman James Rennie, of no fixed address, saw the girl Rebecca Lee and followed her from her home towards the Richard Road shops." Is that accurate, Norman?'

'Yes.'

'"I asked her to come with me, to see where I lived, and she accompanied me to the spot, one hundred yards east of the Frederick Street intersection." Norman?'

'Don't I get some fella to talk to?'

'Who?'

'Lawyer fella.'

'You, my friend, are lucky we don't cut off your balls and send them to that little girl's mother and father. Got it? Now: "Once there I was overcome with the need to satisfy my sexual urges, and consequently . . ."'

A confession, in pidgin English, Aranda, and the Queen's English (transcribed). Followed by a six-day trial, and a death sentence. Norman saying, 'What they reckon they gonna do with me?'

And X: 'They're gonna do to you what you did to her, Norman. 'Cept you won't suffer half as much, will you?'

No problems. Everyone happy. Parents, public, politicians, the public prosecutor and (it has to be said) defender. But then Norman said, 'Hang me? I didn't do nothing.'

'You confessed. You signed. See here?'

'But I had to.'

'Why?'

'They woulda hit me more.'

Still, it was too late. It had all been decided. And anyway, you'd expect a condemned man to try his luck. But no, it was all in writing.

Then this Catholic priest (who'd been sent to help Norman get ready for the big day), an Irish bloke, wrote to Father saying there was something wrong with the confession, the whole trial. 'No way Norman could've said those words, written that confession. They don't sound like him. It doesn't follow.'

That's the story Father told me and Mother: there was a little girl, and a black man had raped and killed her – although, he told us, it couldn't have been true.

Back in the kitchen, Father said, 'Who knows when we'll be back, Trish. Weeks. Months. Never. If we can get someone to pick up our gear from Hermannsburg . . . maybe Pastor Stolz will arrange it?'

Gale said to me, 'What's your favourite sort of history?'

Trying to listen to two things at once. 'I don't know . . . Vikings.'

'Me, too!'

Ignatz looked over, narrowed his eyes, returned to his book.

Father said, 'Then it'd be up to Allen or Lou or Gus or someone to fetch him, bring him to Horseshoe Bend. Far more sensible that he comes now.'

Mother screwed up the letter, threw it out the door, and it settled at my feet.

'Well,' Trish said, 'we should concede, Alma. If it's gonna cause problems.'

So, the story continued. Me, Mother, Ignatz and Father sitting at the table one night. Father and Ignatz had just returned from Adelaide. Ignatz had been with Father when he'd given his evidence. He'd been there since the beginning, since the letter had arrived from the Irishman asking if Father could offer a professional opinion. As we ate, Father said to Mother, 'I knew from the beginning it'd been made up.'

'How?'

'Syntax. Aranda has a special word order. It wasn't there. It was English. Subject, verb, object. Clauses, all of it. Perfect.'

Mother said, 'What if it *was* him?'

'It wasn't.'

'Maybe the police just tidied it up? Maybe this fella said it, and it wasn't clear, so they put it into proper English?'

'They can't do that. And anyway, I never believed he did it.'

'Why?'

'Talking to him. Whatever you said, he'd agree. Night's day. Black's white. He'd just nod. A congenial idiot. Like that girl, what's her name . . . Allen's daughter?'

'Gale?'

'Like Gale.'

'That's a nasty thing to say.'

'He sat there, those detectives told him what to say and he agreed, or else . . . That's what happened. That's why the confession's a load of shit.'

Father swearing. I think I smiled, and I think Mother told me not to and I think Father said, 'So what? If it comes down to a man being hanged, Alma, you've got to do everything you can. Everything.'

'Not if he killed that girl.'

Then Ignatz had said, 'It's the lesser of two evils, Alma.'

'How's that?'

The last thing said that night, although over the years, Rebecca Lee's ghost kept appearing around our dinner table, Father saying to Ignatz: 'We avoided a bad, bad error, didn't we, Ignatz?'

'We did.'

And for twenty-odd years, this is all I knew: a girl had been killed, the wrong man convicted, Father, through his mastery of the native language, had saved Norman's life (although no one else was ever arrested). Twenty-odd years. Until sometime in the seventies, when I found a pile of Father's notes, a few newspaper clippings (one with a photo of a doll, sitting in sand in the Todd River), and at the bottom of one: '16 October 1922. This article tells the truth. The girl was murdered. Norman got off, and the detectives charged with fabricating the confession. Pity. But necessary. Maybe if a man does wrong he should be punished. But not by death.'

As a series of wheels and cogs fell into place. The realisation that Father knew, that Ignatz knew, that they'd discussed it and set it in motion. To find a way to save the life of a black man who'd done wrong, but not so much that God couldn't, wouldn't forgive him.

Me, sitting in my hot shed, reading these words over and over, piecing together what he'd written on that day in the Harmstorf's house, when no one was watching or listening. And a second clipping, the edges all worn, the quarters in pieces. 'This is a fair record of what Norman told the police. Fair. Although what was fair about hanging an idiot?'

Inside, I heard Father saying, 'The point is, he's stuck with me for all these years. When no one else . . . who else was there, Alma?'

Ignatz called over: 'Just about ready to leave?'

I shrugged.

But Gale said, 'You gotta tell your dad then.'

'What?'

'About the Vikings. About me going to, where was it, what was it called?'

'Immanuel.'

As Ignatz just read.

It would've been nice, of course, if Father had told me. If he'd pulled me close and said, 'All that business about Rebecca Lee. Do you remember? I have to tell you something, Benno.'

But he didn't. It didn't work like that. There were no revelations or neat endings, and the chapters never resolved like *David Copperfield*. But I guess Father thought he'd done the right thing. After all, no one was going to bring Rebecca Lee back to life.

Mother stood on the porch and handed me the last box. 'And when that's on, Benno, pack your clothes, and give them to Lou.'

'Is Ignatz coming?' I asked.

'Apparently.'

The Wallaby Skin Coat

The last of the sun, as Father finally decided: 'That's it, we're off!' Ignatz and Ludwig helped him down the front steps, across the compound to the dray. He said, 'I don't know how to thank you for your hospitality, Allen.'

'It was nothing.'

'*Something*. In the middle of this awful journey. Benno, you coming?'

'I forgot.' I ran back behind the house, grabbed the didgeridoo, returned and slid it into a gap between the boxes. 'All ready.'

'This reminds me of Steinwerder,' Father said, smiling. 'Goodbye, children!'

'Martin!' Mother said, turning to Trish and saying, 'He's reverting to childhood.'

'Goodbye, Michael! Goodbye, Alwin!' Waving to his children, standing on the dock at Hamburg with Opa and Oma. 'Charlotte, take care of your grandparents!'

Ignatz helped him up, one step at a time, slowly reaching the top and shuffling over to his chair, easing himself down and saying, 'And Julius. Goodbye, son!' Waving again, standing high on the deck of the Schwendau, as we surveyed the last of the Gerlachs. Five sets of sad eyes staring up at me, thinking (I guessed), Why does it have to be like this?

Silas settled into his usual spot beside Father and said, 'This time tomorrow, Pastor!'

Father was waving, tears in his eyes. The ship was moving, and he turned to Mother and said, 'I hope we've done the right thing.' She said,

'None of that now. Benno, wave to your brothers and sister.'

Ignatz sat on the back of the dray so he'd have the best view of where we'd been, what we were leaving behind. Ludwig up front with Mother, me standing, waiting, before Father said, 'Here, beside me, son.'

People were throwing streamers from the ship to shore, shore to ship. Some made it, others dropped into the sea. Father said to me, 'You and me, a team.' Although he didn't seem sure. 'We can conquer Australia, civilise the damn place, eh, Benno?'

'I reckon.'

The streamers settled in the swell, or stuck to the side of the ship. More waving, more kisses, as people became an outline, a blur, a notion, then nothing.

Father said to Allen, 'We're sure to return soon.'

'If we see you we see you,' he said.

Gale stood on the porch holding Etsy. From this distance I couldn't see her scratches and bruises – just a pale, glowing girl, pink-skinned and wide-eyed, a little wave, and I waved back. And beside her, Kurt, turning to her and saying something, both of them talking like nothing had ever happened.

'See you later,' I said to Kurt, but he didn't reply. Just watched me go. And Trish saying, 'I think it'll cool,' and Mother saying she agreed, it was sure to, it was sure to be a nice night.

Kurt had filled two kerosene lamps, and Allen had secured them to the dray. Now they glowed, cheesy-yellow, Royal Dutch. Our over-secured load, mail for town, a wedding dress (wrapped in muslin) Gale and Trish had made for Gus's oldest daughter. The usual cast in the usual configuration, Mother refusing to talk to Ignatz, telling Father (as we made our final preparations), 'If he so much as looks at me.'

'Don't be dramatic.'

'And when we get to Horseshoe Bend I'm going to tell him what I think of him. And he can pack his bags. He can get to town, not on our train, and find another job and disappear from our lives.'

How it would be: making our way through the coolest part of the night so we only had a few hours of daylight before Horseshoe Bend. We'd be tired tomorrow, but at least we'd make it intact, sane, safe, alive. And anyway, as we'd prepared to go Father had said, 'There's something romantic about the night, isn't there, Alma?'

Mother had laughed, and said to Trish, 'I wouldn't know. That was too long ago.'

'Something of Goethe and Shakespeare. Maybe we could have some poetry as we go, Ignatz?'

Silas offered Psalms, the Book of Songs, but Father said, 'Something more pastoral.' Bottom and Puck and the old donkeys left to weather and die in the Harmstorf's yards as our new horses waited, kicking and jumping, ready for the journey.

'No point lingering,' Father said. 'Ludwig?'

Ludwig flicked the reins, the horses pulled and the dray moved forward. Thomas, Caleb and Ezekiel appeared from the shadows and started following us along the track.

'Happy travels!' Trish called.

'We'll be in contact,' Mother said, waving back, as the Harmstorfs became smaller, their little house blurring into bush. The boys running beside us and saying, 'We can follow you all the way.'

'Go back to your parents,' Mother said.

'Got a horse for me?' Thomas said to Jamy, on one of the two spares.

'Get out of it, you kids!'

'Hope your legs get better,' Caleb said to Father, but he just waved them away, and said, 'And Anton, I forgot to mention Anton. Did you see him, Alma?'

'He was there. Behind the other kids.'

'Why, do you think?'

'I don't know, Martin.'

'I hope he wasn't upset. Did you see him, Benno?'

'He was waving.'

'Good. He'll be fine, won't he, Alma? If anything, it'll teach them responsibility. One day they might thank us, mightn't they, Alma?'

The last of the streamers fluttered in the breeze before a purser walked along the side and cut them all, and they dropped into the black ocean.

A series of low hills led away from Idracowra. The dray passed in the folds, the gaps between them. The horses hardly had to pull. Mother said, 'It's a blessing, what Gus did.'

Father didn't reply.

'Martin?'

'What?'

'Gus. Lou. Bringing the horses.'

'I agree.'

'If not for that . . .'

If not. Lou had returned ahead of us at six, a little later – her and her blacks on a couple of horses Allen had lent them. Mounting up, saying she'd tell the others we were travelling through the night. Riding off without any dramas.

Low, open grassland. Father sat back and said, 'Not at all unpleasant.'

Silas said, '"How I long for the months gone by, for the days when God watched over me . . ."' But Father waved his hand and said, 'None of that now, Silas.'

There was enough moon to see where we were going. Each clump of grass, each pile of rocks, a bustard settling on cliffs. A man-made landscape with beach sand, bits of stuck-together grass, painted clouds. Nothing authentic. A stuffed cormorant, a label with its common and binomial name, its shape, size and colour. Behind glass, and you could smell the formaldehyde. Temperature- and humidity-controlled cabinets, worn carpet where generations of kids and their dads and granddads had stood and said, 'That's exactly the same bird I saw when I was your age, Tom.'

Tom said to Jack, 'Shouldn't they replace it?'

'About time. We pay our taxes.'

'Grandpa?'

'Look, you can see where the insects have eaten its feathers.'

We all agreed – they needed a new cormorant, a new gazelle, a new elephant. The place had become (I explained) a museum of a museum, showcasing how people used to stand and look and learn, before computers, before David Attenborough, before anything that made the experience interesting.

This day, only a few weeks ago. My idea: another trip to the city in Jack's car, a Chinese meal, then over to the museum, the same meteorite, the same Polynesian canoes and headdresses, the same six attendants. From the bustard to the tiger, its seams coming open, the lion with a mechanical tail, the life drained out of it by sixty years (I could remember it, from when Father took me) of kids saying, 'Wow, look, its tail moves.'

Tom said, 'What about the night parrot?'

'It's in storage.'

'That's rubbish. Wouldn't you want to show people?'

Father, lying back, nodding off, Mother telling him he should've had a nap. Him saying, 'Why? I can sleep tonight.' Adjusting himself, trying one side then another, realising there was no way he could get comfortable, and calling: '"Oh, for the days when I was in my prime . . ." Benno, don't forget, keep your eyes open for a night parrot.'

'What time do they come out?'

'The last bit of light. See, just the moon. So they'll be sticking their snouts out, making sure it's safe, trying to sniff a bit of water. Watch out for them, son.'

'There's no water.'

'It doesn't matter. Just listen. Can you hear them?'

'Can't hear anything.'

'Listen . . . Ignatz?'

'You'd have to be lucky.'

'Ludwig?'

'No, Pastor.'

'Give it time. Wait. Be patient, Benno, and you're sure to see one.'

Never had. Never would. I said to Tom, 'Damn it!' I approached the desk and said to a young man, 'I was wondering, I know there's a night parrot here somewhere . . .'

'A what?'

'A night parrot.'

'Never seen one.'

'I know. It's in storage. I was wondering whether I could see it?'

He just smiled and shook his head. 'If it isn't out then you can't see it.'

'But can I *arrange* to see it?'

'It doesn't work like that. There are tens of thousands of things in storage, and we can't go get them whenever someone wants to see them.'

'Why not?'

'I just said. There are lots of things. And anyway, they're kept in an off-site store at Richmond and it'd take weeks, even if someone agreed.'

'Weeks? Fine. So who'd have to agree?'

He sighed. A proper, big sigh. Then he went away, talked to an older man standing doing nothing, and they both looked at me and Jack said, 'They're gonna love you, Dad.'

'I don't care. I want to see the night parrot. Don't you, Tom?'

'Absolutely.'

'See. Your son wants to see the night parrot. He shouldn't be denied. I shouldn't. If it's there why can't we look at it?'

'You're making their lives difficult.'

'Fuck them. Sorry, Tom. Bugger them. If it's there, and they're too lazy to get off their arses . . .'

The young man came back and said, 'Apparently you have to go to the admin office.'

'Where's that?'

'Upstairs. But it's only open Monday to Friday, nine to four.'

'Four? Why four? Why not five? People want to see things. They want to come here to learn. They don't want to have to go through this every time—'

Jack took me by the arm and said to the young man, 'Thanks. Nine to four. Dad?' When we got far enough away, he said, 'You're a difficult old bastard, aren't you?'

'You haven't seen anything yet.'

'I've seen it. I remember it. Plenty of times . . . you and Mum arguing.'

'That was different.'

'*No, they're not coming out with you, Benno*. I remember. Nothing much's changed, eh, Dad?'

'Well . . . she wouldn't let me see my own kids.'

'I'm sure Tom won't care if he can't see a parrot.'

'It's not just a parrot.'

'Yeah, Dad,' Tom said. 'It's a night parrot. They're the rarest in the world.'

'How do you know?'

Tom had already told me. When I'd first told him, he'd gone to his school library and checked, made notes, traced a picture, and yes, he told his father, 'It'd be great to see one, wouldn't it, Grandpa?'

'Exactly.' Messing his hair, taking him around the shoulder and squeezing him.

That ended the night parrot business. Except for Father, shirt open to the moonlight, sipping cold barley water, Mother standing and wiping his forehead as he said, 'Any luck, Benno?'

'Not yet.'

'Keep looking. Told you, didn't I, this fella shot one and took it back to Holland, and they've got it in a museum there. Strange, eh? All these Dutchmen admiring it, but we can't. That's the problem with Australia, with Australians. Not interested in what's around them.'

'Not much to get excited about,' Mother said to Father, sitting, handing Silas the flannel.

'Plenty,' he said, 'if you're looking. We just want to see polar bears, but there's not many of them around here, eh, Benno?'

'No.'

'We refuse to look,' he said.

'How's that?' Ignatz asked.

'There are termites and even smaller insects, but who cares? There are blind moles tunnelling under us right now, but who cares? There are a hundred rodents, and there are . . . it's endless, and it needs recording, but I guess I won't get to it now.'

'You might.'

'It just needs recording. Maybe it's too early. Maybe all of that will happen one day, and there'll be night parrots, thousands of them, as far as you can see.' Indicating.

One of the kero lamps flickered and Mother sat forward and adjusted it. Father said, 'Perhaps someone should start with a survey of the birds?'

No one replied. Just the grind of wheels on hard ground, the creaking of spokes, the huffing and snorting of horses, settling into a rhythm.

'Or perhaps the people. Perhaps that's what we need to understand first. The people. Unless we can do that . . . Benno, do you think?'

'I reckon.'

'Course you do.' Smiling. 'Infinitely more interesting than we give them credit for . . . but I wasted so much time on God.'

'Don't say that,' Mother said.

'I did. If I could have my time again . . . have you seen it, Benno?'

'No.'

'But it's out there somewhere.'

Same thing I said to Jack and Tom, standing in the museum. 'Made special, I guess, because of its rarity. What do you think, Tom?'

'I read it might not even exist.'

'That's not right. It exists. Plenty of people have seen it. Anyway, let's get on, these animals depress me.'

We went into the Indigenous Gallery (with its list of corporate sponsors) and I stopped in front of another cabinet, knelt, studied a few labels and said, 'There, look. Your great-grandfather.'

A collection of string beads, trinkets, explanations of where they'd come from, and below all of this: 'Collected by Martin Gerlach. c. 1909'.

'Cool,' Tom said, kneeling beside me, reading all of the labels, finding Martin again and again, and saying, 'Did you know?'

'Of course. Read the rest.'

'"Donated by James Elder-Smith". Who was that?'

'He was what you kids call an arsehole, Tom.'

Though by now, neither of them were shocked.

'This Elder-Smith character. Arrived at Hermannsburg around 1906, worked with Father, collected trinkets, spears, shields, a load of stuff, then one day Father got up and he was gone, took it all with him, never asked us, the owners, no one. Just took it to town, then it appeared here. Father kept asking for them to send it back, but they wouldn't. Donated, they said. So it stayed. And what was worse, half of it was Father's, so it was stolen. But do you think anyone cared? Father eventually went to the police, but they just laughed. Said something like, *A loada old spears*.'

'It's *still* here?' Jack said.

'I had a go, but they said the same. The museum owned it. Not me. Not Father. Not the blacks. None of us. They owned it. It was *theirs*. Like a car or a house or a washing machine. *Theirs*.'

The tour continued. I showed Tom some sacred stones, digging sticks, boomerangs. 'Collected by Benjamin Gerlach. Western Desert. c. 1959'. Tom said the same: 'Wow, that's cool, Grandpa. You got this?' I said yes, and he wanted to know the story, so I told him. 'Years trawling the desert, getting to know the people, earning their trust. That was the hard part. So much time . . .' Turning to Jack and saying, 'As you noticed.'

'And was it worth it?' Studying a shield.

'Well, I thought, at the time, and maybe it was but . . . maybe not.'

He didn't continue. Perhaps it didn't matter.

We got to a wallaby skin coat and Tom saw my name and said, 'What about this one?' I said, 'This woman came to the mission from the desert, and she was wearing it, and Ignatz, you know I told you about Ignatz?'

'I know.'

'He ripped it from her shoulders and said, *None of that here*. She grabbed it back but he said, *If you want to stay at Hermannsburg you must follow our rules*.'

'What a prick, sorry, you said he was a prick, didn't you?'

'A prick. Exactly, Tom. So Ignatz hands her this dress, you know, white, linen, for all the women to wear when they're working in the kitchens, and says, *This is what you'll wear now.* There was this terrible argument, and she was shouting, and he told her she could leave but eventually . . . Ignatz won. He always won.'

'And how did it get here?' Tom asked.

I shrugged. 'I can't remember. I suppose Ignatz put it in a box and it stayed there, but I found it a few years ago and donated it. Why, I can't say. If they're not going to put out the parrot, eh, Tom?'

'Exactly.'

'I should ask for all of this back, shouldn't I?' Indicating a room full of artefacts, a quarter, perhaps, that had come from Father and me.

'You should. We should. Should we go tell them now?'

'Come on.'

But Jack said, 'I don't think they're going to return anything, Dad. You gave it to them, didn't you?'

'Of course, Tom. The parrot. We'll write a letter. We'll *demand* they put it on display.'

He just held up a thumb, smiling.

Back on the dray, Father said to me, 'If somehow you can attune your ears to it, Benno.'

'Sorry?'

'It's a quiet call . . . but the longer you listen, the more chance you'll have of hearing it.'

I tried. I listened. Hard. I watched, but I realised I wasn't going to see or hear anything. Like it was some promise, some dream, Father had given me. And if it ever became real, then everything we'd ever hoped for would be lost.

Tuesday 17 October (Day 8)

There was nothing to do except close your eyes, breathe the night, the sticks and termite mounds, the soggy armpit of endless mulga, the sizzle of eucalyptus oil from the box gums. To go with the motion of the dray, allow your body to relax, to sway. Father said, 'This is where Death came into the world.'

Nothing to do except let go of every thought, every worry, every fear. To open your eyes, see the gathering storm, spit the dust (blowing up around us), snort it, like the horses, already tired, already confused (I guess) why they were walking at night. Nothing but little shards of sky the clouds had left behind, a few stars, and Kate saying to me, 'I don't want to get poetic . . .'

'Well, don't.'

'But that one there, see . . . maybe fifteen light-years away.'

Because we'd been here before, in 1960, in an open tourer we'd bought with an inheritance (hers), driving across the same plains, then a flat tyre, Kate telling me there was no rush to change it. Pointing up at the stars and saying, 'See, Venus, there . . .'

And me: 'We passed this place on the way to Horseshoe Bend.'

'Ah, *Horseshoe Bend*.'

'If you don't want to hear about it . . .'

'Of course, go ahead. Fill in the few remaining blanks.'

'It was after midnight and we were all tired and there was a dust storm brewing, out that way, and I said to Father, *Do you think it's going to get to us*, and he said, *No, we'll be fine*. But by then he was sort of . . . potty . . . remembering the old stories about Death.'

'Death?'

'Yes. This is where Death came into the world.'

'Do tell.'

'You're so patronising.'

'Me?' Smiling, laughing, and I think we might've kissed.

But years earlier, on the dray, it wasn't so funny. Me seeking reassurance about the storm, because it was getting closer, the wind stronger, the sand in my eyes. 'What happens if . . .?'

Father wobbled, clung to the handles, winced and said, 'These winds, Benno. At the beginning of time. The shell parrot, I've told you about her?'

'I think.'

'These winds made her pregnant.' Descending, head rolling on his shoulders, Silas trying to wipe his forehead with the flannel. 'They implanted the seed, the twins, surely I've told you about the twins?'

'I don't think so.'

'Maybe just try and sleep,' Mother said to him.

'The parrot gave birth to twins and they became snakes. Then she flew up into the sky, up, up' – showing us with his hands – 'and left them to fend for themselves. Which was her first mistake, I suppose. If she'd stayed and watched out for them and . . .'

'The problem wasn't the shell parrot,' Mother said. 'The problem was the Board. Twelve men, and every time we sent a letter they read it, decided they didn't care, and that's why we're here now, Martin.'

He just shook his head. 'No, no.'

Kringka watercourse ran in a dogleg from the Finke River. We followed a pair of wheel ruts, avoiding soft sand, the marshiest ground spreading out before us. And filling the void, a not-so-distant curtain of dust dragging across the wasteland. Just the place to set a story about Death. As we limped along, and Father hummed Mozart, and Silas mumbled Job, understanding (at last) that no one wanted to hear. Ludwig said, 'Hour till Nine Mile Creek.'

'That long?' Mother said.

'If we had a car, ten minutes,' Ignatz said. 'Wonder what happened to Gotthold?'

'*We were told*,' Mother said to him. 'He broke down. The car couldn't be repaired. He returned to Oodnadatta.'

'Anything can be fixed.'

'Apparently not. I can't see why, after going to all that trouble, he'd lie to us, Herr Beck.'

Ignatz was right. Cars were the way to go. The same journey took me and Kate two days. And on that starry night I tried to get out, to change the tyre by lamplight, but Kate said, 'Leave it till the morning, till you can see.'

'Where we gonna sleep?'

'Who needs to sleep? It's an adventure, isn't it? Isn't that what you said you wanted? An adventure? The old country? The journey to Horseshoe Bend?'

'We could pitch the tent?'

But she just indicated another star. 'If we set off on a rocket we'd get there, no, our great-grandkids would get there when they're a thousand years old. We'd eat and root around and have kids and die, and that'd keep going, again and again, and that's how big it is, Benjamin Gerlach.'

'Not sure we'd have any kids.'

'Why not?'

'The first two didn't . . . maybe if they'd talk to me.'

'Give them time. They could come. All the way to Alpha Centauri?'

'They won't even . . .' I stopped and listened and let the cogs detach and spin in the air, and it was like I could hear the Earth turning on its axle (smoothly, like the bearings had been greased). I tried to make the moment last, but couldn't. 'It'll get worse. It's Terese. I'm sure it's Terese. Jack even said. He reckons she said I should've . . . But you wanted Horseshoe Bend?'

'Something about a parrot. A night parrot?'

'A shell parrot. Two kids, let's just call them Jack and Sharon, and they became snakes, dangerous, venomous snakes. They were unhappy with the world because their mother, the shell parrot, had flown away and left them. But they were determined to get revenge.'

'Just skip to the memories, Ben. You on the dray . . .'

'Humour me.'

Back on the dray, Father explained: 'They just went around biting people, I guess.'

'Who?' Mother asked.

'The twins. You wouldn't want to cross them.'

Now we were on the edge of the storm. Sandpapering us, but Ludwig kept going, and we dropped our heads, closed our eyes, tried to shake it off. Mother said stop, but Ignatz said it would pass: *Keep going, Ludwig, keep going.* I pulled my shirt over my nose, and breathed easy. I asked Father if he was okay, but he just said, 'Eventually she returned . . .'

'Who?'

'The parrot, but now she turned herself into a woman. And the snakes were men, young men, angry young men. She offered them her breast . . .'

'Martin,' Mother said, 'we can't keep going in this.' Covering her head with her dress.

'It'll pass,' Ignatz said.

'No one asked you.'

Jamy, a few yards behind, but he didn't seem to care. Just plodded along, oblivious.

'. . . her breast' – Father said, turning to me, wincing with pain, lifting his arse from the chair and re-depositing it – 'she offered them her breast. See, even then, Benno. Maybe she thought it wasn't too late?'

'What happened?' Although by now I'd remembered. The bird, the woman, the breast, the mutilation.

'The younger brother bit it off!' He sat back, slapped his leg, and laughed louder than the storm. 'He bit it off! He grabbed it and threw it as far as he could, all the way to Bagatia, and that explains the hill, you know the one?'

I shrugged. I doubted he saw me.

'The son was so angry . . .' Father said. 'So angry he bit off his mother's breast. Imagine!'

Just after one am we drew up under a tree, helped Father down, settled close to the trunk, and Mother and Ludwig and Ignatz found rugs, opened a swag, a groundsheet, and covered us. The horses gathered together, hid their heads in a little gap of air, and waited. Father said to God, 'What, you want to try a bit of this, too?'

Mother: 'Martin.'

'He's testing us,' Silas said.

'Show yourself!' And intoning: '"Why hast thou set me as a mark against thee . . . so that I am a burden to myself?"'

We sat for half an hour perhaps, under the creaking boughs, Silas warning us they might break, drop, kill us anyway – laughing at the idea. As the heavens stirred, and Father said, 'If this is how it ends . . .'

But it did. Soon after. We gathered the covers and rugs and Silas said, 'See, it's passing,' and Ignatz said, 'We're making good time.' We helped Father up, and the horses shook the sand from their faces, and we continued into the night. Towards Nine Mile Creek.

Mother told Father he should try and sleep. He said he wasn't tired anymore. He just held the chair handles, took long, deep breaths, clutched his jaw and sucked air over his bottom teeth. I knew, we all knew, what he was feeling. Like a mark. Set against the world, the weather, the heavens, God, everything. Like he was some imposition, a bother, a burden to himself and us. Like he was thinking it couldn't continue, and if he could just fly off, change form, he would. He said, 'If it'd cool a few degrees, just enough. Your lot,' he said to Silas, 'brought Death into the world.'

'That's not what the Bible says.'

'That was written years before anyone knew about the blacks . . . why we're all here, eh, Alma?'

'I just did what you asked, Martin.'

'You should've stopped me. You should've said no, we won't go, we won't leave them. What thanks will we get in fifty years? He hasn't cared a bit about . . . set his mark, his mark, his mark . . .' He repeated these words ten, fifteen times.

'We were both wrong,' Mother consoled.

'You did good,' Silas said to Father. 'All them people . . .'

Father closed his eyes, and was calm. He didn't fight the terrain, the movement, the rocking. Just went with it, despite (I guess) the pain. 'His mark . . .' Dropping his head onto his chest.

I stood, took a few steps, placed my hand under Father's chin and tried to lift his head. It fell back, and I looked at Mother, but she just said, 'Go on.' So I took the flannel from Silas and started wiping his face, but Father roared, 'What?' Opened his eyes, saw me, without seeing me, and struck me across the face. Hard, too. I'll always remember. Hard. I backed off, and almost straight away he realised what he'd done. 'Jesus, Benno.' He put out his hand, took my arm, pulled me close and said, 'Sorry . . . I hit you, did I hit you?'

'It was an accident,' Mother said.

'No, it wasn't. I hit you. Benno.' Pulling me closer, holding me, like something between us had changed, just holding and squeezing as I said, 'It's fine,' and Mother said it was an accident, and Silas said it was an accident, Ludwig, even Jamy, calling, 'You're getting confused, Martin.'

'I am . . . confused.' Slowly releasing me and saying, 'Is that a bruise?'

I rubbed it. 'No. See.'

'I thought you were . . .' Taking a deep breath, releasing it. 'I didn't mean to, Benno.'

'I know,' I said. 'It's fine. I'm fine. It's gone.'

'I don't believe . . .' And he cried. That quickly. He put his face in his hand and said, 'I didn't mean to.'

Uralterinja

Nine Mile Creek. The dust storm had subsided, the air was clear, a breeze through cane grass flats spreading out from the watercourse. A little before two am, grey clouds gathering in the east, and Ignatz, his legs over the back of the dray: 'Looks like that's coming our way, too.'

Mother checked and said, 'Miles away.' Although the flashes of lightning made it clear – high clouds with mushroom tops, snatches of blue and black as the smell of rain intensified. The memory of it, sitting at my window, watching it drift towards Hermannsburg, the blacks securing their humpies and huts, Ludwig and Jamy and the others bringing in the calves, Mother and Pauline gathering the washing. Always the best. And always late on a Saturday evening, with Schubert blaring, the smell of boiled cabbage from the kitchen, a half-finished balsa wood ketch on my desk. But now, just the stirring of cane grass and mulga and the big branches of a few trees surviving in a liminal zone of life and death. Ignatz said, 'It's coming closer.' And Mother, 'So what should we do about it?'

By now, she wasn't even disguising her contempt. Short, sharp words and the inner workings of her frustration, and hate, her disgust with the man she'd tolerated for too long.

We arrived at Uralterinja sometime after three. The outline of the waterhole, until our eyes adjusted, then more reeds, more shrubs; birds drinking, a few wallabies darting into the bush. Father said he needed to stop, so we pulled up, and Jamy and Ludwig unharnessed the horses and led them to water. Ludwig rubbed them down, and they started searching for grass.

A few camp stools, a log, and we all settled. I fetched kindling and started a fire. A well-drilled procedure – water, kettle, and soon I was making tea, handing it around. Father again, asking for milk and saying, 'The rain ancestress . . .'

'Yes, we know,' Mother said. 'Around here, wasn't it?'

'Close by.'

'Well . . .' Drinking her tea, telling me I hadn't put enough sugar in – I never put enough sugar in.

A few drops on our faces, in the fire. Father said, 'Smit, remember him, Alma?'

'I never met him,' Mother said.

'He was the best. *He* made me decide to become a pastor.' He recited the baptismal prayer. 'He was the single most . . . you must remember that, Benno? Pastor Smit. He was the one who changed my life, for the better, I think.'

I'd heard about him. How he'd baptised Father, confirmed him, the life-changing chats about God, the power of religion and love and how this, and only this, could give these people, poor people, these natives, savages, some reason to live.

'Before that . . .' Father said. 'Is it getting heavier, Ignatz?'

'I believe.'

The lightning matched the thunder, and the smell of wet grass drifted around us.

'We shouldn't be sitting so close to a tree,' Mother said, and Silas agreed – one good strike and we'd all be dead. But Father didn't care. 'I might've ended up a mason. Imagine that, Alma. Back in Leipzig . . . you and me and the children . . . although I'd probably be too old to do that now.'

'I'm getting wet,' Mother said.

'I could put up a groundsheet?' Ludwig offered, but no one replied.

'If I hadn't met him,' Father said. 'He was a grand old man, Benno. No nonsense, a deep well of love. I think I've tried to be a little like him, but I suspect I've failed.'

'You haven't failed,' Mother said.

'He was natural, Benno. A child would see him and be drawn to him, go up to him and talk to him like . . . magnetism. I think it was this *lightness* he had. Like nothing mattered. Except God's love. He'd say, Come here, son, and some boy would go over and he'd tell him a joke and they'd laugh and it was like a spider catching a fly. I've always tried to be like that, like *him*, but . . .'

He seemed concerned about this. Like there was someone he should've been, some way he should've acted, but failed. 'You could say the worst things to him . . . you could tell him you'd done something awful but it never mattered.' He reached out, tried to touch the gathering storm. 'He'd be surprised to see me here.' Smiling. 'That's one thing I achieved. Although he was the one who told me to go somewhere I might make a difference. And I have, I think. I have made a difference, haven't I, Alma?'

'You have.'

'You have,' Silas agreed. Ignatz didn't say anything.

'I think he'd be proud of me, Benno.'

'I reckon.'

'I remember one day when the class had been playing up (he taught at St Thomas's too), he pretended to be God.' He laughed. 'He put out his arms and shouted, *What was I thinking? Why did I bother? I think I'll unmake the world.* Then someone said, *You can't unmake the world.* So Smit (his name was Joseph, but everyone called him Jo-Jo) picked up a chair and threw it across the room and it shattered into a hundred pieces and we all fell silent, terrified, and he said, *Okay, what's next? You, Herr Gerlach?*' Laughing. 'That kept us quiet for weeks. But I could see him, Benno, standing at the front, grinning as he wrote our Latin verbs. He was a genius. With children, especially.'

The rain fell solidly, but no one seemed to care. At least there was no more Job.

'You've been just as good as him,' Silas said, holding out his hand for the rain.

'No sort of match, I'm afraid.' His head rolling on his shoulders, gathering rain and wetting his face and hair. 'More than anything, he was decent. That's the most important thing. Remember that, Benno. Don't worry about dictionaries. Don't worry about the emu callers. Just be decent.'

I can still remember sitting with my too-strong tea, trying to work out why Father was telling me (because it was meant for me) about Smit. 'I don't think it really matters, does it, Benno?'

'What?'

'Building a church. Teaching kids grammar. Making a few pounds from cattle. Who'll remember any of it?'

'Plenty of people,' Silas said.

'No. In a hundred years. No one. What someone'll remember is the touch, the laugh, the *lightness* . . . that's all.'

'Enough!' Mother said. 'Or should I just dig a hole and bury you now?'

Ludwig looked at Mother like, *Even now, you old cow*. I was thinking the same thing. If Father was a feather, then Mother was an anvil. These two things had started the same (somewhere, years ago) but grown apart until there was no similarity. The same happened to me and Terese. Because we'd been here, at this waterhole, in 1952. We'd been here with a car full of half-caste kids. We'd stopped during the day, and it was hot, and I'd said, 'Ten minutes for a swim, kids.' And they (I could list them all if you'd like) had stripped off, jumped in, splashed about, and Terese had said, 'You're going to get in a lot of trouble.'

'No.'

'We should take them back.'

'It'll be fine.'

Because I'd broken a few rules, a few laws, perhaps. So what? I'd packed the kids in the car (I knew they were coming for them the next day) and said, 'We're going on a trip.'

'Where?' (Isaiah).

'A surprise. Come on.'

I'd driven them all this way because I knew what was in store for them at Semaphore. I knew about the mops and lathes, the big pots of watery soup, and the hundreds, thousands, millions of buttons they'd have to sew onto shirts. I'd told their parents I was taking them for a week, and I'd bring them back when the Protector had returned to Adelaide. Just a short holiday, to a few friends in Alice. My little act of grace. Of defiance (though I paid for it later). But despite this, and even then, Terese, watching them splash about in the waterhole, said, 'You could lose your job.'

'So what?'

'You're still on probation.'

'Does that matter? You know what'll happen to them?'

'Maybe it's best for them?'

'You reckon?' Just watching them shouting, full of life and love. 'You want them to be locked up and taught to make stews and . . .?'

'You could be arrested. You could be prosecuted.'

'A holiday? How was I to know the Protector was coming?'

By now, the rain had slowed. Father said, 'Pity.'

'I didn't think there'd be much in it,' Ignatz said, throwing the last of his cold tea into the bush.

Father said, 'The water looks nice.'

No one replied.

'Maybe . . . Silas?'

'We should keep moving,' Ignatz said.

'Silas?'

Silas helped Father up. Mother said, 'Martin . . .' But he ignored her. He walked towards the waterhole, then into it (bare feet, and cut-down pants), up to his knees, his thighs. He reached down, splashed the water and said, 'I remember.'

'Does it help?' Silas said.

'It does, Silas. It helps my old legs.' And up at us: 'Who's coming in?'

I didn't feel like getting wet. Father told me to strip off, come in, you'll feel better. He said to Silas, 'Do you accept the spirit of Jesus?'

'Yes, Pastor.'

He tried to lower him into the water, but Silas finished the job and came up and said, 'Off we go again, Pastor!'

'We do! What do I say next? Damn. Alma?'

'You're the pastor.'

'The spirit of God lives in these waters, Silas. He washes away the sins of man and allows you to start again. Do you want to start again, Silas?'

'I reckon.'

Maybe, about now, I was laughing. But maybe Mother poked me. I remember Ludwig leaning over and saying to me, 'He's remembering a lot of things now, Benno.'

Father said, 'Someone doesn't *have* to be baptised, does he, Father Smit, if he wants to be with God? No, he doesn't. It's all a bit of a show, Benno. A bit of theatre. A few songs perhaps. God'd like a song, I reckon.'

Ludwig got closer and whispered, 'Not that it's a concern, Benno.'

'What?'

Checking Mother couldn't hear. 'He just wants to know everything will be okay. So go with it.'

'What?'

'Whatever he wants. Go with it. If he wants you to finish his dictionary . . . just say you will. That's all he wants to hear. No one's saying you gotta do it. Do you understand?'

The rain getting heavier. Mother called for Father to come in, but he said his legs were feeling fine. 'This was you, Benno.'

'What was?'

'Your christening. I was scared you weren't going to make it. They said I had to hurry and rush you, express, to Heaven, before you died. And look now!'

'What did I look like?'

'You looked like a calf born a month too early. All red and slippery. But I had faith, son. I knew you'd be alright.'

The rain came down heavy, spread across the land, the darkness lit up with flashes. Mother and Ignatz stood under a tree, and Mother called, 'Martin!' I didn't care. I just sat there. It was fun. I was back in my bedroom, smelling the glue from the balsa boat, as happy as I'd ever been. Mother told me to stop sitting in the rain, but somehow, even then, I realised my best chance at happiness lay in ignoring her.

'Do your best!' Father shouted up to the heavens. 'Go on. I dare you!'

Then he slipped and fell into the water. He bobbed up and down, and Silas reached for him, but couldn't find him. I ran in, grabbed his big body, grappled with it, lifted it from the water. Ignatz and Mother and Jamy waited at the edge. I helped Father up, and he stood, walked out of the water and, of course, Mother asked him what the hell he was thinking. 'You could've drowned.'

'But I didn't, Alma. See, it feels good. Doesn't it, Benno?'

He took off his shirt and handed it to Mother and she said she was getting wet, we were all getting wet, and why, Martin? So you can play in the water? But she didn't get it. She said if he wasn't sick before he would be now, and he turned to her and laughed and said, 'How much worse can it get?'

Bony Bream

I can never get to sleep. Into bed, lie there an hour, two, get up and read a few pages of Dickens, back to bed, toss and turn, and I say to myself, *Benno, you idiot, what are you doing? What does it matter if you can't sleep? You can sleep tomorrow*. But this logic never works. My miserable little brain saying *I'll decide when we get to sleep*. Sometimes I wonder if this has anything to do with that trip, that night, three, four am, keeping myself awake, my head slipping from my shoulders, a little start, and Mother saying, 'Go lie down on the back, Benno.'

'I'm fine.'

Ten minutes, an hour, shaking my head, stamping my feet, determined to see it through. I could sleep at Horseshoe Bend. But now, we had to watch Father. Groaning, slipping from his chair, pulling himself up, Silas placing a box under his feet, and a few minutes later: 'This isn't working.' Slipping into memory, talking to Smit about Africa, or singing the parrot song.

I decided to cut my losses, again. I found *David Copperfield* in his box, opened to Chapter sixteen and continued reading. Five am, perhaps, and still no sign of light. '"Next morning, after breakfast, I entered on school life again . . ."'

Father said, 'All too neat.'

'What?' I asked.

'David's life. *I am born. I observe.* It's not like that.'

'What *is* it like?' I said.

'*I travel through the desert at five am* . . . uneven is what I mean, Benno. Uneven. Messy. Life is messy, isn't it, Silas?'

'Yes, Pastor.'

'And good intentions are never . . . but go on, read.'

'"I went, accompanied by Mr Wickfield, to the scene of my favourite studies . . ."'

It lightened just after six, and we stopped an hour later. We kept the horses harnessed, boiled a quick billy, sipped warm tea and ate more biscuits. Ludwig said, 'Last breakfast, eh, Pastor?'

'True,' Father said, from up on his throne, because we hadn't bothered getting him down.

'Tomorrow we'll have bacon . . . Gus's hotel?'

'We will.'

'We've made it,' Mother said.

'Nearly,' Father said. 'Nearly.'

'What time, do you think?' Mother asked Ignatz, and he said, 'Six, perhaps, depending on the day. I think it'll be hot again.'

After breakfast we continued, with some sense of hope, at last. Although the closer we got, the worse Father looked. He just sat mumbling: 'If we can get enough of those cattle sold, Silas.'

'What cattle, Pastor?'

'The young ones. That should get us through until . . . although Mr Wurst . . . did I tell you, Alma, he sent me a cheque?'

'That was years ago, Martin.'

'Two hundred pounds. Did you add it to the total, Ignatz?'

'Yes, Pastor.'

'Because every cent was accounted for. I checked myself. The cattle. The payments from Trenwood. The subscriptions, the money from our few, our *very* few donors, and the piddly bit from the Board. Every penny and every pound.'

Mother glared at Ignatz. He noticed and said, 'What?'

'Did you put that in your letter?'

He refused to answer.

And Father: 'What did you tell Pastor Klein, Ignatz?'

'Nothing.'

'We saw the letter,' Mother barked.

'That was private.'

'So what? We saw it. Luckily, we're nearly there, we're nearly fine, we're fine, aren't we, Martin? But not because of *you*,' she said to Ignatz. 'Worked and sacrificed and . . .'

'Do you want to hear more *Copperfield*?' I said to Father.

'No, it's all nonsense,' he said, waving me away. '*I am born.* So what? It was never like that, was it, Silas?'

Eventually we stopped for lunch. Father said he needed the toilet. Mother took him, through low grass, sedges, and I watched as she helped him with his pants, waited for him to squat, said, 'Do you need any help?'

'I'm not crippled.'

Leaving him with a dozen squares of newspaper. 'Watch for snakes.' Returning to us and saying: 'That'd be the go. A taipan. Six hours from Horseshoe Bend.'

A few minutes later we were all sitting in a circle, tackling a flan Trish had cooked for us, washed down with barley water, and the promise (from Ludwig): 'No more of this stuff. How about a roast pig tonight, eh, Benno?'

'If they've got one.'

'It's a hotel, isn't it? Let's see, what should I order?' Pretending to read the menu. 'Mm, duck, that'd be the go.'

'Do they have pork pies?'

'Here, look.' Indicating. 'Pork pies and mashed potato. What do you say?'

And Mother: 'Hear that, Martin? Pork pies. Your favourite.'

'Where?'

She shook her head and said, 'There's no menu, Ludwig. They've got roast beef and Yorkshire pudding every day.'

'That'd be okay.' Deciding he didn't like the flan, and flinging it into the bush.

Like I said, an insomniac. Lying there for sixty-six years, counting the hours, dissecting my own life, chopping it up and seeing where I went wrong. Adding up to nothing. Like Father (it occurred to me then), reaching into the darkness, trying to hold onto the past, make sense of it, find a way forward (tomorrow, in the light of day). 'This paper's as rough as hell, Alma.'

She tried not to laugh. 'It'll have to do.'

Like Tom, emerging from the small toilet beside my third-floor bed, and saying, 'Neat.'

And me: 'You reckon?'

Jack was there, and he said, 'I'll go and get a picture.'

'No, you won't,' I said to him. 'It was my own fault.'

This time he'd brought Steph (it was a Saturday afternoon). She's a nice kid, and good-looking. Brown hair, brown eyes, little, peepy slits where she looked at me and said, 'It's quite a gash, Benno.'

'It's not so bad.'

She's tall, with broad shoulders, and even then I was thinking: *If only I were forty years younger*. She said, 'Surely they'll have to stitch it?'

'They reckon not. Look at my skin. Barbecued chicken, eh, Tom?'

He stood close by, studied my leg. 'It looks bad.'

This happened three weeks ago. I was searching for specials in John Martin's basement when I went around a corner and there was this woman, shocked, pointing at me, and I looked down and there, a gash, and blood streaming out. I said: 'What's this?' A sales assistant came over and said, 'What have you done?'

'It's not that bad.'

It was. Three inches, maybe four. The blood kept flowing down my leg, into my sock, soaking my sandal, gathering in a pool on the lino floor. I said, 'I didn't feel it.' The first woman pointed at the sharp corner of the display cabinet and said, 'No wonder. That shoulda been fixed. You oughta go them.'

The sales assistant fetched a towel, wrapped it around my leg and called, 'Julie, can you phone an ambulance?'

Two hours later I was admitted to hospital. A nurse asked if there was anyone she should contact, and I said, 'I don't want to bother him.'

'Who?'

'My son. But he's probably . . .'

She got it out of me anyway, and an hour later there he was, and Steph, and Tom, looking at the wound, saying, 'Your skin looks funny.'

Steph giving him a smack behind the ear: 'Tom.'

'I just meant . . .'

'I'm eighty years old,' I said to him.

'So you were around when Hitler was *killing* everyone?'

'I was.'

'That's pretty old.' Examining my bony, bleached-white legs and saying, 'Do you eat much?'

'Of course.'

'You're pretty thin. Maybe you need some junk food. Dad?'

'What?'

'We could get a couple of Whoppers.'

I said, 'This is what happens, Tom, when you get old. All of your bits and pieces . . .'

Father, calling from the bushes: 'It's a bloody mess.'

'Do you want a hand?' Mother said.

'Wait.'

We waited. A minute, more, then Mother called, 'We're nearly there.'

'If I make it.'

'You've made it this far.'

Maybe that's what I was thinking. Maybe I was remembering Father, that morning, squatting in the bushes (as best he could), cursing the world. 'If I can get back up . . .'

'Do you need help?' Mother.

'I'll go.' Ludwig, standing, but Mother told him to wait.

That's what I was trying to tell Tom. 'You're lucky. Look at you. Big biceps.' And I squeezed one. 'Clear eyes. Sharp brain. But it doesn't last forever.'

'That's what I was thinking,' Jack said. 'We were talking, weren't we, Steph?'

She nodded. Looking me over, like she was deciding whether I was worth salvaging.

'What?' I asked, as Tom took my hand, examined each of my fingers and said, 'You need a two-piece feed.'

'It's just, I was thinking, Dad,' Jack said. 'When I was at your place and . . .'

'What?'

'Are you looking after yourself?'

'Of course.'

'I mean, fruit, vegetables . . . I checked the fridge.'

'So?' As I lit up. 'You're saying . . .?'

'Saturday morning. Woolies. Then we could come and help, couldn't we, Steph, Tom, with a bit of cleaning. That place's a big job for someone your age.'

'I keep it clean.'

'Well, some of it. When I went to the bathroom there was a bit of mould . . . a lot of mould.'

Tom had finished with my hands. He examined my face. 'You got big cheekbones.'

Again, Steph told him off, but he just said, 'If you came shopping with us, Grandpa, we could buy plenty of things so you could put on a bit of weight.'

'I'm perfectly fine.'

He told me my arms were bony and I needed some muscle. I said, 'Listen, I know you care, but I'm able to look after myself.'

'Okay, let me pay for someone to come in,' Jack said. 'Six hours a week. I know someone. She's good. She does our place every Thursday.'

'She's reliable,' Steph said. 'Thorough.'

'No.'

'It's fifteen dollars an hour. Give you some peace of mind, me . . . us, eh, Tom?'

I just said, 'It was a sharp corner. It's already healing.'

'Who's your doctor?' Jack asked. 'That's what kills most people. Infections. You in that dirty old bathroom.'

'It's fine. I clean it. Once a week.'

Tom wasn't happy. 'I've had a grandfather for three weeks and then . . . how about a cleaner, Grandpa?'

'How about you . . .?' *Mind your own business*. But I couldn't say it. He was right. Three weeks wasn't long. 'Alright! Maybe . . . once a fortnight.'

'And my doctor,' Jack said. 'He's good.'

'So's mine.'

'Who?'

I couldn't think of a name. It'd been a few years. Some Indian guy I'd seen when I couldn't stop shitting. 'Dr White.'

'*White*?' Smiling. 'There's no Doctor White. I'll take you to mine. He's good. He can look at this.' And to the nurse, checking my chart. 'When can he go home?'

'In the morning.'

'Good,' Jack said. 'Clean the joint up, get a doctor. Then we can start on that shed. I saw a rat.'

'That's Mrs Wright. I've had a word with her, but she's dotty, she doesn't listen, and her son, who lives with her, he's off with the fairies.'

'Pest controller.'

'You lot have been talking about all this, haven't you?'

'We have.'

'I'm not helpless.'

'Didn't say you were.'

'I appreciate all this,' I said. 'You at the front door, and Tom' – cupping his chin in my weak old hand – 'but you've gotta understand, I've always taken care of myself.'

'No, you haven't. Socks and sandals?'

'I'm fine!'

Similar to what Father said. As he walked from the bush: 'Eighty, ninety, at least, eh, Ignatz?'

'Martin!' Mother, rushing towards him.

But it was too late. Father, his pants around his ankles, his underwear, and his old bloke dangling in the breeze as he emerged from the cane grass. I looked away. But I'd seen. And once seen. Mother pulled up his pants, but there was paper stuck to his arse. 'You haven't finished.'

'Ignatz, have you been looking after them?'

'Who?' he asked.

'The ones we hid away . . . Benno, what do you think?'

'I don't know.' Looking at the distant ranges.

'Come on,' Mother said, and she led him back to the bushes, pulled down his pants, helped him finish the job. Say what you want about my mother, but she always finished a job. Two, three am in the camp, the dorms, some kid lying in a bed full of shit, or some old bloke coughing up his lungs. It was her. Father standing back, arms crossed, discussing the logistics. Her. Like now, saying to Father, 'All you have to do is call, Martin.'

But Father just shouted, 'Ignatz, another hour till the Bend?'

'A few.'

'Maybe you could show the Protector where we keep them?'

'Keep still,' Mother said.

Eventually Father and Mother returned. Father sat on a lump of granite and rubbed his legs. 'That's done.' Mother fetched water, and helped wash his hands. She said, 'From now on . . .' As she noticed me, and said, 'It's fine, Benno. It's the heat. Once he cools . . . don't you think, Martin?'

I said, 'It's just too hot, isn't it, Father?'

What can I say? You live, you shit, you fail, you come to an abrupt and undignified end. You lose control. You gash your leg and everyone thinks it's because you're old and stupid and no good for anything anymore. But you are. You're just as good as when you started. No difference. Just the cogs wearing out. It's all there still. Right up until the end. Which is what I wanted to say to my father that day, although I didn't have the words, and even if I did, the sense to say them.

'It's enough to feel faint,' Father said, and he put his head back, then fell to the ground, and Mother and Ignatz, Ludwig, me, Silas, all of us rushed over to him, sat him up, asked if he was okay. He just said, 'Faint.'

'Drink this.' Mother gave him water.

Father said, 'You just have to get on with it. Ludwig, the horses are fine?'

'All ready, Pastor.'

'Then we should go.' Trying to stand, wobbly again, Ignatz telling us to help him.

I had the same approach. I said to Tom, 'Get a pad, Tom. Find one . . . nurse?'

A minute later, Tom was sitting beside my bed, clutching a pen, waiting. I said, 'What sort of approach, do you think?'

'Conciliatory,' Jack said.

'*Dear* (we'll insert his name later) . . . *I am writing on behalf of my grandson, Thomas Gerlach.*' I waited. Tom wrote. Block letters, and I told Jack it was a shame, wasn't it, they didn't teach the kids cursive anymore. '*Recently, on a visit to your museum, Tom told me he'd be interested in seeing a specimen of the night parrot* (leave the rest, I'll add the binomial later). *Upon asking . . .*'

Like this, for ten minutes, Tom adding suggestions, scribbling out and changing words, lines. Until finally I said, '*The path forward seems clear. One of your employees finds the parrot, adds it to the diorama, labels it, perhaps a pre-recorded call? Then I, Benjamin Gerlach, son of Pastor Gerlach, donor, owner of the hundreds of specimens presently on display in your museum, will renounce any claim to said items. Forever. I await your timely reply. Sincerely, Etcetera, etcetera. Benjamin Gerlach*. Got that?'

'Hold on.' Biting his lip, writing as fast as he could.

'Righto. Read it back.'

When we were done, I said to Jack, 'You wouldn't mind typing that up and sending it to the director of the museum. I think his name is Jones?'

'Fine, Dad.'

'And in return . . .' I said.

'What?'

'Thursday morning. Nine to twelve. But if she gabbles, she's out. Eh, Tom?'

'I reckon.'

'And in return,' Jack said, 'First check-up. Next week. I noticed the old heart pills in your bathroom. When did you last take them?'

Tom, glaring at me.

'I have a script somewhere.'

'Somewhere?'

'A few years old, perhaps.'

'The doctor, Monday, right?'

I said to Tom, 'Your father got where he is by bullying weak people.'

Back beside the Finke, we packed up our few things. We set off into another hot day. So far. Like this trip had no beginning, middle or end.

Charms against injury or sickness

This was when we should've felt our happiest, or at least most hopeful. Another hour under the belt, as we crossed stony country towards Horseshoe Bend. When we should've felt most excited, most convinced we'd make it. Although it didn't feel this way. Just like we'd been in battle, and we were returning to our country, our homes, to see what could be salvaged.

'Couple of hours, Pastor,' Ludwig said.

Father sat on his throne, slumped forward, head low. His arms on the rests, as he cleared his throat, spat the result in a handkerchief that Silas kept offering. In the end he tired of this and just spat it, blood and all, over the side. Mother told him not to, but he didn't care. He just didn't care.

'Long trip, but we did it,' Ludwig said, trying to inject some enthusiasm.

Father held tight to the chair that had carried him hundreds of miles; stretched out his legs, tried to stop the pain (I guess) and said, 'They won't have time to be looking after us.'

'Course they will,' Mother said.

'Gus has got a station to run . . . not a hospital.'

'Lou won't mind . . . for a few days.'

I sat cross-legged beside Father, watching camels running beside us, stopping, drinking from a spring, observing us like *we* were the intruders. I'd thought about what Ludwig had said. About showing Father I was interested, cared about his work, and intended carrying on. Although I wasn't interested in anything at fourteen. At fifteen, sixteen. Even at university, until one day, C.F. Lewis (Professor of Classics) stopped me (undergraduate Gerlach) in a hallway, held my arm, said, 'I've been meaning to talk to you.'

'Sir?'

'I was reading some of your father's monographs.'

I told him I was more interested in European languages, but he said, 'Bullshit. If anyone can know or write about Aboriginal people . . .'

He explained he could organise it all: Masters, PhD. 'Let me know what you'd like to study, Gerlach.'

'Sir?'

'Your thesis.'

'I was thinking, maybe, Italian?'

'Anyone can study Italian. Millions. So what? But we've got one person who can go out into the desert and study Aranda, other languages, record them . . . and don't you want to continue your father's work?' He handed me an application for a scholarship. 'I realise you might not have a lot of money.'

I wasn't sure. I put off telling Mother for weeks, but when I did: 'If they're going to cover eighty per cent of your costs . . .'

'But I love Italian.' I'd topped the state in my Leaving exams.

She just repeated: 'Eighty per cent.'

Later, Lewis stopped me again and said, 'I was reading your father's notes about Aranda language. Fascinating, Benno. The use of image as word . . . completely unique.' Waiting a few moments. 'But I still haven't seen that application.'

Although I'd filled it in. Mother had watched me do it. Sitting there, telling me what to write, as I told her to butt out. As she said, 'Eighty per cent is a lot.' Eventually taking the completed application and signing it and telling me, 'Give it to him, tomorrow.'

Back on the dray, it had begun. Me sitting with the hand-scribbled booklet Father had managed, somehow, to complete. I read what he'd written. His beautiful *Sütterlin* script. '"A good example is the Old English charm *For a sudden stitch*."'

He sang a few lines, then said, 'It's important, Benno, to make *connections*. Every song has its equivalent in another culture.' Singing a few lines, but then dropping his head again, staring down at the boards, coughing up another mouthful and spitting it, the leftovers striking Mother. 'Silas, give him his handkerchief!'

Father was defeated. His pants cut up the sides, across the front, held up with a belt. And the faint, shitty whiff that kept coming over. Although what could I say? Did he smell it? Mother? Were we in a conspiracy of silence? God granting Father another indignity.

'If maybe, one day . . .' he said to me.

'Of course,' I replied. 'They've been singing these songs a long time, I guess?'

'Thousands and thousands of years, eh, Silas?'

'Thousands.'

Father stared at me like he wasn't quite sure. Why, suddenly, I'd taken an interest. But he could be convinced. I said, '"Chanted words have the power to bring spirits to life."'

'Do you understand?' Father said, cautiously.

'Like . . . they only have power when they're sung?'

'Exactly. True, isn't it, Silas?'

'Gotta sing them, Benno.'

'If you're interested?' Father said.

'I could help you finish. I don't know all this, but I could learn. You could tell me.'

'That's what you're thinking?' Looking up.

'I reckon.'

Maybe Father could be helped, fixed up, wounds treated. Maybe he could return to what he'd been, standing in front of the congregation, thundering Matthew, a homily about blazing bushes and the power of faith. Or walking around the blacks' camp – do this, do that, take this child in and feed her, have those boys completed their work? Because it's important to remember that's how he was, most of the time, most of my childhood. A warrior, a stormtrooper for God, full of endless energy and drive and *tomorrow we'll finish rendering that wall*, or *I must get to town to buy more books.*

'It's all there,' Father said. 'Boxes of it, if anyone's interested.'

'You've got a lot of work to do when we return to civilisation,' Mother said.

'I have.' Conceding.

'Years of it, Martin. Something for your old age.'

'I think.' Although he looked at me differently. 'It'd take a brave man, Benno.'

'Why?'

'Because every time you start something you discover another hundred facts, songs, stories, and you keep writing them down, but it never gets to the point where you think you've got everything. More and more. That's why I haven't finished. Or barely started, I think.'

Maybe he was thinking: *You reckon I'll die, and I'll die with regrets, and this is your attempt to fool me, to pacify me*. He said to Ludwig, 'It should be written down, shouldn't it, Ludwig?'

'Yes.'

'So people can know your stories, like you know ours. Like Dickens. Like *David Copperfield*. There's a hundred Copperfields in those carts' – indicating – 'eh, Ludwig?'

'There is.'

He turned to me and said, 'Maybe those charms will help.'

'Medicine'd be more useful,' Ignatz said.

'Charms,' Father said to him. 'If you don't want to believe . . . if you don't have any faith, Ludwig.'

I could still smell him. Why didn't Mother say anything? She would, normally. She was only too happy to tell me about my shortcomings, my body odour and bad breath. But not now. Father's shirt, half of its buttons missing, none of them done up anyway. He dropped his head again, and studied his fingers. I was reminded of Allen Harmstorf sitting at his table – the way he watched his daughter. Not shame, but some sort of acceptance. 'I'm not in great condition, Benno.'

'It doesn't matter.'

But it did, to him. As he held and squeezed each of his fingers, like he wanted to pull them from his hand.

'Not great. I think I might've . . .' And to Mother. 'Perhaps we should stop?'

But she said, 'Let's just get there, Martin. We can deal with it then.'

I said, 'It's just cos it's been such a long trip, Father.'

'Yes. And difficult. Floods and storms and dust . . . all of it, eh, Benno?'

The way Father paraded around the mission, gave orders, lifted sacks onto the back of the dray, told kids to get shoes on. And he was always well-presented. Always, in his black pants and frock coat, freshly pressed, courtesy of Pauline or Adele. Not like this. His big, flat feet plastered across the boards. His uncut toenails. 'What it might take, Benno, is a common touch. Someone to simplify the ideas, pick out the best, write something . . . popular. It could be done. People have a keen interest in these parts.'

I saw a spark. Like he'd decided I was genuine, and might agree, might *want* to carry on.

'And maybe if it could be published with photographs – I have plenty, of course, don't I, Alma? – but I mean high quality photographs that show the landscape like we're seeing it, with all these colours and . . . the brilliance . . . if people could see that, Benno.'

So, to make an observation. I (at eighty years of age) am not sure it was all worthwhile. Father's work, mine (which was only ever an adjunct). I'll give you an example: 1957. I received a phone call from Professor Lewis. 'Ben, how are you?'

'Fine.'

Although hardly, with a couple of kids who refused to talk to me, a wife who hated me, child maintenance, stuck in the desert patrolling and photographing and recording, making notes, always notes, to add to Father's never-to-be-finished compendium of all things Aranda.

'I was ringing, Benno, with news of another scholarship.'

'What's that?'

As I sat in my Hillcrest lounge room, Kate cooking tea, asking who was calling. I said, 'More free money, eh?'

'You could say. But it's a travelling scholarship.'

'Travel? Where?'

'Wherever you want. To lecture. Tell people about your work. And your father's work.'

So there I was, six months later, in a dimly-lit basement in London. Thirty rows of chairs set out. A tape recording of the flowering crests of the countless stalks, the Honey Ant song playing in the background to welcome the crowd, as it was, or wasn't. Me in a suit and tie and Kate sitting at the back, smiling, blowing me a kiss. I'd had a photo of Father blown up, and I'd stuck it up. Another of a sacred ceremony. And along the side of the room – boomerangs, a didgeridoo (Tom's), necklaces and digging sticks, all set out with little labels Kate had helped me type before we'd left Australia. The Royal Society (who'd agreed to host me) had supplied an urn, cups, a few biscuits in a box.

And there we sat, waiting. Two, three, four people. Thirty minutes after the advertised starting time, and Kate said, 'Should we just . . .?'

So I began. Ten people. Two lives worth of work; six crates worth of material, seen off from Port Adelaide docks; an ocean journey; months of organisation, and ten people. And it was worse in Liverpool (six). And Birmingham (five). At the end of all this, on the way home, standing on the deck gazing out at the endless desert of water, Kate said to me, 'Would you do it again?'

I laughed. 'I was sure people would be interested.'

'People are only interested in what they know.'

'All this way. I thought there'd be people waiting outside to get in. Isn't anyone in England curious?'

'Just about what they'll be eating tomorrow.'

That's the story I wanted to tell you. There are plenty more, but that one makes it clear. That just because *you're* interested in something doesn't mean . . . And maybe that was Father's fear, that last day of our journey, on the dray? That despite anything he or I or anyone might write down, or record, illustrate . . . no one would care.

'And what about the Honey Ant song?' I asked Father. 'And these words . . . like, thirty letters? How do you say that?'

'You'll learn. Given time. Just listen, ask people to repeat it.'

Eventually Father came good. He asked Ignatz how much further, and scanned the horizon. He sat up, like all of this sickness was nothing, and he pounded his leg, like he would when he was in Sunday school and trying to make a point about Paul on the road to Damascus. He said, 'If we could just get back, Alma.'

'Where?'

'Hermannsburg. There's work left unfinished.'

'Are you joking?'

Ignatz called, 'There it is.' Indicating the Horseshoe Bend Hotel, small and shiny and *real*, on the horizon.

It took another hour to get there. As we went, Father said, 'I could be made well, Alma.'

'We've decided.'

'Perhaps.' But then lost in the detail of the hotel. The walls covered in iron, the few trees growing close to the house. 'I never thought.'

'You gotta have a bitta faith,' Ludwig said.

There was Lou, out the front waving. And her husband, Gus. A few blacks standing behind them, and what looked like a character from Dickens – big, round and pot-bellied. 'It's Pastor Stolz,' Father said.

'See!' Mother said. 'We made it, Martin.'

There was a boy, too, about fifteen, sitting on the porch, watching our progress.

'I thought it'd kill me,' Father said. 'I thought . . .'

Mother stood, held him, and said, 'You were right to come, Martin.'

But she was distracted by the last hundred yards, these people gaining definition. 'I never would've thought . . .'

Gus and Lou waved back, the boy wiped his nose on his arm, and the blacks studied us like we'd just arrived from Mars.

So we stopped. The dust settled. The horses waited, content. Greetings, then Ludwig and Ignatz helped Father down from his chair, for the last time. The boy approached me and said, 'I'm Harry.'

'Benno.'

We shook.

He said, 'What's Benno mean?'

'Benjamin. Ben.'

'Why aren't you just called that, then?'

'Ask my mum.'

Lou was hugging Mother, and Gus was almost pulling Father up the front steps of his small hotel. Silas and Ludwig and Ignatz and Jamy, standing watching. Then Father stopped, turned to them and said, 'We've done it.'

Harry sniffed the air and said, 'Did someone shit themselves?'

Riders of the Purple Sage

'Here,' Harry said, showing me the old bath on the back porch of the Horseshoe Bend Hotel. 'Plenty of room for a swim.'

I didn't fancy getting in – a third full, a brown soup of Mother's and Father's dirt, sweat and god knows whatever else. 'Can I get some clean water?'

'It *is* clean, mostly.' Indicating.

Because, he explained, the tanks were nearly dry, people had to drink, Ruby had to cook. And even muddy water, he said, left you cleaner than before.

'Right.' I took off my shirt, waited for him to leave, but he just sat and said, 'Jack Fountain reckons your dad's in bad nick.'

'He'll be okay.'

'Real bad . . . you shy?'

'No.'

He turned around, stared out across the compound, to the stables, the horses back in their stalls. 'But they got something for it?' he asked.

The porch was open to the yards, the house, the dining room. I turned away, slipped off my pants, my underpants, got in. Luckily the dirt hid everything, but Harry went into the kitchen and returned with a bucket of hot water, stood over me, poured it in. 'Just tell me if I hit anything.'

I picked up the old flannel, wiped my chest, legs, all over, as Harry settled in again and said, 'Pastor Stolz was worried.'

'Was he?'

'He came all the way with that Gotthold bloke, but they broke down at Stevenson Crossing, and Stolz borrowed a horse to get here, to see your dad. He reckons he's important.'

I cleaned my face, spat dirt from my mouth. 'Maybe.'

'I went to Hermannsburg once.'

'When?'

'When I was baptised. You were just little. That Silas bloke did some sermon . . . he's still got the same suit on. He's a bit funny, I reckon. The place looked as boring as batshit. But this is, too. But I'm not staying here for long.'

'What you gonna do?'

He didn't say. He just went in, filled the bucket, returned and topped me up. 'Not as bad as you.'

'What?'

'Stuck out here, like them ringers. At least I go back next week.'

'Where?'

'School. Immanuel. I board.'

So what? 'Dad's thinking of sending me. Maybe we could live together?'

But he just said, 'It's fun. On the weekend we piss off to Glenelg and go swimming and plenty of other things.'

'Like what?'

He just smiled. 'Plenty. They try to keep the boys and girls apart, but they can't. They'd love you, Benno. There's this one called Tracey . . . she's the worst of the lot.'

'The worst what?'

He ran across the backyard, past a dead ribbon gum, into some sheds. A moment later he re-emerged, returned and said, 'Try this.' Producing a bottle of whiskey, taking a swig and handing it to me.

'I dunno.'

'If you're going to Immanuel. There's plenty of this. The shop on Colley Reserve sells it to us cheap.'

I took it, smelt it, then tasted some. 'Jesus!' Spitting it into the water. Harry took another swig, hid the bottle under the bath and produced a few smokes from his pocket. 'Want one?'

'They're just inside.'

'So what?' Matches, but we heard footsteps and he shoved the lot in his pocket. Pastor Stolz, big and round and sweaty, wiping his forehead with a handkerchief. He asked if we'd seen Ignatz, we said no, he went in and Harry said, 'Perhaps tomorrow.'

He returned to the shed. I waited, watching a flock of cockatoos fly low over the hotel, drowning out *Don Giovanni*. Father had already discussed it with Gus as we sat eating a meal of pickled onions and cold pork. Gus telling him he'd tried popular songs, underneath the mellow moon and *Daisy*, but they didn't stick in your head like this stuff, eh, Martin?

I thought of getting out. Noticed my pants, imagined the move – but by then Harry was on his way back. He sat down beside me and said, 'It's only cos they want to get rid of me.'

'What?'

'Immanuel. They think I'm a pain in the arse.' And he shrugged. 'Cos I'm not interested in sweaty old balls. So they ship me off every term.'

'But you like it?'

He took a few moments to decide, then said, 'Doesn't make sense, Ben.'

'What?'

'They don't send me to boarding school cos they think I like it. They send me because . . . why do I give a shit? Look at it. That's our house over there. See, and the station sheds, and that's where I'm meant to work when I'm . . . I think Dad's already given up on me.'

'Why?'

He smiled. 'Would you prefer their thing, or the other thing.'

'Sorry?'

'Girls. They got two things.' He sat back on the porch railing, put his feet up. 'Fuck stayin' here.'

'I reckon I'll go to university.'

'Why?'

'Dunno. I might study languages.'

'You don't need any of that.' Grinning.

I moved my hands through the muddy water. 'I'm going to help Father with his books, his notes. He's written a dictionary.'

'Who's *Father*?'

'Dad. My dad. A dictionary. And I'm going to finish it.'

'Fuck.' He shook his head. 'Why would you want to write a dictionary?'

'Not just. Maybe other books.'

Mother appeared at the door and said, 'You're not going to get clean in that, Benno.'

'It's all that's left, after you and Father.'

'*Father*,' Harry mocked. And then to Mother: 'It's all the water we've got, Mother.'

'Pardon?'

'*Mrs Gerlach*.'

She just shook her head and said, 'Come and sit with your father, Benno.' And went in.

A moment later, Harry said, '. . . *sit with your father, Benno*. What a battleaxe.'

'She's my mother.'

He grinned, like he'd been successful at whatever he was trying to do. 'Oh, I'm sorry, Master Gerlach. Have I upset you? Shall I powder your bottom, dear?'

I just sat, defiant.

'If you're gonna survive at Immanuel . . .'

'I might not be going there. I might return to Germany, to my brothers and sister in Leipzig. Not this shithole. Not Adelaide. Not Immanuel. Little town . . . little people.'

He said, 'You've got claws. Good work. Now we can get started, *Benno*.'

I don't think I've ever met someone so instantly unlikeable. Someone who existed, even then, despite others, not because of them. I said, 'I forgot to get a towel.'

Harry indicated one on the back of a chair, already wet, already brown. 'But you're shy, aren't you?'

'No.'

'Can't be shy at Immanuel. We gotta club. You can join if you like. See who can get the furthest.'

Bugger it. I stood, stepped out, claimed the towel and started drying myself. He said, 'Shit, you got it all happening downstairs, eh? Trace'll be mighty impressed.'

Fifteen minutes later I went into the sitting room. Empty, apart from Gus Elliot, who told me to sit down. A smokers' stand, *The Bulletin*, a few books by Zane Grey. He stared at me sideways, like he didn't understand something. Like he didn't know why I was dressed in clean pyjamas. He said, 'Talkin' to Harry?'

'Yes.'

'He gets some strange ideas. You feeling better?'

'Thanks.'

A long way from seven bodies, stumbling in the front door, stripped, cleaned, scrubbed, dressed in fresh clothes, prodded and poked and examined for signs of life. Lou saying things like, 'I wasn't sure you'd get here in one piece.' Mother saying it was incredibly generous, what she'd done for us, Gus telling us it's what anyone would do, and he would've come, but he'd had a flare up, and he showed us his gouty foot. 'See, you're not the only daft bugger, Martin.'

Then there'd been pudding and tea and brandy and Mother had put Father to bed. Room three. The biggest, Lou had explained. King-sized bed, with a view across the hills, French doors, freshly-washed curtains. Two pounds a night, but for us, nothing.

Gus said to me, 'I've done the trip before, but not with all that gear, that many people. Quite an achievement, Benno, and your Father tells me it was all down to you.'

'How?'

'Keeping him company. Keeping him sane. Reading. Someone that makes sense.'

'What about me?' Mother called, coming out of the room, an armful of dirty clothes. 'Where's the copper, Gus?'

Gus indicated, waited until Mother left, then said, 'When you're only fourteen, eh?'

'Pardon?'

'All that way.' He leaned forward. 'With him that ill. But don't let it play on yer brain, Benno. It is what it is, and you've done well, for a boy of fourteen.'

He seemed happy with this. He'd said what needed saying, so he reclined, scratched his belly, took a puff from his pipe and said, 'D'yer like Mozart?'

'Dad's got a music box.'

'I know. He showed me. You like music?'

'The bit we've got.'

Sideways, like there was something he couldn't understand. 'When Jack told me the cart had bust and you were on the dray and the donks . . . that must have been something.'

I shrugged.

'You don't give much away, do you, Benno?'

'Ludwig and Jamy did all the work.'

'They're good horsemen. You were lucky you had them along. But your dad said it was you—'

'What's that?' Mother asked, passing through the room with a bottle of laudanum.

'What, you trying to poison him?' Gus said.

'It's the only way he can sleep.'

Gus leaned forward and said, 'I was just saying, Benno's done a good job, hasn't he, Alma?'

'He has.'

'Boy his age. His father sick.'

'That's why we brought him along, Gus.' Returning to Father.

More Mozart, more smoke from the pipe. Gus said, 'I had a mother like her.' He pulled a face. I laughed. I whispered, 'It was a long trip.'

Mother called, and I went into Father's room. The blinds drawn, a candle burning beside his bed. Someone had gathered a bunch of lavender, a few roses, a Bible open to *Genesis*. Mother helped Father settle, then he said to me, 'At last . . .'

'Call me if you need me, Benno. He should sleep now.'

'Don't talk about me like I'm not in the room,' Father said.

Mother went out, and I sat beside Father. 'The bath was dirty.'

'You should've gone first.'

'You needed it more.'

He smiled. 'It's been a while since I shat myself, Benno. But, of course, you . . .'

'What?'

'Changed you plenty of times. Three in the morning . . . just remember that.'

He closed his eyes and started taking long, laboured breaths. I said, 'Good of Pastor Stolz to come.' But I knew this sounded fake, forced, small talk.

'Good,' he managed. 'It's good to see what people will do . . . what they *want* to do, Benno.'

'You feel okay?' I said, leaning forward.

'Fine, fine.' Like he sensed my anxiety. 'I was just thinking . . . when we get back to town we should go to the theatre. It's been so long? Remember *Richard the Third*?'

'Sort of.'

I knew *of* it. I recalled the program, sitting in our kitchen drawer for years, remembered reading about the theatre, the cast (J. Maggs as Richard), the sponsor (Penfolds Wines), the governor and his wife attending the opening. A yellowing memory of the only play they'd taken me to.

'I can still remember,' Father said. 'The stage was all dark, and out he pops, Richard, and he looks at us, at me and Mother in the front row, and he says, "Now is the winter of our discontent, made glorious summer by this sun of York . . ."' Smiling. 'Can you remember, Benno?'

'Sort of.'

'Honest. He looked me in the eyes and said, "And all the clouds that lowered upon our house are deep in the ocean's bosom buried . . ." I've often thought about what we've missed, Benno.'

'That doesn't matter.'

'It does. But we can go again, can't we?'

'I reckon they'd have another play by Shakespeare, eh?'

'He saw you, and he looked at you, and he was saying how he was going to kill his brother and become the king . . . you must remember him looking at you, Benno?'

'A bit.'

'Your mother didn't think much of it. Halfway through, during the intermission, she said this is as boring as hell, come on, let's go. But I said no. I said we're staying. If it kills me, I'm sitting through it, Alma. Because the people up there on the stage . . . that was something special.' Gazing up at the pressed tin ceiling, like the ghosts had followed him here. Then he closed his eyes again. Gus came in and asked if everything was okay, and I said fine. I told him to go to bed, because I wasn't tired, and I'd stay up, and it was after midnight and everyone else was asleep. But he just looked at me. Sideways. 'Let him sleep, Benno.' Before going out.

So Father slept. Deep. Mouth open. Dragging in every breath, holding it, like he was about to stop breathing, as I put my hand on his arm, shook him a little. Over and over.

I couldn't remember *Richard the Third*. I couldn't remember most of what had happened those fourteen years. I searched for it among the sheets, on his arms (all pale and scabby), his chest (the few old freckles), his fat cheeks, hairs flaring from his nostrils, the wax in his ears. I couldn't remember much at all. Plays, concerts, most of what had happened in Germany, and before. I couldn't remember my baptism, having my shitty nappy changed at three in the morning, the first time I spoke, or wrote a word, all of which must have happened. And if all of this were the case, then what was left?

I could still smell the pipe smoke coming from the sitting room.

Father stirred, and I said, 'I remember going to the museum though.'

'You do?'

'The display cases, with all of the stuffed animals, and the way the lion's tail moved, I can remember that. And where they kept all the Aboriginal stuff, remember?'

'That's right, I showed you.' He smiled.

'The string necklaces, remember? Ignatz got the women to make them, and you sent them to the museum, and they were right there, and there was a label and it said your name, I remember that.'

Then, I guess, he must have drifted off again. But this time there was no drama, no noise, no struggle. Just a deep sleep, like he was dreaming about the actors, floating on and off stage, the ghosts, the smoke, the smell of make-up and oil from the footlights. I guess I must have fallen asleep, too. Because the next thing I remember was Gus Elliot shaking me awake, looking up at him and wondering who he was, my eyes adjusting, checking Father to see he was alright.

Gus led me back out to the sitting room, sat me down in his rocker, handed me a glass of milk he'd warmed. 'Time for bed.'

'I gotta watch Father.'

'I'll watch him. I can't sleep with this foot anyway.'

He waited as I drank milk. Then he said, 'My father was an idiot, Benno.'

I just waited.

'He built a rig and raced it around a track (I'll show you tomorrow) and the thing fell on him and the horse . . . big bloody mare, Benno.'

'Was he okay?'

'No. Dead as a dodo. I was your age, a year or two younger.'

'Did you see it?'

'Yes. I was first there. But he was already gone.'

'How did you feel?'

'I'm not sure. I was too busy . . . I pulled him out. I was only this little runt, but I had to because there was no one else around. I tried to wake him up but he wouldn't so I ran back to the house and told the maid but she was no help, so I saddled a horse and rode all the way . . . for an hour . . . I don't even know what I was thinking.' He waited, remembering. 'I think I was trying to get to Oodnadatta. But I stopped, and thought, and realised . . . he was dead.'

'So what did you do?'

'I turned around and rode back. An hour. See, that's how stupid I was.'

I'm not sure why he told me the story, or if it was true. But maybe it didn't matter. Maybe this is what he thought it'd be like, to have a horse fall on your father when you were a kid.

Then he helped me stand, led me into Room two, where I fell into bed beside Mother.

Wednesday 18 October (Day 9)

A ring of scones, Pastor Stolz drinking tea from his saucer, spilling it down his front, excusing himself. 'All of them would say the same, Martin.' Although Father didn't care. Sitting in a pyjama top, belly out, a sheet draped over his midriff and legs, the only way, he'd told us, he could bear the pain. Mother sitting close to him, holding his cup, helping him drink.

'I'll attest to each one of them,' Stolz said. 'That's why I came, Martin. I thought it important you see, you know.'

A ring of people: Mother, Father, me, Lou and Gus, Harry looking sideways at Father, like he was planning something. And in an outer ring, an orbit of moons – Jamy (playing solitaire on the sideboard) and Ludwig, Ignatz, one of the station girls, because Lou reckoned it was important to include them.

It'd been a hot night. I'd slept, on and off, through sheer exhaustion. Woke, every hour or so, wiped sweat from my face and neck, laid back, studying the pressed-tin planets and stars. I'd heard Gus talking to Father. Practical things: Hermannsburg in five years' time; how they'd find someone to look after the blacks; the intrusion of the outside world, the stray ringers and grog and loss of the old ways ('Our fault, perhaps, Gus') that, at least for a while, had made the job easier. Father had said, 'We should've been making them more independent, Gus.'

'There's only so much you can do for them.'

'*More*. Not less. Relying on us. It'll have to be fixed.'

'Not by you. You just have to get well, Martin.'

Father hadn't slept. And now he sat, dressed like some Roman emperor, nodding his head, a few moments' sleep, snoring, waking and saying, 'What?'

And Mother: 'You're snoring.'

'Shit of a night.'

Gus said, 'The place was never built with insulation, Martin. It needs to be replaced. Knocked down, the whole lot. You can't cool a hotel with iron walls, tin ceilings . . .'

'Martin?' Stolz asked, shaking a letter in the air.

And Father: 'So what did they say?'

'"In grateful thanks for fifty years' service at Hermannsburg Mission, we, the undersigned, express our gratitude and ongoing support for Pastor Martin Gerlach."'

'Pity the Board didn't write something . . .'

'That was never going to happen,' Stolz said.

'What sort of people are they, Pastor?'

'They're administrators. Small people, Martin. People who have emerged from *the machinery*, you understand? Nothing of the vision you've had . . . let alone the perseverance. "In honour of the work, also, bettering the lives of the native people of Central Australia. To cater to their health, wellbeing, education, their understanding of God's message. That their lives may be enriched. Again, we thank you."' Looking up at Father and saying, 'I thought that was rather special, Martin.'

'It is, it means a lot,' Father said, as Mother offered him more scones, but he shook his head.

Silas said, 'I'm among them, Pastor Gerlach.'

'You needn't call me that, Silas. Martin . . .'

Ignatz watched Father, like he needed to clear up a few details. The letters he'd sent to the Board had made it clear. The old man had tried, but failed, and no one had held him to account.

Father said, 'It's just a letter.'

'It's not just a letter,' Mother said.

Stolz read the names. '"Gotthold Wurst." I think he might have organised it, Martin.'

Harry jerked his head towards the door, mouthing: 'Want to get out of here?' Then he said, 'I might show Benno around.'

Father turned to me and said, 'Are you tired, Benno?'

'No.'

'I kept you up. Did I keep you up?'

'No.'

Although it was three, maybe later, when I woke to Gus laughing, telling Father about some woman named Stephanie, remember, Martin, every time you asked her she'd say, 'Not unless I can have a go.' Father said, 'She was the old-fashioned type.' A silent gap, then a whisper, listening carefully to hear them, as I lay there, staring out of the window, poking Mother to stop her snoring.

Ten minutes later, Harry and I were walking along a dry creek bed. Kicking polished stones, Harry finding a skink, admiring it, pulling off its legs, putting it on a rock and saying, 'See how far you can go.'

'Why'd you do that?'

'Why not?'

As I watched this half-curious boy. 'I heard our dads talking last night.'

He didn't reply.

'Your dad's pretty old.'

'Sixty. They had me when he was forty-five, and Mum was forty-six. Which is sorta . . .' And he screwed up his nose.

'My dad's fifty.'

'*Forty-five*. Can you imagine, at that age?' He flicked the skink from the rock, and it went flying. 'Come on.'

Continuing around the yards. Horseshoe Bend had originally been Pfeiffer Station, and people (farmers, tourists, Jack Fountain and his camels) had needed somewhere to stay, so the owner at the time (Theo Pfeiffer) had decided to build a hotel to accommodate them, make extra money. A frame was erected, tin salvaged, a few weeks' work and there it was – plain and simple, but adequate. A dining room for the few guests, a long drop and a kitchen for roast beef sandwiches. And now Gus (who'd inherited the hotel with the station) always had someone to talk to.

Harry said, 'Can you imagine . . .'

'What?'

'At that age.' Like he was spitting it out. 'Disgusting.'

A few minutes later we saw a small calf, stuck in dried mud. Trying to pull itself free, but failing. I went to get it, but Harry stopped me and said, 'Where are you going?'

'She's stuck.'

'Come on, I'll show you the Abos.'

No, I thought. I jumped down into the dry creek, the baked mud, reached out, took her around the belly and said, 'She's all bone.'

'What are you doing? Come on.'

I pulled, her legs stretched, eventually she emerged. I laid her on the ground and watched her heart beating fast, staring at me, bleating, over and over, as Harry said, 'It's just a friggin' cow.'

'Should we take her back?'

'Come on, I'll show you the boongs.'

But I was more interested in the calf. You could count the ribs. A little sucked-in belly, and a face that was mostly skull. 'How come she's here?' I said.

'You're soft. She's gonna die anyway. Leave her.'

'No.' Glaring at him.

'Tell you've never lived on a farm.'

'I have,' I said. 'We run two hundred cattle. But *our* blacks look after them properly. You can't just leave her here. It's cruel.'

'So what you gonna do?'

I thought about it. The ten, fifteen minute walk back to the hotel. I picked her up, but she was limp, no muscle, no will to live, just a soft cry, her tail moving.

'Come on, Benno.'

There wasn't much life left in her. She was cold.

'Anyway,' Harry said, 'that's just cruel. Trying to feed her, and she lives a day, and dies. If you reckon you know how to watch animals . . .'

So I put the calf down. She moved her head to see me, the light, something – as her cries quietened, and Harry called, 'Come on. Lois gets around without a top on.'

I leaned down, put my hand over her muzzle, her mouth. She didn't object to dying. Just went loose, quietened. Harry was laughing, he was saying, 'Nice work, Benno.'

'It's not funny.'

'Come on, before the old girl calls.'

So I went with him, past a grove of native pines, a sweet, honey-flavoured breeze coming off the desert. A few minutes later we were standing, ten yards short of the blacks' huts, and Harry said, 'Give it a minute.'

We waited. A few extended families, mothers, fathers, uncles, aunts, kids and cousins, in their own ring, talking in Aranda, a quick explosion of argument, then laughing. Kids coming in and out of the part-iron, part foliage huts. Dogs sniffing bones, and starting on them. 'The girls start early,' Harry whispered.

'Start what?'

'They're pregnant at fourteen. Our age, Benno. Can you imagine? Can you imagine being a father at our age? It's cos they can't keep their hands off each other.'

'I don't want kids . . . ever.'

'Why?'

'Too much trouble. I've got four brothers and a sister in Germany.'

'See, your parents are smart. Root your brains out, have kids, leave them with someone else.' He pointed to a girl, fifteen, sixteen, coming out of a hut, everything showing. 'How bloody good is that? You can't tell me you wouldn't wanna get your hands on them. Makes you all . . .' A long, deep breath.

I said, 'Lucky Ignatz isn't here.'

'The teacher?' Although he didn't take his eyes off her. 'Why's that?'

'I don't reckon *he* likes girls.'

He turned to me, puzzled. 'What?'

'You know, Jamy?'

'Yeah?' Dawning on him. 'No?'

I started walking back to the hotel, and Harry called, 'Where you going?' The blacks asked what was happening, but seemed to know, because one of them chased him off. And then he caught up to me and said, 'Don't worry about them.'

'Who?'

'The abos. You just let them breed, and give them some food, and they work for you.'

I didn't reply. If he didn't get it, I couldn't tell him. 'They *are* people.'

'Just.'

We walked back in silence, went inside and reclaimed our spots around the table. I could hear Gus in the hallway, talking on the telephone. 'No, you don't reckon?' And a long pause.

Lou said, 'Harry show you around, Benno?'

'Yes.' Darting a look at him, him grinning, saying, 'Benno had to kill a calf, didn't you, Benno?'

I said, 'She was stuck in the mud for days by the look of it. All ribs.'

Gus said, 'Well, that seems like the smartest approach, Dr James. Yes . . . no, I fully intend to . . . you wouldn't want to be doing that trip by yerself.'

'It's good you two are the same age, Benno,' Lou said. 'Harry said maybe if you ended up at Immanuel, you two—'

'Presently,' Gus said. 'And in the meantime?'

'You two could share a room, perhaps? He could look out for you, couldn't you, Harry?'

'Of course.' Grinning again.

Gus rang off, returned to the table, finished his cold tea and said, 'It's all taken care of, Martin. There's a spare car, and he can come in two days. He just wants to take care of the patients he's got now.'

In Oodnadatta. At the base hospital.

'I told him it wasn't a trip for the faint-hearted, and he's not used to this country, so I said I'd ride to Oodnadatta and drive back with him.'

'You needn't do that,' Mother said.

'Done that trip a thousand times,' he said. 'I'm not worried, Alma. Get me outta this place for a while. Away from that thing.' Indicating Harry, and laughing.

Mother said she didn't want anyone put out, and we could wait, take the horses and dray to Oodnadatta. But Gus said, 'No, Martin can't do no more travelling, eh, Pastor?'

We all waited for Father – eyes closed, lost in his own thoughts, concentrating on each breath. Eventually Mother agreed. 'If you reckon, Gus?'

'He reckons, in the meantime . . . where's the medicine kept these days, Lou?'

She told him, and he went out.

Father opened his eyes, rejoined the conversation. 'Pastor Stolz came all this way, Benno.' Showing me the letter again.

'I know,' I said. 'I was here.'

'You must be proud of your father?' Stolz asked.

'Of course,' I said, watching him watching me, the sheet slipping from his body, Mother pulling it up, Father saying, 'Benno's agreed to help me with my notes. Maybe get a few things ready for publication. The dictionary, in particular, I thought . . . if people could understand the language they'd understand the culture, the people . . . and things might improve between the blacks and whites.'

'That's quite an ask,' Gus said, returning, searching through the medicine basket.

'We have to start somewhere,' Father said. 'As things are, it's not very satisfactory.'

'How's that?' Gus asked.

Father thought for a moment. 'I decided to come out here, Gus, because I thought, we thought, didn't we, Alma, that every man, every woman, every child, made in the image of God . . .' Confused – like he wasn't sure anymore. 'People were made equal, in the eyes of God.'

Harry laughed.

Either Father didn't hear this, or he ignored it. 'And there were ways,' he said, 'there *are* ways for things to be improved.'

I watched Harry. I could see what he was thinking.

'That's why I came to this godforsaken place, Gus, Pastor Stolz.'

'I can only agree,' Stolz said.

'One day, perhaps, we'll have a native prime minister,' Father added.

'Hardly,' Harry said.

Everyone looked at him, and he said, 'They're not the same as us, are they? I mean, upstairs?' He tapped his head.

'Given time,' Father said.

'It's just how they are, eh, Dad?'

But he just said, 'Harry . . .'

'I mean, they're stone age, aren't they? They just breed. They have to be looked after. That's what you said, Dad.'

A few moments' silence.

'I'm not saying it's bad. What you done is good, Pastor Gerlach. But prime minister?'

Gus struck the table and the cutlery rattled. The medicines in their basket. The cups in their saucers. He said to Harry, 'You need to check the troughs.'

Harry shrugged. 'I was just saying.' Then he stood, and went out.

Gus said, 'I never reckoned that, Martin.' He found what he was looking for. A tube of asthma medication. He handed it to Mother, who inspected it and said it was the wrong thing. But Gus said, 'He reckons it's worth trying.'

Shane

Gus picked his two best horses and brought them around to the front of the house. He tied them to the porch, saddled the first, saying to me (sitting in the old rocker), 'Tomorrow . . . if we can get the car. Main thing is, don't worry, Benno.' Then he came up and sat next to me.

A little *Shane* moment. Alan Ladd riding in from the desert, offering me life lessons. Poor old Father, inside, incapable of more than a few words of protest. As it was, I remember, sometime in the fifties, me, Kate, Sharon and Jack at the drive-in. Shane's face consuming the screen, as Sharon said, 'This is boring as shit,' got out of the car, wandered back to the candy bar. Kate said to Jack, 'Not a real success.'

And Jack: 'She's just pissed off.'

'Why?'

He shrugged. The Gerlach shrug. Always the same.

'Cosa me?'

'You'd have to ask her.'

Joey watching Shane polish his gun, saying (something like), 'You gonna help Dad with them men?'

And Shane, low and guttural: 'Man shouldn't put up with things that aren't right, aren't fair.'

'She's just thinking of Mum, I guess,' Jack said.

Silence. Just spurs. And a storm.

'I'm trying my best,' I said.

'I know. Tell her. Plus, I don't think she likes Westerns.'

'*I asked.*'

When Sharon got back in with a Coke and chips she said, 'How much longer's it go?'

'It's just started,' I told her.

'It's dull.'

'You wanted to come.'

She sipped, and stared at Kate, and Kate said, 'What's wrong, Sharon?'

'Nothing.'

'If there's a problem?'

And me: 'Kate . . .'

Sharon: 'There's only one problem.'

I said to her, 'If you want, we can go home.'

But she just shrugged and said, 'I don't care. Your choice.'

Jack told her to stop being such a pussy. 'If you didn't want to come you shouldn't have. I wanted to see it.' Indicating the screen, full of tumbleweed and close-ups.

But Kate had had enough. 'Just cos things don't suit you . . .'

'It's not me. It's my mum. *His* wife.' Pointing at me.

'Enough!' I said.

But I knew everything would be alright. It was in the script. Things always ended that way. The good guys got rewarded, the bad guys got a bullet between the eyes. It was just a matter of waiting – introduction, complication, resolution. Of eating the overpriced popcorn and guessing the ending, which always involved a bit of fear.

Back on the porch, Gus said to me, 'You could come with me, Benno?'

'I'd rather stay.'

'Good point. Best you stay and keep things sane.' He slapped a knee, and checked the horizon. 'Just think of next year. Just think of living in town . . . or better still, back with Julius and Anton and the others. You looking forward to that?'

'I guess.'

'Why's it always guessing? Course you are. You're all glum. But you gotta perk up. Your dad wants to see it. He needs to, I reckon.'

'Okay.'

'Just go in and talk to him like nothing's happening. No big deal. About . . . something funny. Something to cheer him up.'

Shane. Please. I get it. Just saddle up and ride off into the afternoon sun. Bring help. Solve this problem.

Saturday night at the drive-in, and Sharon said, 'What did you say you do, Kate?'

'I'm a research assistant.'

'What do you research?'

'The same as your father. Languages. Culture. Aranda.'

'That's handy.'

So I started the car. 'I'll take you home.'

'No!' Jack said. 'It's just getting good.' Turning to his sister and saying, 'Stop being such a pain in the arse.'

I waited. 'Sharon?'

'I'll watch it, I guess.' Slurping the last of the drink.

'You guess?'

'I'll watch your stupid movie. But I know what happens. Shane pisses off.'

'Shut up!' Jack said, and Sharon laughed, and Kate shook her head and I said, 'I won't be in a rush to do this again.'

Mother and Lou came out to the porch, sat on either side of me, waited as Gus got on his horse. 'Like I said, Benno.'

'Okay.'

'What's that?' Mother asked.

'A coupla stories, funny ones, eh?' Gus said, flicking the reins, turning the horses and heading down the road.

'Don't dawdle,' Lou called. 'Tell him it'd be better on Friday.'

'I can't make no one do nothing.'

'Yes, you can.'

But Gus just waved. He didn't look back. Didn't say a thing.

'I might go in then?' I said, standing.

Mother pulled me back down. 'He's asleep.'

'I can wait with him.'

'Let him go.'

Because that's all he did now – sleep. Long, deep sleep. Emerging for a while to work out where he was, who was with him, before drifting off again.

Lou said, 'What you heard before, Benno . . . you gotta expect a bit of that.'

Earlier. I'd been waiting outside Father's room, trying to make out whispered voices. Father (who'd summoned Lou) saying, 'It's not the point, Lou. It is what it is. I've been over it and I've accepted it.' Then all I could hear was a needle scratching a finished disc. 'So someone's gotta listen. You're the only one who'll be able to . . .'

'We can talk about this later.'

'No, we can't. *Now* . . . she's gonna need someone to look after her, Lou.'

'Don't worry about Alma.'

'She's in charge of this and that, but come the time . . . And Benno. It's going to hit him. You watch. All I ask. Help them get to Oodnadatta, to town, and on that boat. It's the best chance for both of them.'

Then silence, and it was like he could sense me, and he said, 'That you, Benno?'

I just turned, quietly walked from the house, ran across the yard to the old waterhole where they dumped their rubbish, sat on an old wringer and said, '"I observe. The first objects that assume a distinct presence . . ."'

Lou was on the porch, and she called to me, 'You just come out, did yer, Benno?'

'". . . as I look back, far into the blank of my infancy . . ."'

'Do you think we oughta have a word?'

Back on the porch with Mother and Lou, I studied the stables, the yards, the machine sheds, all of it, just like Hermannsburg. Fifteen, twenty dog pelts hung out to dry on a line. A few blacks wandering around and Silas sitting cross-legged under a gum singing about honey ants.

'It's just a case of . . . being so worried,' Lou said. 'He wants everything taken care of. But I tried to tell him, Benno. Tried to tell him he was being silly.'

'It's not *silly*,' I said.

'Not silly, but . . . there's no *need* for it.'

Mother sat kicking her legs, watching Silas. 'We've been through worse, Benno.'

'Like what?'

'You, for one, with the flu. Eleven years old. We thought we might lose you.'

'It wasn't that bad.'

'No? Millions dead? You don't remember how your father was.' Turning to me. 'Either way. We've got through worse.' And calling: 'Silas, what are you doing?'

But he just ignored her.

'But he *mightn't* be okay?' I said to her. 'He *mightn't* . . . that's what he was saying.'

'Things have been much worse,' Mother repeated.

'He said *come the time* . . . he wants to *fix* things . . . he wants to be sure.' I couldn't understand how she couldn't see it. She'd married him. She was meant to understand him more than anyone. But she didn't. 'You should listen to him,' I said to her.

'You don't give in to all that, Benno.'

'To all what?'

'You don't complicate it.' And she shooed me away. 'Silas, come out of the sun!'

'But that's what he thinks, eh, Mrs Elliot?'

She patted my knee, pointed to a couple of rabbits emerging from under the house, and said, 'They're breeding up again. Harry?'

Harry emerged, saw the rabbits, didn't need any encouragement. He went inside, fetched his rifle, returned and said, 'Where did they go?'

Lou indicated, and he ran off around the house.

Rabbits. Still a problem sixty years later. Me and Tom on a hot Hillcrest morning discussing the way things change. 'This headdress was one of the last things Father collected.'

Tom carefully lifted it, admired the feathers, the sewn rings of colour around the frame. 'It's heavy.'

'Only worn on special occasions.'

'They gave it to him?'

'A gift. Because he was the only one they trusted to look after it, and after he went, it came to me, and that's a big responsibility.'

'So maybe,' Tom said, studying the details, 'maybe you should give it back to them?'

'Maybe I should.'

The two of us, a few days ago, sitting in a room that had once been a study, now a storeroom for my ceremonial objects, shields and spears and boxes, photos and films, handwritten notes of the Father and son, slides (from my trip to England), Amgoorie tins full of carved rocks and postcards I'd never got around to reading. Leaving me with one hope. The same hope, I guess, Father had. I said, 'This is from the ingkaia totem, remember?'

'The bandicoot?'

'Exactly. You're getting it. Even in those days there weren't many left. Bandicoots, I mean. Furry-eared bandicoots. The rabbits had forced them out. So Father thought this was special.' Running my hand over a few old feathers.

'And now there are rabbits everywhere?' Tom said.

'Exactly. No more bandicoots, but plenty of people. Whiteys, like us, Tom. Sailing our boats across the harbour. But hardly anyone stops to think about the poor old bandicoot.'

I handed him a spear, told him it was still sharp, be careful. He pretended to throw it, said, 'Got him, Grandpa, right in the guts!' Then he sat and said, 'You still got a lot to do.'

'I know. Every day I get up and think I'll go through such and such today, write it all up, do this or that but . . .'

'You're doing it all wrong.'

'What?'

'There's this new computer. Apple. Have you heard of Apple? It has this word processor. You know what that is?'

'Type things up?'

'That's it.' Smiling. 'Dad's gonna get me one to help with my school work. A word processor. Word.'

'What word?'

'That's what it's called. But here's what we could do. I could set it up here and when I come over, you bring out a bunch of notes and read them out and I type them up and save them, then there's a record, right?'

'Okay.'

'And the good thing is you can change things, so if you do something and reckon it's shit, then you can change stuff.'

'Sounds like the go. But it's *your* computer.'

'No, you don't get parents, Grandpa. I tell them you're good with English, you've got this degree and all, and if they drop me at your place you can help me, see? That's what you say. Simple.'

'But what about your school work?'

'*What I did in my summer holidays*. Easy. Meanwhile, we can start on this lot.'

I explained. I said I was ashamed because I'd had a similar conversation with Father in 1922, and here I was sixty-six years later with even more stuff I'd collected, put away for the day when I got to it. 'But if, *if*, say, I dropped dead with a heart attack tomorrow . . .?'

'That's not likely, is it?'

'It's possible. Look at my father.'

'He was different.'

'How?'

He tried to think, but just said, 'Lots of ways.'

'But *if*?' I said.

He surveyed the room. 'It'd be easier if you just kept going for a while.'

I squeezed his arm and said, 'Word?'

He told me how it worked. Type. Save. If it's shit, delete. A hundred different fonts, and I asked if they'd have Aranda, and he said no, but we could always draw them in. This seemed fair. It took Father years to find someone to print his book of songs.

A knock on the door, and I called, 'In here.'

Footsteps in the hallway, then Jack came into the room, surveyed the mess and said, 'What have you two been up to?'

Tom told him. About his new Commodore 64. About how he'd rather set it up here, and Grandpa could help with homework. Jack didn't seem interested. He sat down on a spare seat, leaned forward, elbows on his knees. 'You remember that day, Dad, when I knocked on your door?'

'Yes.'

'You must have been surprised?'

'I was.'

'It'd been a while. And the way we'd left things . . .?'

'I know,' I said. 'I'm a lazy old man, aren't I, Tom? I leave things too long. Just look at this lot.' Indicating.

'Things take time,' Jack said.

I didn't know what he meant. But then he called, 'In here.'

I heard footsteps in the hallway, then I saw Sharon standing, for the first time in thirty years, in the doorway. She said, 'Hello.'

I said, 'Sharon? You . . .? It's a bit of a mess but . . . Jesus!'

'Go on, give her a kiss,' Tom said, pushing me.

I managed to stand, and she managed to take a few steps through the mess. Then she touched my arm, pecked my cheek. 'All because of this?'

'Not just,' I said.

'There's a shed full of it,' Jack told his sister.

So we went out to the shed, and Sharon had the same look of surprise as everyone else. Then we came in and I put on the kettle and we sat for an hour as Tom told his aunty about the bandicoot and the rabbit and the didgeridoo (which, he said, he'd almost mastered), the sacred stones that held the answers to everything, didn't they, Grandpa? As I just sat, watching my daughter, wondering what she was thinking. As Tom explained how, when he first saw me walking past the butcher outside Woolies, this was his idea – to fix things. And when he'd gone home and told Steph and Tom, and when he'd said to them, 'Maybe not, the old bastard doesn't deserve it,' Tom had said, 'But it's probably not like you think. He's probably okay, Dad. People are never as bad as you reckon.'

The Night Parrots

'Unlike you to throw something away,' Father said.

I tried to decide whether I should tell him I still had it.

'We could start again?'

'Mother said you should sleep.'

'I'm not sure about all that *Mother*,' he said. 'And *Father*. The way I've always talked to my parents. Things have changed, haven't they, Benno? The times. Things aren't as . . . formal anymore.'

He left it there. Perhaps it was too late to worry about naming things, seeing them differently.

'I had a very different relationship with my father,' he said, glancing sideways at me, lying back on his pillow and staring at the ceiling. 'He never saw that I was any different to the cat or dog or pigs.'

'Really?'

'Maybe not pigs. Maybe the organ, the sideboard . . . possessions. Children were possessions.' And trying again. 'I hope it's more than that now.'

I didn't reply. I thought so.

'So you haven't got it?' Father said.

'I'm not sure.'

'I was hoping we could send it to them.'

'Hold on.'

I went out of Room three, waited in the hallway for a few minutes, smelled the lamb fat, the suet, the ale that Gus had brewed in his laundry. Waited, as one of the kitchen girls went past and asked if I was okay.

Then I took the letter from my pocket and went back to Father. Showing him, saying it was in my other shirt.

'*Good.*' He glowed. 'So let's finish it.'

He tried to sit up, but couldn't. I told him to stay where he was, but he wanted to do it properly. A few inches, but by then his face was red, little capillaries pumping blood around his face, his neck. I said, 'You should rest.'

'Damn this thing!' Sitting half up. 'I never asked for any of this, Benno.'

'I know.'

'Take advantage of your strength while you can. It doesn't last long . . . so little time since I was skiing with your mother. We went to Switzerland. I told you about that?'

'I think.'

'We caught the lift . . . but no sooner had it started rising than I had this feeling, I swear, like the world was going to end. Everything moving, my head about to . . . sick to the guts. I was shouting at your mother to get me down but she just said, *We're stuck here now*. Ten minutes, and I closed my eyes, but when I opened them . . . so there's another piece of advice. Heights. Gerlachs can't take heights. Don't find out the hard way, like I did. When we got to the top I sat in the cafeteria and told your mother to go by herself, but she said, *What's the point?* So ten minutes later, there we were waiting for the next lift down.'

He relaxed. He smiled. His singlet, his shorts, and the same light sheet. Not that he needed it. It was hot. But it was there, I guess, so Mother, I, no one would see his big, red balloon body, about to burst. I knew, I know now, he must have been in pain. But all this time, he didn't say a word. Not a word. That's how you learn. Not from being told – but from seeing. Working it out for yourself.

A scratchy string quartet from the sitting room, Lou talking to Mother. Just an occasional word, a snatch of conversation, as they sat eating oranges, licking their fingers, discussing knitting patterns, like none of this was happening.

Father said, 'Shall we continue?'

I opened the letter on the bedside drawer, flattened it and said, 'Ready.'

'What was the last thing?'

'The hope is that we can be home for Christmas. With Oma and Opa. And Benno playing up. That we can eat six turkeys, nineteen chickens, a pig, three cows, a million sheep – for you, Julius, sheep, your favourite . . .'

He smiled. He seemed to like this. 'Out of all you children, Julius was the biggest worry. So how about . . . *And here we are* . . . four, five days later, is it, Benno?'

I shrugged.

'Four, five days . . . and I'm resting at Horseshoe Bend. Your mother outside with Mrs Elliot, Ludwig and Jamy out . . . fill that in later, Benno . . . *And Ignatz* . . . later.'

'You'll have to slow down,' I said. 'I can't write that fast.'

He looked over. 'You shouldn't print. Use cursive.'

'I hate cursive.'

'It's faster. Promise me, practise.'

'Promise you? Why?'

But he wouldn't say. It was starting to grate. Like everything was about to end, and I'd be left with instructions, carry on, set things right. Like he'd decided something, but even then, wouldn't tell me.

'Julius, I hope you have been behaving. Adventure is all well and good, but you know how your mother responds to . . . what's the word, Benno?'

'For what?'

'Risk! That's it. Risk. Write that down, Benno.'

I said, 'You'll get to see them soon. You can tell them all this. It's a lot to write down.'

He just turned his head and said, 'I want a record, Benno.'

So I wrote. Adventure. Well and good. Mother responds. Then he said, *'I should remind you of that time at Troubridge Island. You should remember.'*

'Slower.'

But he didn't listen. *'All in that small boat, and the water, four feet deep, and you jumping out and saying you could walk all the way back to the beach.'*

'I can't keep up.' Looking up. 'You can tell him this.'

He just waved his hand for me to keep going. '*But then the rip, we couldn't see the rip, and you're taken out, and there's me* . . . it's lucky I had good legs in those days, Benno. Do you remember?'

'I can't write that fast.'

'I can wait. We haven't anything else to do. I doubt I'll sleep again.'

So we continued. The story of Julius drifting out to sea, Father swimming after him, managing to grab him, turning around and heading back to us, throwing Julius in, clinging to the side while he tried to get his breath, while Mother shouted at Julius: 'Stupid boy! Not enough you want to kill yourself, but your father, too!' Julius sitting breathless, shivering, hands clasped between his legs. Father wanted all of this in a letter, but I said, 'Can we stop for a while?'

He saw that the letter-writing was having the opposite effect to what he'd intended (I suppose) and said, 'Rest your hands.'

I shook them out. 'Wouldn't people prefer to hear what's happening *now*?'

'What's to say?'

'We're resting, and soon we're going to Oodnadatta, and we'll get the train.'

'Yes, maybe . . . maybe write all of that down,' he said.

So I began, but within a few minutes he said, 'It's the things I want people to remember.'

'What?'

'I don't want you to remember me lying here.'

I didn't understand. 'But Mother said, Lou said, Gus said Dr James is coming, and if people are doing all of this for you . . .'

'Yes, you're right,' he said. 'I'm sorry, Benno. There's nothing worse than drama, is there?'

Something under the floorboards, so I kicked them, and there was silence. I said, 'Rabbits,' but Father was gazing out the window, squinting. 'We've worked as a very good team,' he said.

I just waited.

'I had this idea for a story.'

'A novel?'

'Perhaps. Not *Shock-Headed Peter*. Not *David Copperfield*. More . . . about that time we went to Trenwood, remember? I thought that would make a fine story. I was going to write it down.'

'You still can.'

'Yes.' Remembering. 'I could have all the details as they happened. That'd be enough to make a good yarn. It'd sell, too. Just the facts, starting with that black fella, Clark, Clarkson at our back door that night. Do you remember that?'

I did. Barely. I was eight, nine, perhaps, sitting up in bed reading, and someone knocked on the back door and said Mr Trenwood was nearly dead and he wanted to talk to the pastor before he went. So Father gathered his stuff, his Bible, and Ludwig got a couple of horses ready and harnessed them to this small cart we had at the time.

'A fine story,' Father said. 'Chapter one would have you and me, Benno, travelling through the desert at night. Clear sky. Stars. Remember?'

This wasn't so bad. I didn't have to write anything down. I just sat back in my chair, and listened.

'I could leave all the details out,' Father said. 'No one wants to read about them. About you, in your pyjamas, with a coat over the top, telling me you had to stop and pee, and me pulling up the horses . . . none of that.'

I said, 'That would make it believable.'

'Good point. Maybe that's exactly what I'd put in. Travelling, what was it, five hours, stopping to water the horses, and there was a bad dust storm, wasn't there?'

'Yes.'

'All of that. Imagine people sitting in town reading about it. Then they'd really get a sense of this place. Maybe that'd be even more important than the dictionary, the songs, the rest of it?'

'Maybe,' I said.

'Chapter two, and we break down, remember? The wheel comes off. And the worst place – the stony country out towards Trenwood. We could have me saying to you, *That damn agent sold us a piece of shit*.' Smiling. 'Me spending hours trying to fix it before I gave up. And you, you were a great help, Benno. That's what the book would have to show. How *you* were the one who was always there helping me.'

I just listened, savouring it.

'That's what it would have to show. That this father and son had set off on a great adventure, and they faced many challenges, but by working together they'd overcome everything. What a book, Benno!'

What he *should've* been writing, all those years, I guess. The most obvious, the most simple, the most necessary. But who thinks of doing that? We, me, all of us, mucking around with a thousand things that don't really matter, that no one cares about, that no one will remember, while the most important things are left unsaid, unwritten.

'*You* can write this book,' Father said.

'You can.'

He just smiled. 'Then Chapter three. It's the dawn of another hot day. And we can't fix the wheel. So we start walking towards Trenwood. You remember?'

'Sort of.'

'It was stinking hot, and it was only eight, and we had to keep stopping and resting, and we didn't have enough water because we'd left in a rush. Stupid, thinking back. That's what the readers will think, anyway. *Stupid people. They live out there and they don't think about water.*'

'We had some.'

'A canteen? It could have ended much worse, Benno. The next few chapters would be you and me walking through the heat, sunburnt, thirsty, maybe even a hallucination (although that might not ring true). Father and son. That'd be what it's about. You and me, Benno. Cos we've made a good team, haven't we?'

'We have.'

'Walking all day. Cursing myself. Because every good story is about . . . what happens up here.' Tapping his head. 'If you don't get that, if you can't communicate that, Benno.' He smiled at me and said, 'Were you ever scared, Benno?'

'Maybe.'

'Did you ever think we wouldn't make it? It was a hundred miles. It was a hundred and thirty in the shade. Did you think we wouldn't . . .?'

'No.'

And what I couldn't say: at that age, you, Father, were Lord Kitchener, the Kaiser, Jesus and God and everyone and everything important, and necessary. 'I knew we'd make it.'

'I had doubts. That'll have to be in there. I thought we'd never make it. Die of thirst. They'd find our mummified bodies and everyone would be cursing me, saying how stupid I was, and that's how I'd be remembered.' Taking a moment, closing his eyes. 'I hope that's not how I'm remembered, Benno.'

'But we got there,' I said.

'We did. That'd be the second part of the book. Us arriving, all burnt, hungry and thirsty, but in time to offer Ken the last rites, him dying, the burial, the lot. Remember all that, Benno?'

'Yes.'

'Because she had no one else to help bury him. So it was just her, you, me, standing around this little grave . . . you helped me dig it, as I recall.'

'Did I?'

As he stopped, as he thought, as he said: 'I'm glad it'll end here.'

'What?'

'And the final chapter,' he said, 'would be us harnessing the Trenwood horses to their cart, heading back to Hermannsburg with Mrs Mordaunt . . . maybe an epilogue? Her catching the train to town and never returning. We never saw her again after that.' He turned to me. 'You could write that. Sell millions. And you could keep the money and buy a big house in Prospect.'

'You do it,' I said. 'I couldn't write a book.'

'You could. A few nice touches. That time we stopped at the waterhole, five, six in the morning, and I saw a night parrot.'

'You never did,' I said.

'Yes, I did. It came out from some bush, and just sat there, watching me.'

'I can't remember that.'

'Made a few calls. That could be code for watching out for me, Benno. The smart readers would get it.'

'I think,' I said, 'that would be a bit much.'

'No, no,' he said. 'It happened. And people will believe. They'll *want* to believe, Benno. It'll be like Jesus and the loaves . . . if people *want* to believe.'

Looking back, I can understand. That Father wanted to reach out, touch me, feel my skin, my hot face, my wiry hair, all of this. He wanted to. But it wasn't permitted. He wanted me to know anyway. What he felt, watching me that night, following him across the great, open desert that had filled his life. This forty-year-old man and his son. The thought he'd got it all wrong (and believe me, I've worked that one out for myself). That he saw this child, and in him, in me, everything he'd believed in, and loved. I think if there was another chapter, it would have him telling me he was sorry for mucking up. He'd say, 'I can't afford to lose you, son.' But, of course, that only happens in books. Which is why I'm writing this story, sixty years later, sixty years too late. But Tom will understand, and he'll finish it for me if I fall off the perch before it's done.

'What should I write next?' I said to Father.

But he just said, 'It doesn't ring true, does it, Benno?'

'I don't reckon.'

He reached over, took the letter, and slowly, with the little bit of energy he had, screwed it up and let it drop to the ground.

Then he slept. He lay there, and slept. He took long, deep breaths, held them, and I shook him to remind him. Exhaling. Lying beside me, that night in the desert, listening to him breathing. This big, black mound of a man snoring in the middle of the desert. Later, Mother came in and told me to go to bed, but I said no. Lou, Silas, all of them. No. I just sat there, watching him, listening. After a while his breathing became heavy, laboured, and I got worried and shook him enough to wake him. He just stared at me for a minute, smiled, and said, 'In the drawer.' Indicating.

So I looked. A small, sepia snap. He said, 'Smit . . .'

Father, aged eleven or twelve, and Pastor Smit standing beside him, smiling.

'He told me, he said I shouldn't worry . . .' Studying it. 'Said it never helped.'

'It doesn't.'

'Said I'd do well.'

You have, I thought. *You've done well, Father*. I wanted to say this, but couldn't. Which is why when I see Tom now I say, 'You, my boy, are quite extraordinary.'

'Why?'

I tell him. The dozens of ways. I tell him. I say, 'You will go a long way, my boy.'

'How far?'

'Miles and miles and miles.'

'And what's there when you get there?'

'Ah,' I said, laughing. 'A little waterhole.'

'Oh.'

'And beside it, you know what you'll find?'

So maybe that's enough. Maybe that's all you need to know about Father, and me, and those days. Maybe, one day, I'll write the book, the actual book Father wanted me to. Maybe not. It's *my* story, so you can all piss off. Maybe I'll tell you how Father got sick during the night, and tried to breathe, tried hard, sucking at the world, trying to get air, mouth open . . . but I'd rather not describe all that. What would be the point? Maybe it would be better to pick the story up a week ago. Tom pulling my arm towards the museum, saying, 'You gotta see this, Grandpa.' Jack smiling at me and saying, 'I wanted to check.' Then the Gerlach shrug.

Tom taking my hand and leading me through the animal display, the birds, stopping in front of the newly-restored night parrot and saying, 'See?'

And me: 'I never thought . . .'

'You reckoned it wasn't real,' he said.

'*Me*?'

'*You* said it was just a story, a blackfella story, but look!'

As we stood admiring it, the faded feathers, the ebony beak, the small, brown eyes. The label even: 'Night Parrot. Collected by Pastor Martin Gerlach'.

'No, no, the other way around,' I said to him. '*I* said it was real. *You* reckoned I was making it up.'

'No way!'

'You did.'

Me and this boy, standing in the foyer of the museum, arguing about what was real, and imagined. Until eventually I gave up, said he was right. 'This is just what Pastor Smit reckoned.'

'Who was he?'

'He was the one who got all of this started,' I said.

But I didn't tell him any of this. This history. The past lay before him in a glorious blaze of red and orange and turpentine green. Stretching out forever, or at least as far as his kids, who'd continue, I guess, towards Horseshoe Bend.

Prospect

Do you want to know more? I can't tell you more. I can't tell you about Mother, holding the bottle of asthma medicine, at five in the morning, as Father walked out alone into the desert for the last time. The idea that had consumed him, from a young age. A vast, wild, beautiful country that could only be made more perfect with the blessings of God. I can't tell you about Lou's face, or Silas, sitting in the corner, knees under his chin, waiting. Expecting it, I guess. Having seen, at a too-young age, how life works. I can't tell you about Ignatz who, the next morning, was gone. From his room (the bed left unmade). From the house. Some of the blacks saying his tracks led out into the desert, and should they go search for him? I can't tell you about Gus, arriving in Oodnadatta to be told. I don't know what he did, or said. I reckon he wouldn't have been happy. I can't tell you anything about how I felt, the next morning. No sleep, headache, jaws sore from the clenching, skin raw from the crying, a rip that kept pulling me out into the cold of some strange sea. Lying on my bed with my head in my pillow. The world a hot, dark, airless place that had taken my father, despite all the planning and hoping and pleading and explaining and rationalising, and believing.

But what does the past matter? If it's all about the living and the dead, I know what I'd rather. Tom, in the museum cafeteria, wearing his Scotch College blazer, the badges and medals for this and that. Stuffing a Kitchener bun down his throat as his father growled at him to slow down. Then the trip home. Me up front, the air-conditioner blasting my face, Bach on the stereo, Jack saying, 'You and old gramps must still pull a bit of weight at that place.'

Me shrugging. 'I thought they woulda thrown it years ago.'

And Tom: 'Guess where we're going, Grandpa?'

'What?'

And Jack: 'Shh.'

But I worked it out. Main North Road, and I said, 'This is the long way.'

No reply.

Prescott Street, and the old place. The elm that Jack and Sharon had planted. The same wire fence I'd put up one weekend in 1952, still standing. Jack trying to help, the wire flicking his face, a small cut, an inch below his eyes, Terese running out to tell me to be careful, he only had two eyes.

Jack pulled up in the gravel drive and said, 'Ready?'

'You could've asked.' Crossing my arms.

Jack laughed and said, 'Eh, Tom, the Great Explorer can't even find his own front door.'

Tom got out, came around, opened my door, and waited.

'She's probably not even home,' I said.

'How long's it been since you were here?' Jack asked.

Not that long. Six months, perhaps. I often caught the bus to Prospect, walked past the old place, wondering if I should go up the drive, knock, see what happened. But I could never do it. Too much history waiting for me. I'd often sit in the park across the road and watch, and sometimes I'd see her coming out, locking the door, walking down the street with her basket on the way to Tom the Cheaper grocer. Not that I'd tell my son any of this. But I did. Because everyone leaves one thing undone.

Tom, pulling on my arm, saying, 'Come on, Grandpa.'

'You could've asked, Jack.'

'And you would've said no.'

'I wouldn't have.' I climbed from the car, surveyed the house, the same bushes, the same mock orange (and I could smell it, like it was only yesterday), the same viburnum in front of Jack's window, the same pittosporum in front of Sharon's. Up the steps I'd last painted in 1953 or 1954. To the same door, and the same bell, its ring as crisp as ever, the tune me and Terse had chosen from the hardware shop. Mozart, of course. A flute and a harp and a lifetime of suburban bliss.

Jack rang it. We waited. The same creaking floorboards you could hear a mile off, as she approached the door, as Tom said, 'You nervous?'

'What's to be nervous about, Tom?'

'It's been a long time.'

The door opened. The same smell, tea tree oil and polished wood, musty carpet – the Queen still on the wall, and beside her, the halo Father had placed on my head a lifetime ago. Baby Jesus. And my wife. No older, no greyer, no sadder or happier, or different. Just Terese. Like I'd just got off the bus, walked up the road, down the path, knocked and asked what we were having for dinner. But this time she said, 'I was expecting you sooner.'

Later, on the way home, the window down, the wind in my hair, the smell of wet eucalyptus and burgers and petrol, I said to Tom, 'That was quite a surprise.'

He put his head between the seats and said, 'She was okay, eh?'

As I heard the word repeating in this endless loop. Father reaching over and taking my hand and saying, 'None of it matters, Benno.'

'What?'

'This.' Smiling. Content. 'Whatever you might think, or do . . . it just keeps going.'

I said this to Tom, I said, 'It just keeps going,' and he asked what does, and I said, 'I'm not even sure.'

Author's Note

It's been twenty years since I first heard the story of Hermannsburg Mission, Carl and Frieda Strehlow, their son Theo and their 1922 journey to Horseshoe Bend. One of those moments where the scenes start playing out in your head before you've written a word. I knew it'd be a long slog, and I knew the issues involved with writing a 'three keyboard' book would be significant. I knew I'd need time, lots of time, to tell this story. How, then? My record of winning grants is grim. Still, perpetually unfazed, I submitted an application for a Mid-Career Fellowship to the Copyright Agency and, somehow, I was successful. Without this stroke of good fortune you wouldn't be holding this book in your hands now. I thank them, a lot.

Anyway, it's 2016, I'm teaching English at Pembroke School in Adelaide, I'm busy and tired and never able to write but always wanting to write. I'm Kafka's monster ('a non-writing writer is a monster courting insanity'). I'm getting ready for another lesson when a friend reaches into a bag and says to me, 'I've got so many books to get rid of.' She hands me a 1969 Angus & Robertson first edition of Ted Strehlow's *Journey to Horseshoe Bend* and says, 'Do you want this?' Now, I don't believe in gods, or fate, or magic, or anything really, but at that moment I was ripe for conversion. I studied the book, and inside the front cover: 'To Brend Happy 22nd Birthday, Mate Dick Kimber "The Alice" August 1970'.

Richard 'Dick' Kimber (1939–2024) was a key historian and chronicler of Central Australian life, especially the sort of clash-of-cultures story of *Journey*. I often think it strange how the great stories pass through so many hands, from generation to generation, race to race, tongue to paper to character (to screen, perhaps) to eye. Mostly, I guess, through the power of the story itself, but also, through the work of people like Carl Strehlow. These stories *persist*. Spoken, handed on, trusted, revered in the Indigenous sense, but also, told lightly (I hope) and without a writer's ego in the modern sense (the cult of the writer as so much bullshit).

In 2020, encouraged by the virus, I started writing the story. I used Ted Strehlow's third-person autobiography as a scaffold. I watched the 2016 documentary *Night Parrot Stories*. I made the connection between my characters and the parrot, coaxed both from their holes, gave them things to say and promised them the world would be intrigued, and grateful. I read everything I could find about Carl Strehlow, sat in the State Library of South Australia studying his son's *Songs of Central Australia*. All the time, imagining father and son sitting on a dray headed towards Horseshoe Bend in search of a cure for an incurable condition. My main challenge in writing this book has been, as always, making the real seem magic. As Patrick White explained: 'A novel should heighten life, should give one an illuminating experience; it shouldn't set out what you already know.' To do this, I've let go of some things, changed others, invented within the limits of good faith.

There aren't many commercial publishers who'd take on a *Night Parrots* anymore. Things have changed since I scribbled my first novel in 1995. I have Wakefield Press and Michael Bollen to thank for indulging me, again, Maddy Sexton for the editing, Duncan Blachford for the typesetting and cover, Carney Sims and the rest of the crew at Rose Street, Mile End. Nicola Evans and Catherine Ferrari at the Copyright Agency, Martin Shaw for the tour of Leipzig (and lunch at Auerbach's Cellar). Also, thanks to Caroline Overington, as well as a range of wonderful Oz blogs like *ANZ LitLovers*, *Reading Matters* and *Whispering Gums*.

Many, I guess, will come to this story with doubts. Maybe they'll believe the Catholic, Lutheran and other missions were all bad, the missionaries misguided, the rotten economic models and brainwashing and disease not worth a novel. But bad writers take sides, good ones stand at the parapets, pissing themselves. So perhaps what's described here, as with Carl's attempt to reach Horseshoe Bend, is no more than a journey through inhospitable landscapes. Either way, this is the story of a father and a son. It's been told a thousand times before, and will be told again.

Strehlow, T.G.H. (1969) *Journey to Horseshoe Bend*, Angus & Robertson, Sydney

Strehlow, T.G.H. (1971) *Songs of Central Australia*, Angus & Robertson, Sydney

Night Parrot Stories, Ronin Films, 2016 (Directed, written and photographed by Rob Nugent)

Wakefield Press is an independent publishing and
distribution company based in Adelaide, South Australia.
We love good stories and publish beautiful books.
To see our full range of books, please visit our website at
www.wakefieldpress.com.au
where all titles are available for purchase.
To keep up with our latest releases and news,
subscribe to the Wakefield Weekly at
https://mailchi.mp/wakefieldpress/subscribe

Find us!

Facebook: www.facebook.com/wakefield.press
Instagram: www.instagram.com/wakefieldpress

www.ingramcontent.com/pod-product-compliance
Lightning Source LLC
LaVergne TN
LVHW030913080826
845145LV00011B/2878
* 9 7 8 1 9 2 3 3 8 8 6 7 3 *